Gud

Timothy Top

BOOK ONE
THE GREEN
PIG

Translation, Layout, and Editing by Mike Kennedy

CARACAL™

THE MAGNETIC™ COLLECTION

ISBN: 978-1-942367-87-1

Library of Congress Control Number: 2018941128

10 9 8 7 6 5 4 3 2 1

FOR ALESSANDRO AND FEDERICO: KARAMAZOV!

TO THE FOLKS AT TUNUE WHO BELIEVED IN THIS SERIES,
TO SERENA FOR ALWAYS BEING THERE,
TO SKELETONMONSTER, WITHOUT WHOM THIS BOOK WOULD NOT EXIST,
TO CLAUDIA FOR THE CAREFUL EDITS,
TO MASSIMO FOR SAVING ME FROM A CORNER,
TO FAB FOR HIS GRAPHICAL GENIUS,
TO STEFANO FOR PULLING ME OUT OF THE SWAMP OF CLEAR SHADOWS,
TO WERTHER AND GIORGIO, BECAUSE UNDERNEATH THEY LOVE ME,
TO EMILIO FOR BEING A PERFECT MODEL,
TO ANTONIO FOR BEING PRESIDENT,
AND TO YOU WHO ARE ABOUT TO READ THE FIRST ADVENTURE OF TIMOTHY TOP.

THANK YOU!
-GUD

CHAPTER ONE
TIMOTHY

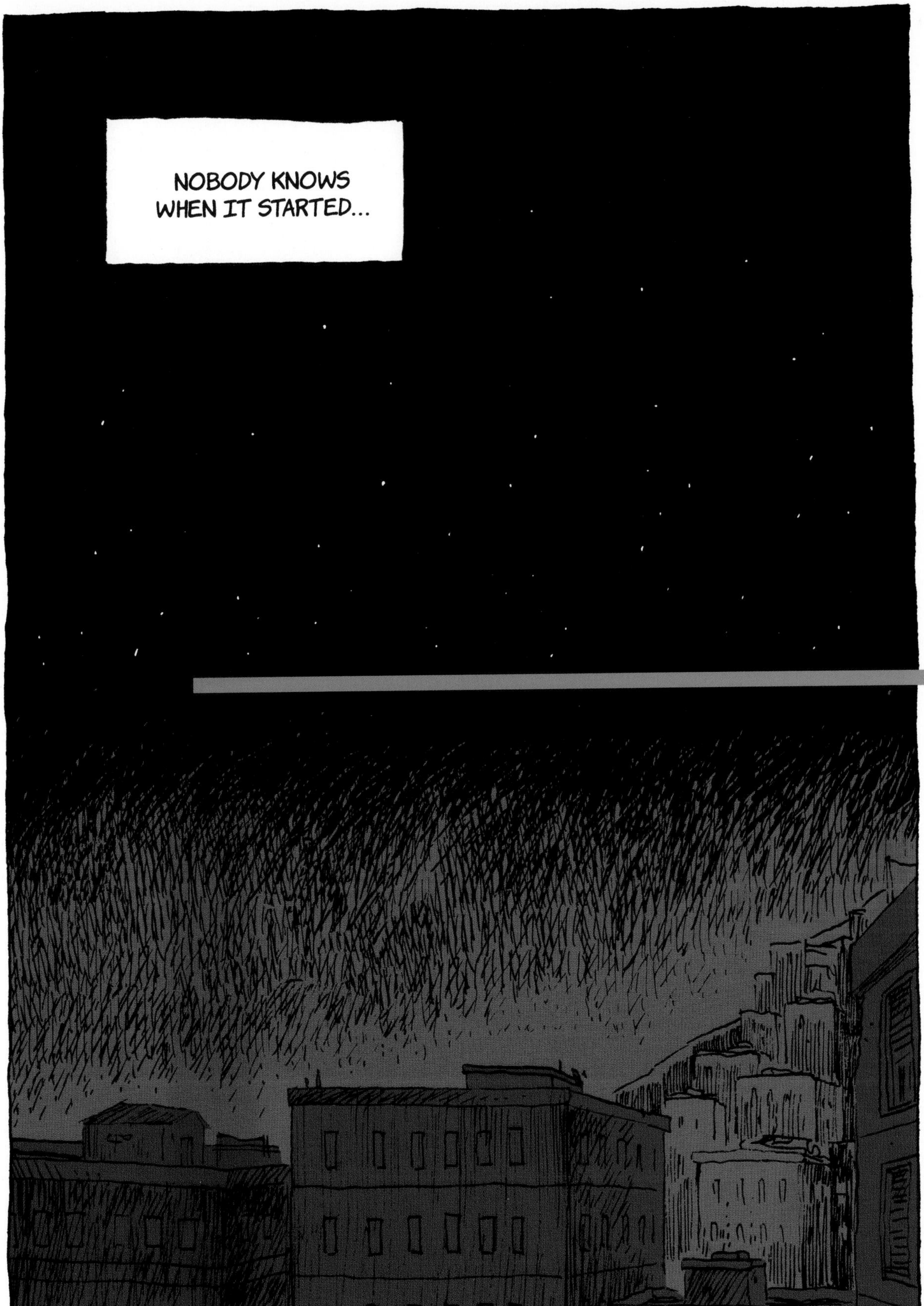
NOBODY KNOWS
WHEN IT STARTED...

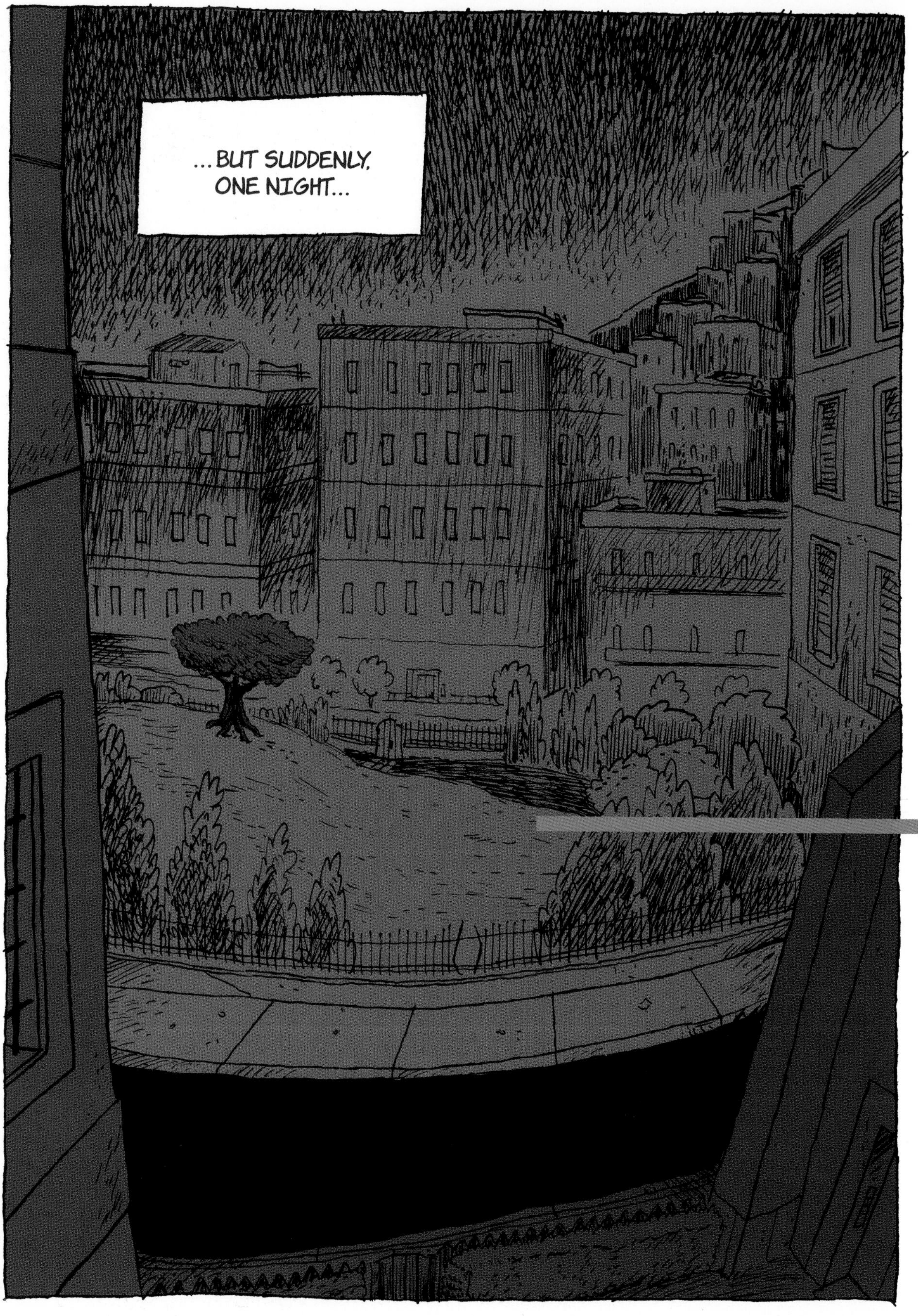
...BUT SUDDENLY, ONE NIGHT...

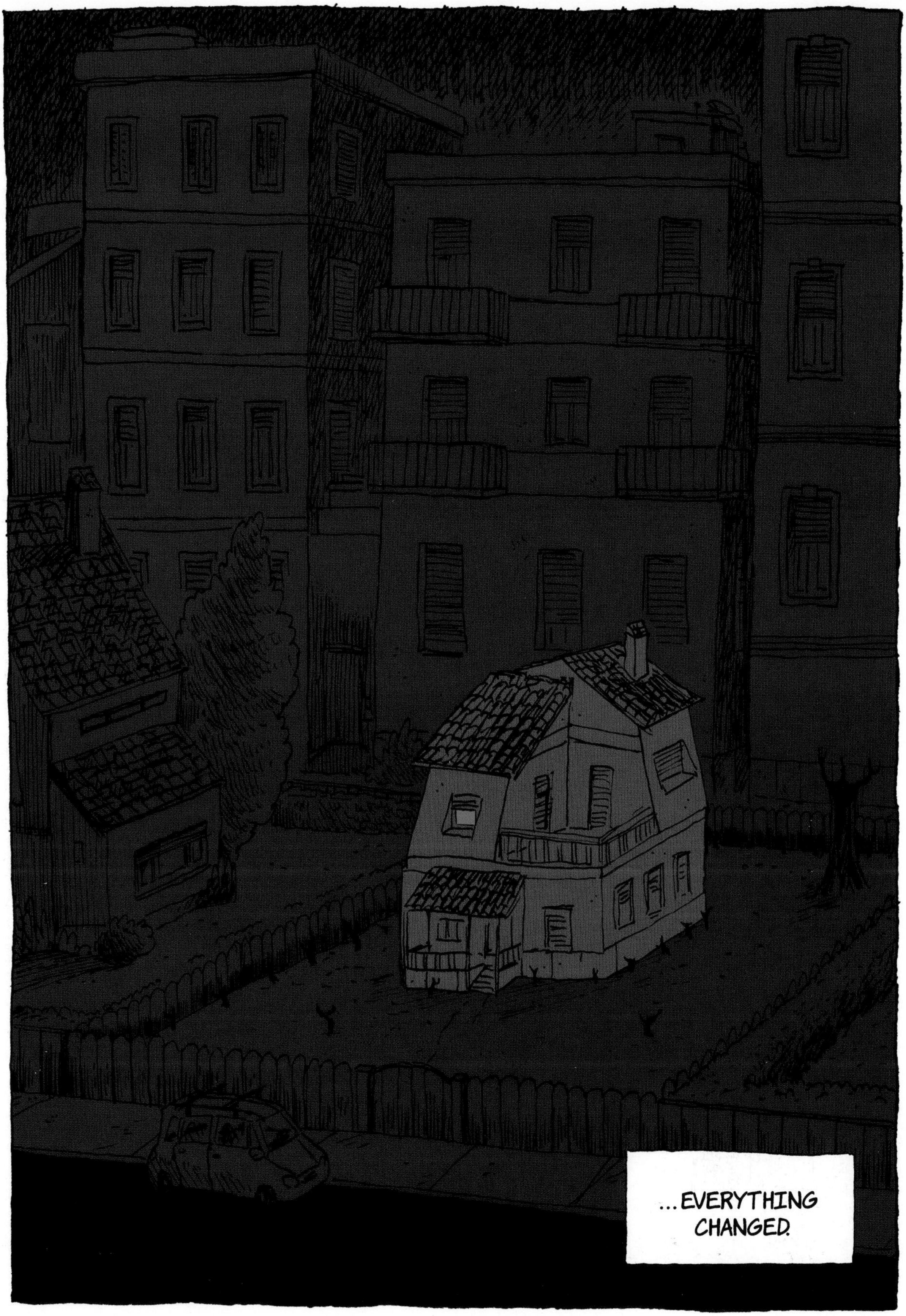
...EVERYTHING CHANGED.

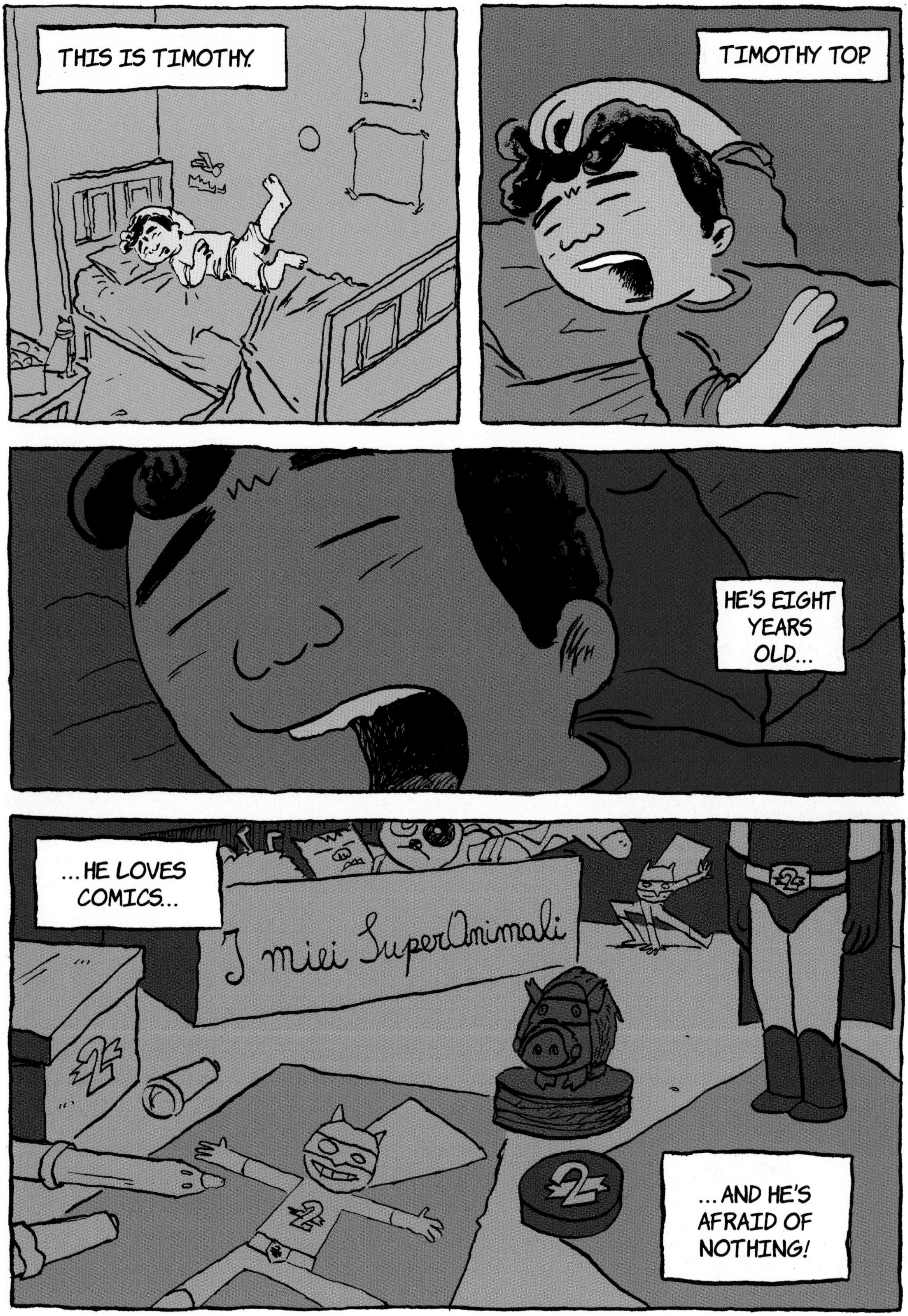
THIS IS TIMOTHY.
TIMOTHY TOP.
HE'S EIGHT YEARS OLD...
...HE LOVES COMICS...
I miei SuperAnimali
...AND HE'S AFRAID OF NOTHING!

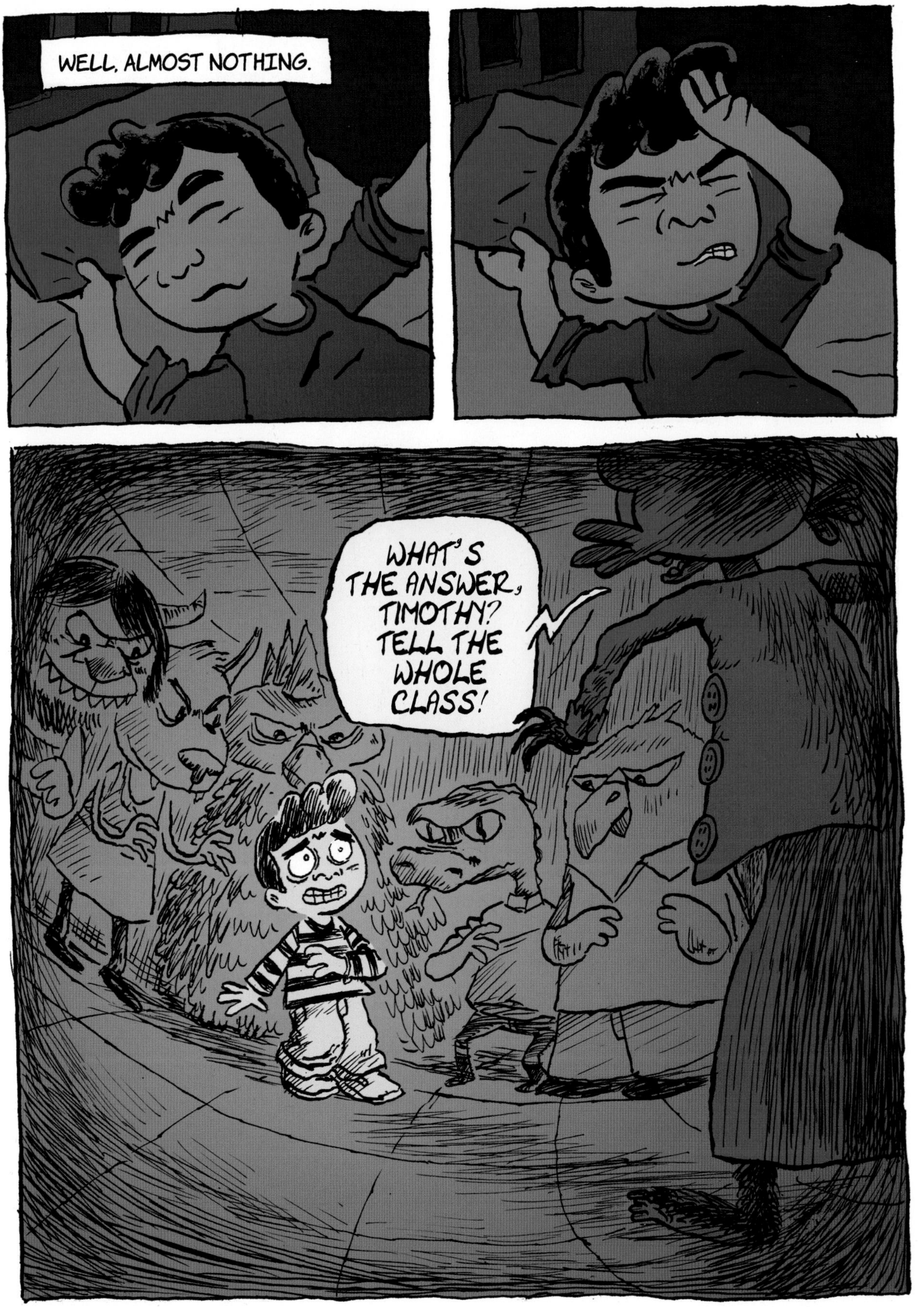
WELL, ALMOST NOTHING.
WHAT'S THE ANSWER, TIMOTHY? TELL THE WHOLE CLASS!

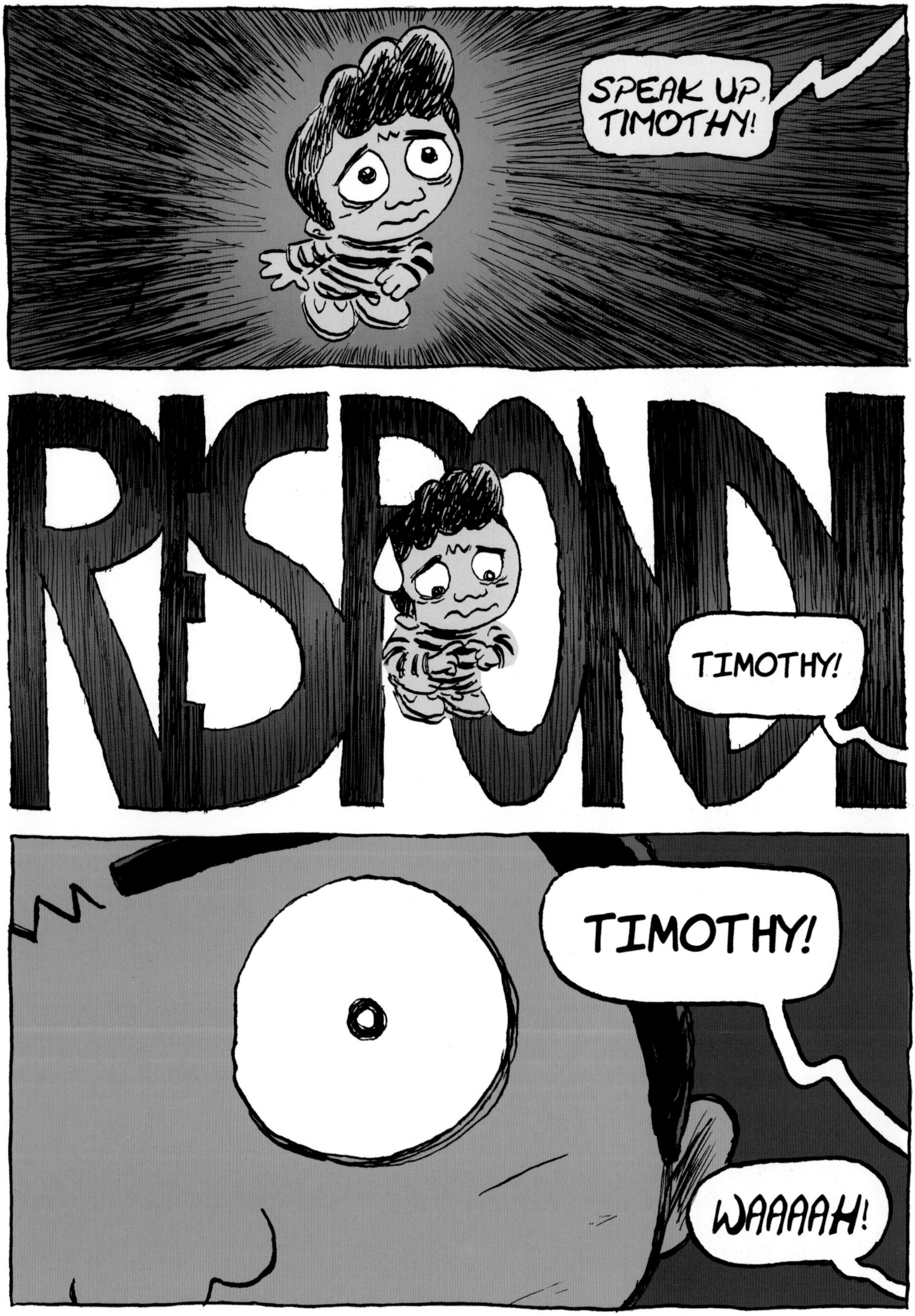
SPEAK UP, TIMOTHY!
RESPOND!
TIMOTHY!
TIMOTHY!
WAAAAH!

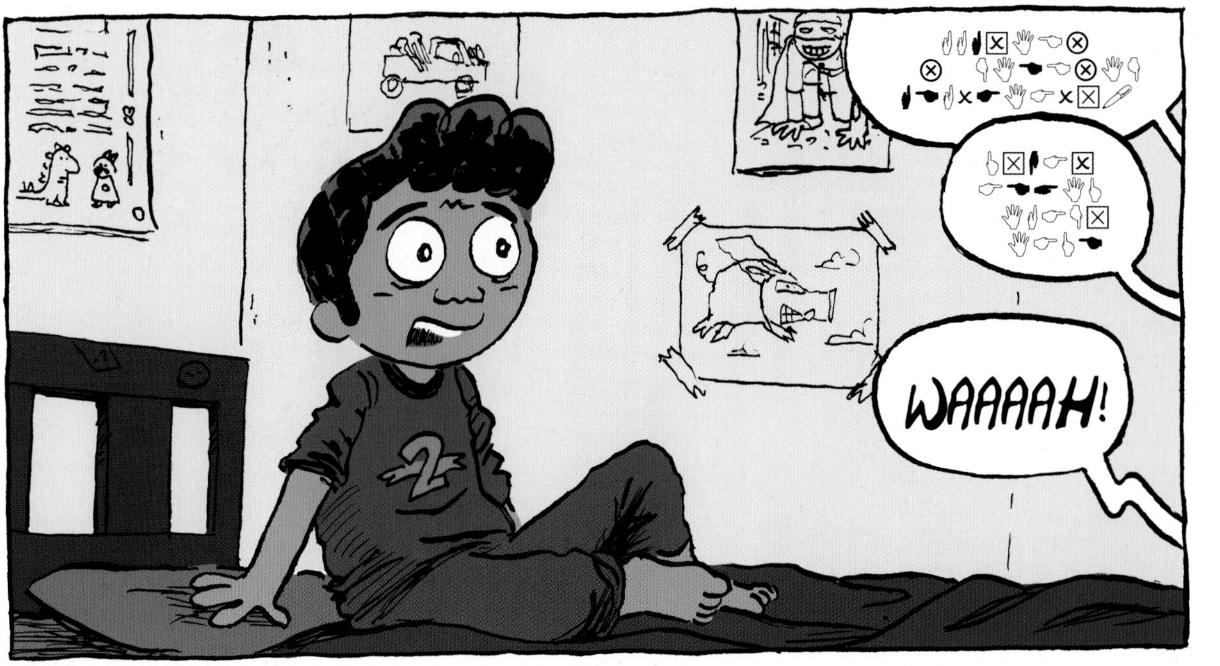
WAAAAH!

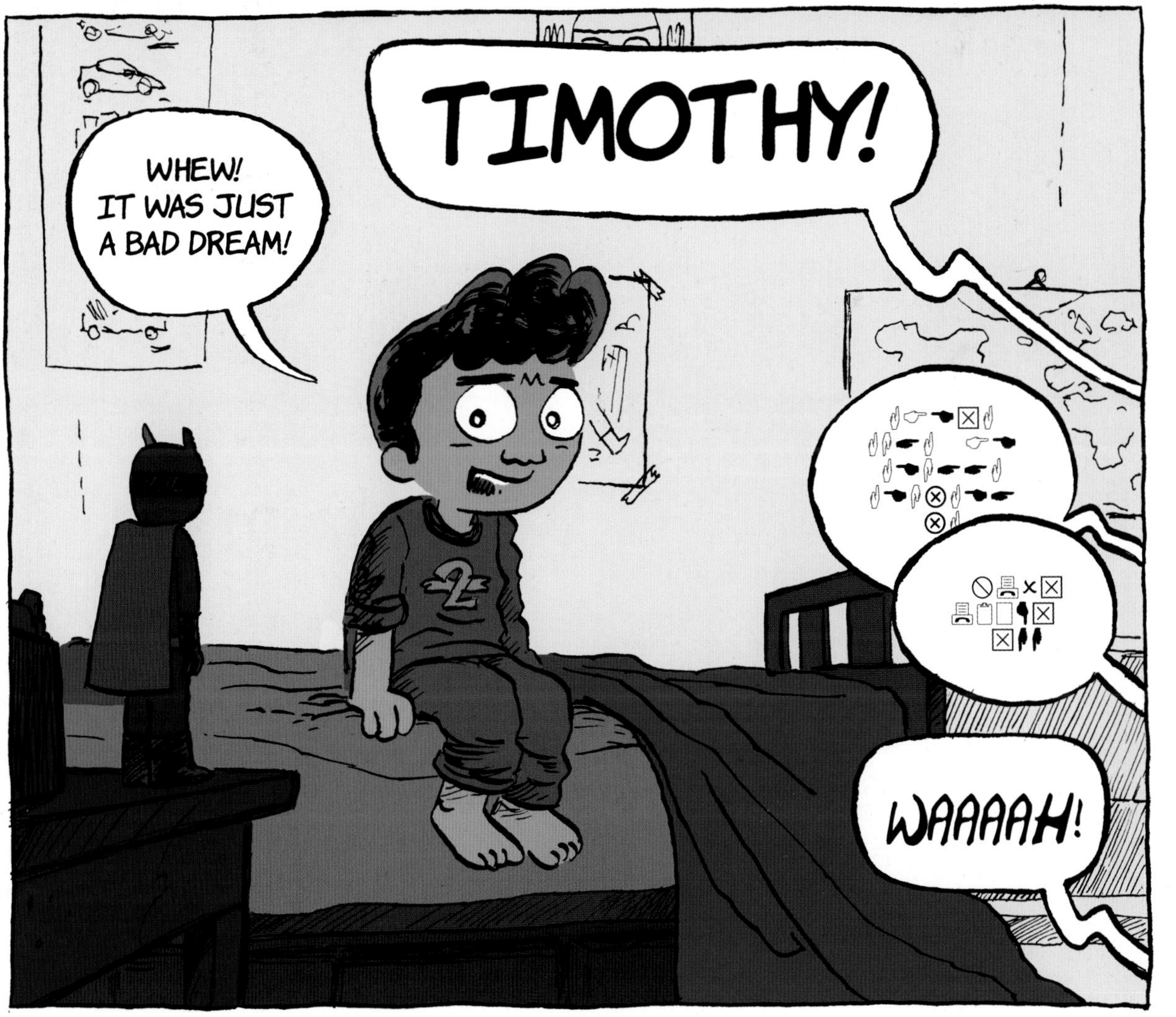
WHEW!
IT WAS JUST
A BAD DREAM!
TIMOTHY!
WAAAAH!

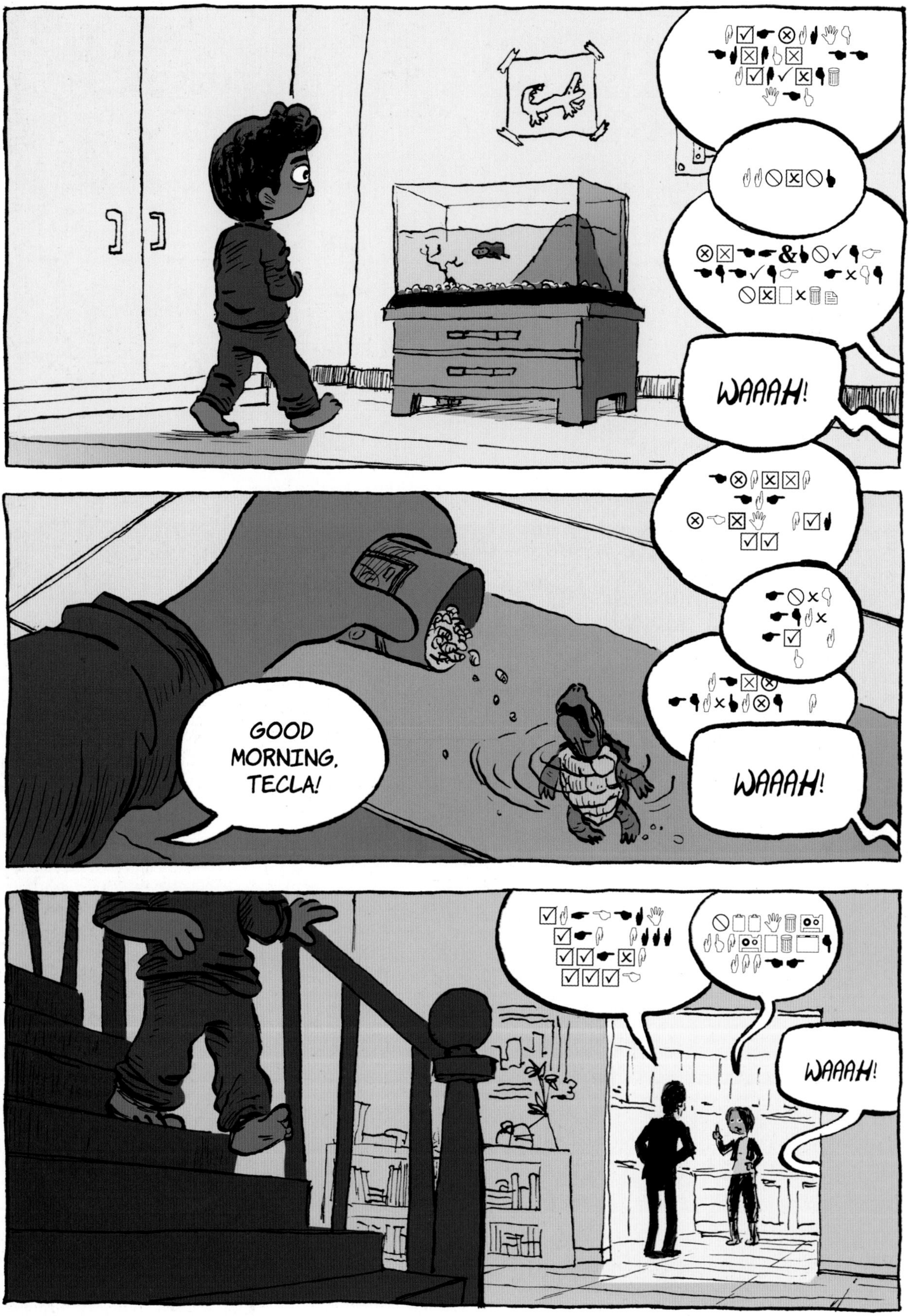
WAAAH!
GOOD MORNING, TECLA!
WAAAH!
WAAAH!

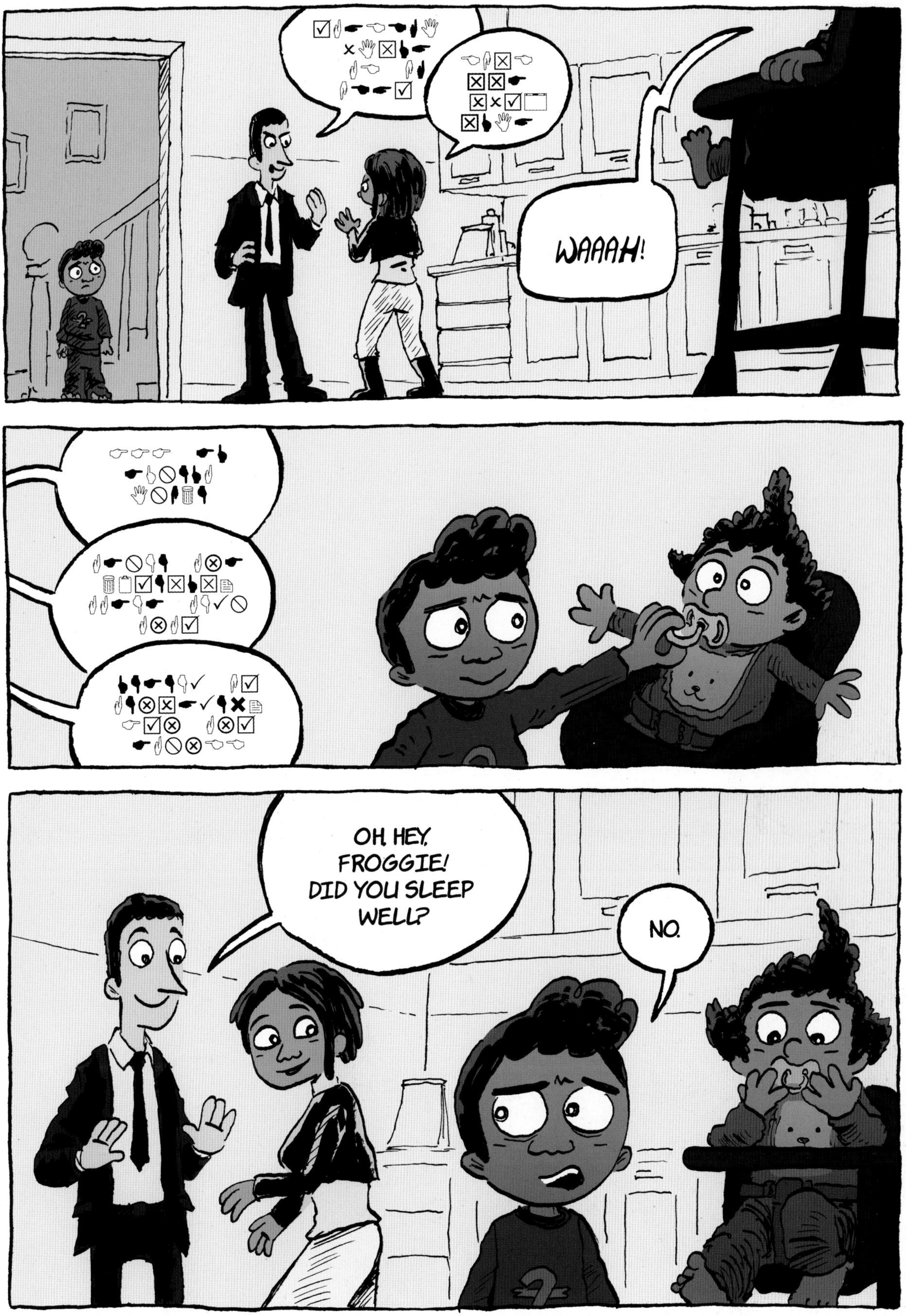
WAAAH!
OH, HEY, FROGGIE! DID YOU SLEEP WELL?
NO.

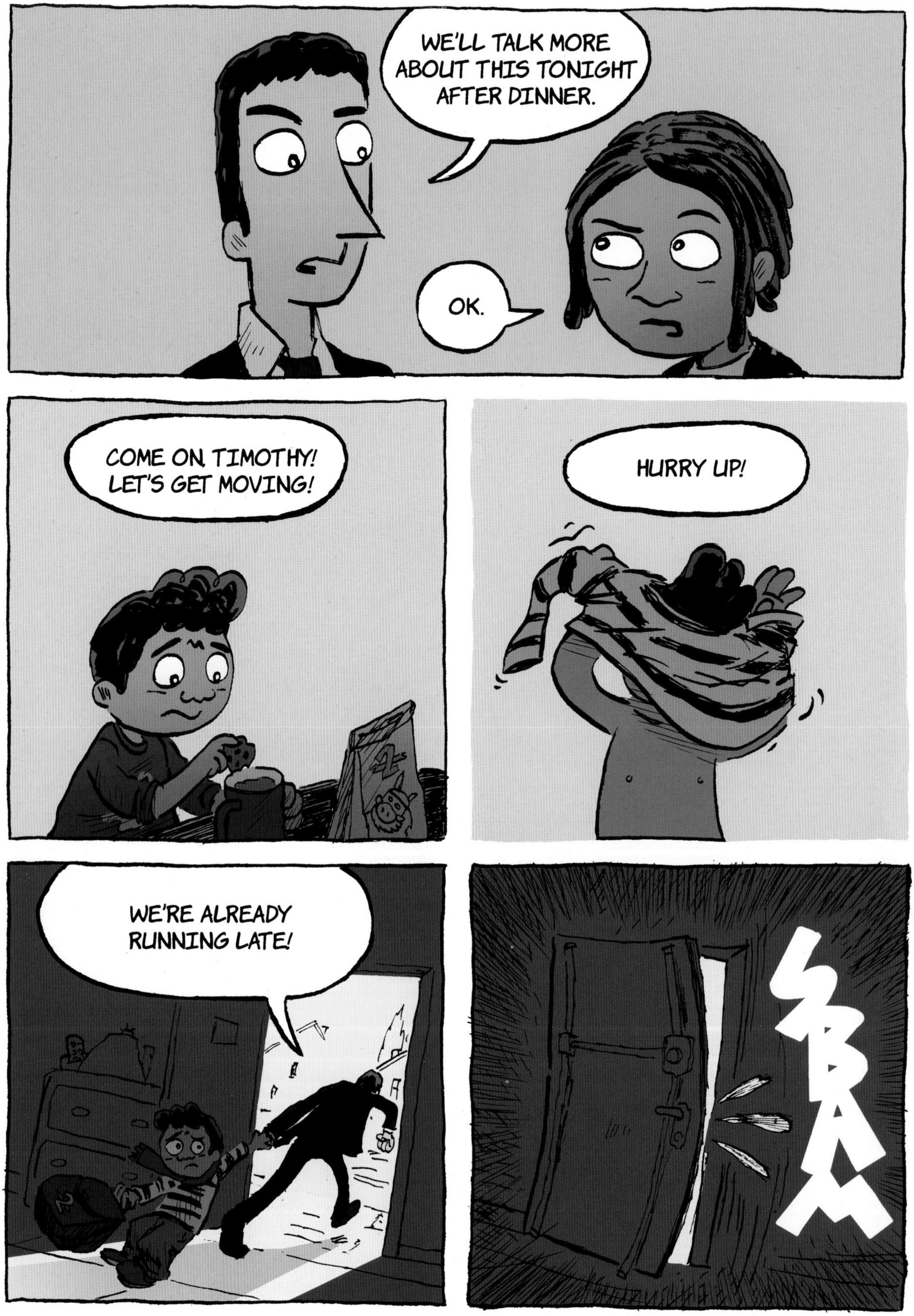

WE'LL TALK MORE ABOUT THIS TONIGHT AFTER DINNER.
OK.
COME ON, TIMOTHY! LET'S GET MOVING!
HURRY UP!
WE'RE ALREADY RUNNING LATE!
SBAM

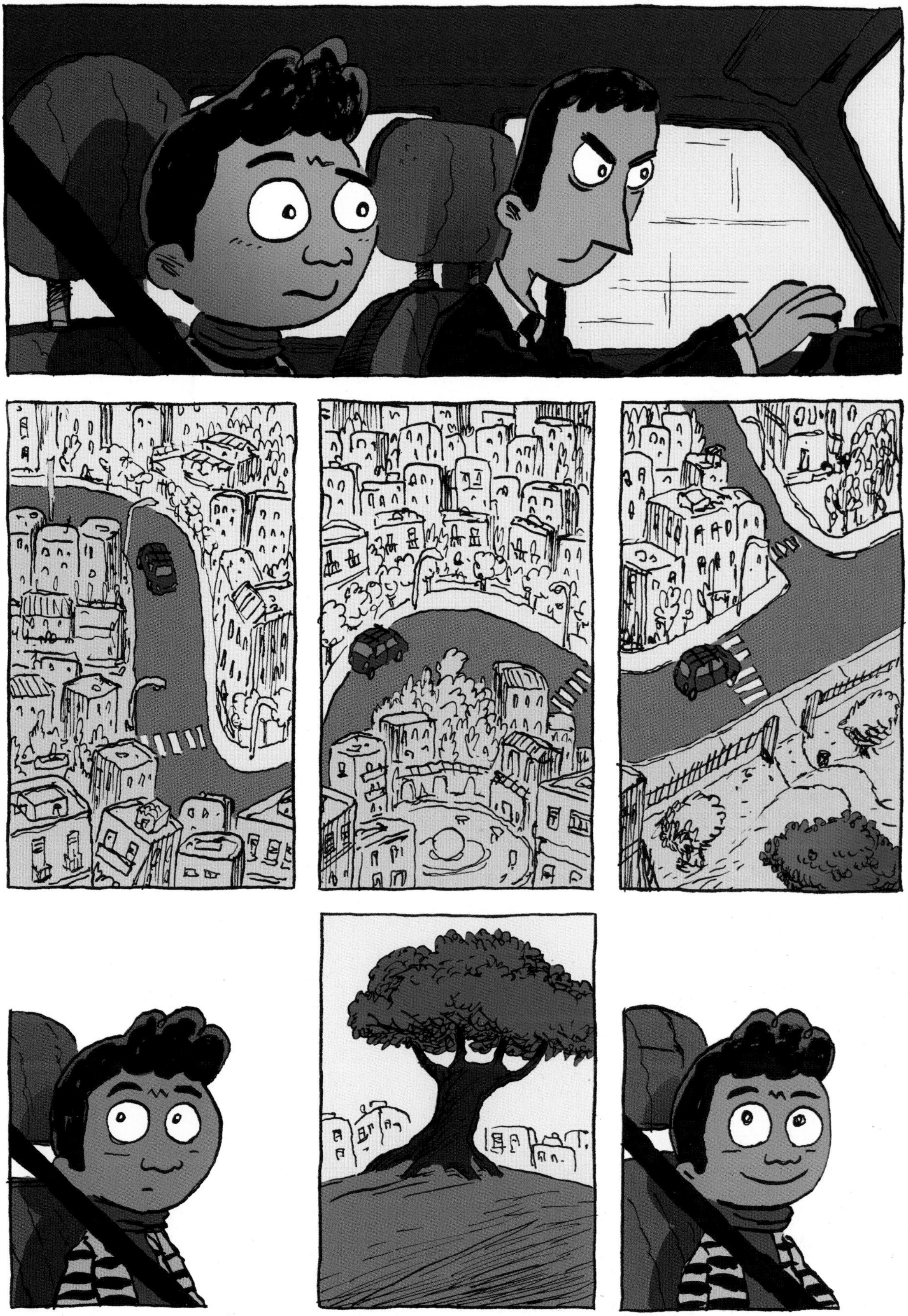

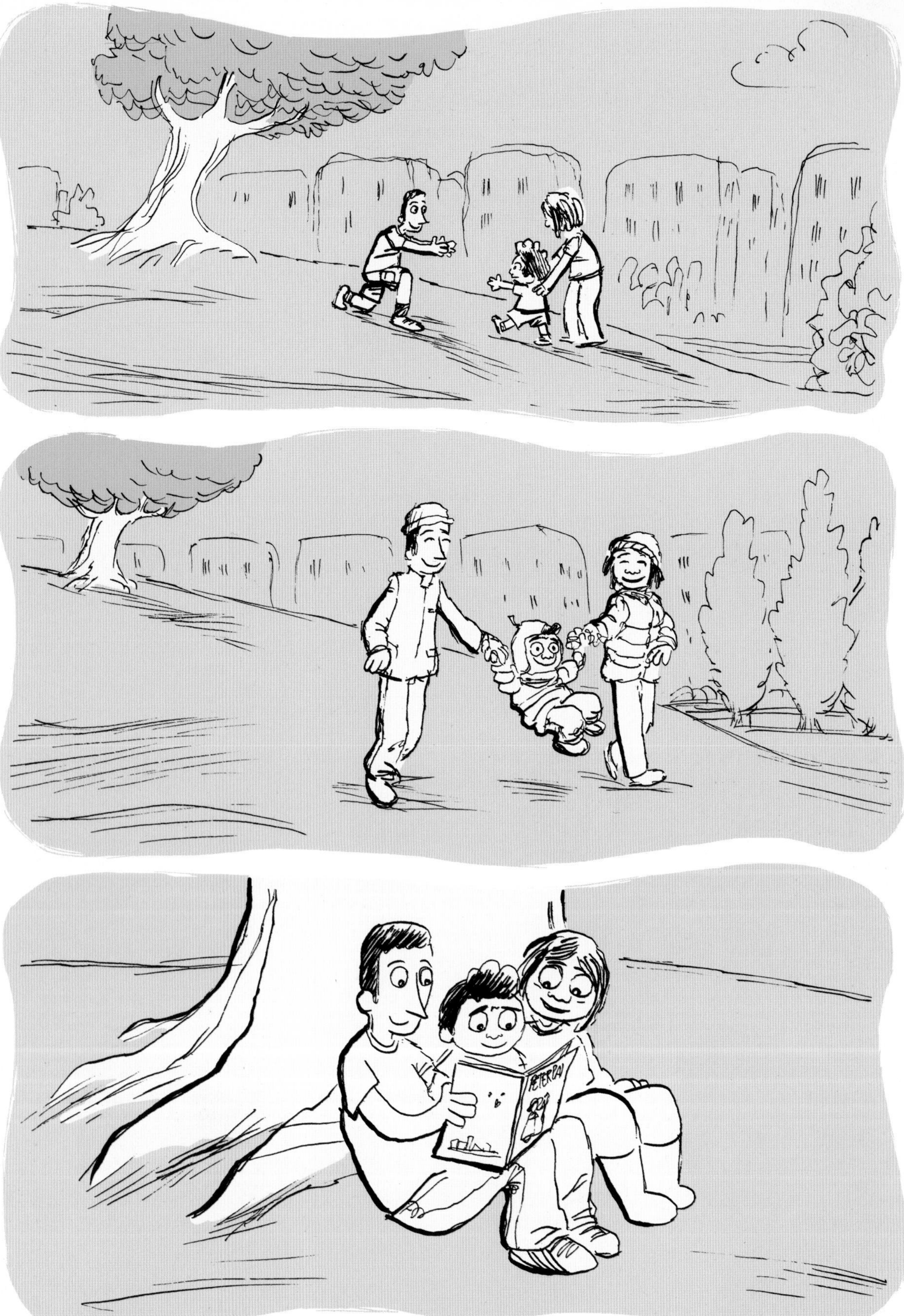
PETER PAN

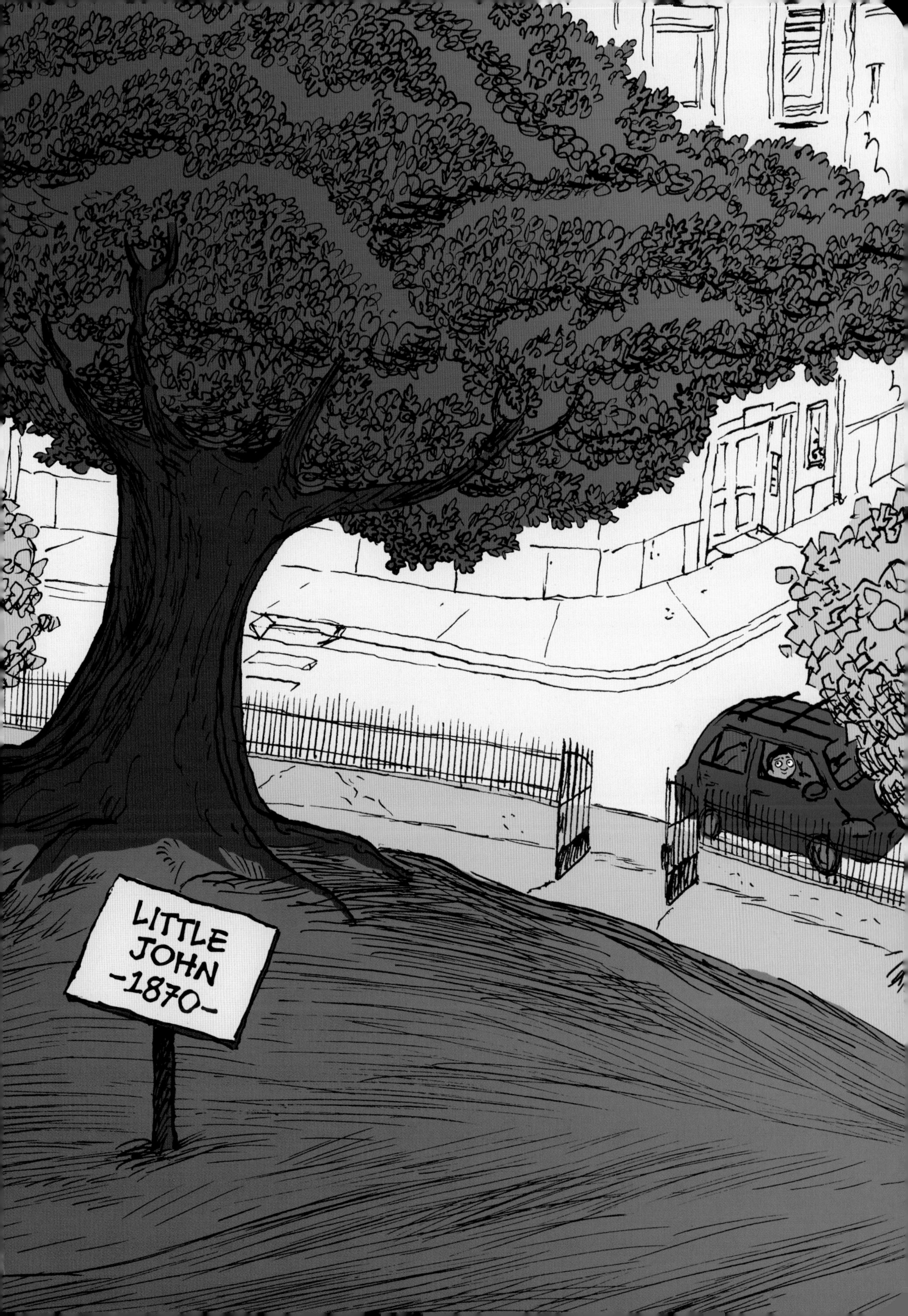
LITTLE
JOHN
-1870-

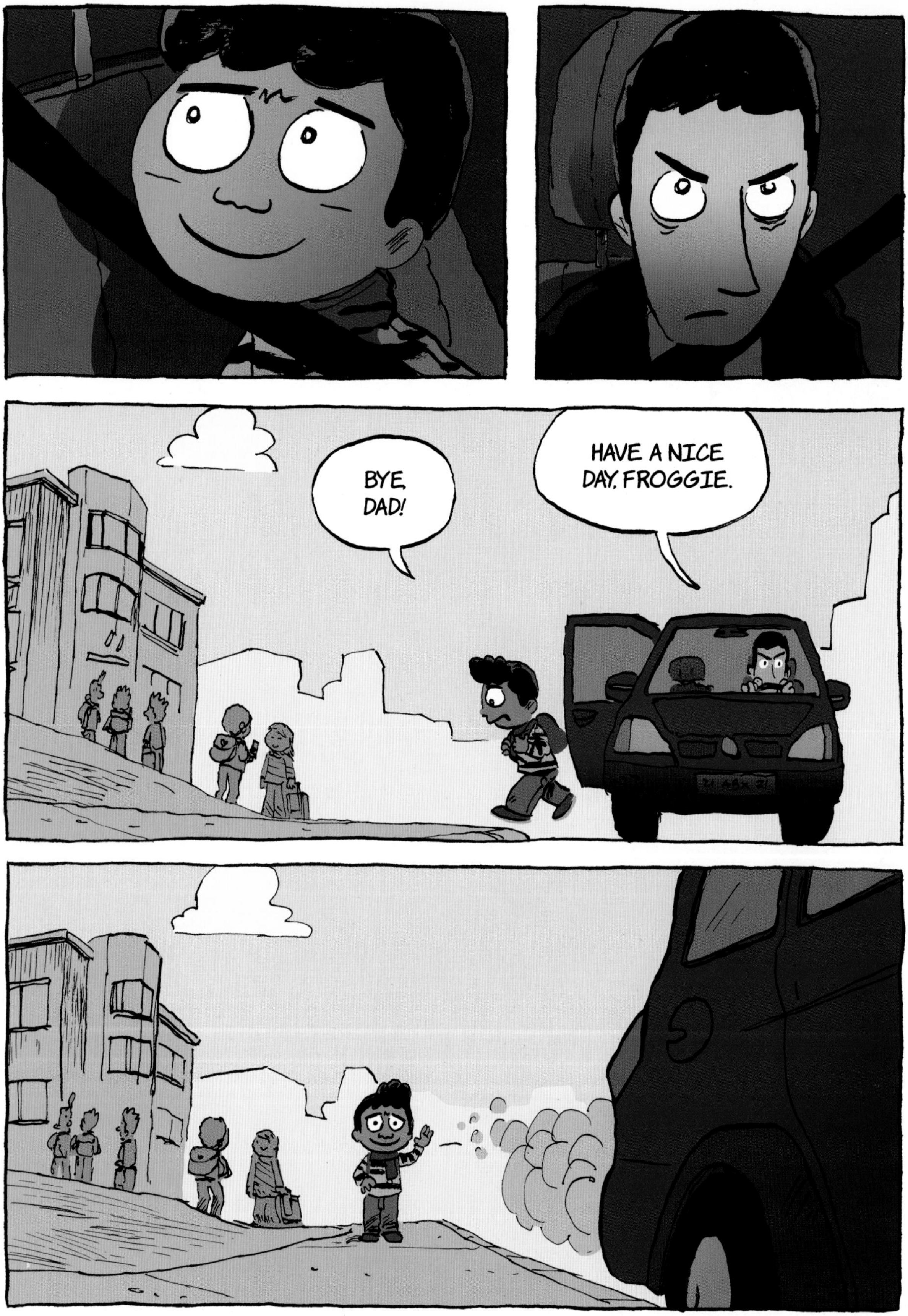
BYE, DAD!
HAVE A NICE DAY, FROGGIE.

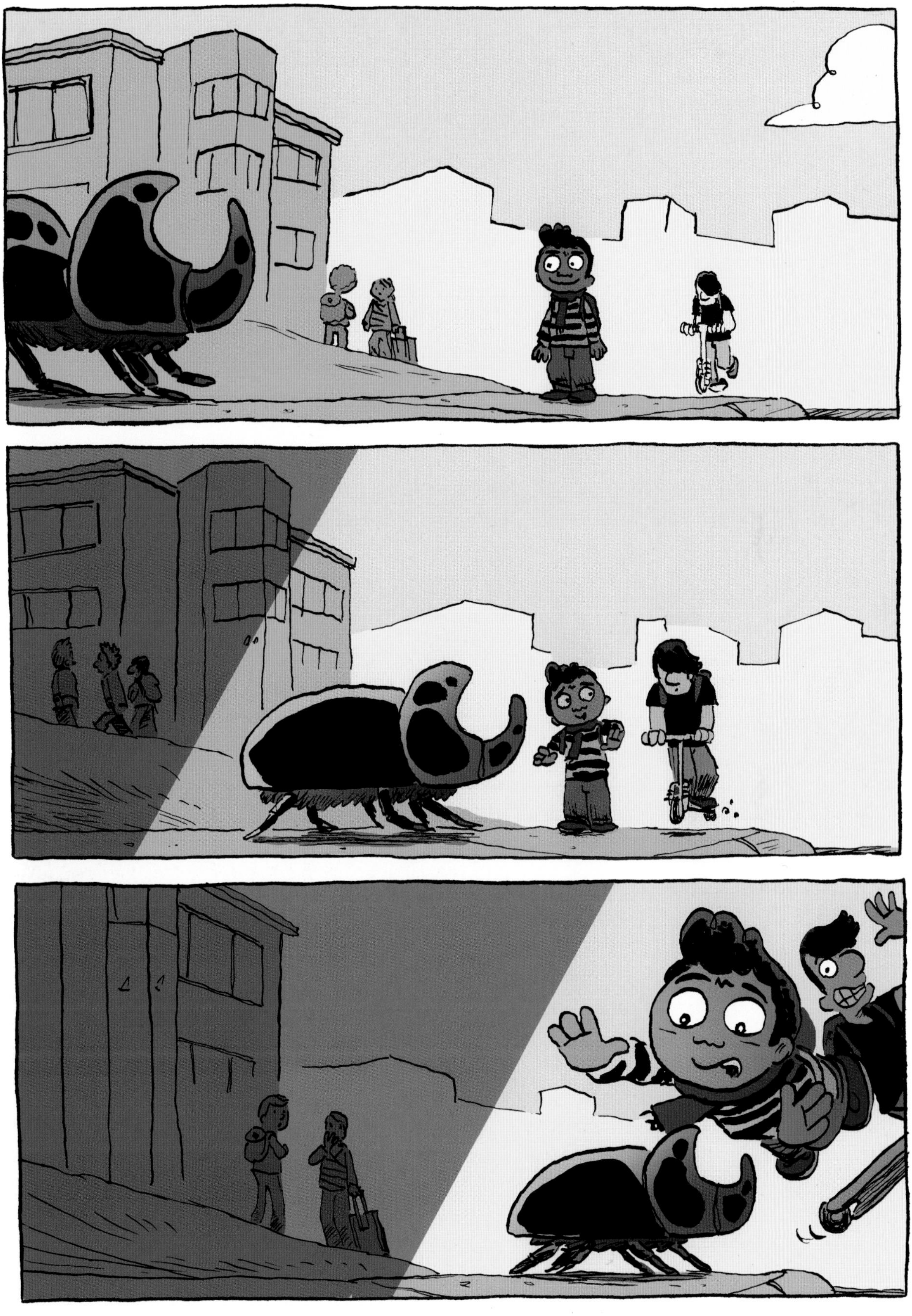

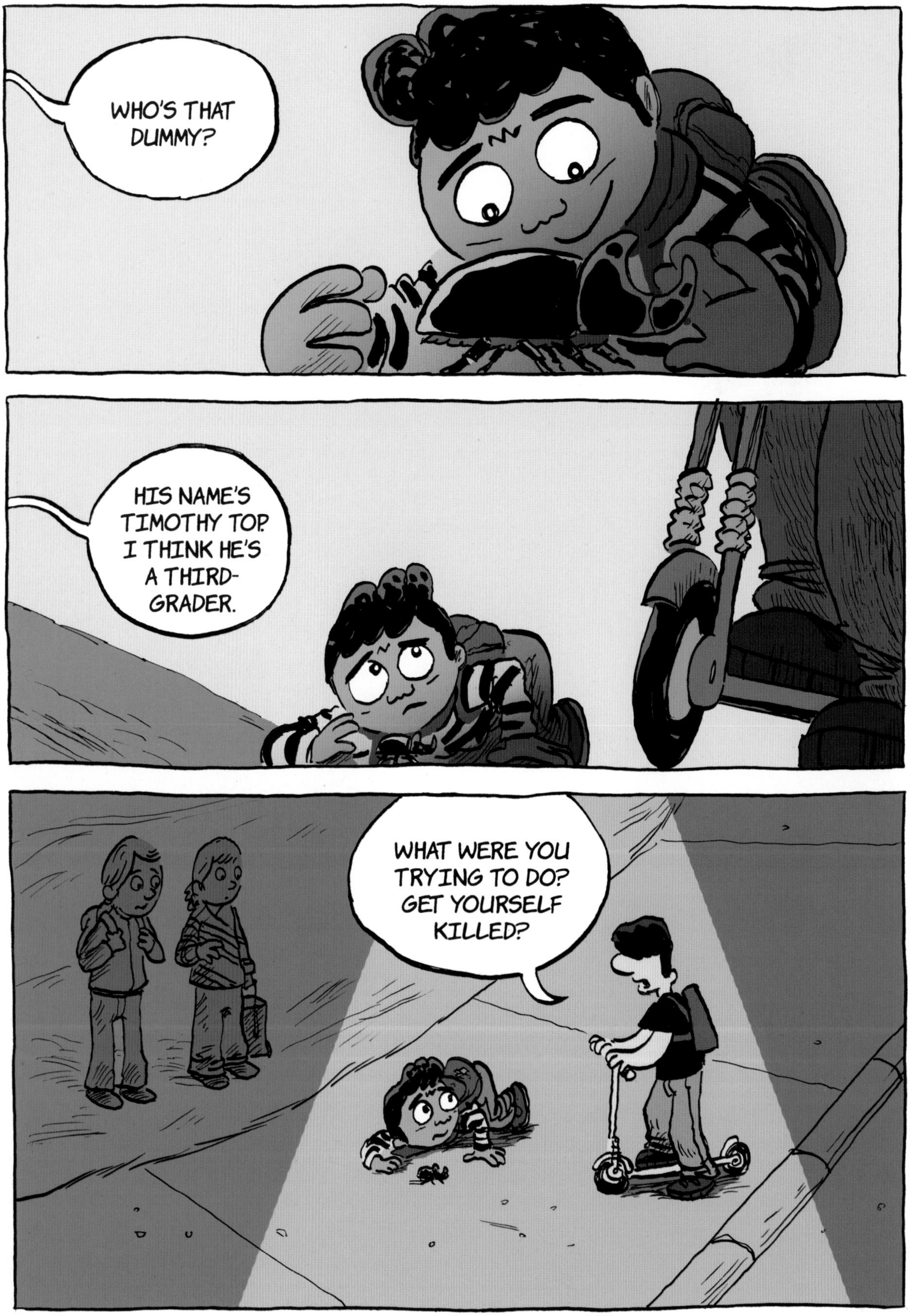
WHO'S THAT DUMMY?
HIS NAME'S TIMOTHY TOP. I THINK HE'S A THIRD-GRADER.
WHAT WERE YOU TRYING TO DO? GET YOURSELF KILLED?

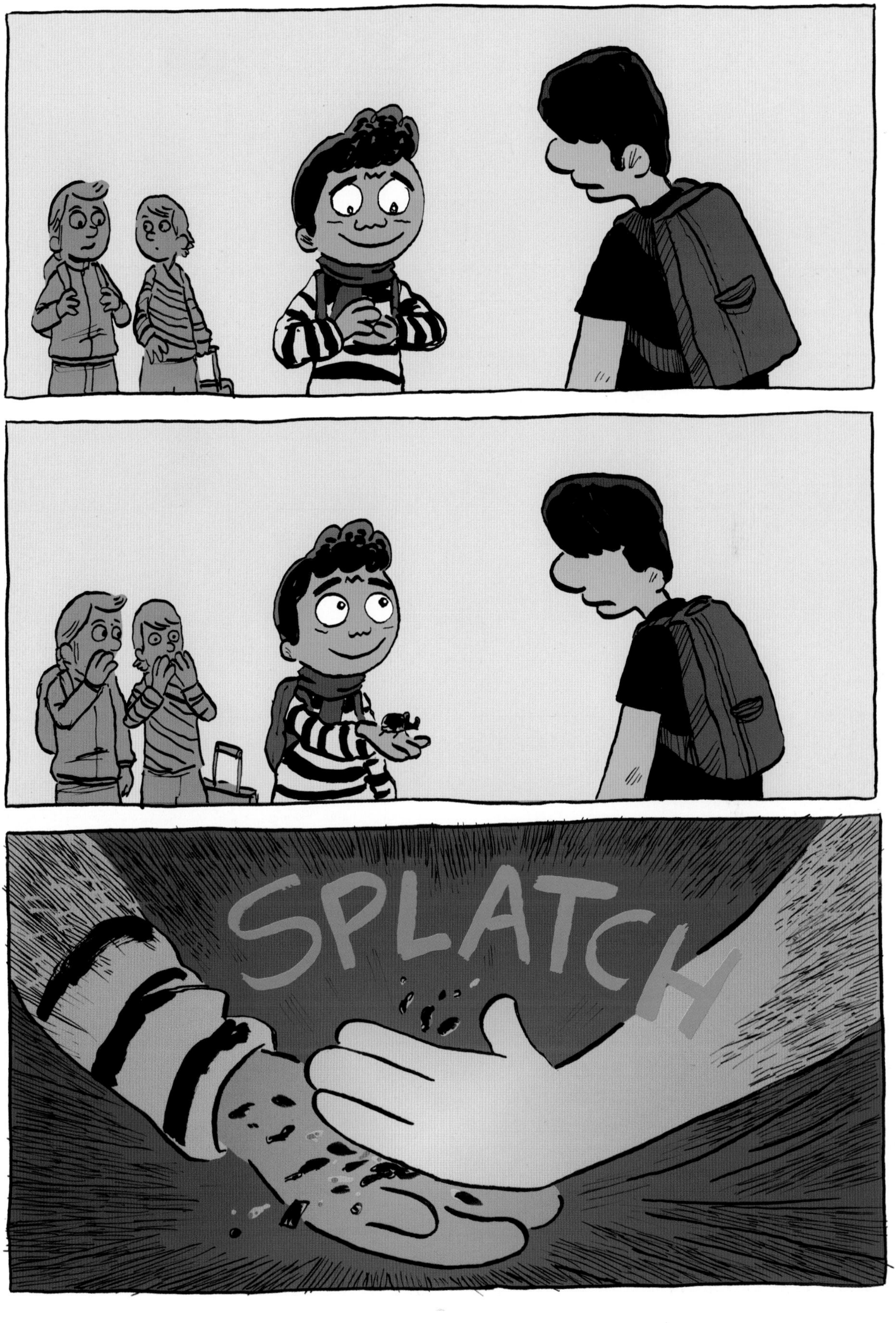
SPLATCH

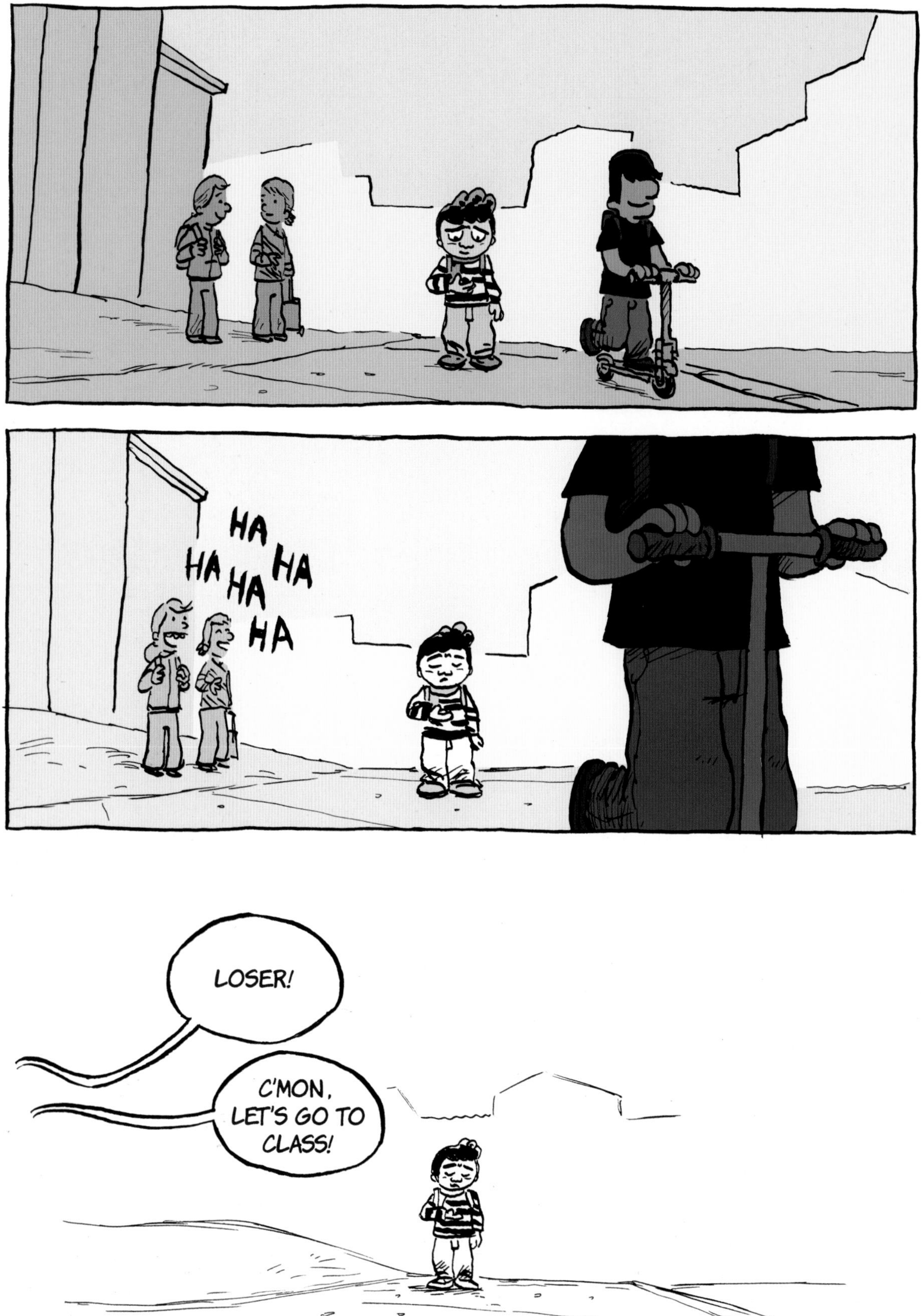
HA HA
HA HA
HA
LOSER!
C'MON, LET'S GO TO CLASS!

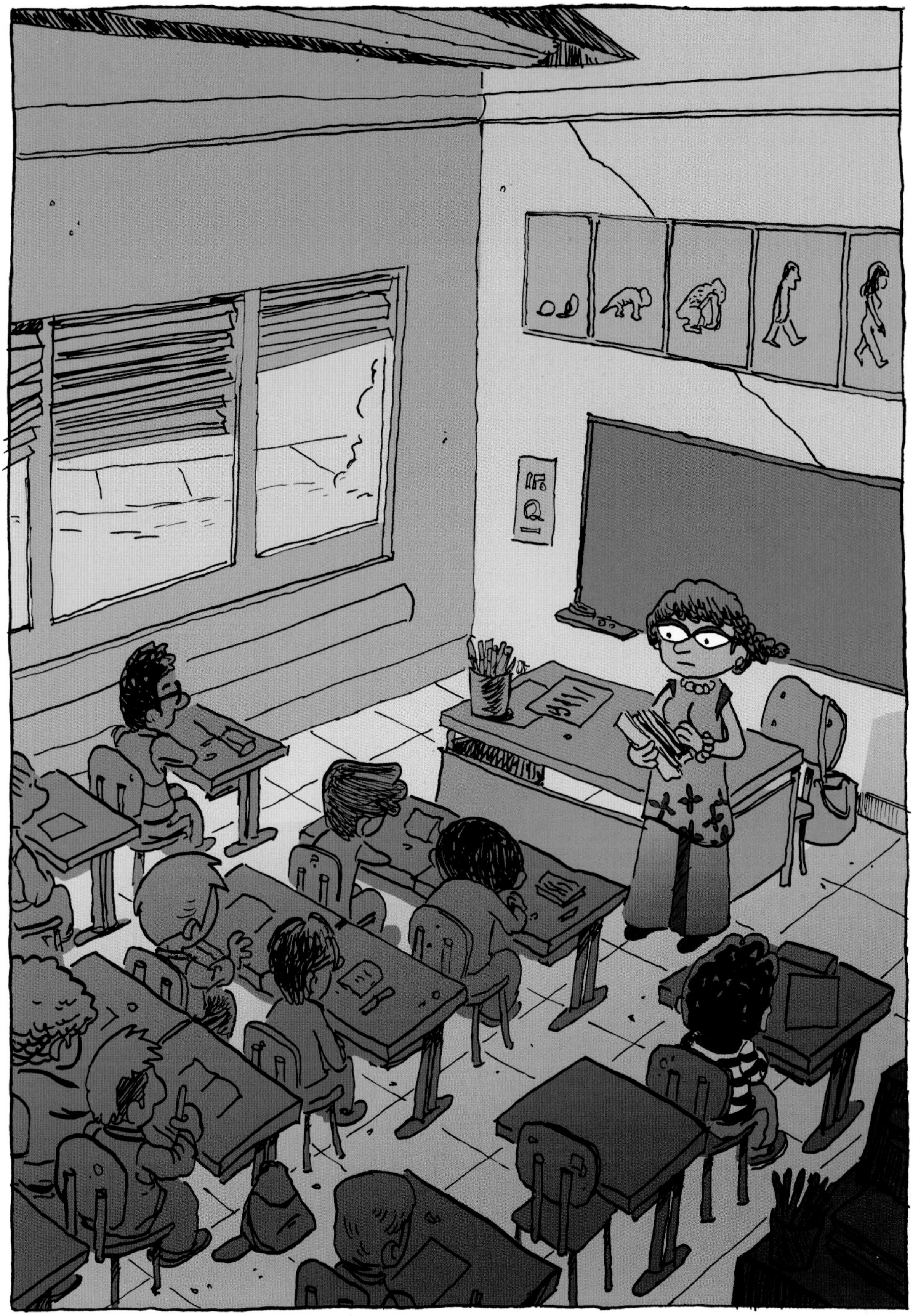

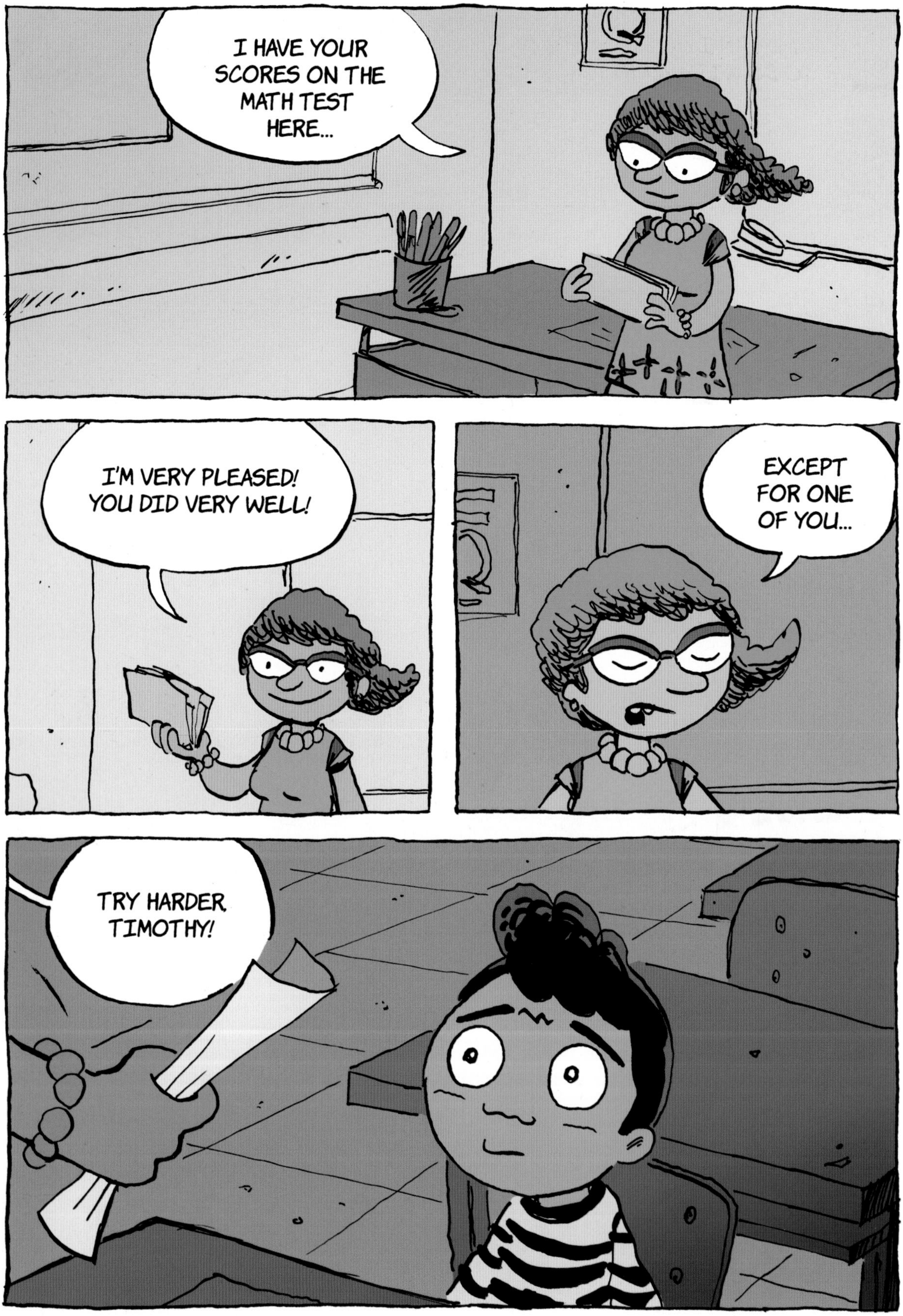
I HAVE YOUR SCORES ON THE MATH TEST HERE...
I'M VERY PLEASED! YOU DID VERY WELL!
EXCEPT FOR ONE OF YOU...
TRY HARDER, TIMOTHY!

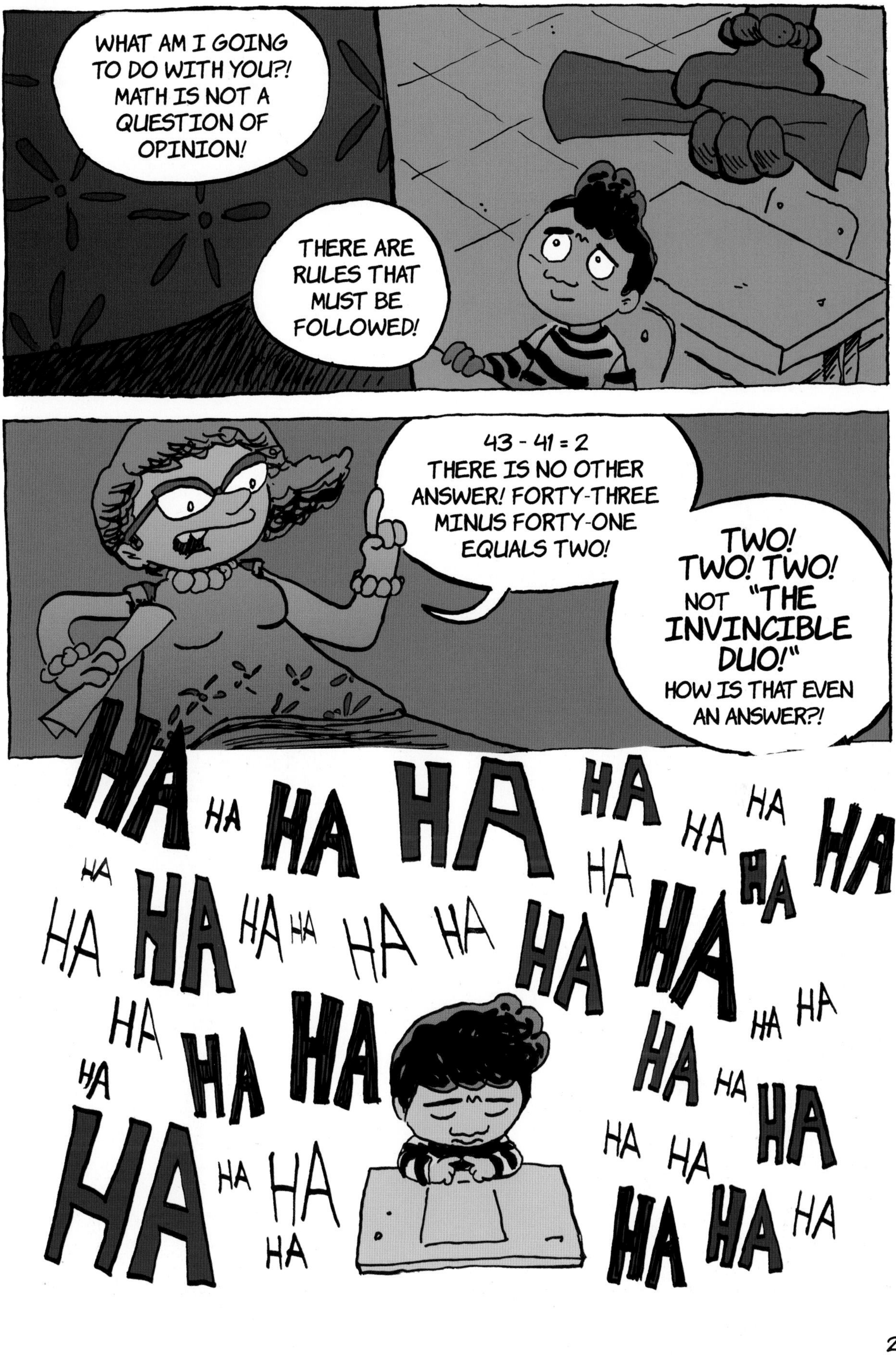
WHAT AM I GOING TO DO WITH YOU?! MATH IS NOT A QUESTION OF OPINION!
THERE ARE RULES THAT MUST BE FOLLOWED!
43 - 41 = 2 THERE IS NO OTHER ANSWER! FORTY-THREE MINUS FORTY-ONE EQUALS TWO!
TWO! TWO! TWO! NOT "THE INVINCIBLE DUO!" HOW IS THAT EVEN AN ANSWER?!
HA HA HA HA HA HA HA HA HA HA HA HA HA HA HA HA HA HA HA HA HA HA HA HA HA HA HA HA HA HA HA HA HA HA HA HA HA

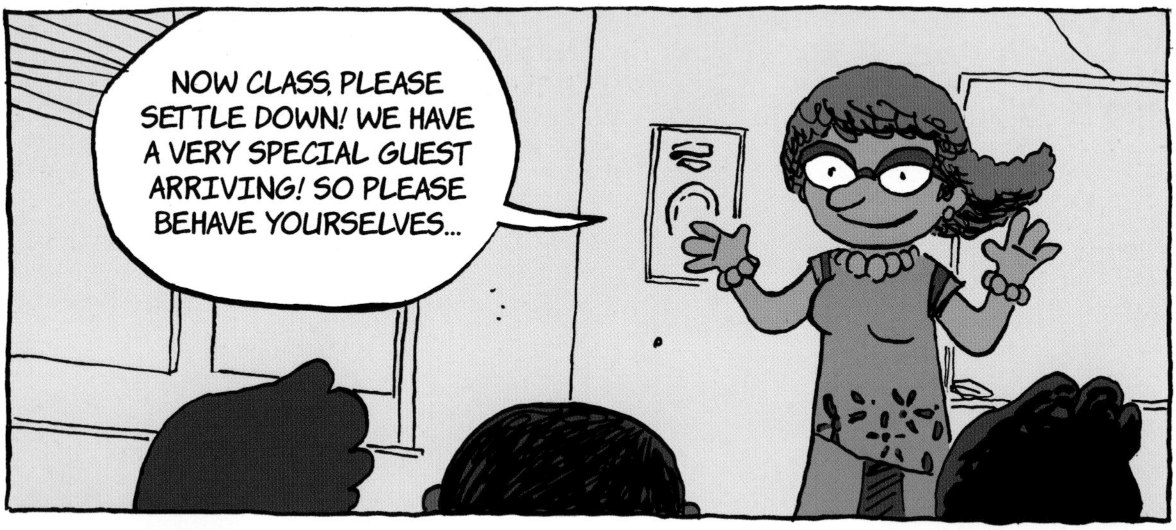
NOW CLASS, PLEASE SETTLE DOWN! WE HAVE A VERY SPECIAL GUEST ARRIVING! SO PLEASE BEHAVE YOURSELVES...

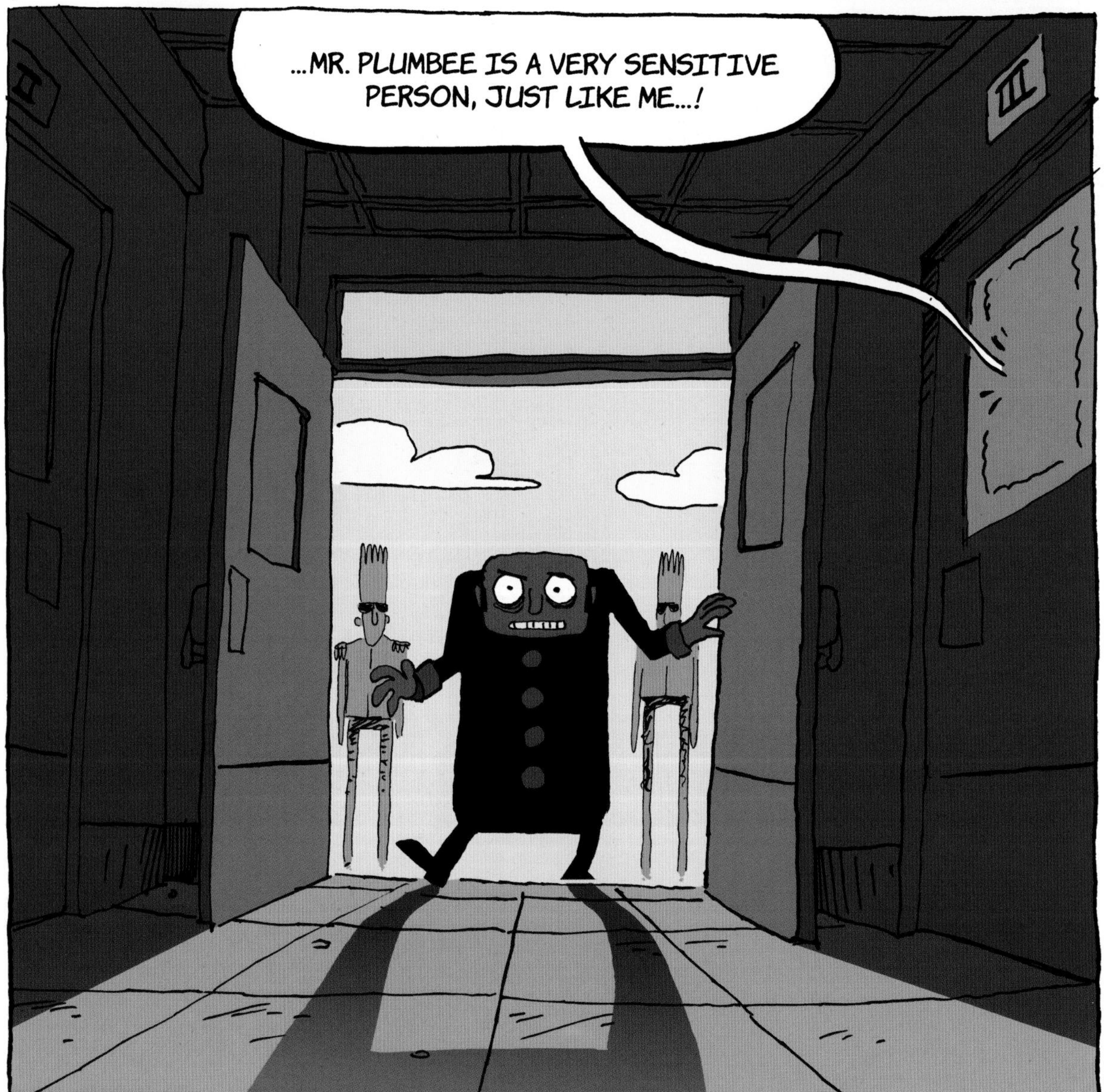
...MR. PLUMBEE IS A VERY SENSITIVE PERSON, JUST LIKE ME...!

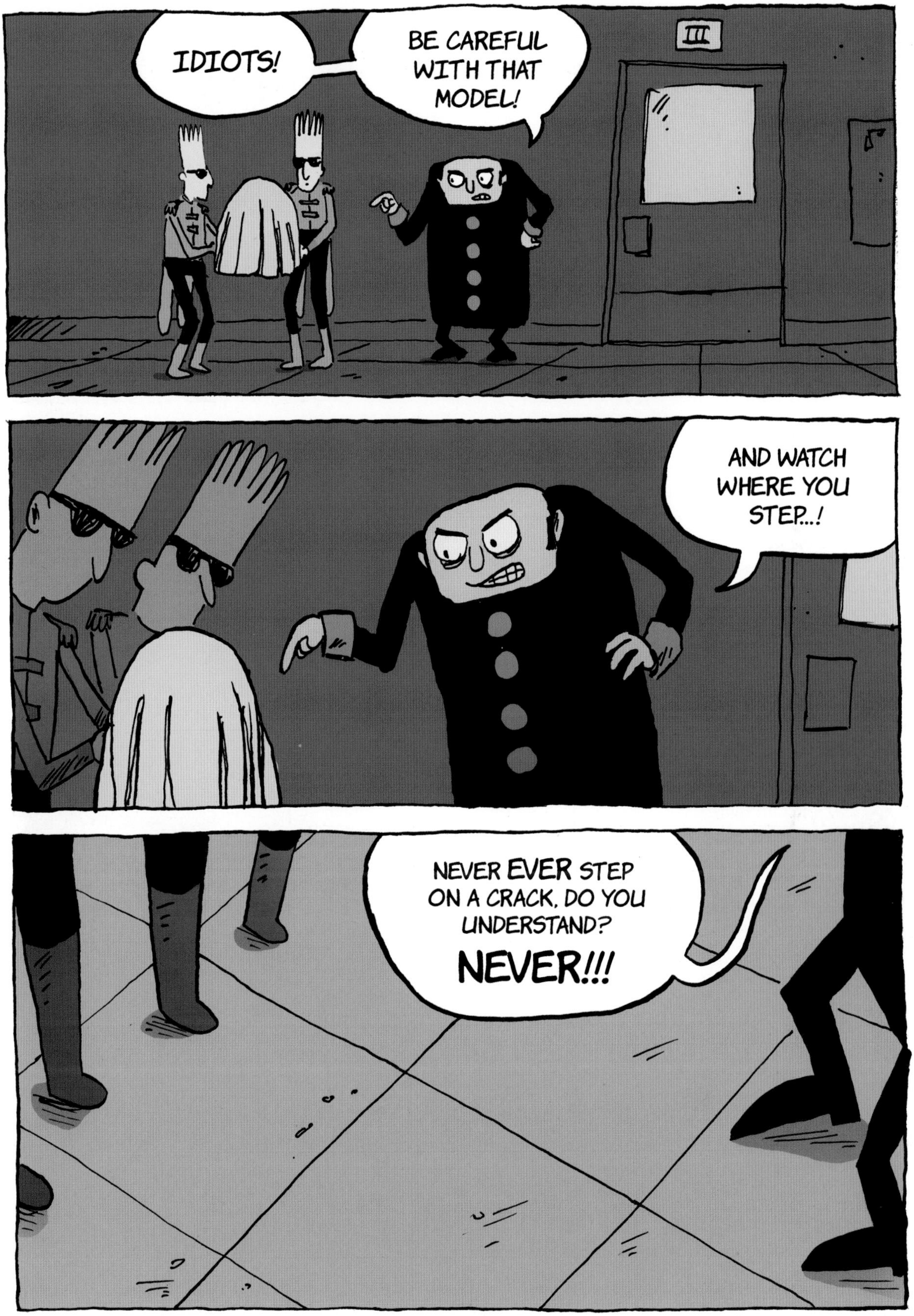
IDIOTS!
BE CAREFUL WITH THAT MODEL!
III
AND WATCH WHERE YOU STEP...!
NEVER **EVER** STEP ON A CRACK, DO YOU UNDERSTAND?
NEVER!!!

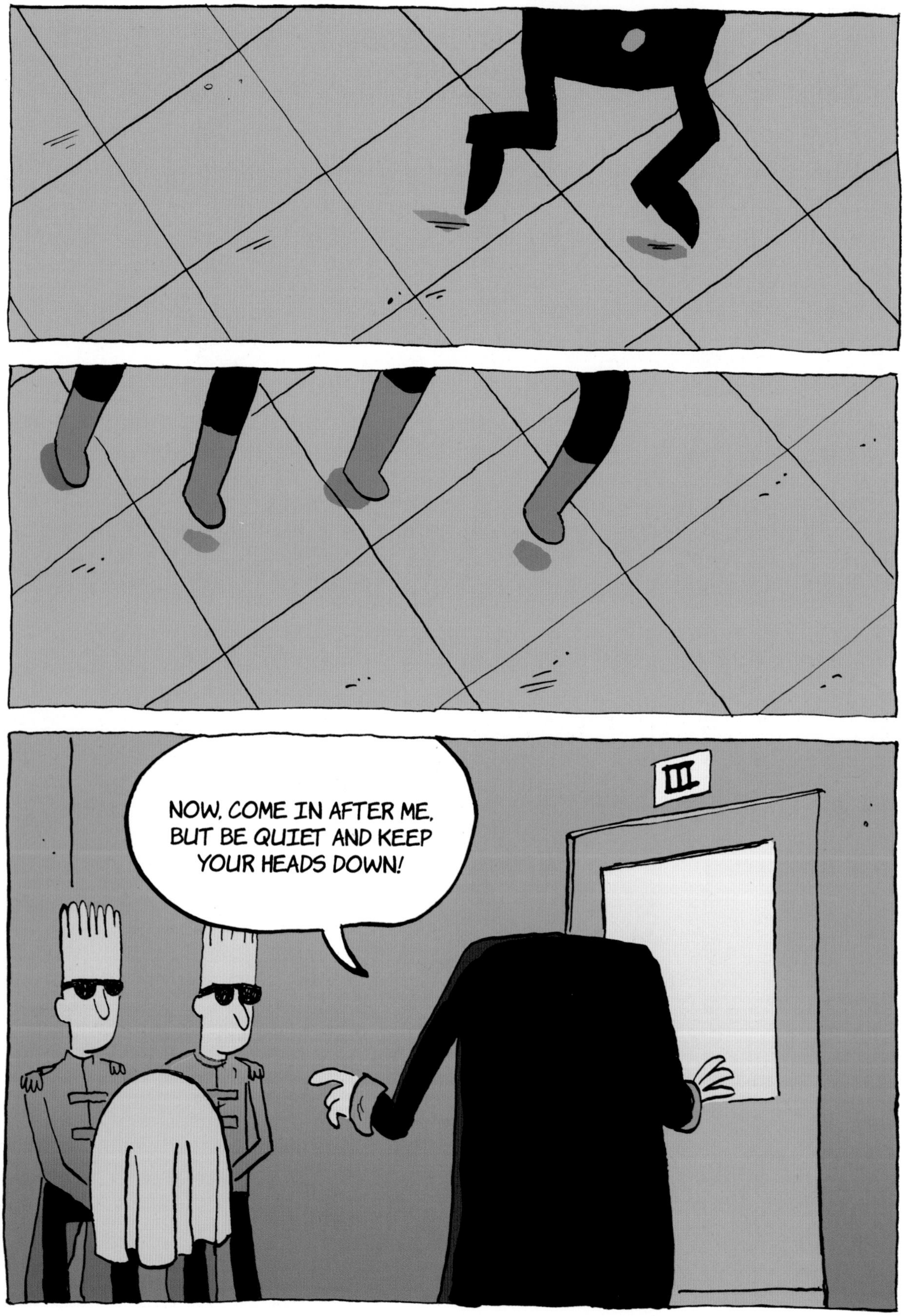
NOW, COME IN AFTER ME, BUT BE QUIET AND KEEP YOUR HEADS DOWN!
III

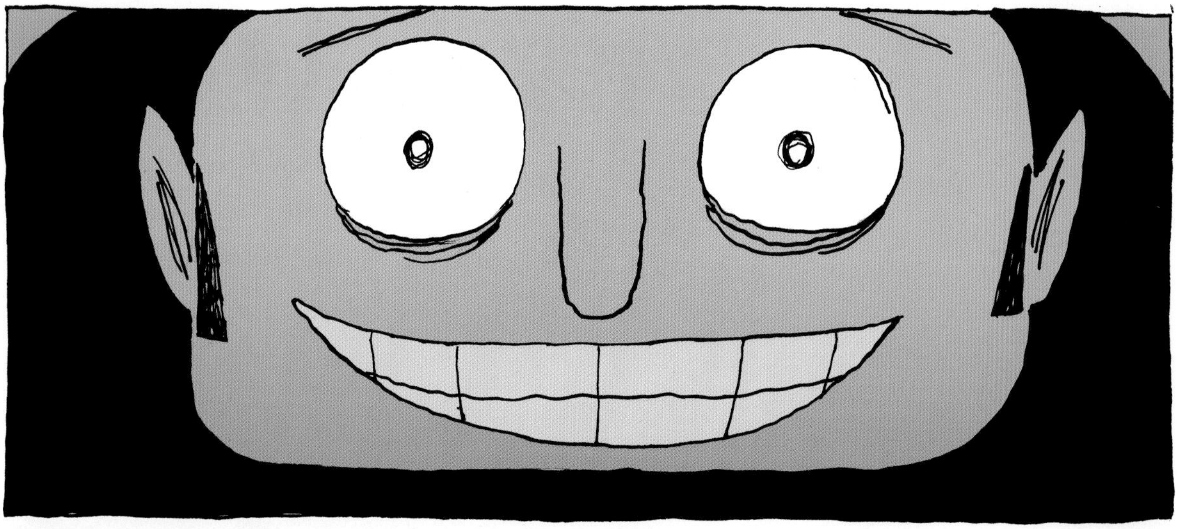

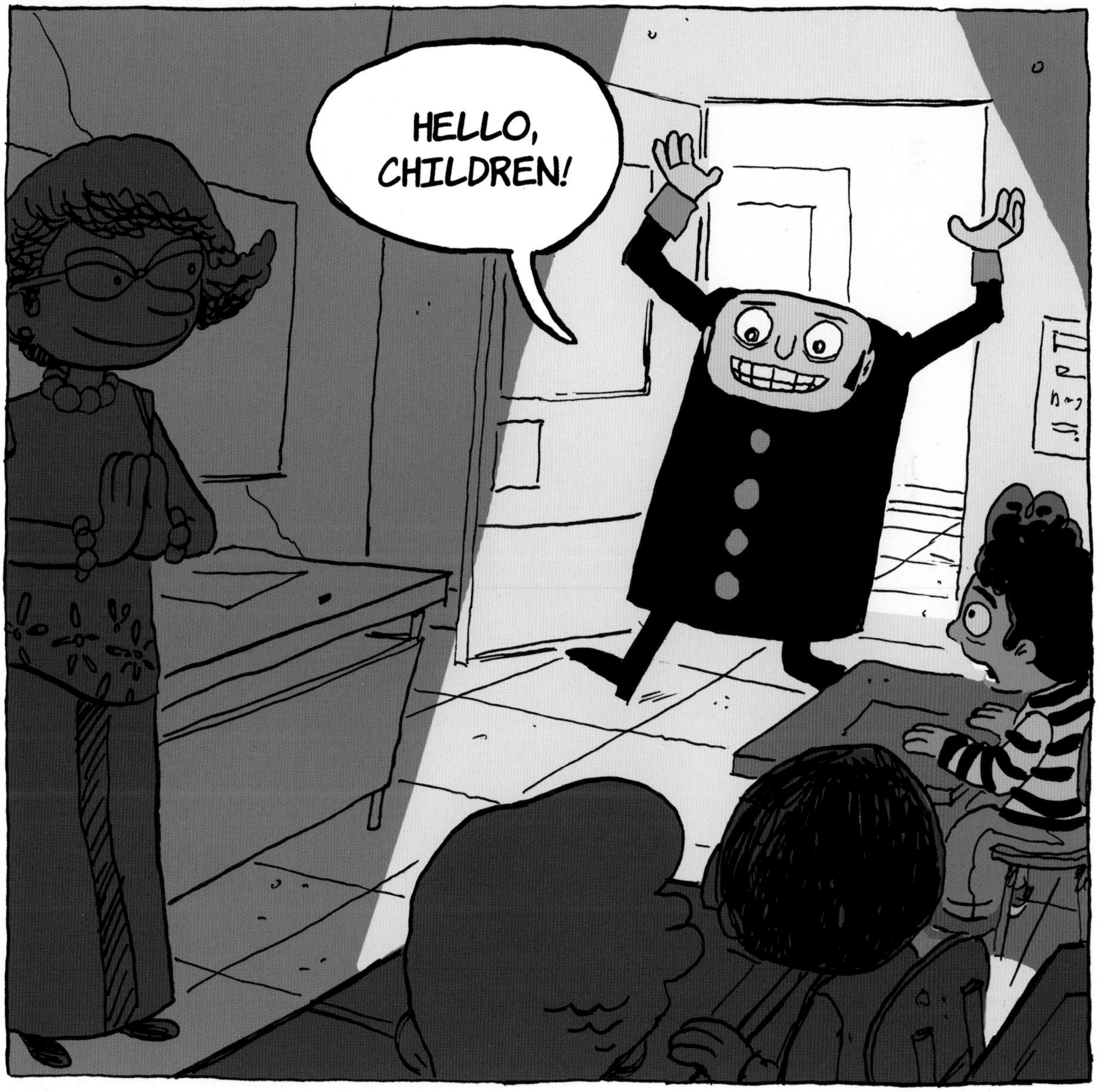
HELLO, CHILDREN!

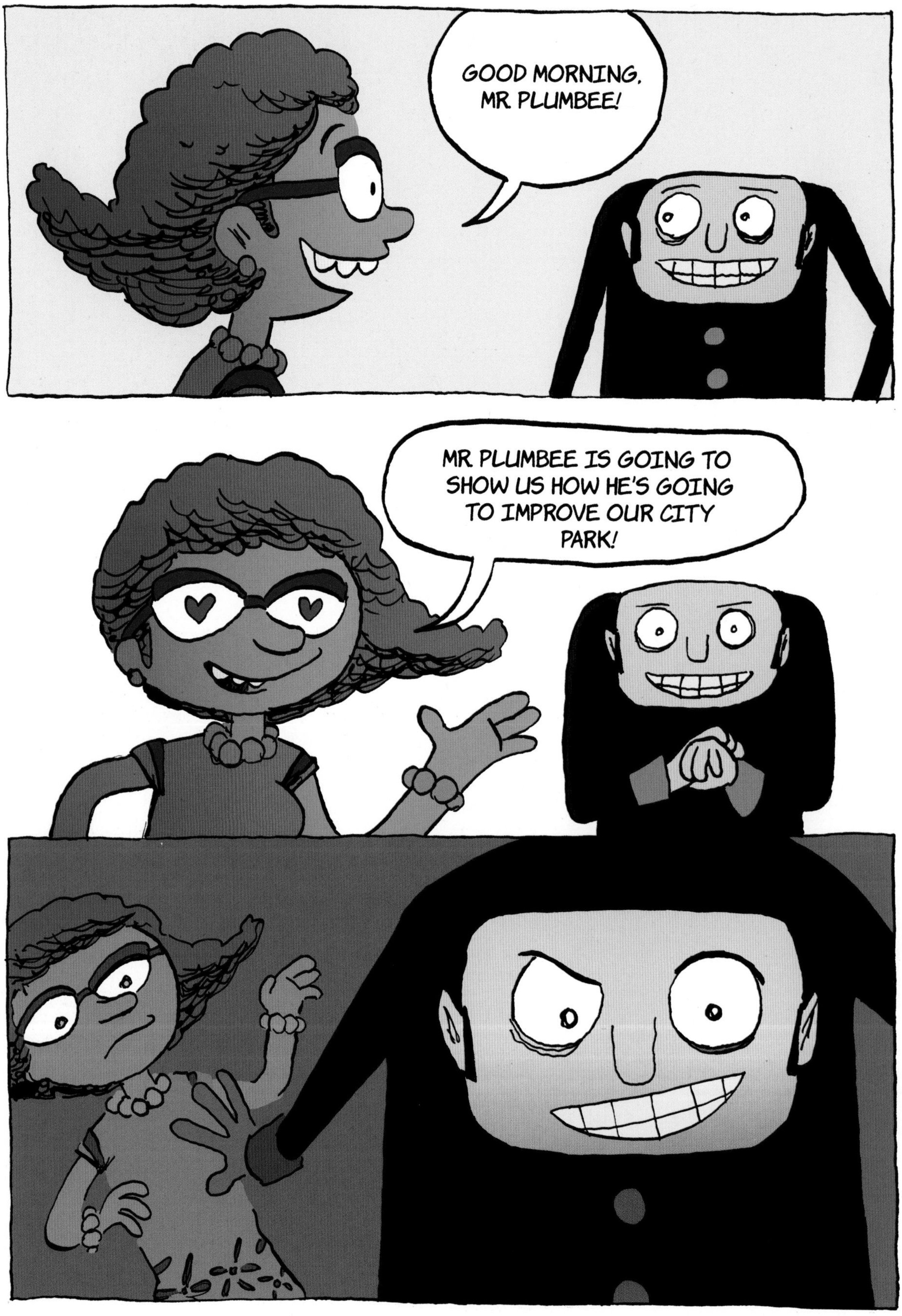
GOOD MORNING, MR. PLUMBEE!
MR. PLUMBEE IS GOING TO SHOW US HOW HE'S GOING TO IMPROVE OUR CITY PARK!

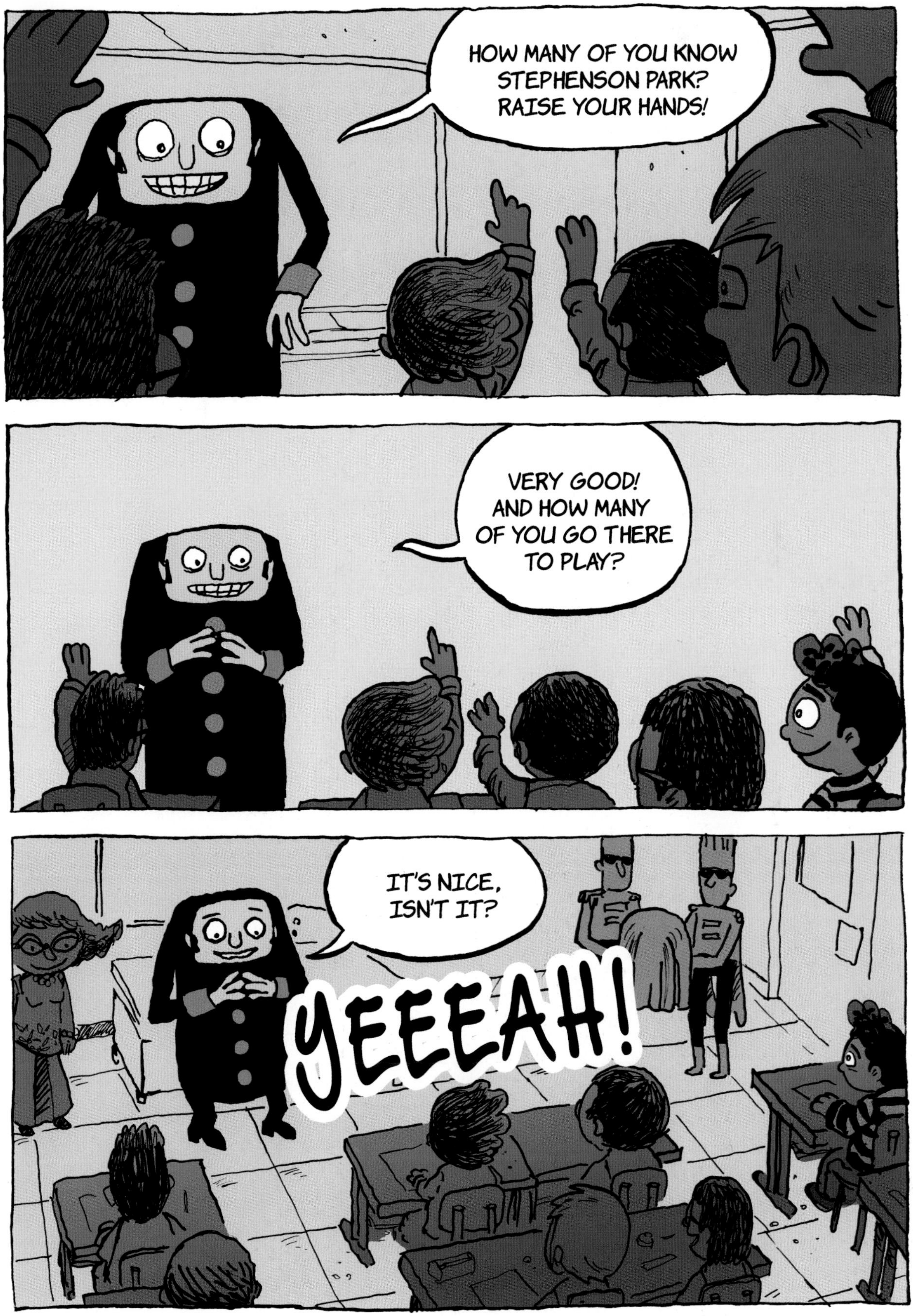
HOW MANY OF YOU KNOW STEPHENSON PARK? RAISE YOUR HANDS!
VERY GOOD! AND HOW MANY OF YOU GO THERE TO PLAY?
IT'S NICE, ISN'T IT?
YEEEAH!

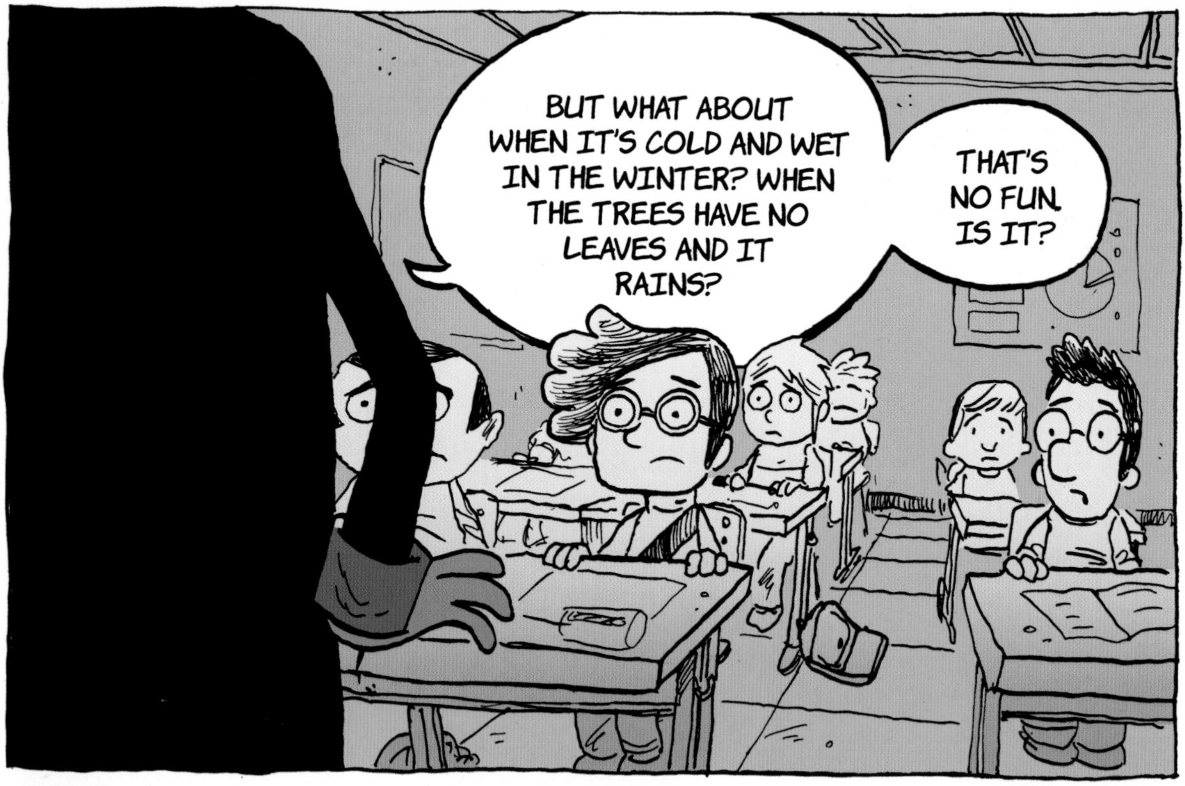
BUT WHAT ABOUT WHEN IT'S COLD AND WET IN THE WINTER? WHEN THE TREES HAVE NO LEAVES AND IT RAINS?
THAT'S NO FUN, IS IT?

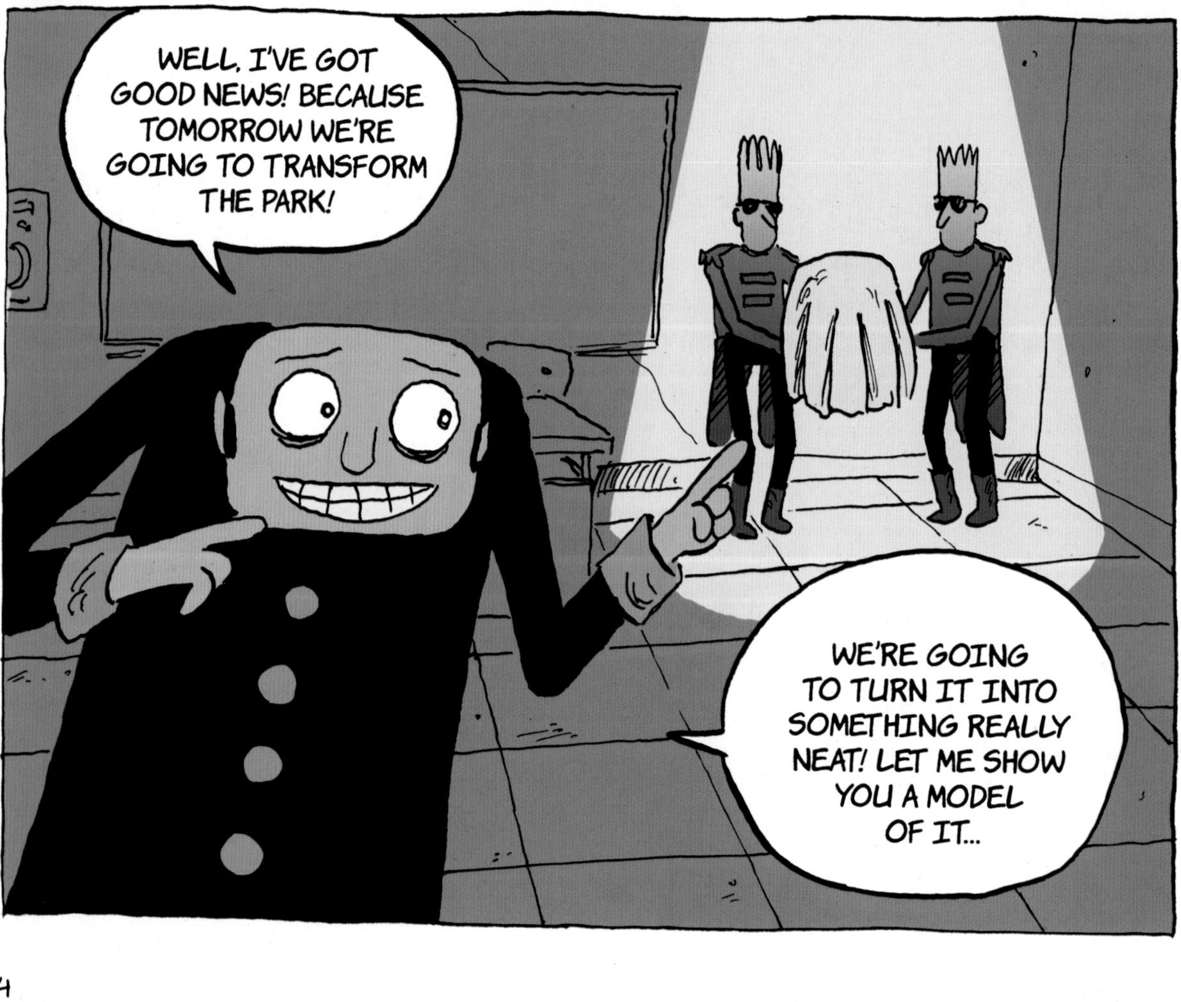
WELL, I'VE GOT GOOD NEWS! BECAUSE TOMORROW WE'RE GOING TO TRANSFORM THE PARK!
WE'RE GOING TO TURN IT INTO SOMETHING REALLY NEAT! LET ME SHOW YOU A MODEL OF IT...

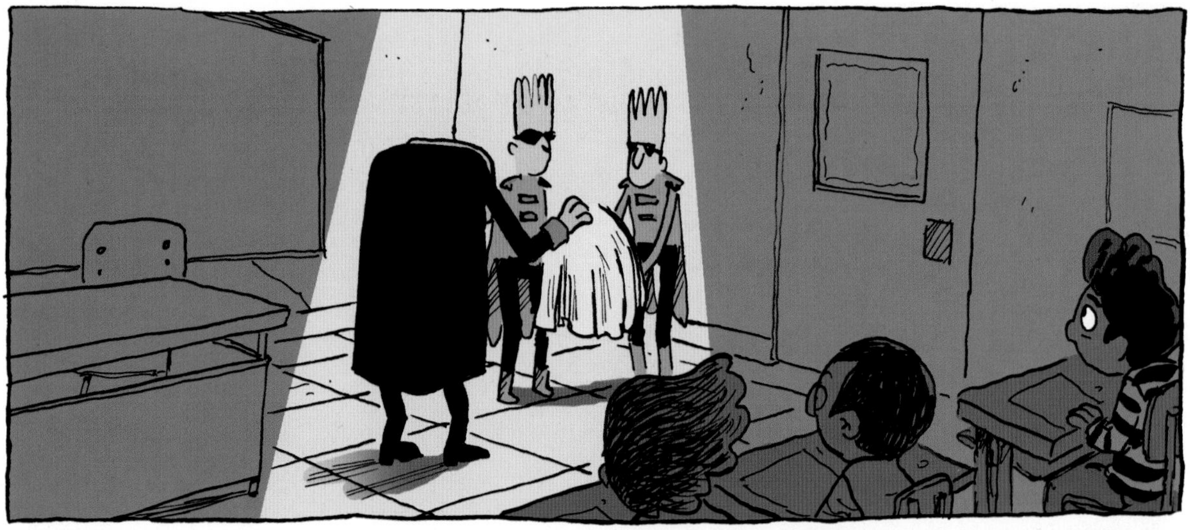

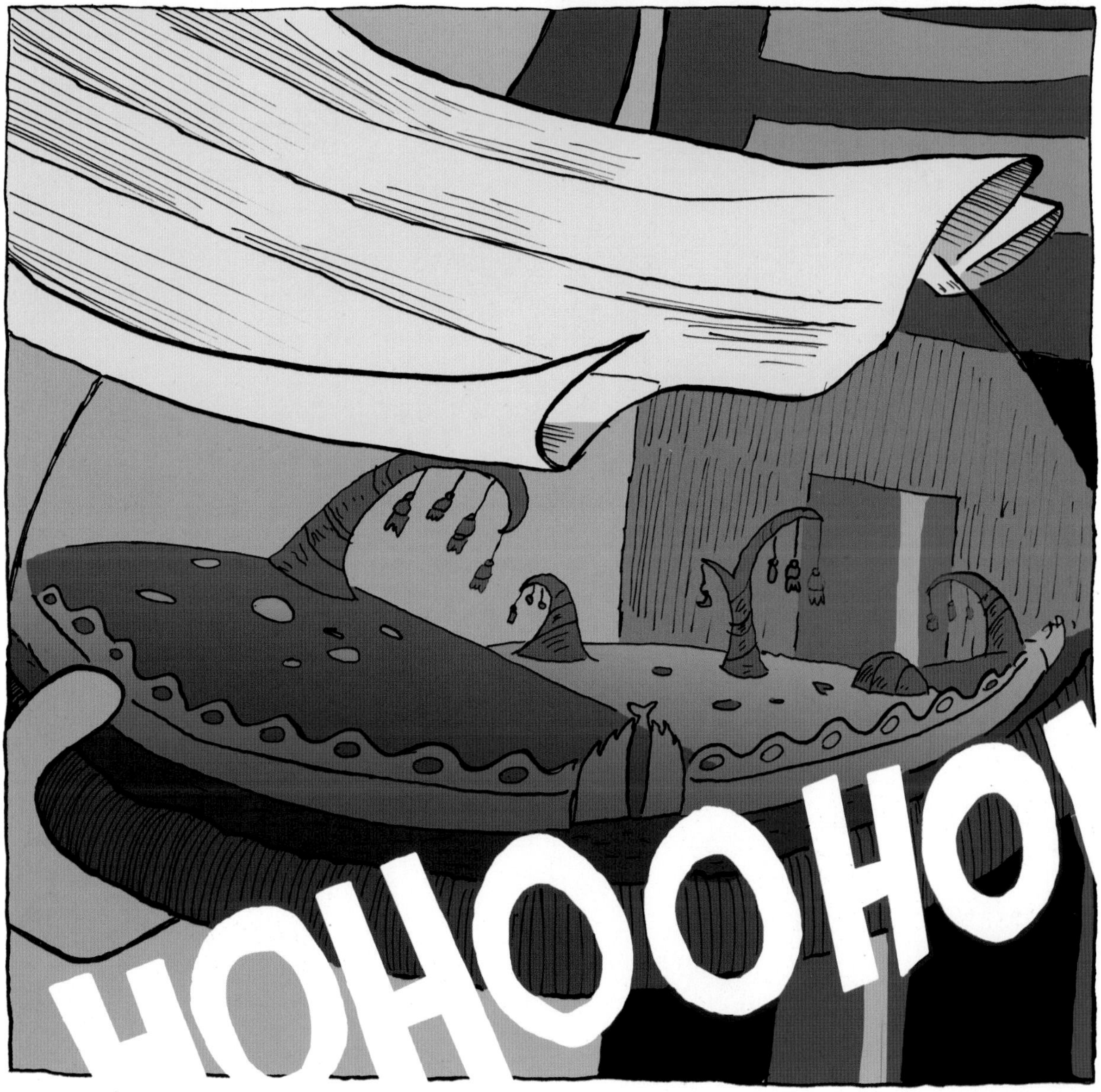
HOHOOHOH

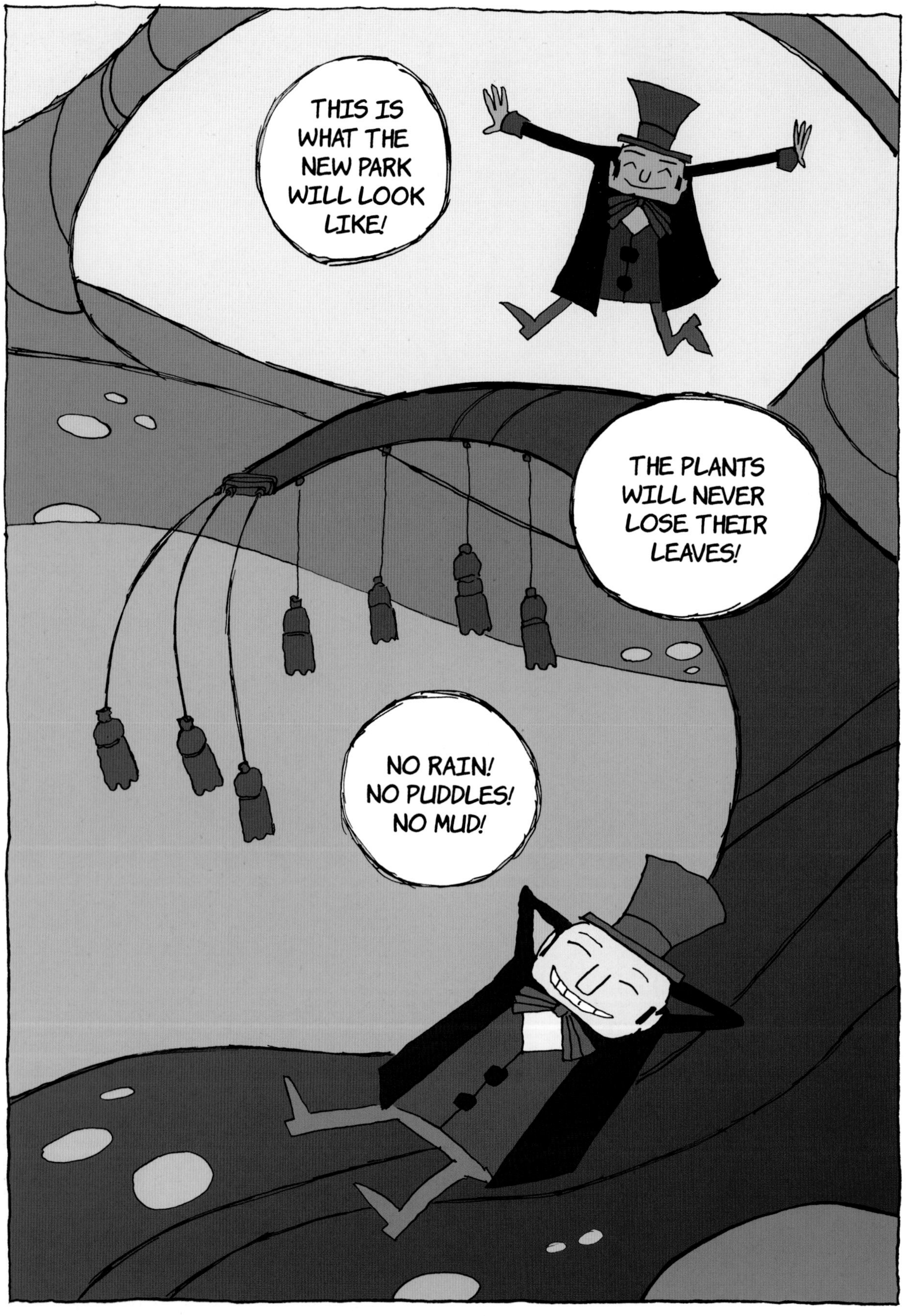
THIS IS WHAT THE NEW PARK WILL LOOK LIKE!
THE PLANTS WILL NEVER LOSE THEIR LEAVES!
NO RAIN! NO PUDDLES! NO MUD!

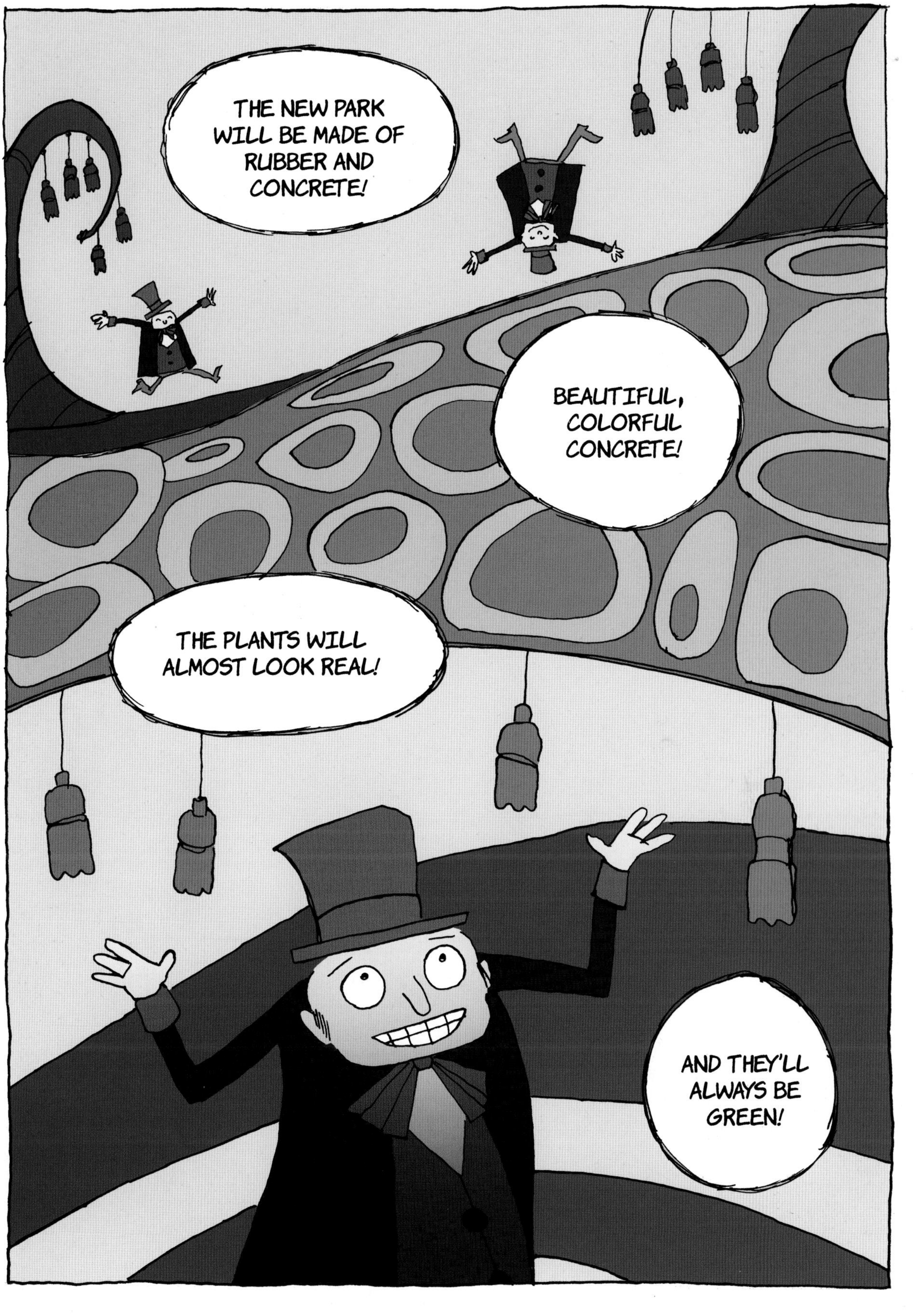
THE NEW PARK WILL BE MADE OF RUBBER AND CONCRETE!
BEAUTIFUL, COLORFUL CONCRETE!
THE PLANTS WILL ALMOST LOOK REAL!
AND THEY'LL ALWAYS BE GREEN!

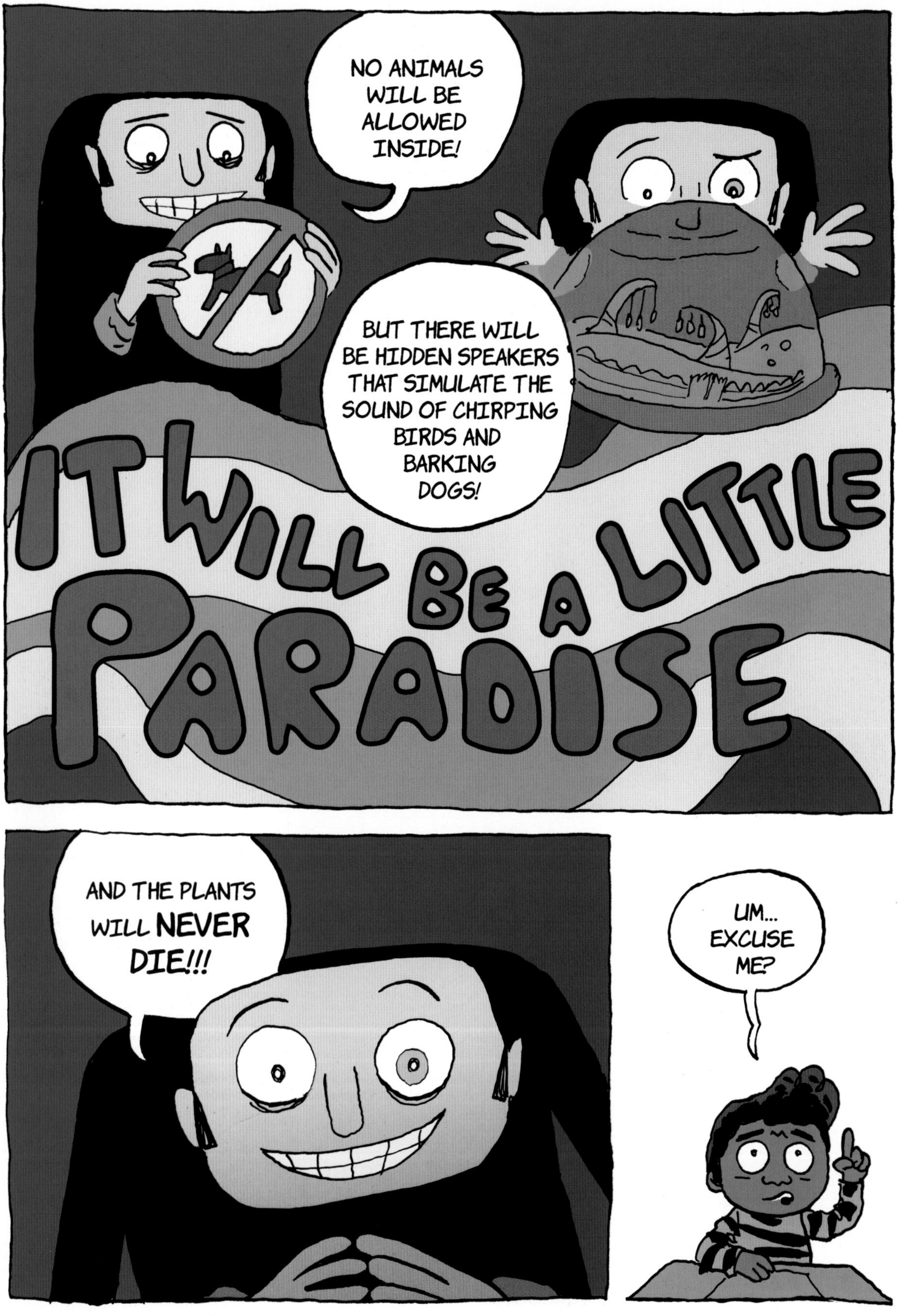
NO ANIMALS WILL BE ALLOWED INSIDE!
BUT THERE WILL BE HIDDEN SPEAKERS THAT SIMULATE THE SOUND OF CHIRPING BIRDS AND BARKING DOGS!
IT WILL BE A LITTLE PARADISE
AND THE PLANTS WILL NEVER DIE!!!
UM... EXCUSE ME?

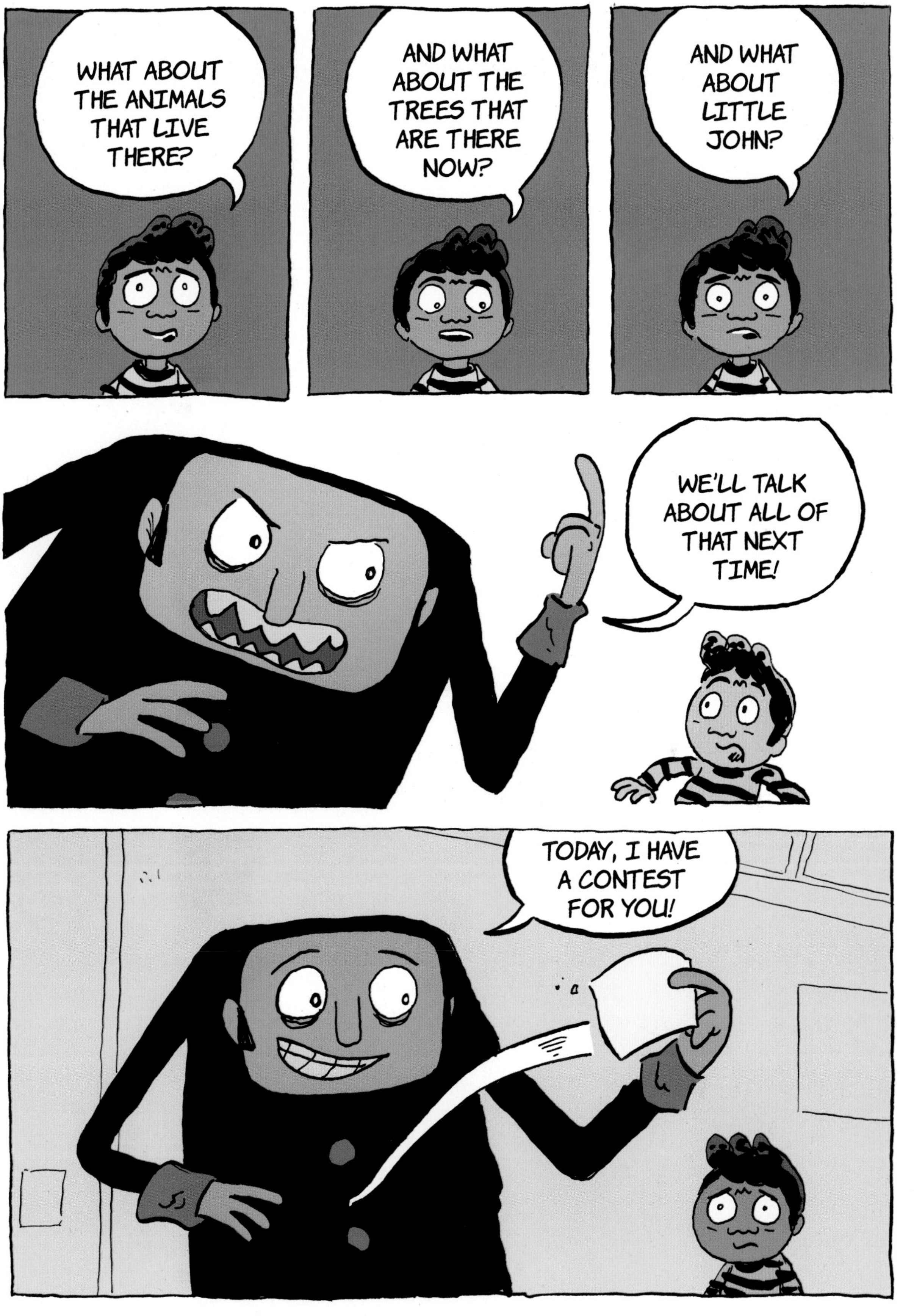
WHAT ABOUT THE ANIMALS THAT LIVE THERE?
AND WHAT ABOUT THE TREES THAT ARE THERE NOW?
AND WHAT ABOUT LITTLE JOHN?
WE'LL TALK ABOUT ALL OF THAT NEXT TIME!
TODAY, I HAVE A CONTEST FOR YOU!

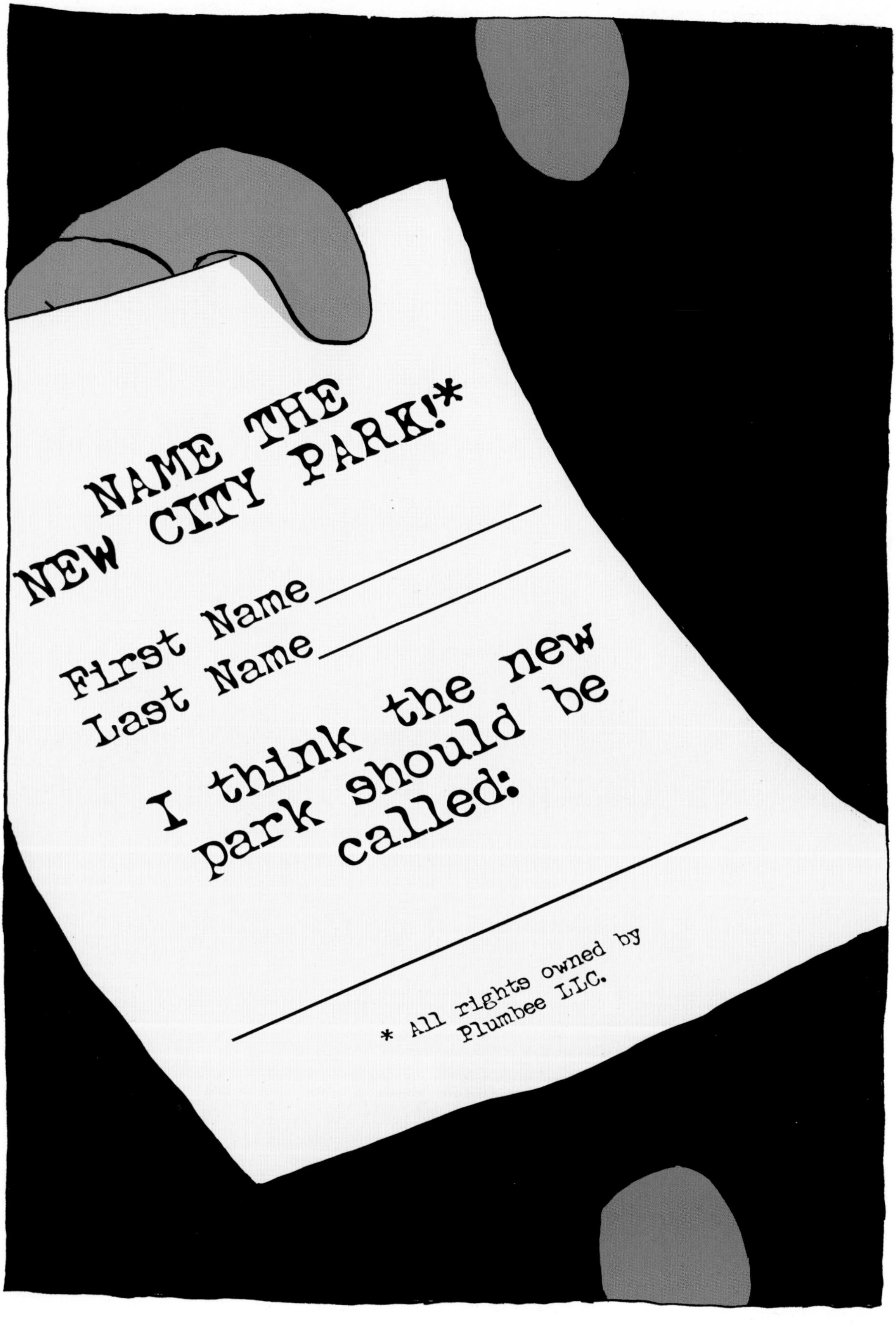
NAME THE
NEW CITY PARK!*
First Name
Last Name
I think the new
park should be
called:
* All rights owned by
Plumbee LLC.

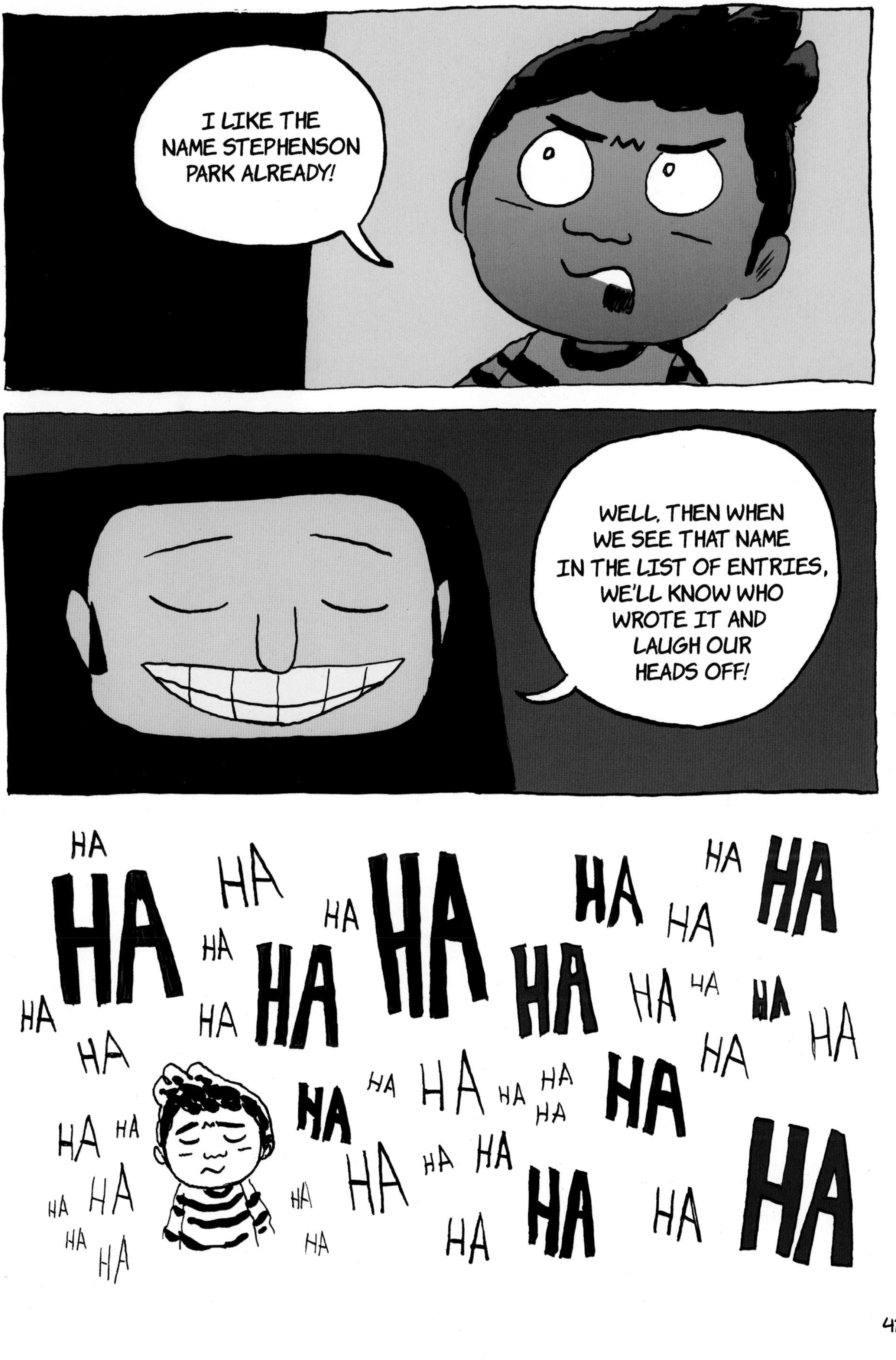
I LIKE THE NAME STEPHENSON PARK ALREADY!
WELL, THEN WHEN WE SEE THAT NAME IN THE LIST OF ENTRIES, WE'LL KNOW WHO WROTE IT AND LAUGH OUR HEADS OFF!
HA HA HA HA HA HA HA HA HA HA HA HA HA HA HA HA HA HA HA HA HA HA HA HA HA HA HA HA HA HA HA HA HA HA HA HA HA HA HA HA HA HA

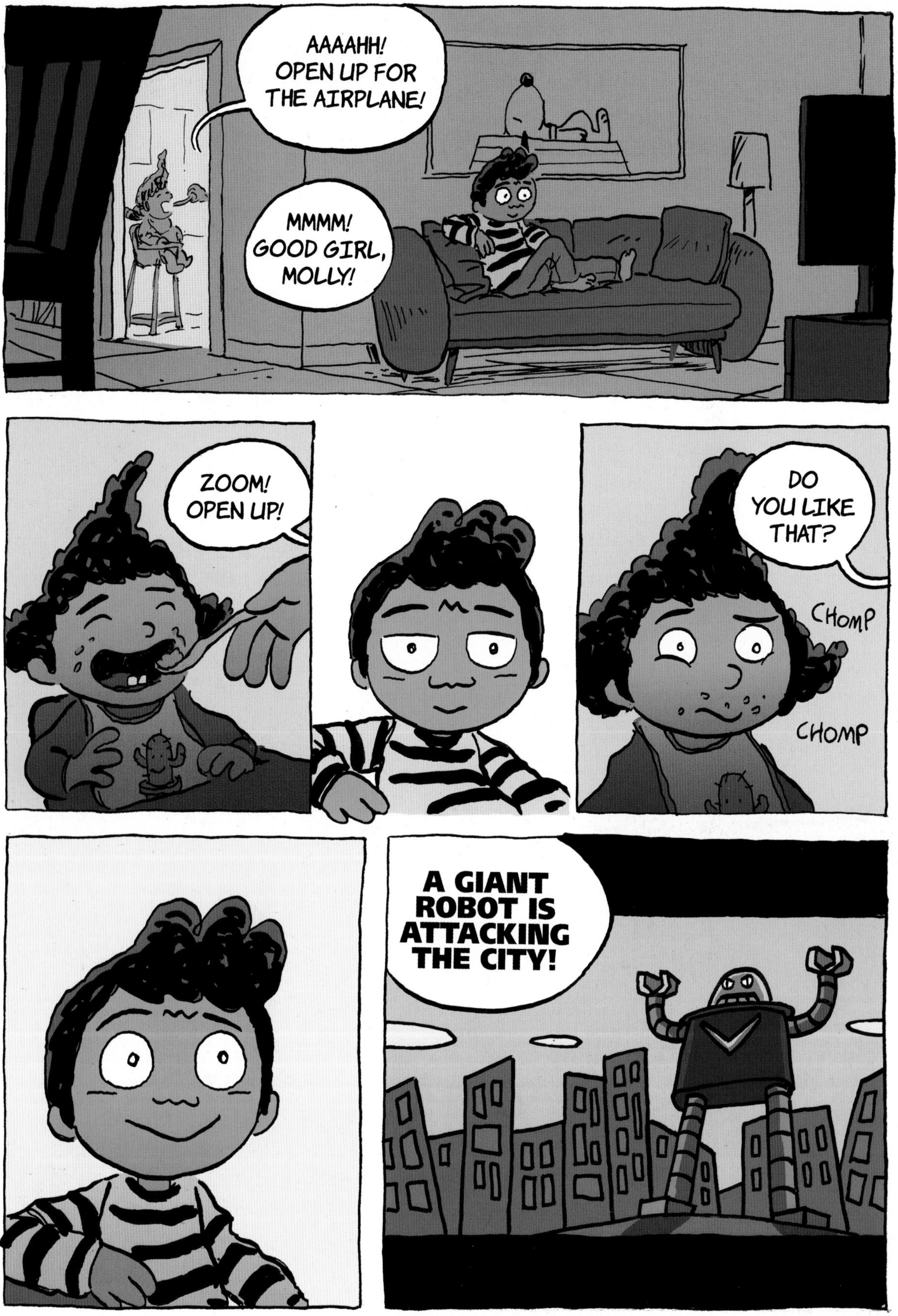
AAAAHH! OPEN UP FOR THE AIRPLANE!
MMMM! GOOD GIRL, MOLLY!
ZOOM! OPEN UP!
DO YOU LIKE THAT?
CHOMP
CHOMP
A GIANT ROBOT IS ATTACKING THE CITY!

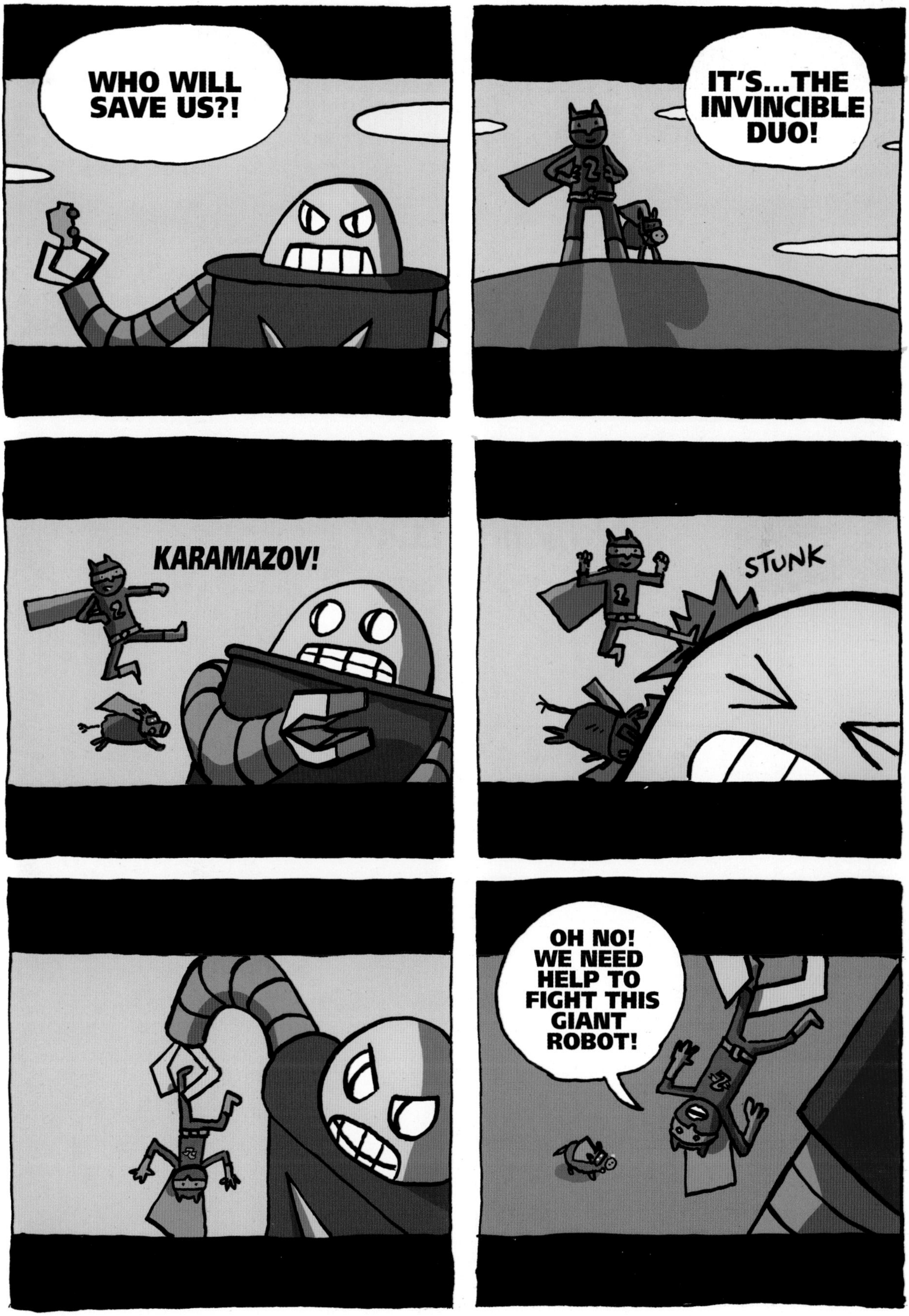
WHO WILL SAVE US?!
IT'S...THE INVINCIBLE DUO!
KARAMAZOV!
STUNK
OH NO! WE NEED HELP TO FIGHT THIS GIANT ROBOT!

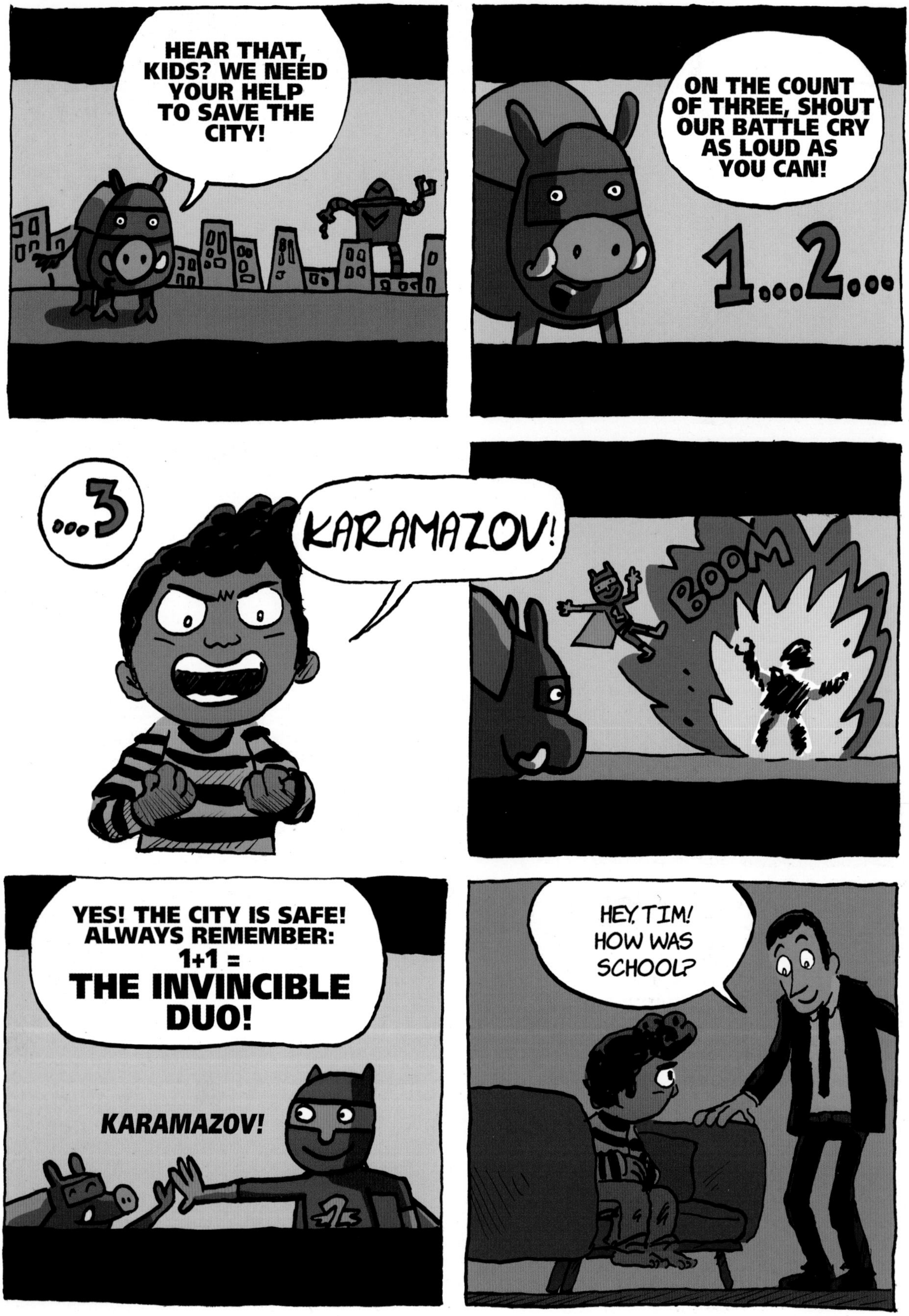
HEAR THAT, KIDS? WE NEED YOUR HELP TO SAVE THE CITY!
ON THE COUNT OF THREE, SHOUT OUR BATTLE CRY AS LOUD AS YOU CAN!
1...2...
...3
KARAMAZOV!
BOOM
YES! THE CITY IS SAFE! ALWAYS REMEMBER: 1+1 = THE INVINCIBLE DUO!
KARAMAZOV!
HEY, TIM! HOW WAS SCHOOL?

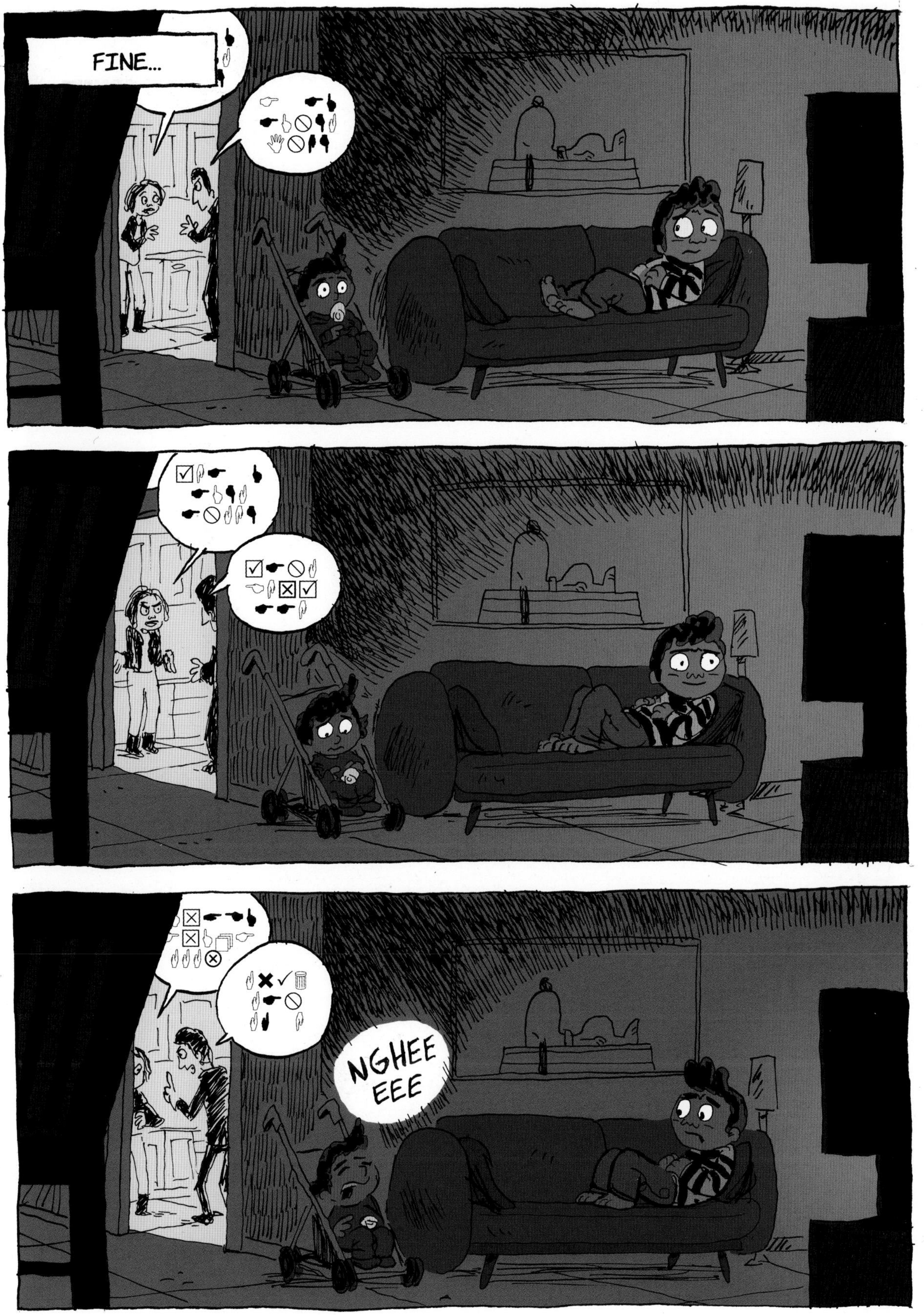
FINE...
NGHEE
EEE

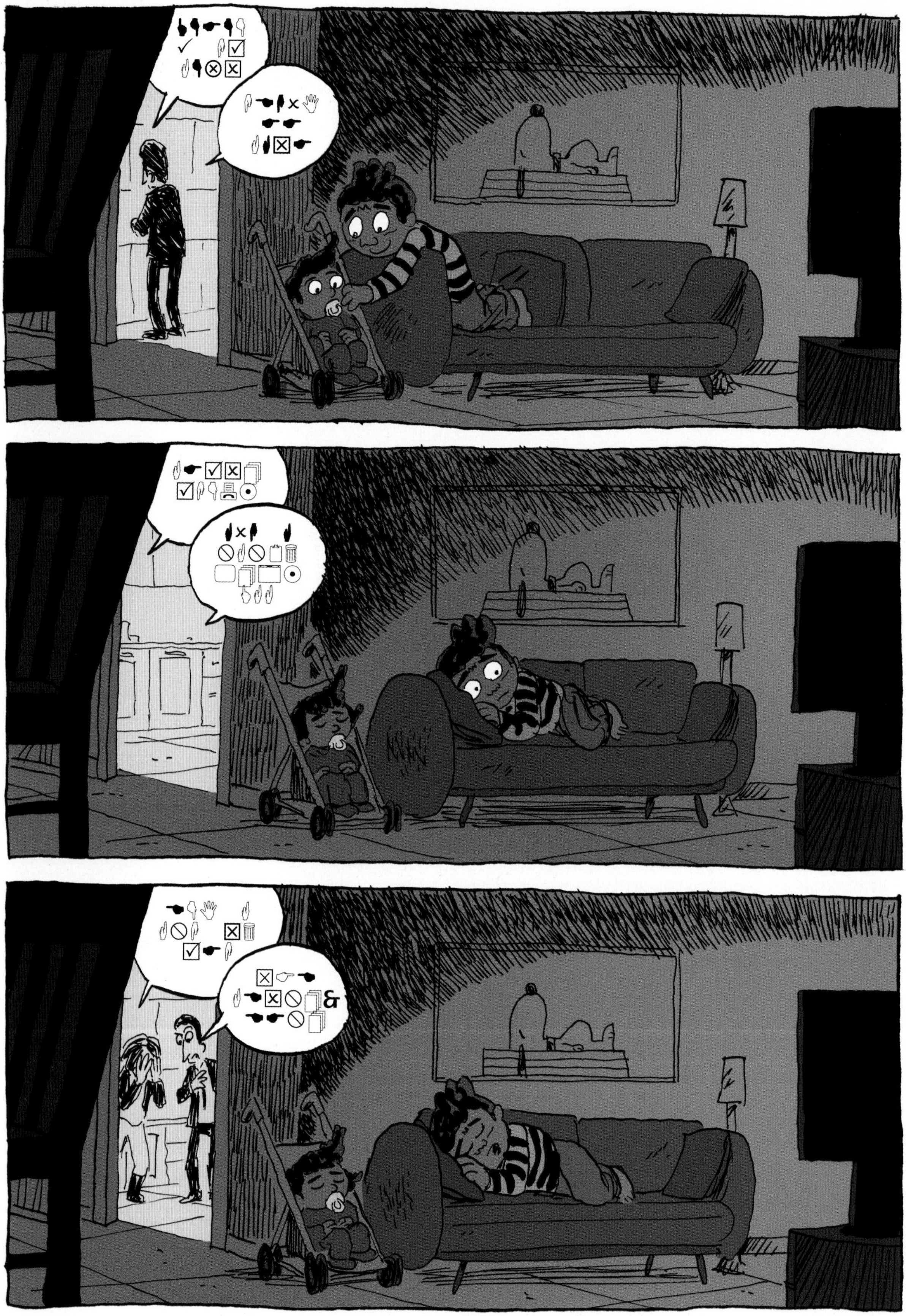

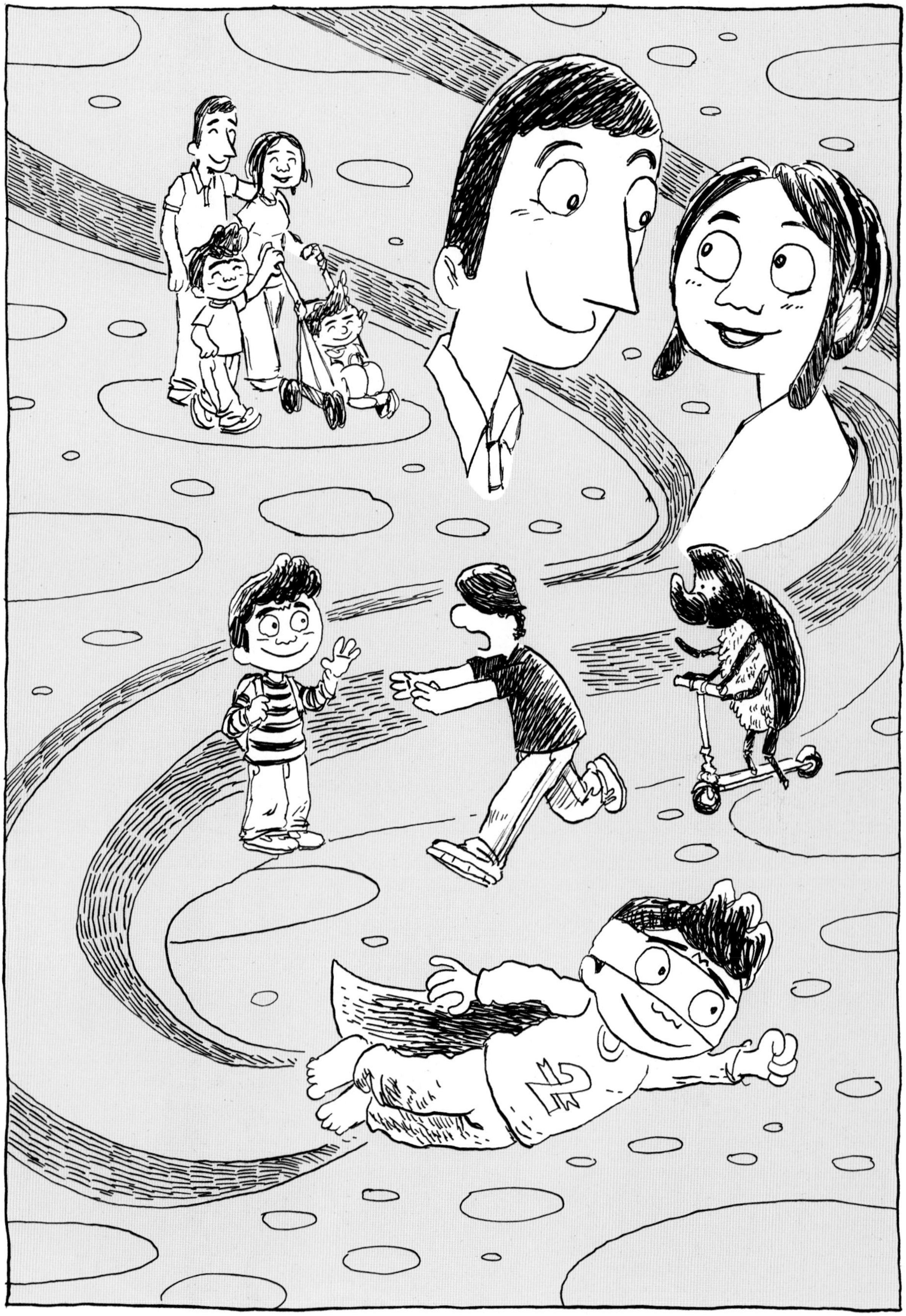

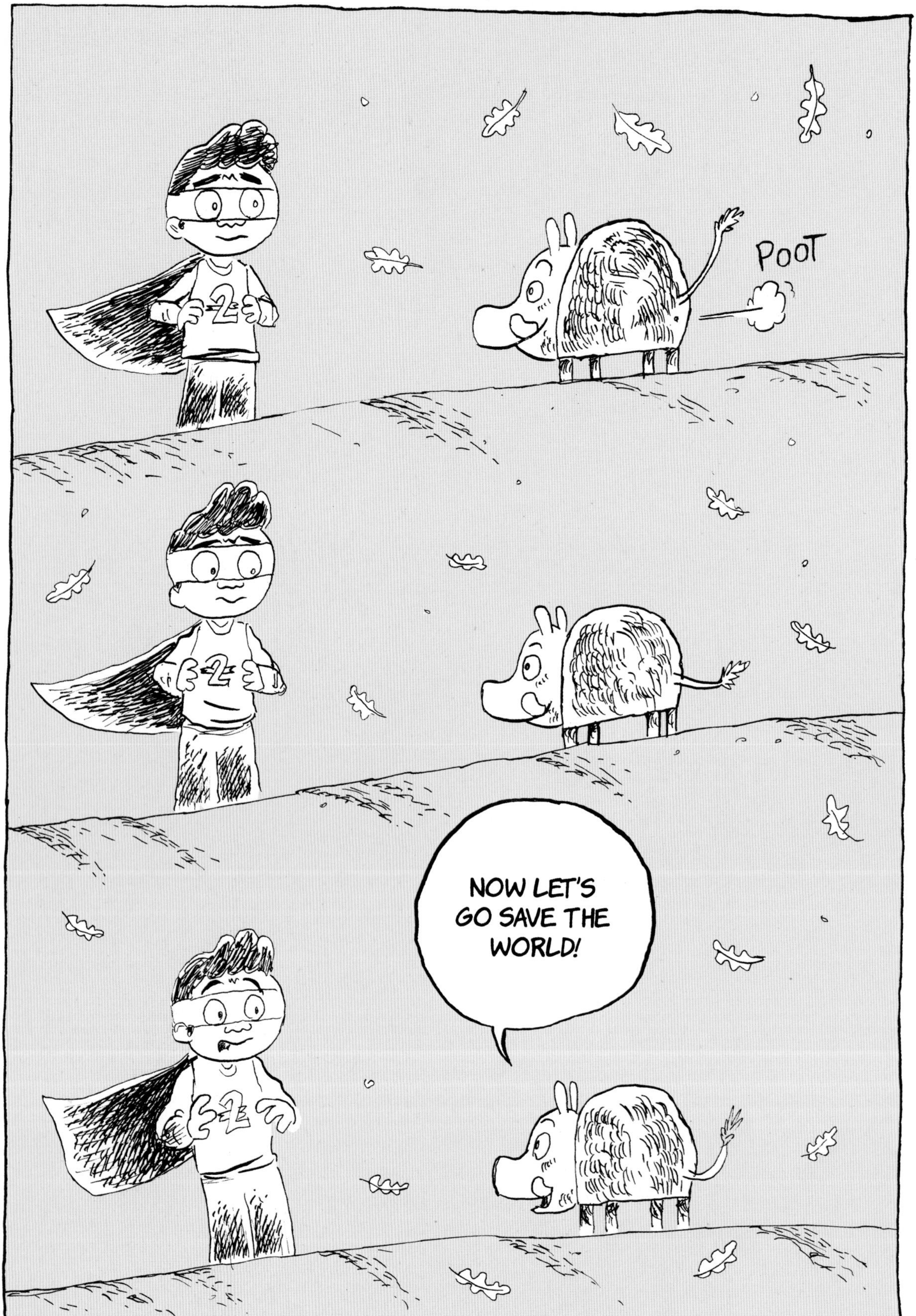
POOT
NOW LET'S GO SAVE THE WORLD!

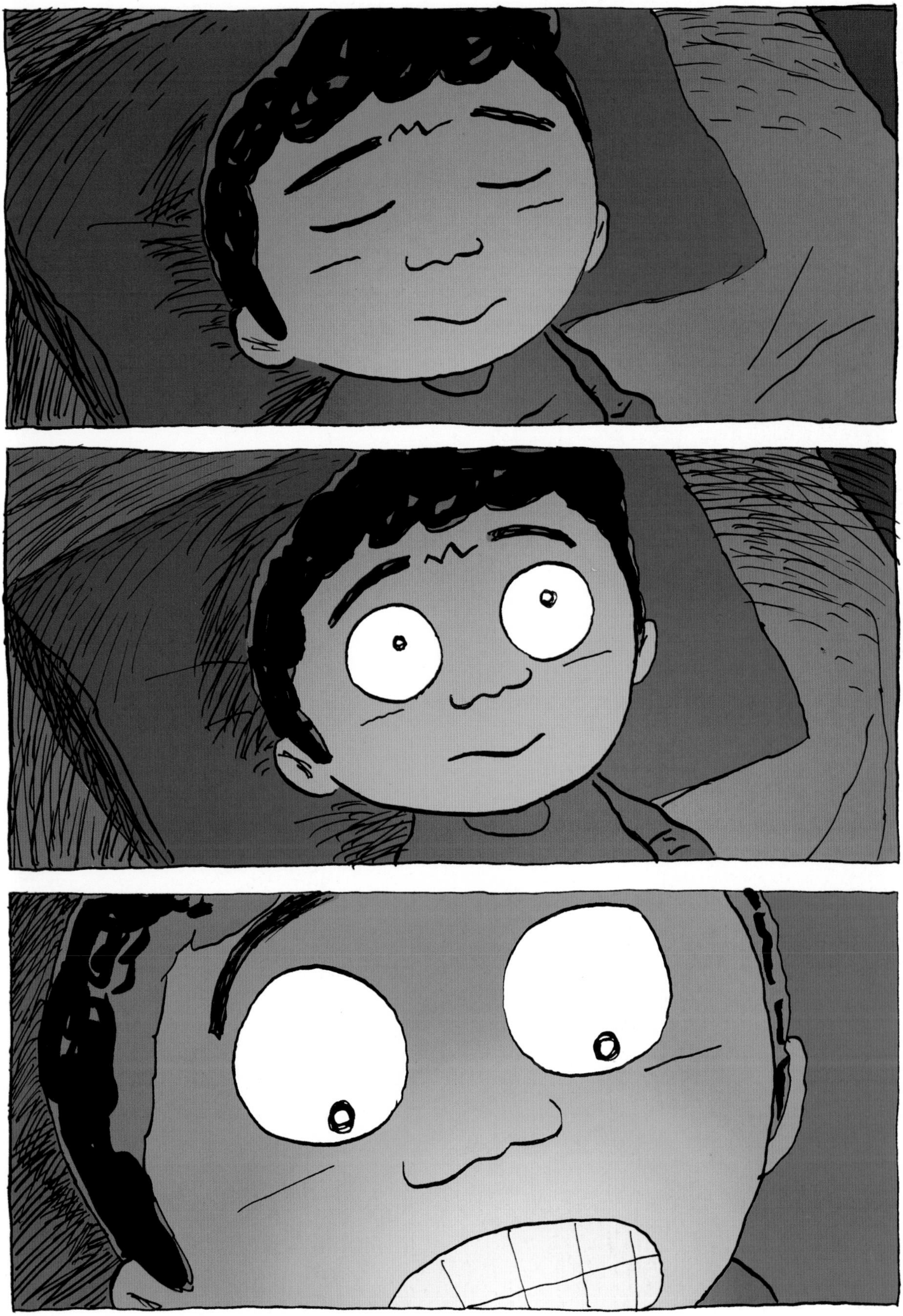

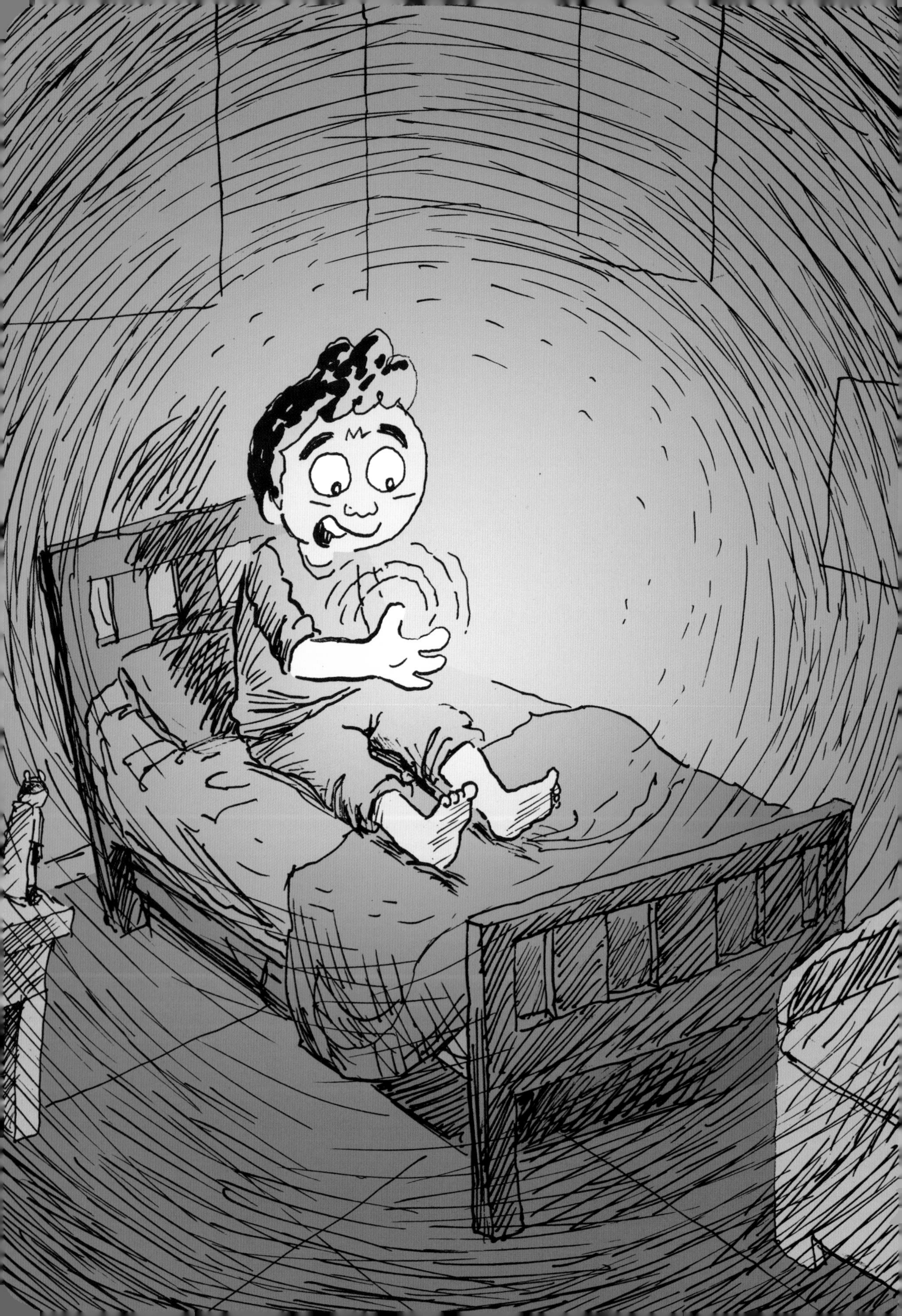

CHAPTER TWO
LITTLE JOHN

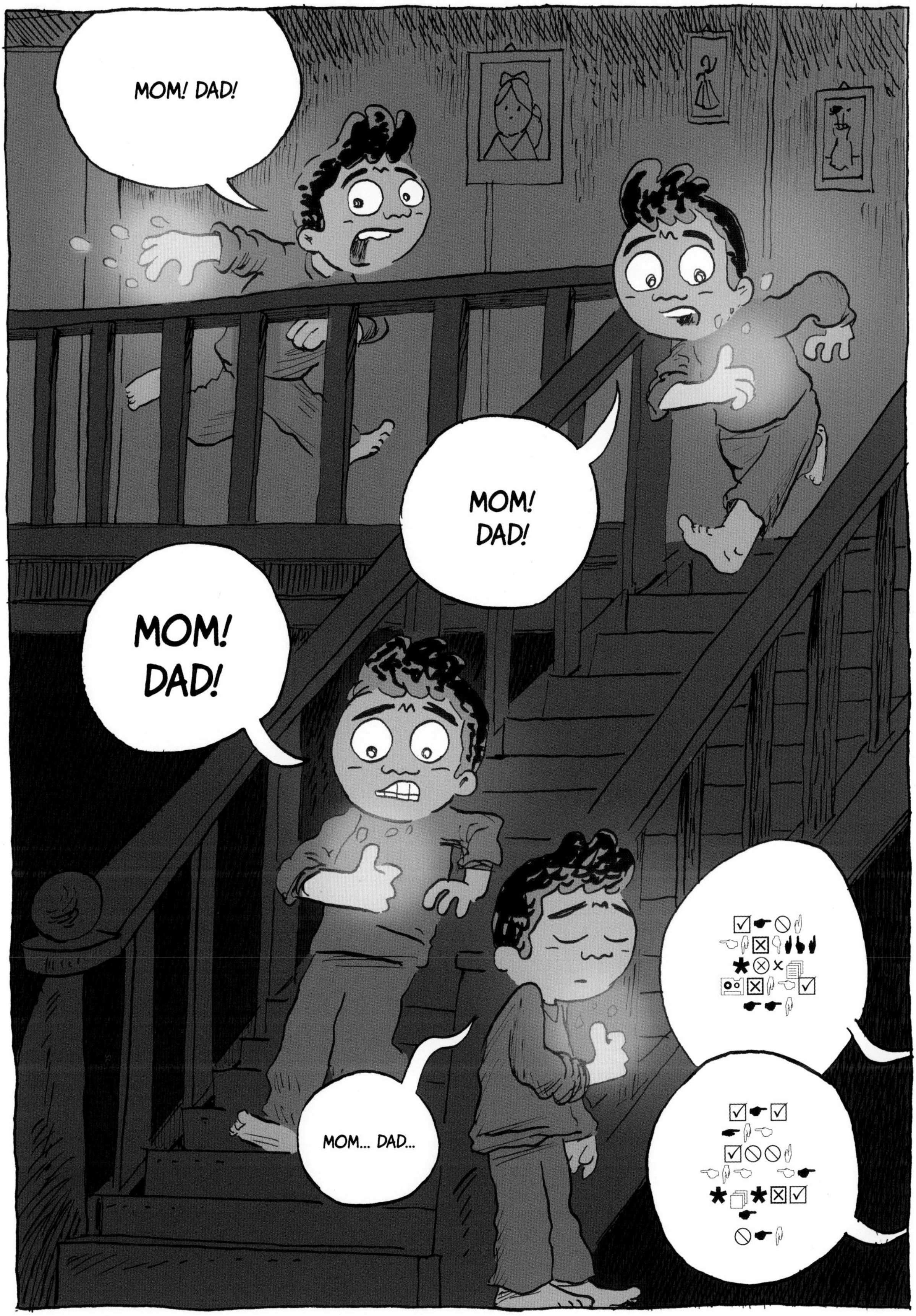
MOM! DAD!
MOM! DAD!
MOM! DAD!
MOM... DAD...

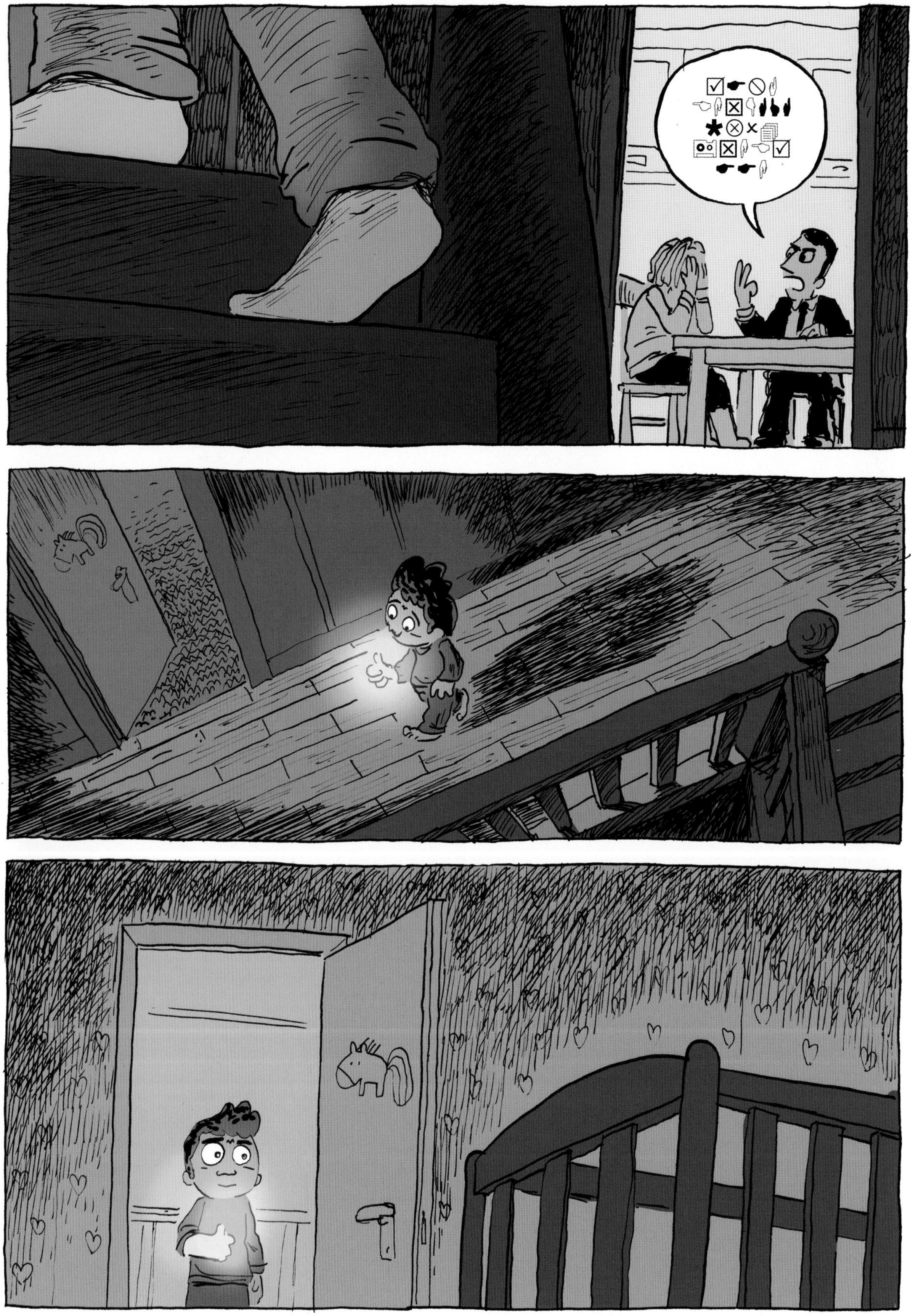

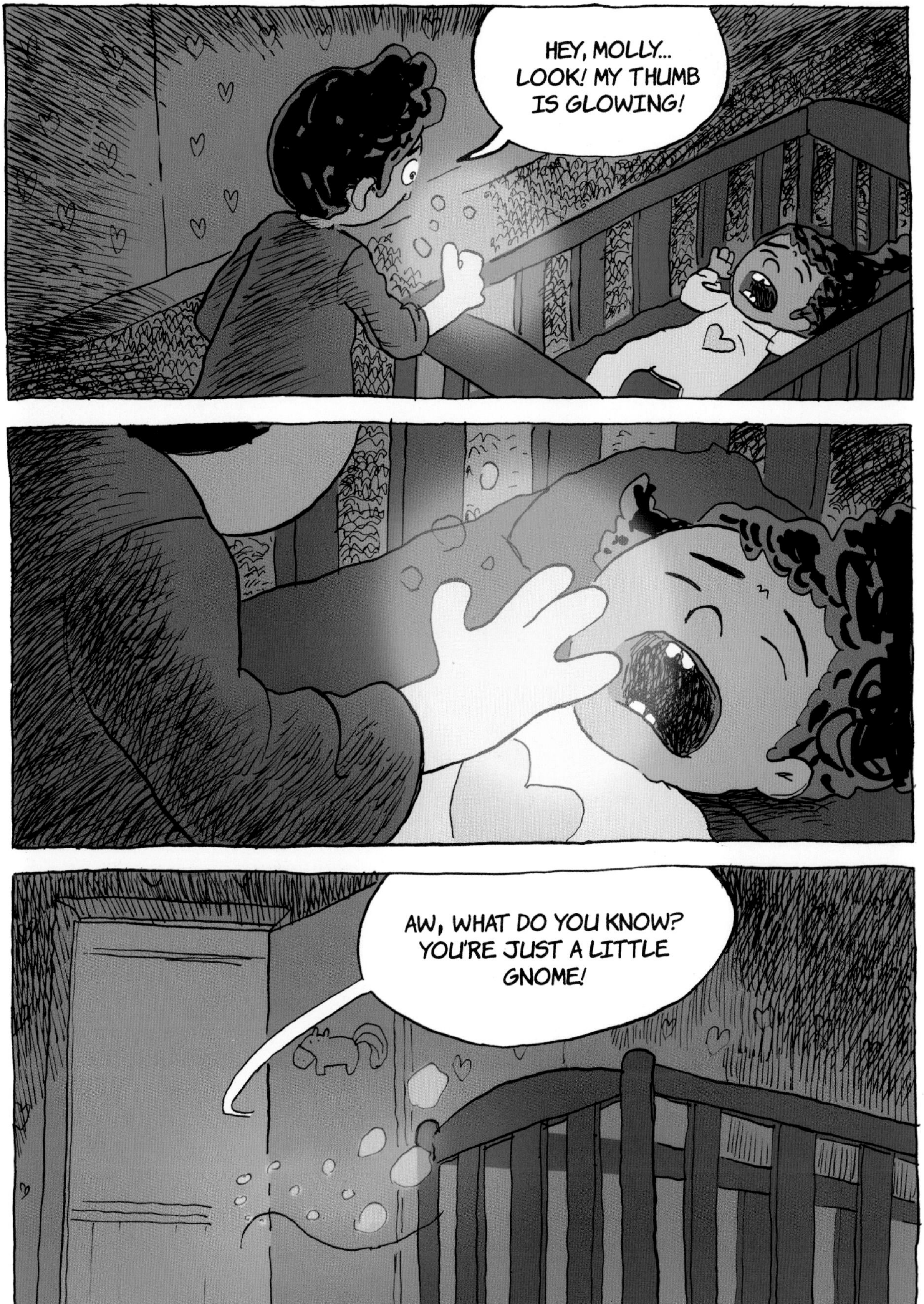
HEY, MOLLY... LOOK! MY THUMB IS GLOWING!
AW, WHAT DO YOU KNOW? YOU'RE JUST A LITTLE GNOME!

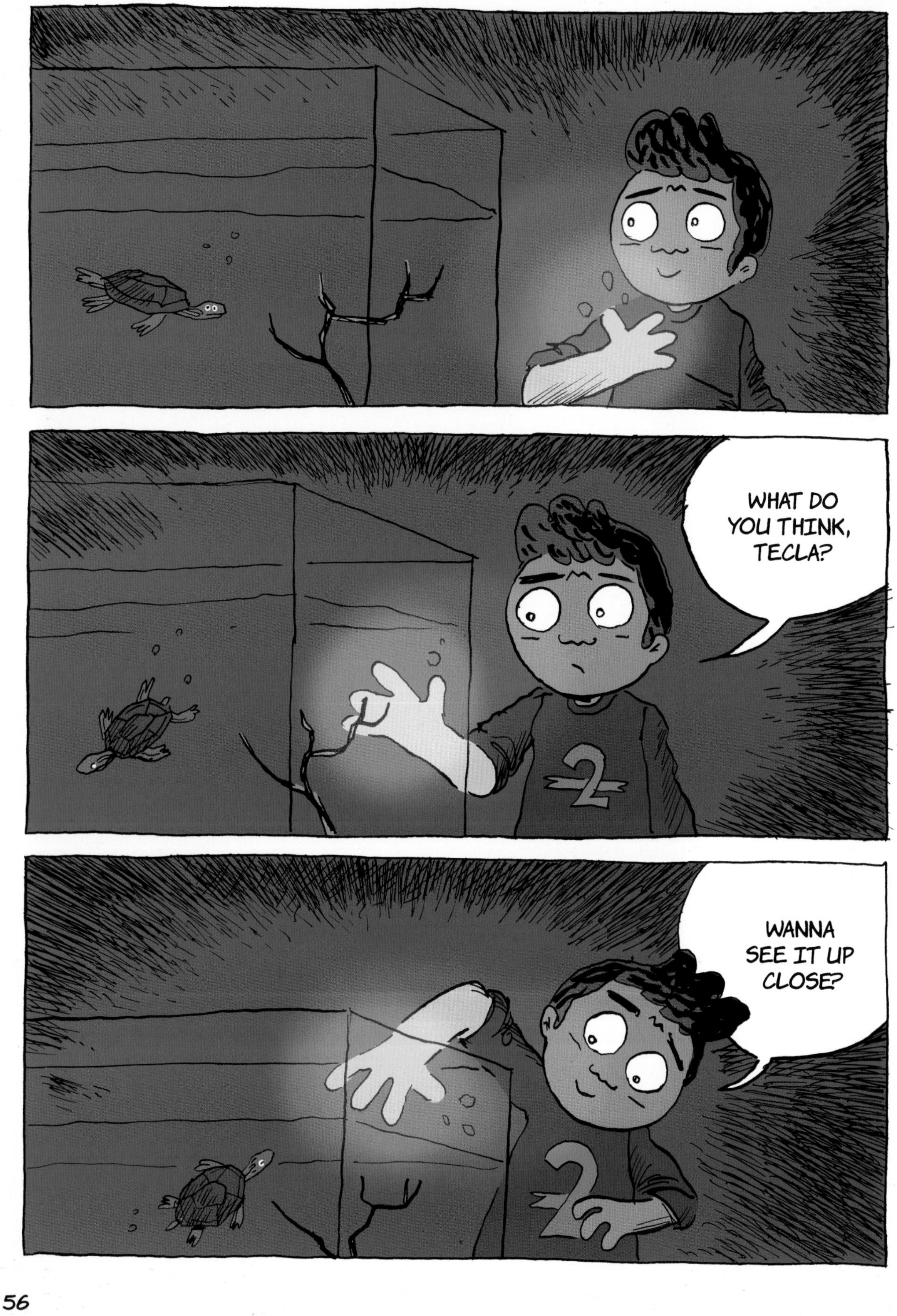
WHAT DO YOU THINK, TECLA?
WANNA SEE IT UP CLOSE?

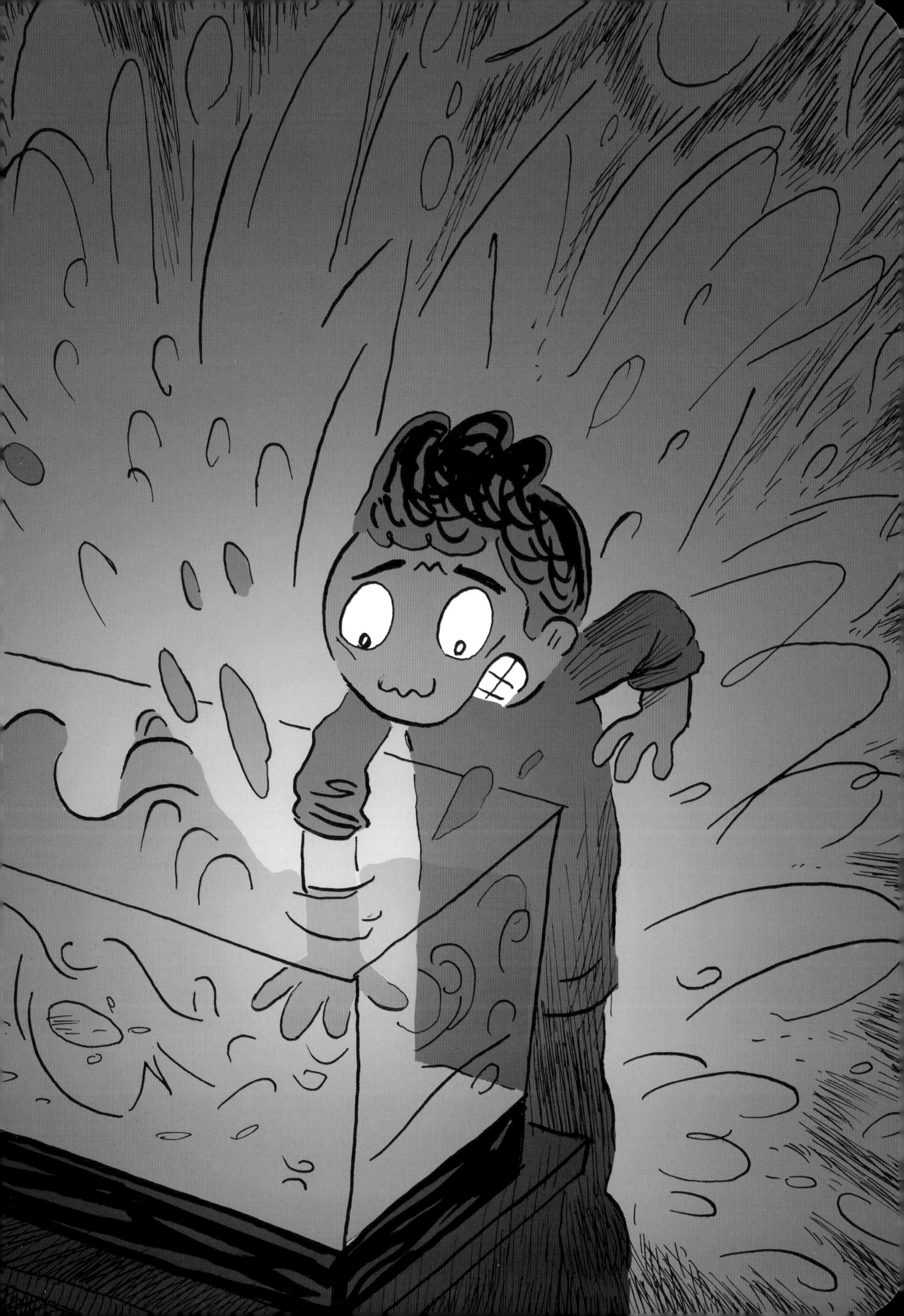

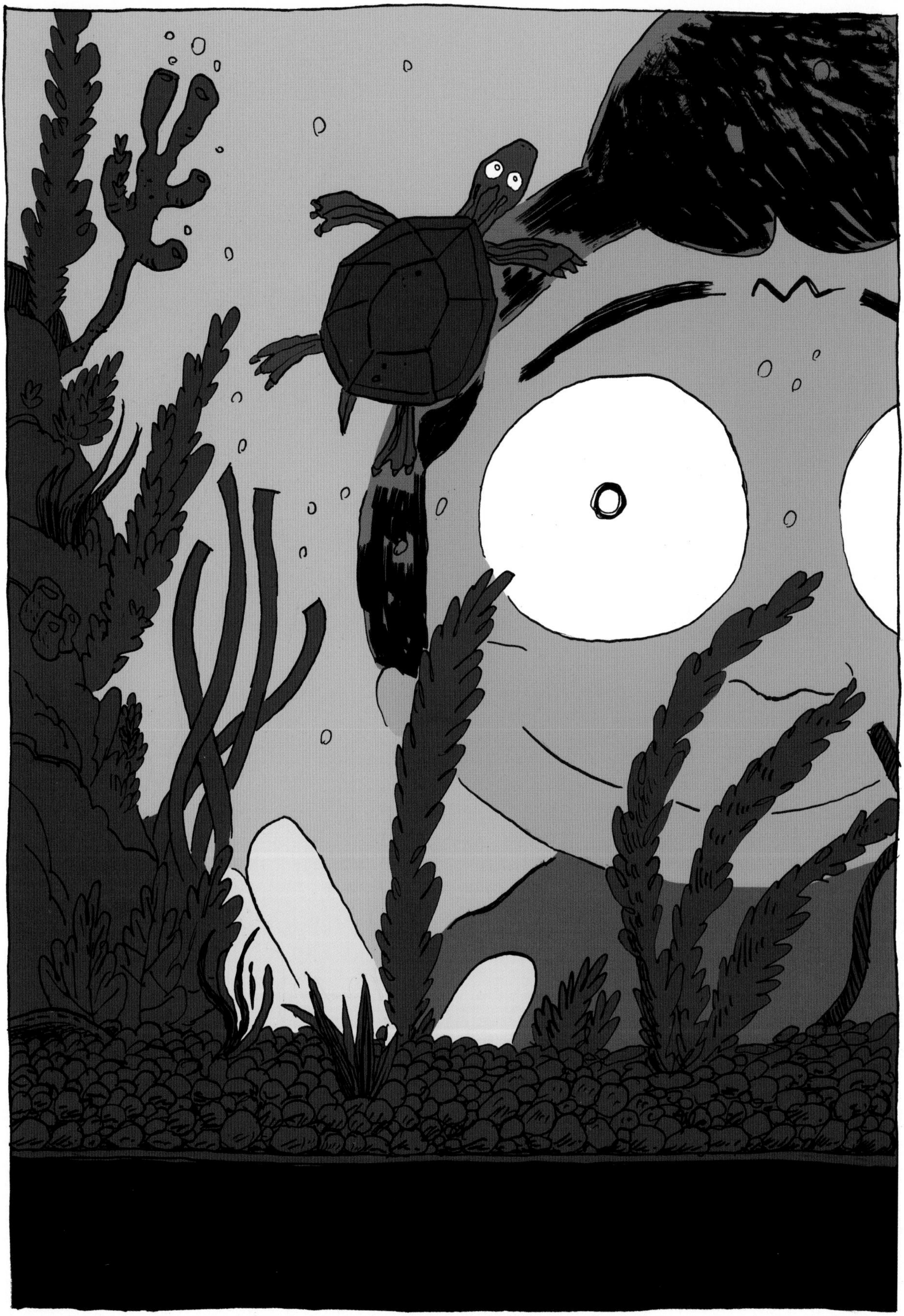

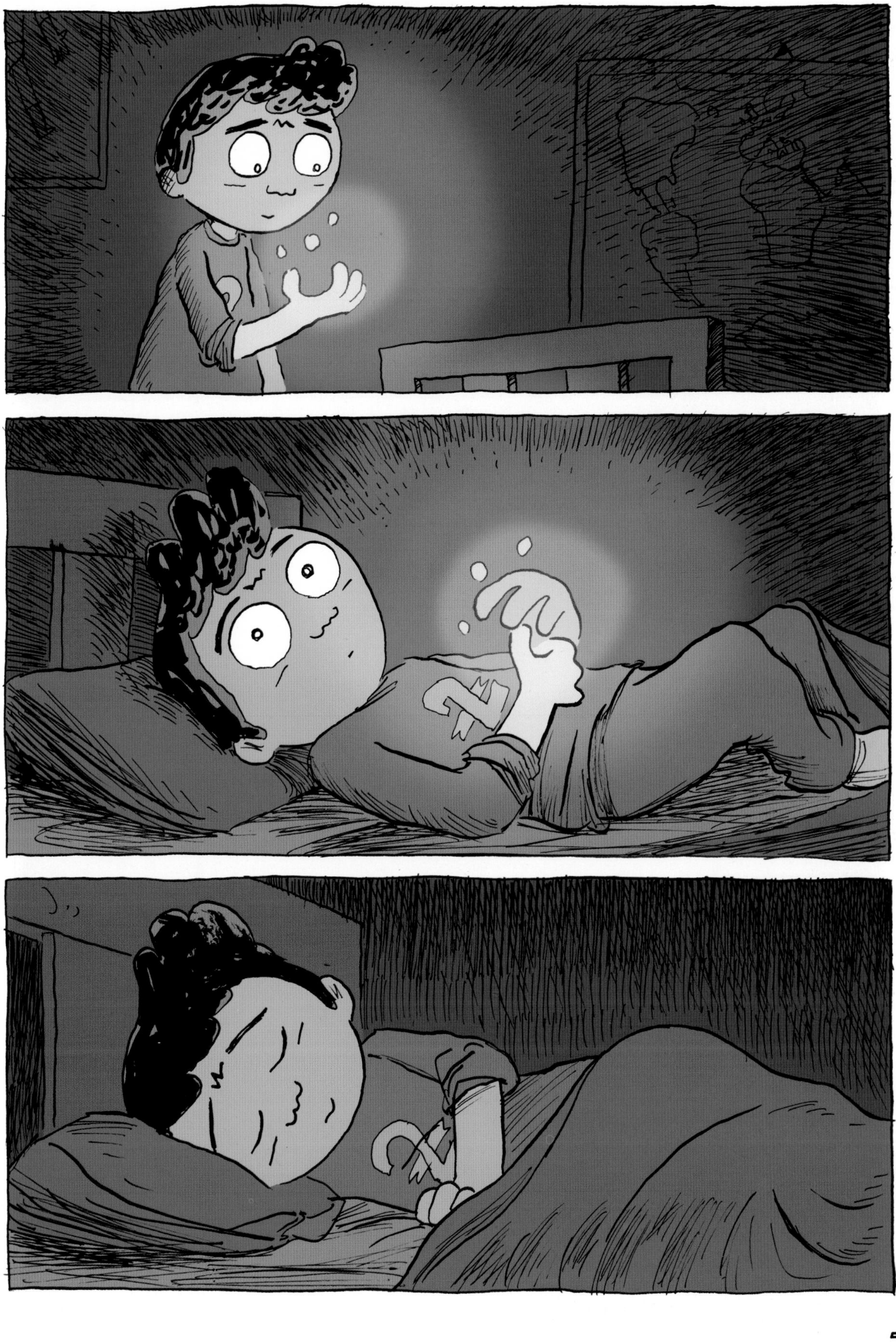

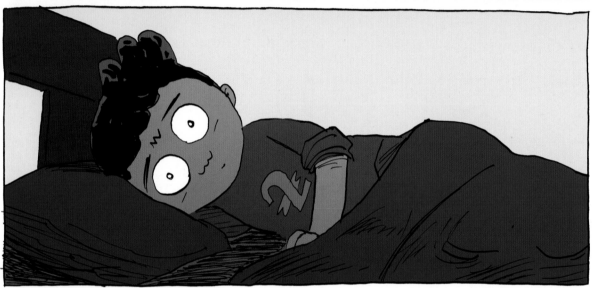

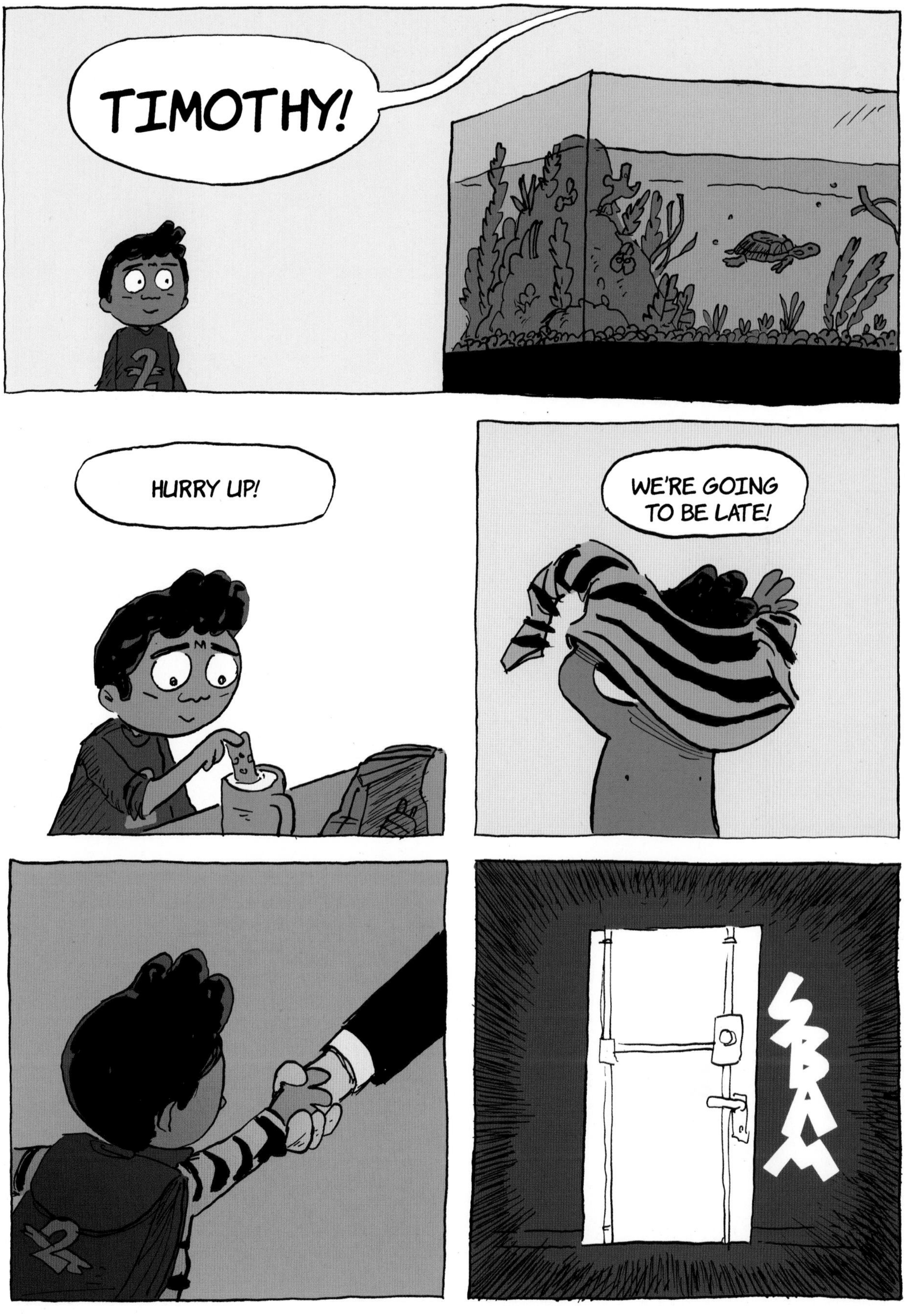
TIMOTHY!
HURRY UP!
WE'RE GOING TO BE LATE!
SBAM

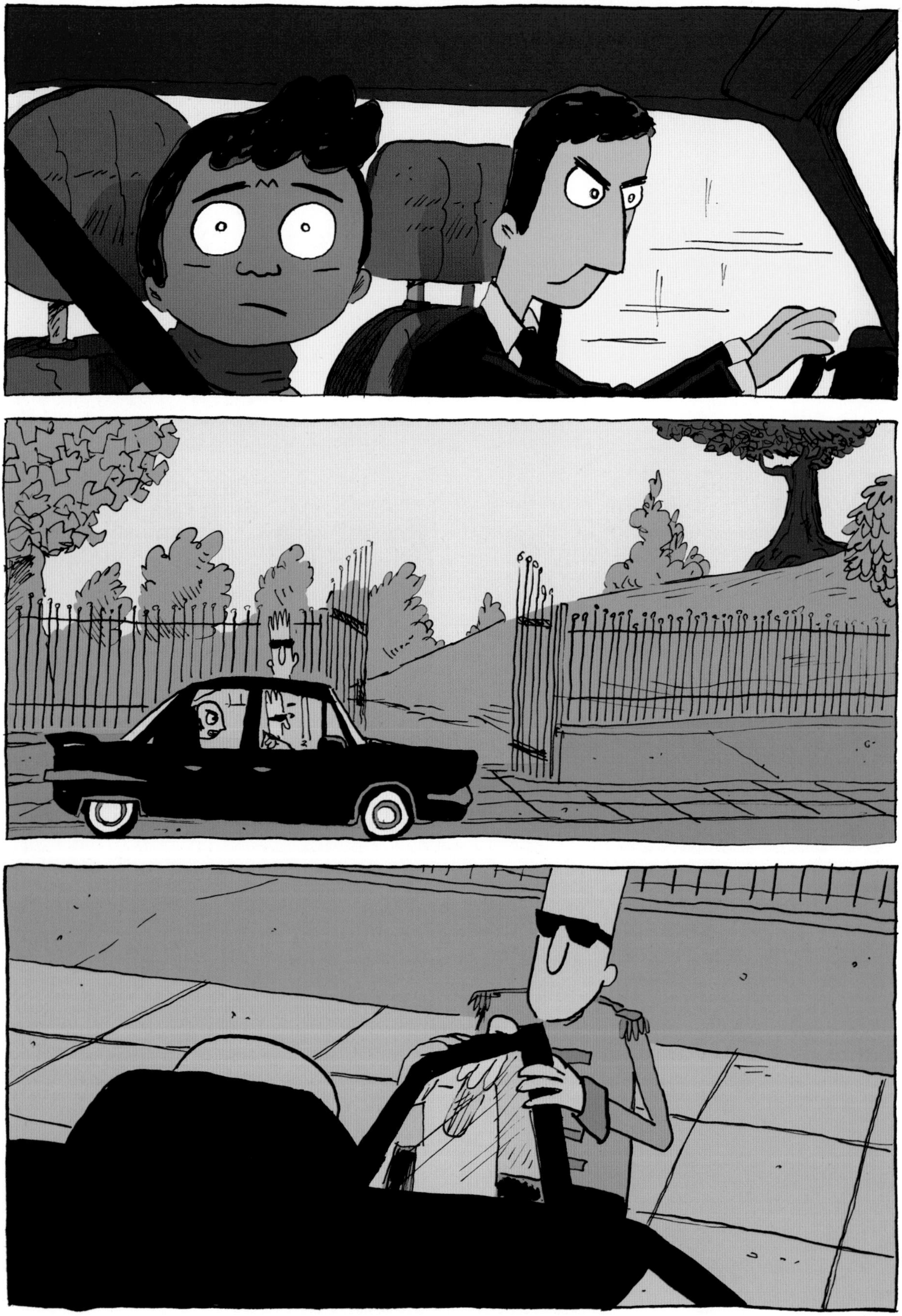

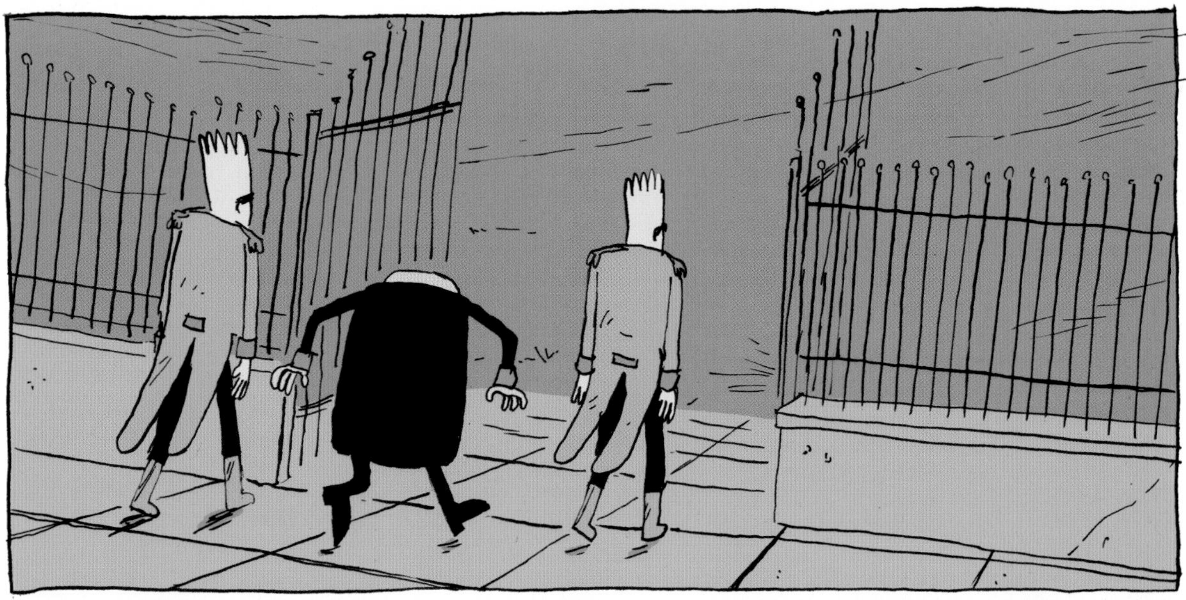

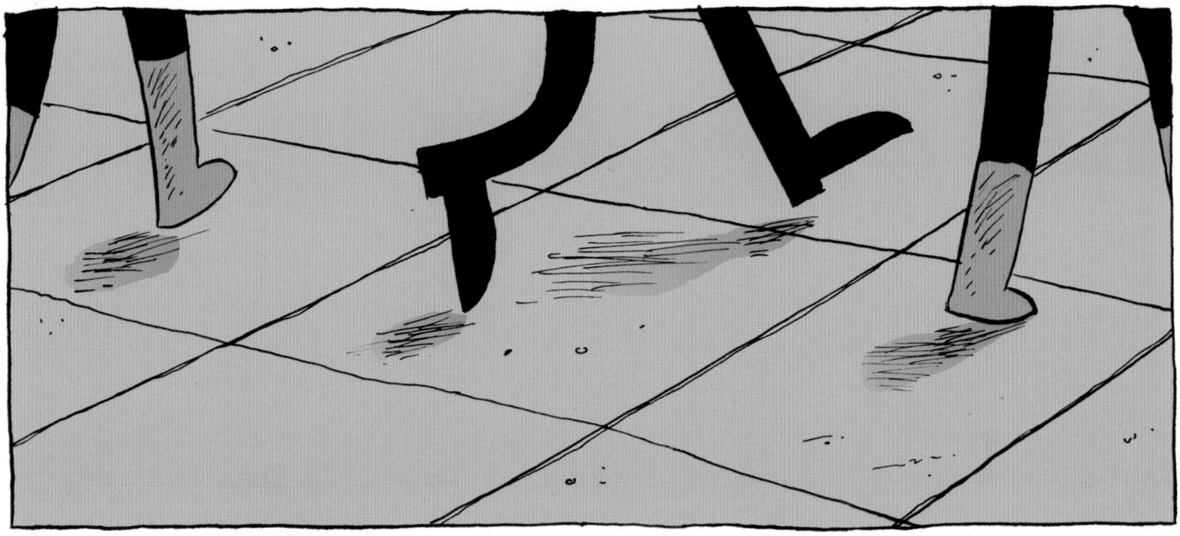

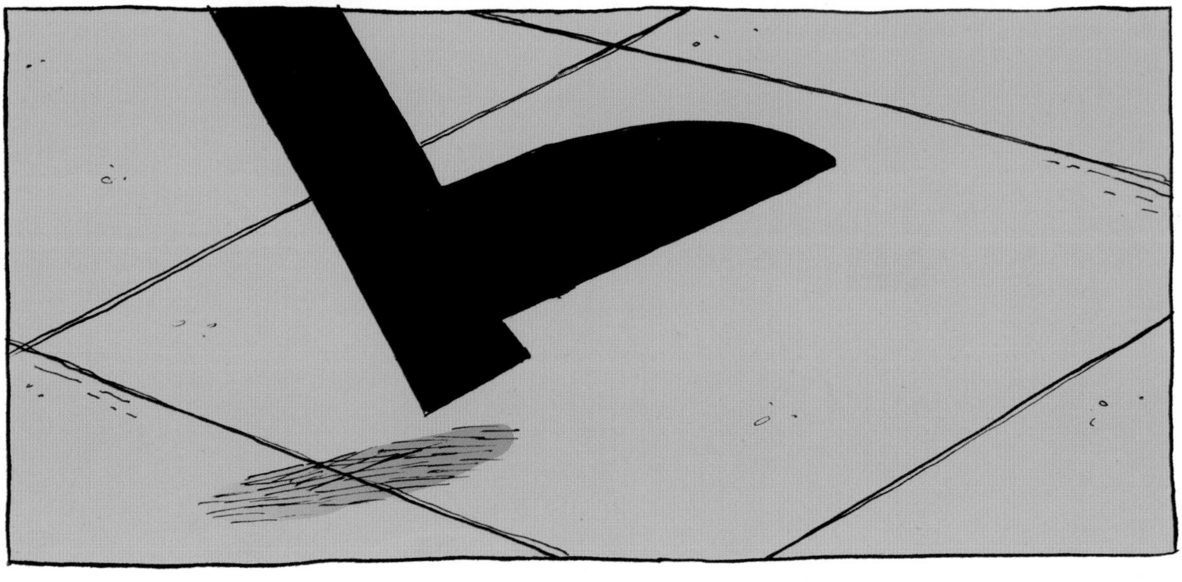

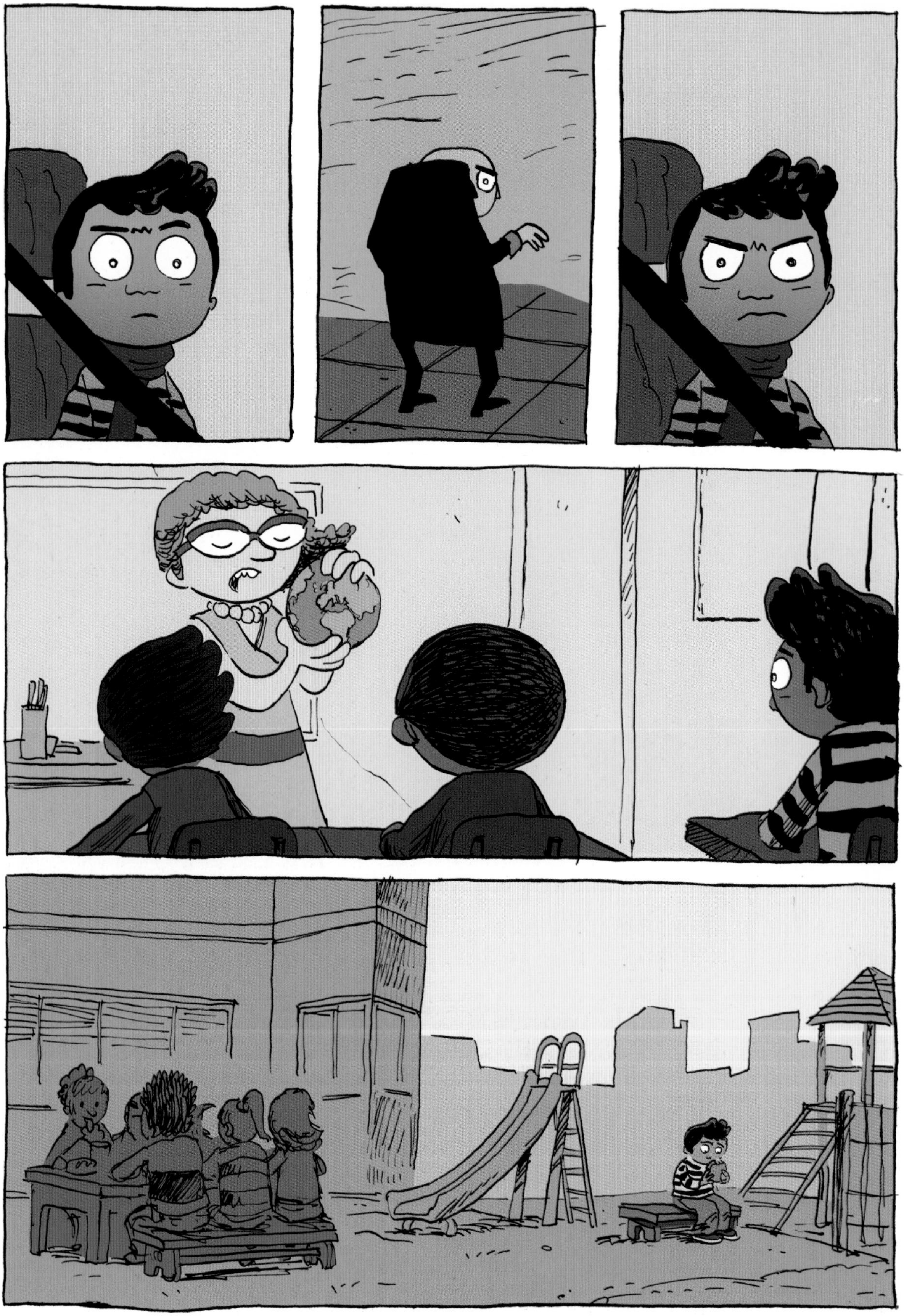

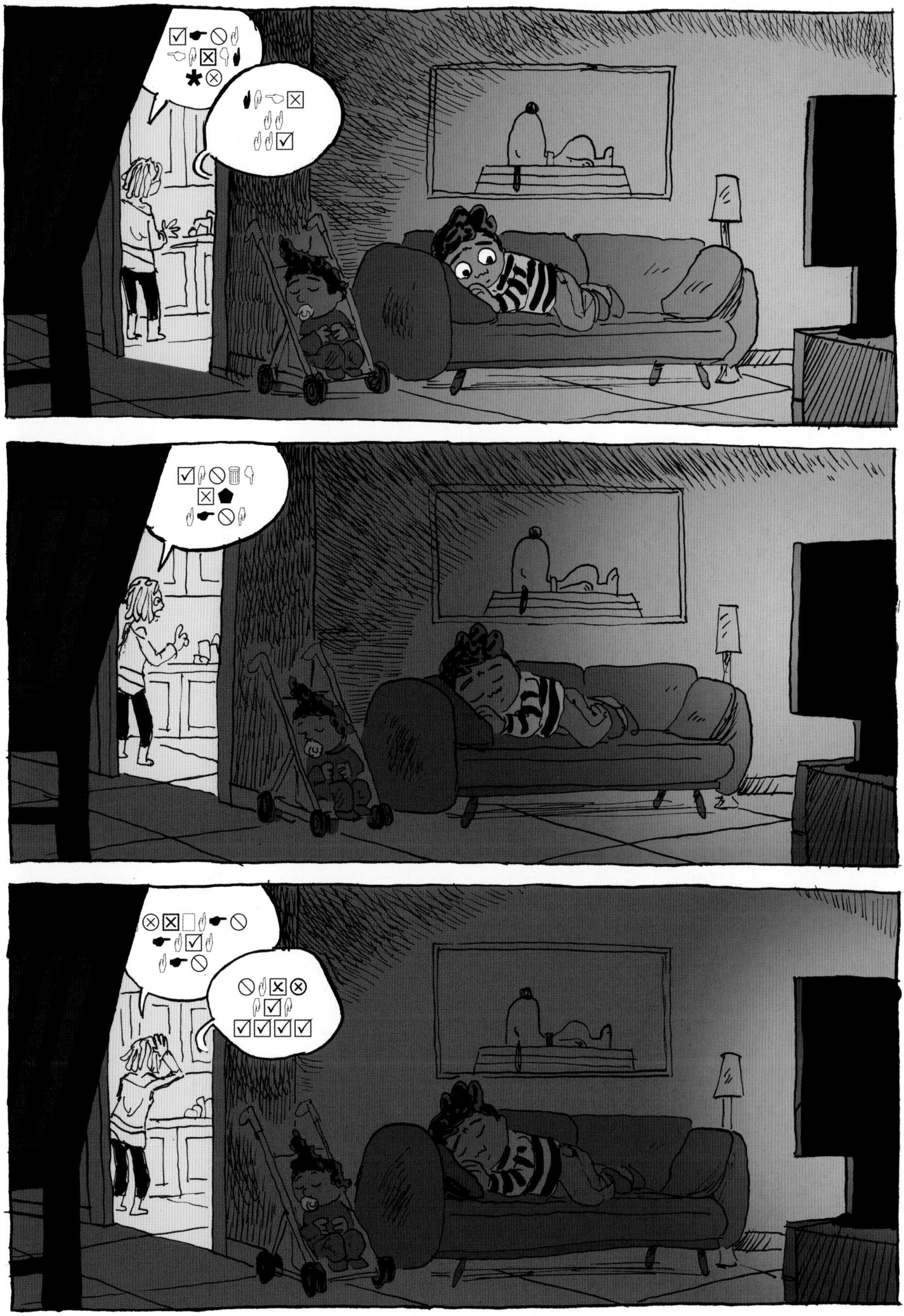

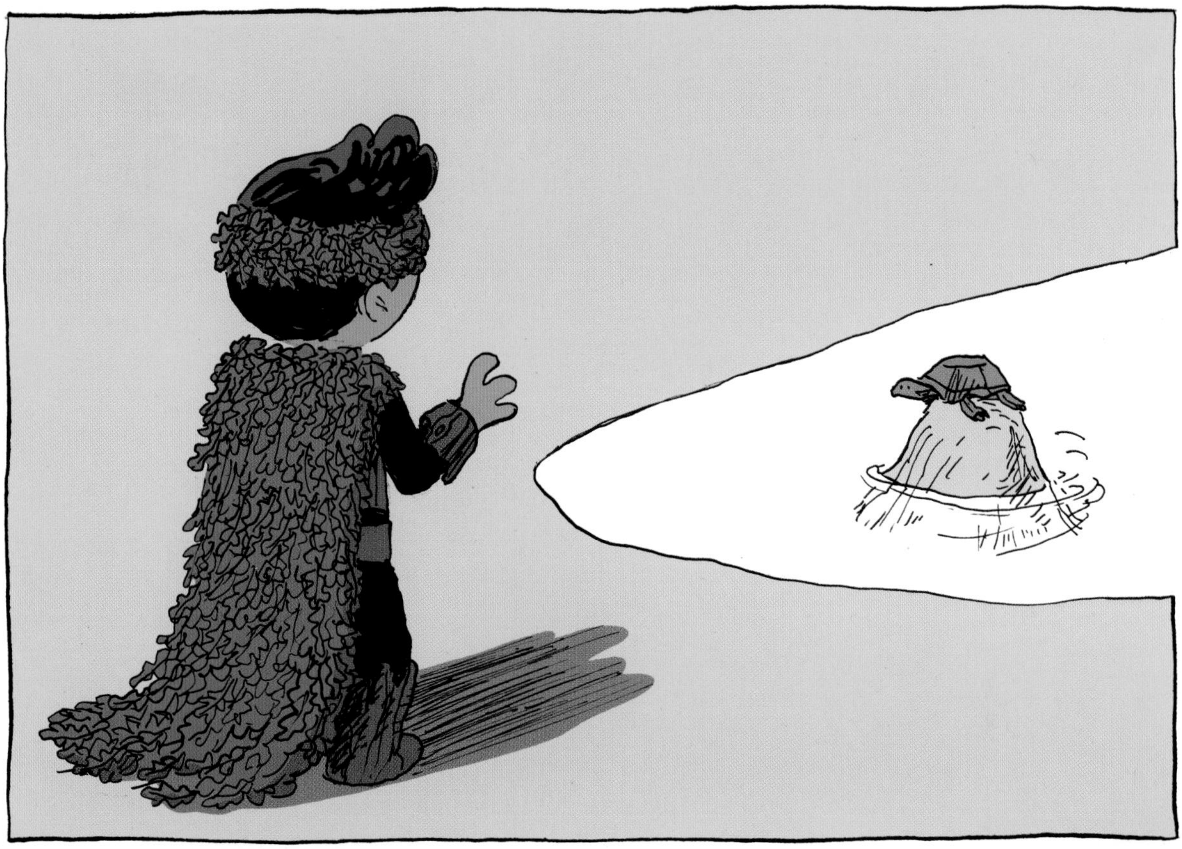

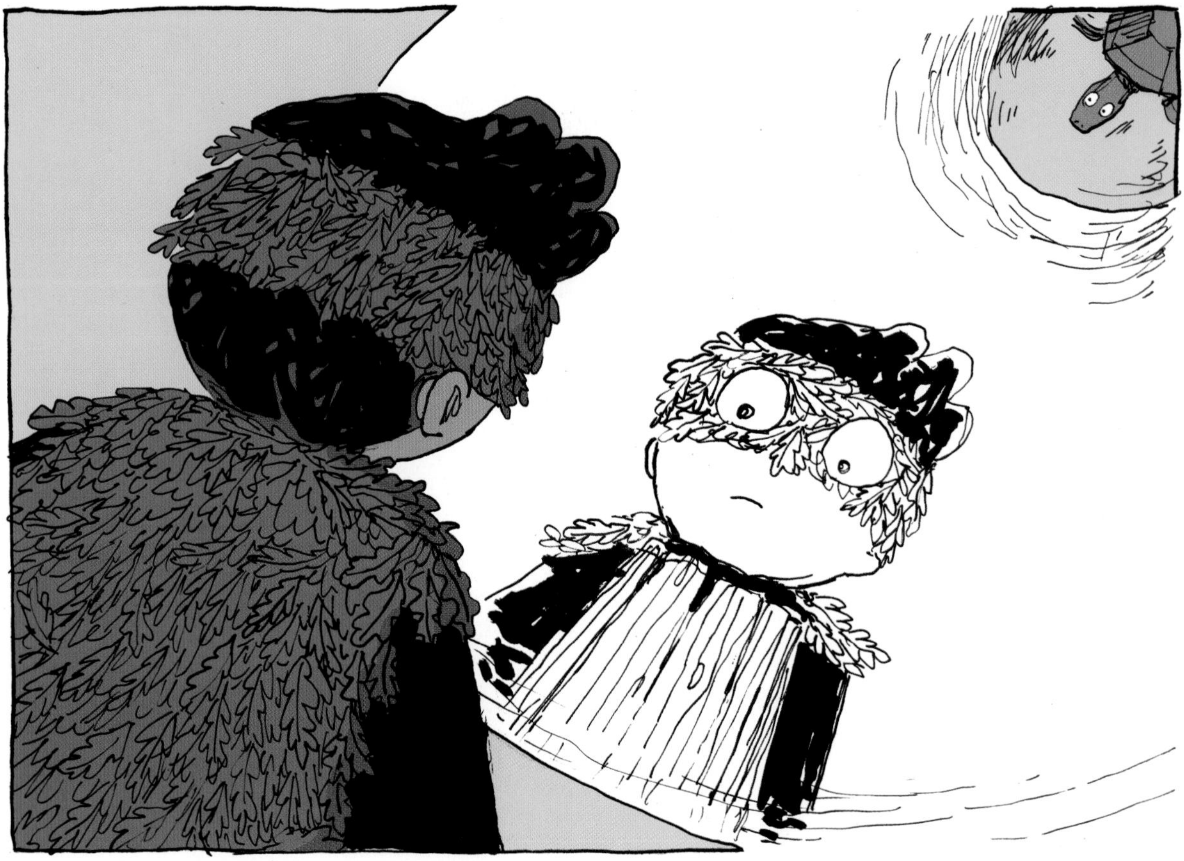

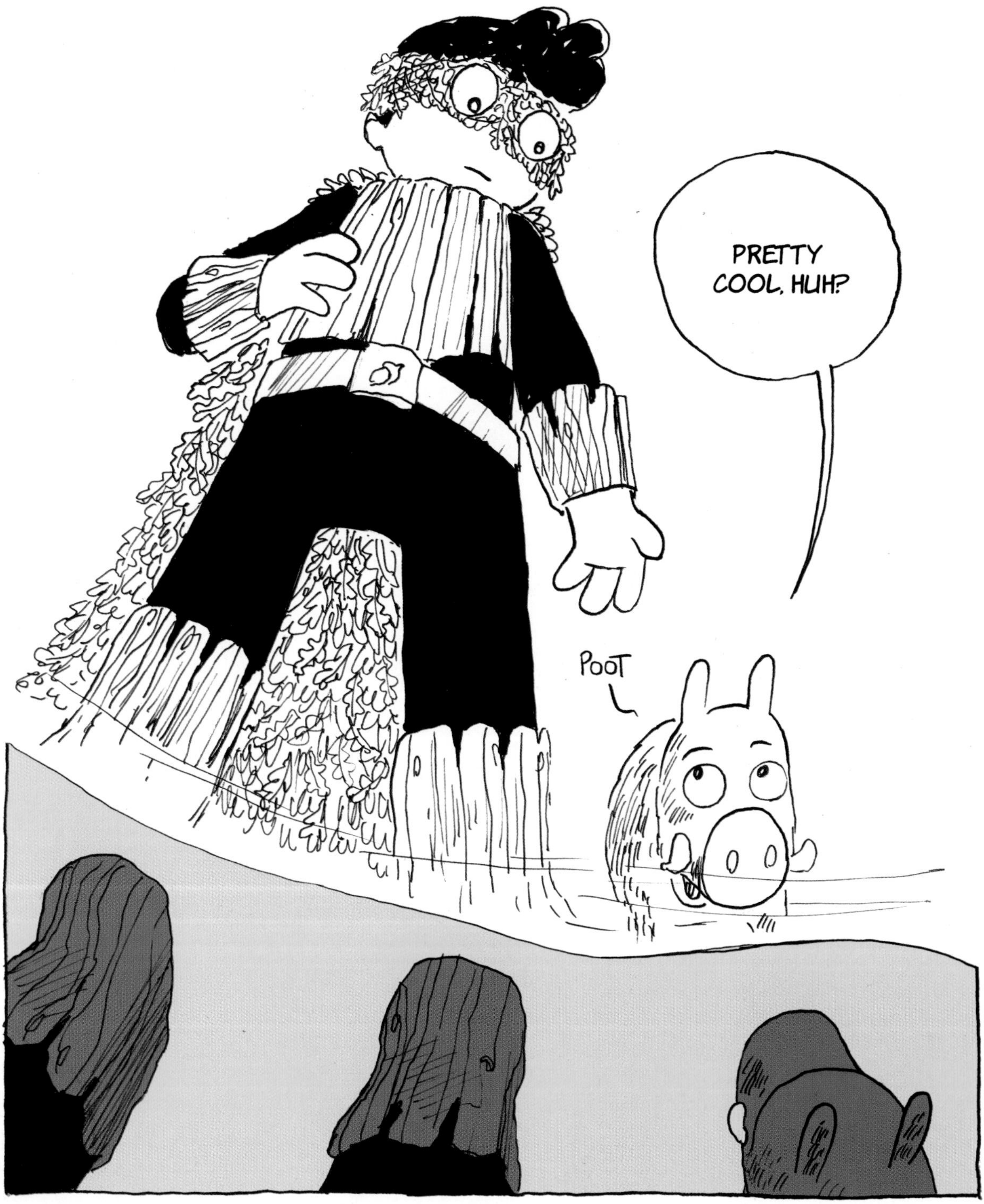
PRETTY COOL, HUH?
POOT

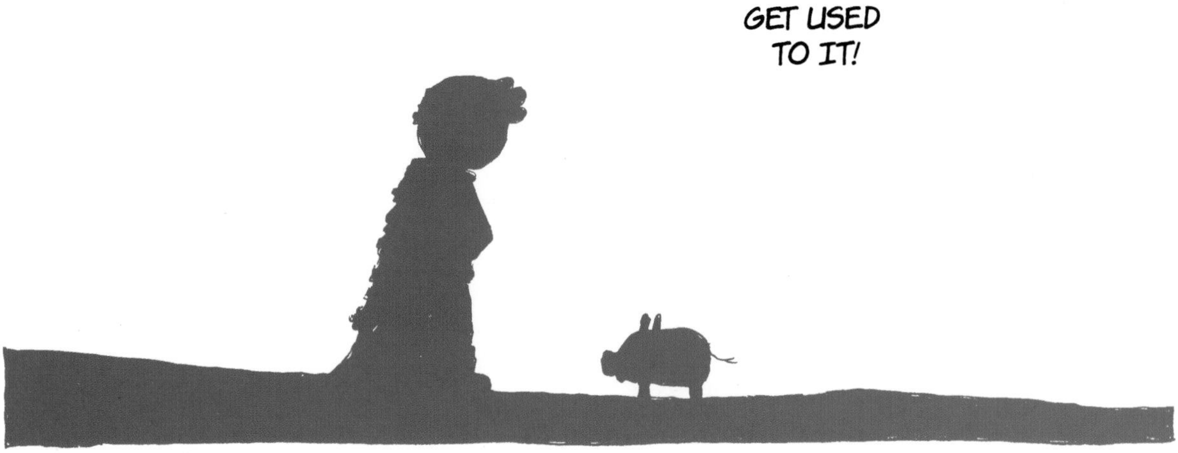
GET USED
TO IT!

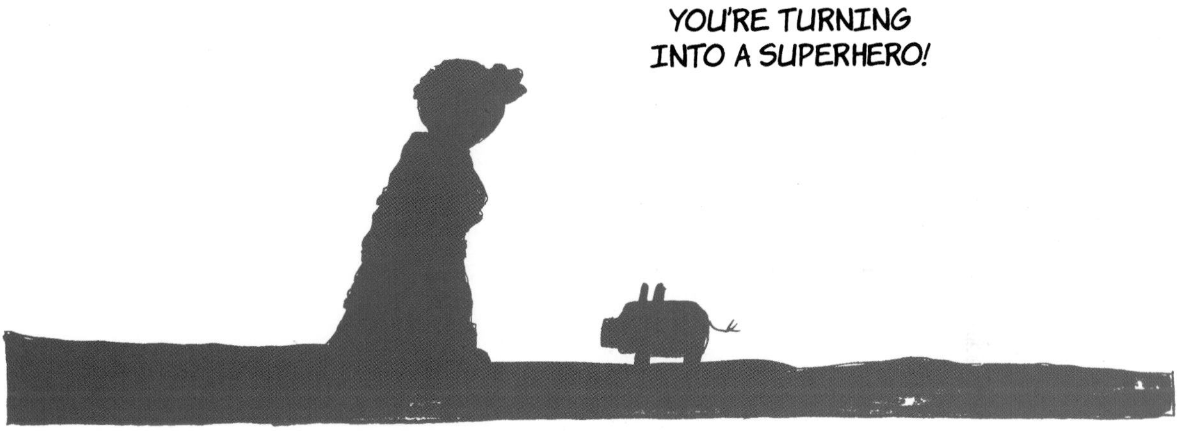
YOU'RE TURNING
INTO A SUPERHERO!

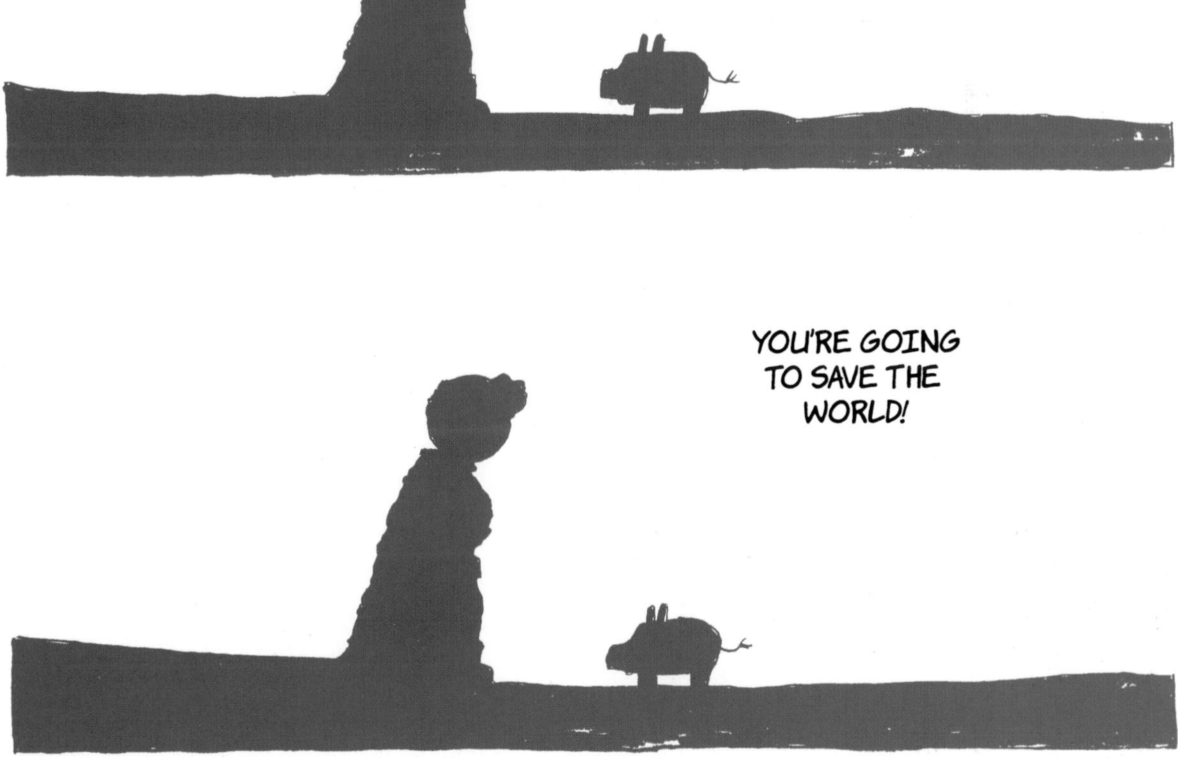
YOU'RE GOING
TO SAVE THE
WORLD!

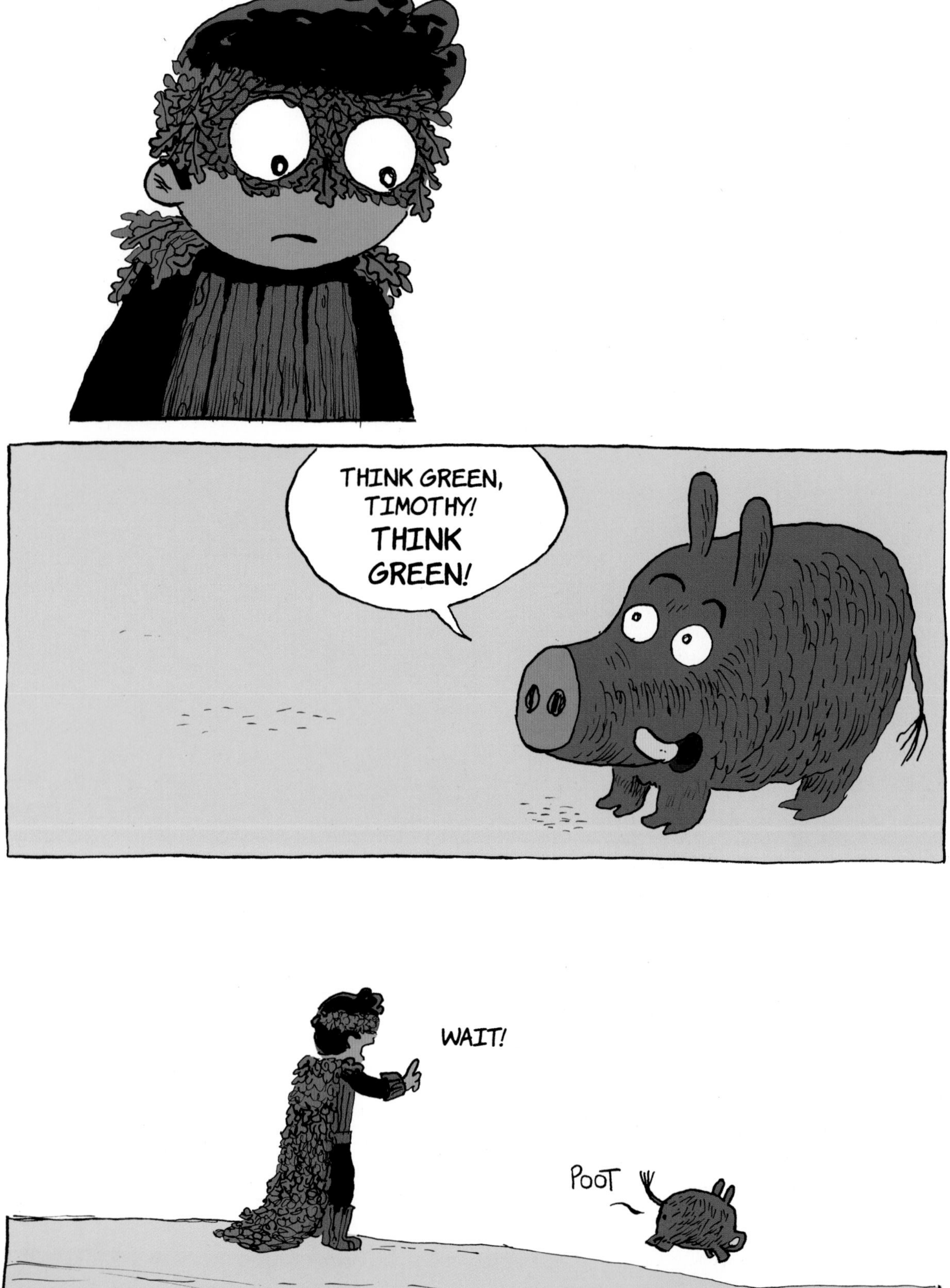
THINK GREEN, TIMOTHY! THINK GREEN!
WAIT!
POOT

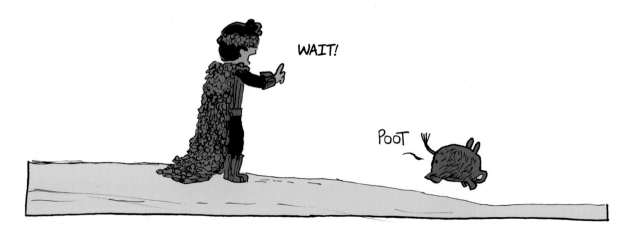

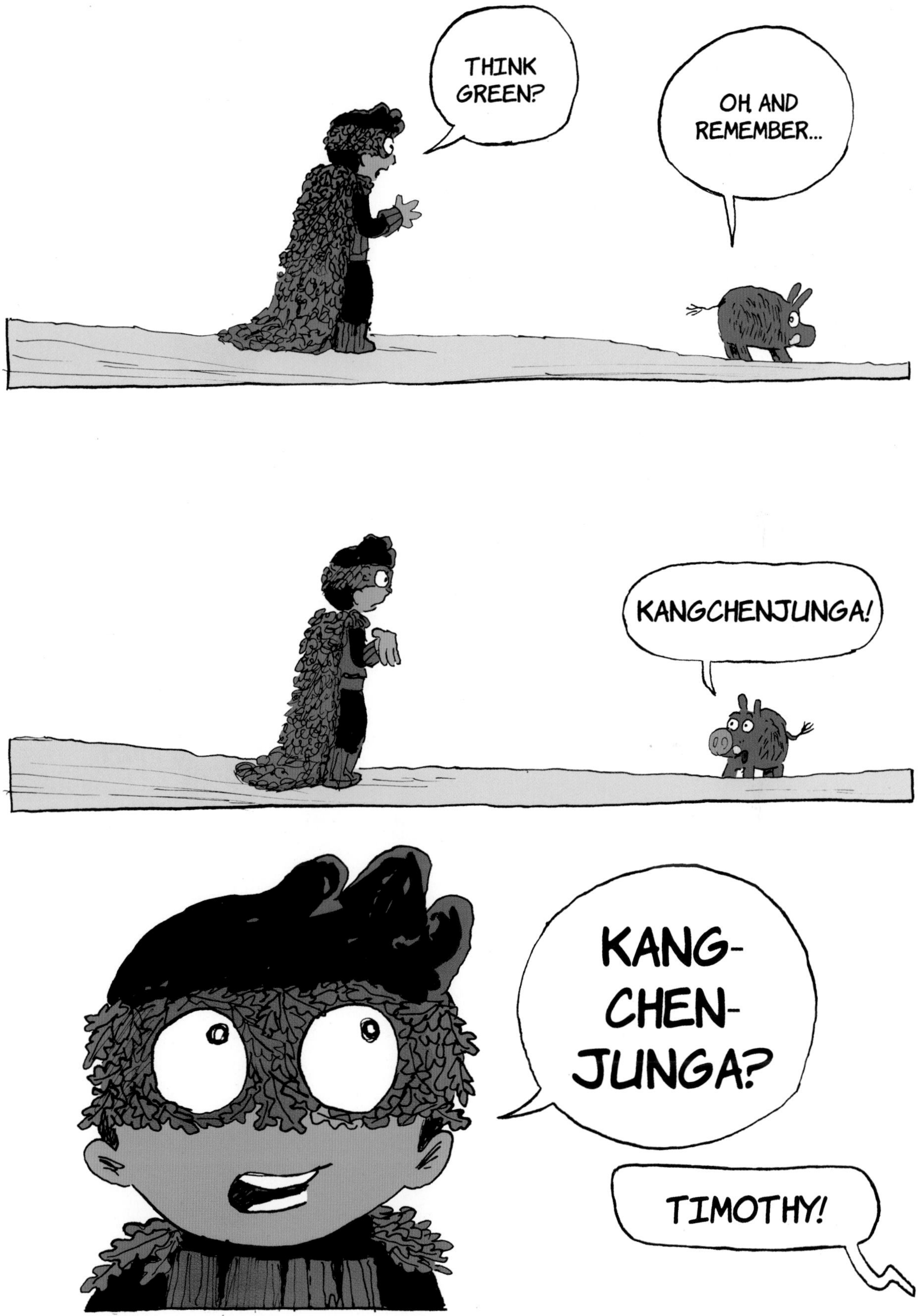
THINK GREEN?
OH, AND REMEMBER...
KANGCHENJUNGA!
KANG-CHEN-JUNGA?
TIMOTHY!

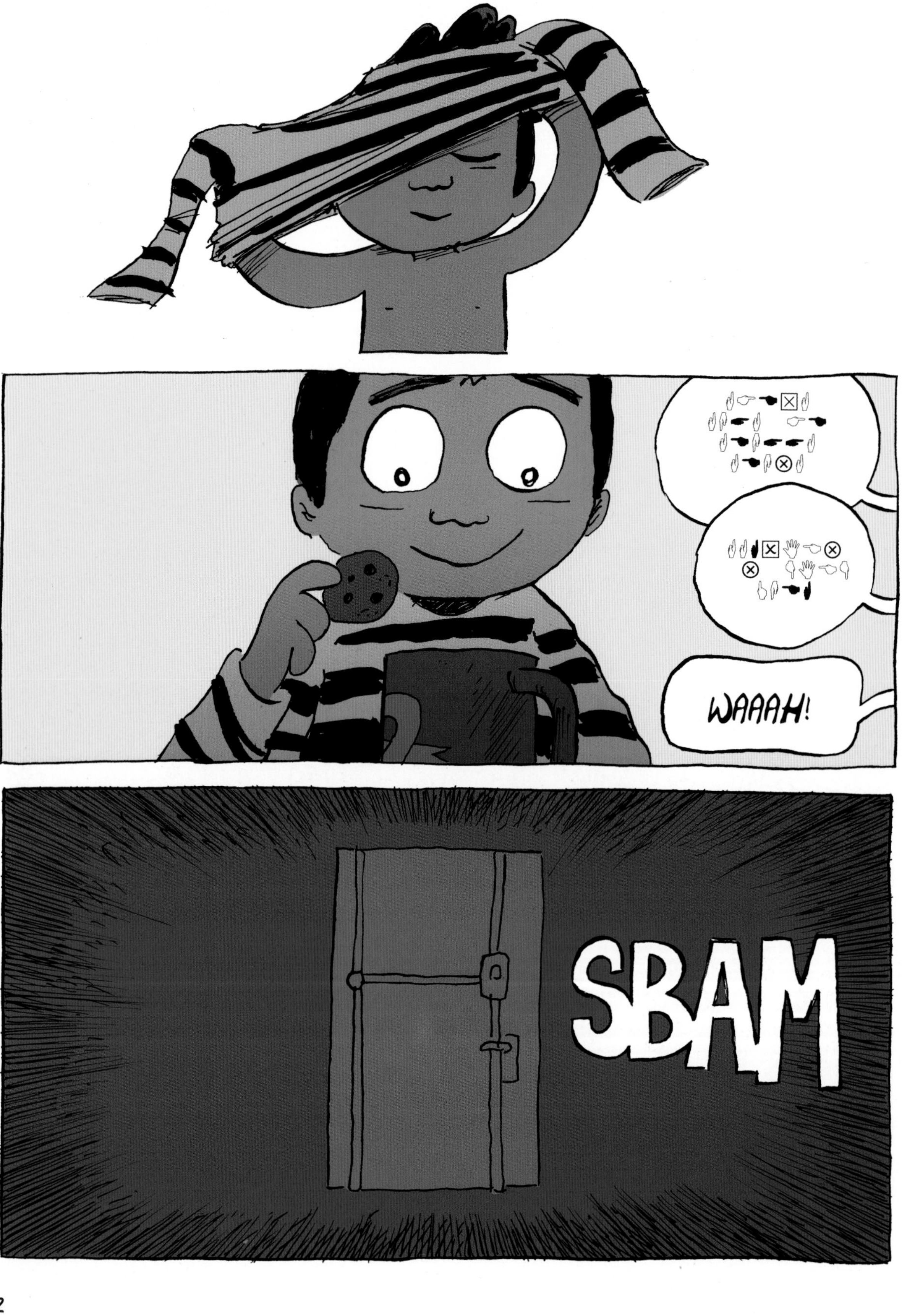
WAAAH!
SBAM

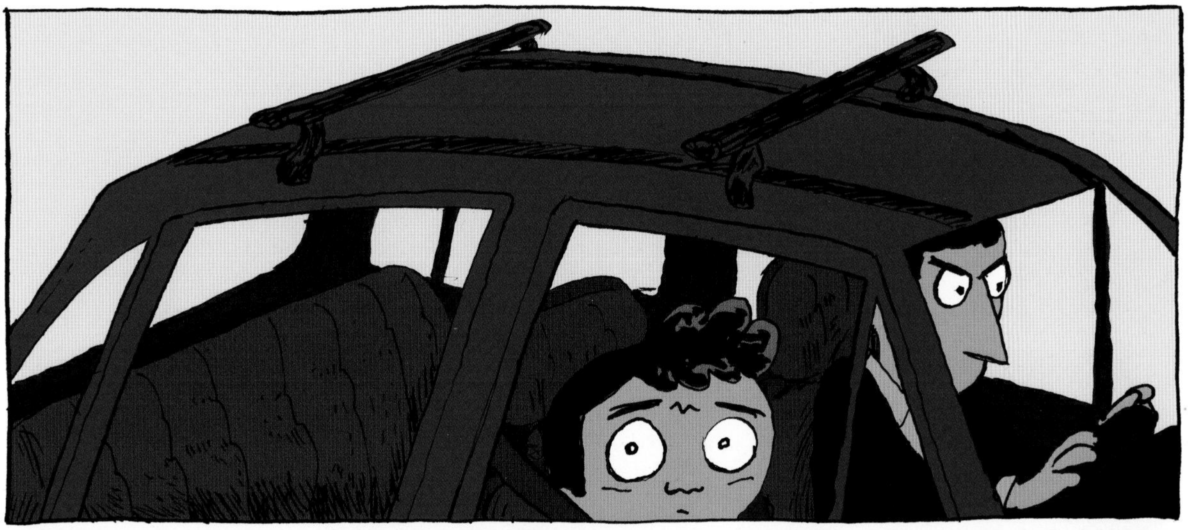

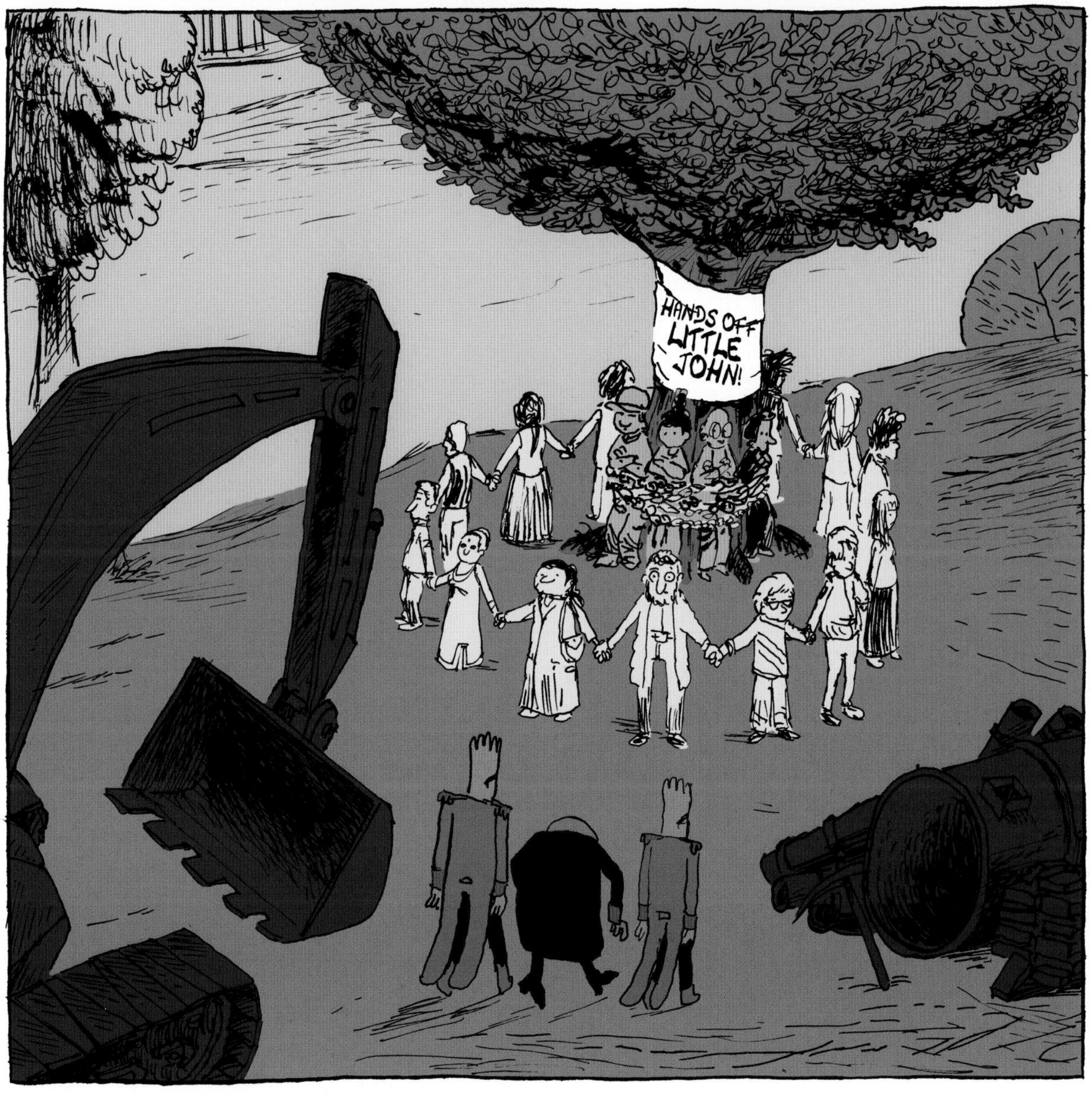
HANDS OFF
LITTLE
JOHN!

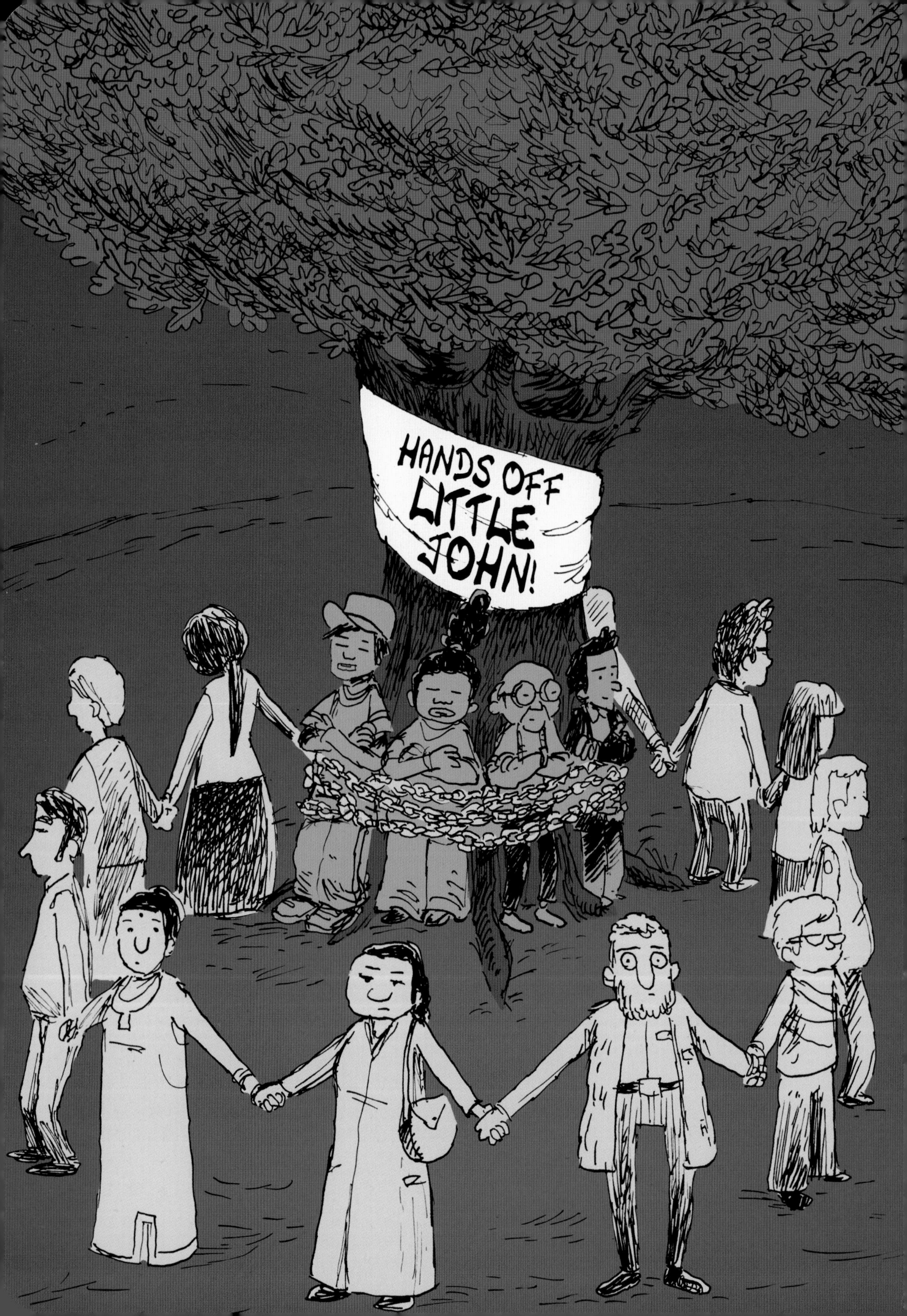
HANDS OFF LITTLE JOHN!

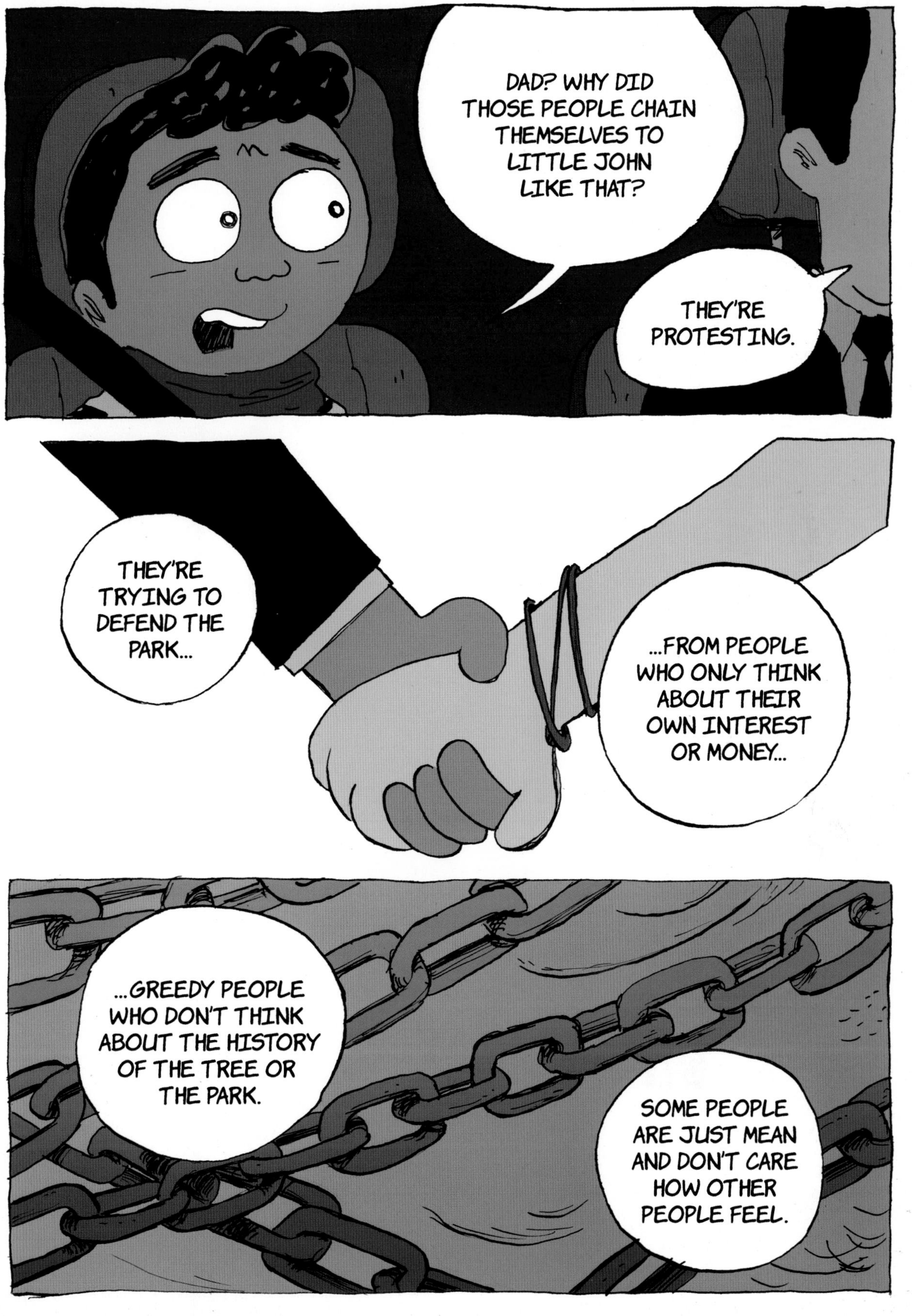
DAD? WHY DID THOSE PEOPLE CHAIN THEMSELVES TO LITTLE JOHN LIKE THAT?
THEY'RE PROTESTING.
THEY'RE TRYING TO DEFEND THE PARK...
...FROM PEOPLE WHO ONLY THINK ABOUT THEIR OWN INTEREST OR MONEY...
...GREEDY PEOPLE WHO DON'T THINK ABOUT THE HISTORY OF THE TREE OR THE PARK.
SOME PEOPLE ARE JUST MEAN AND DON'T CARE HOW OTHER PEOPLE FEEL.

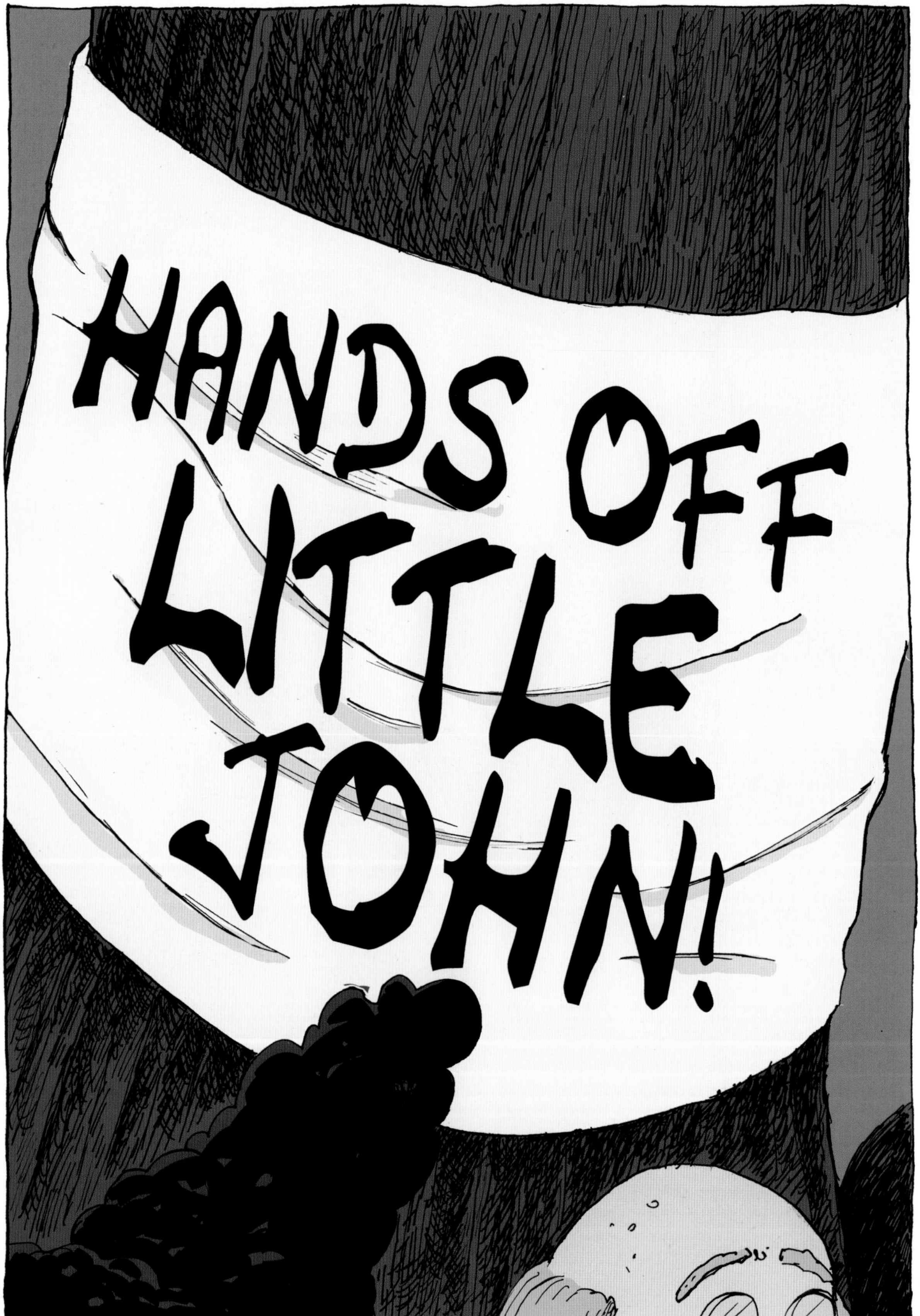
HANDS OFF LITTLE JOHN!

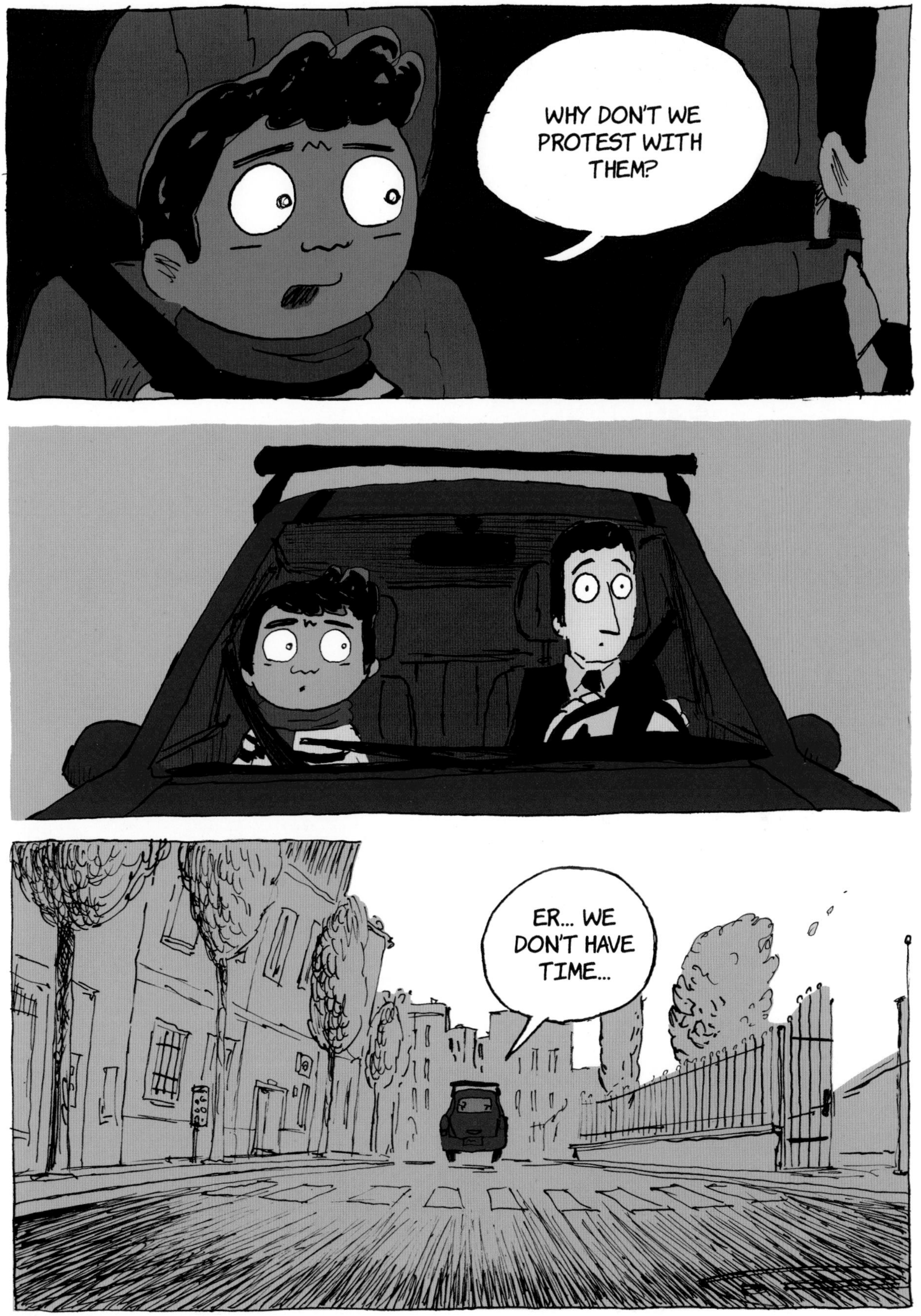
WHY DON'T WE PROTEST WITH THEM?
ER... WE DON'T HAVE TIME...

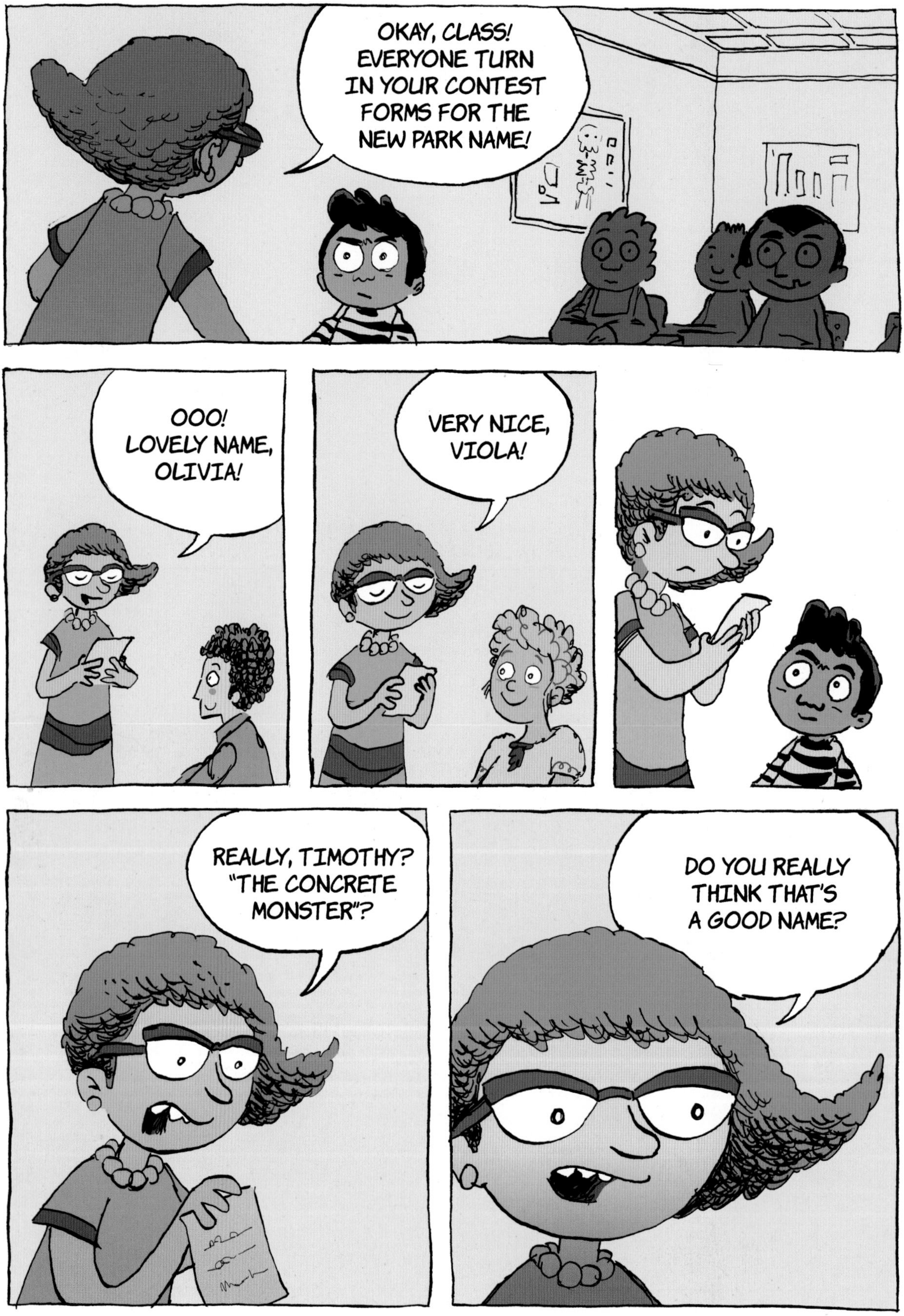
OKAY, CLASS! EVERYONE TURN IN YOUR CONTEST FORMS FOR THE NEW PARK NAME!
OOO! LOVELY NAME, OLIVIA!
VERY NICE, VIOLA!
REALLY, TIMOTHY? "THE CONCRETE MONSTER"?
DO YOU REALLY THINK THAT'S A GOOD NAME?

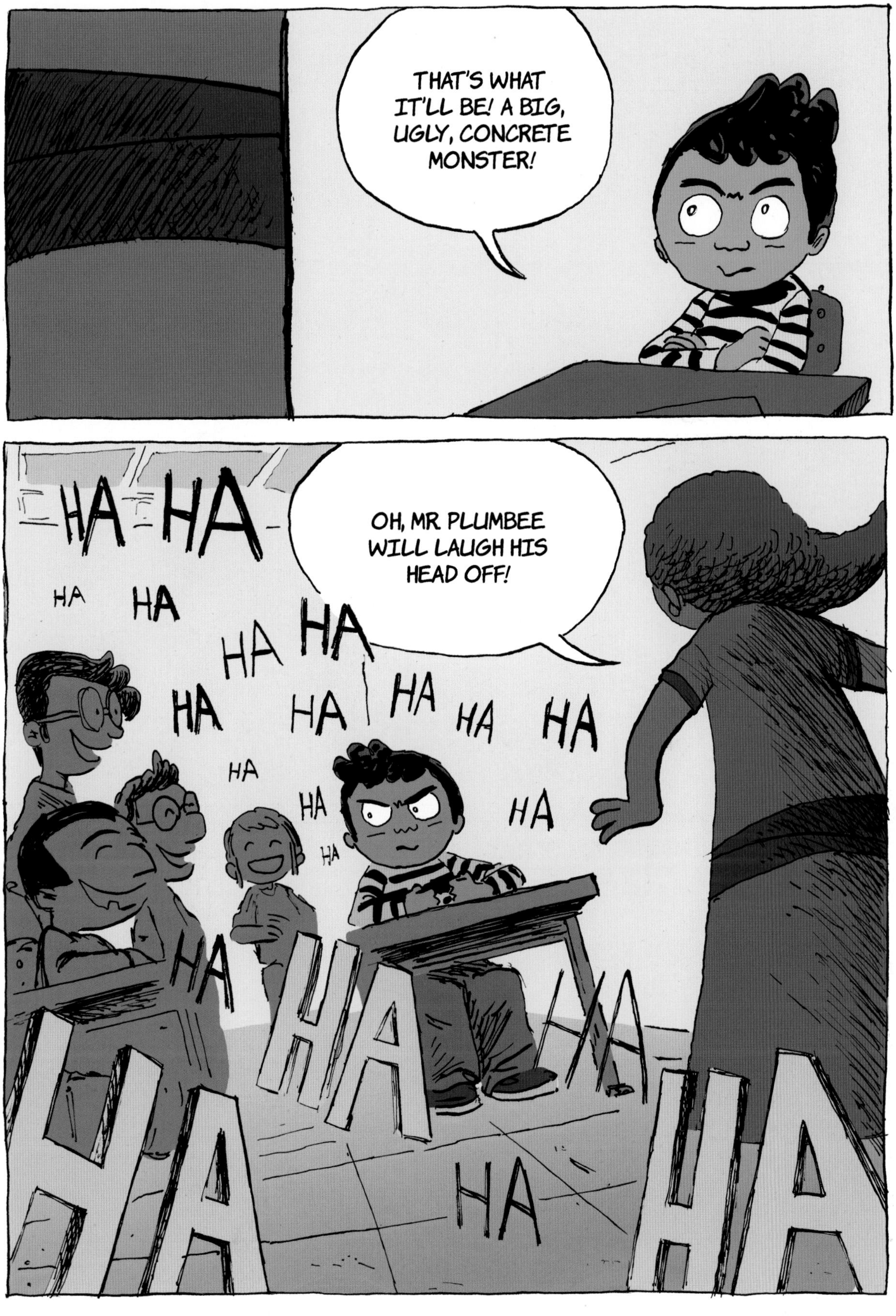
THAT'S WHAT IT'LL BE! A BIG, UGLY, CONCRETE MONSTER!
HA HA
HA HA
HA HA
HA HA HA HA HA
HA HA HA
HA
HA
OH, MR PLUMBEE WILL LAUGH HIS HEAD OFF!
HA HA HA HA HA HA

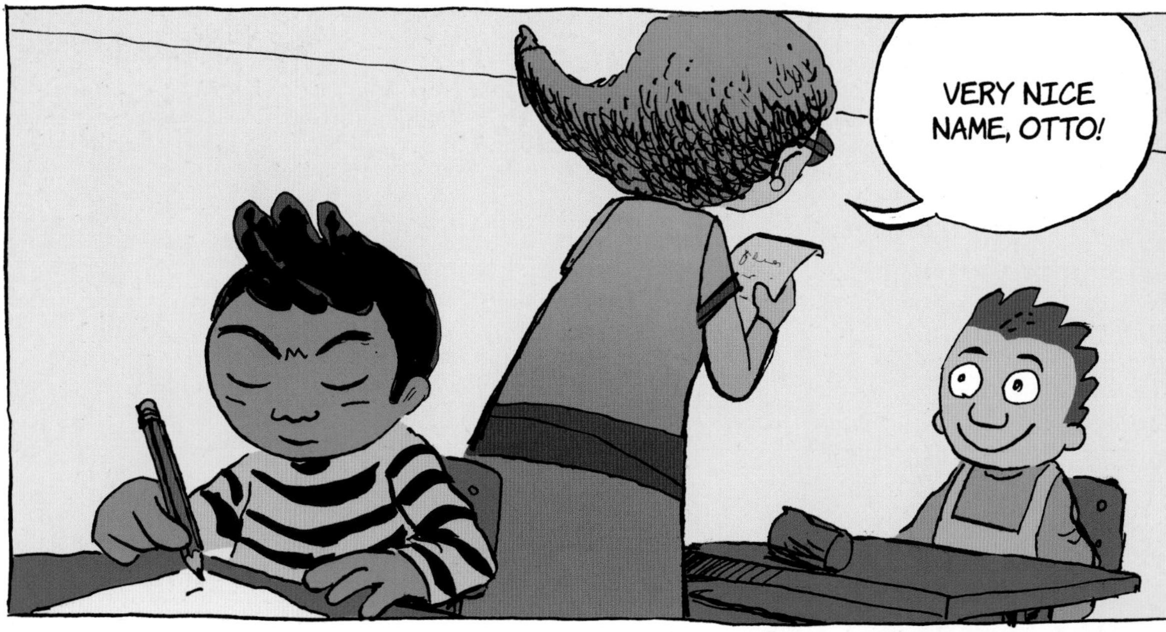
VERY NICE NAME, OTTO!

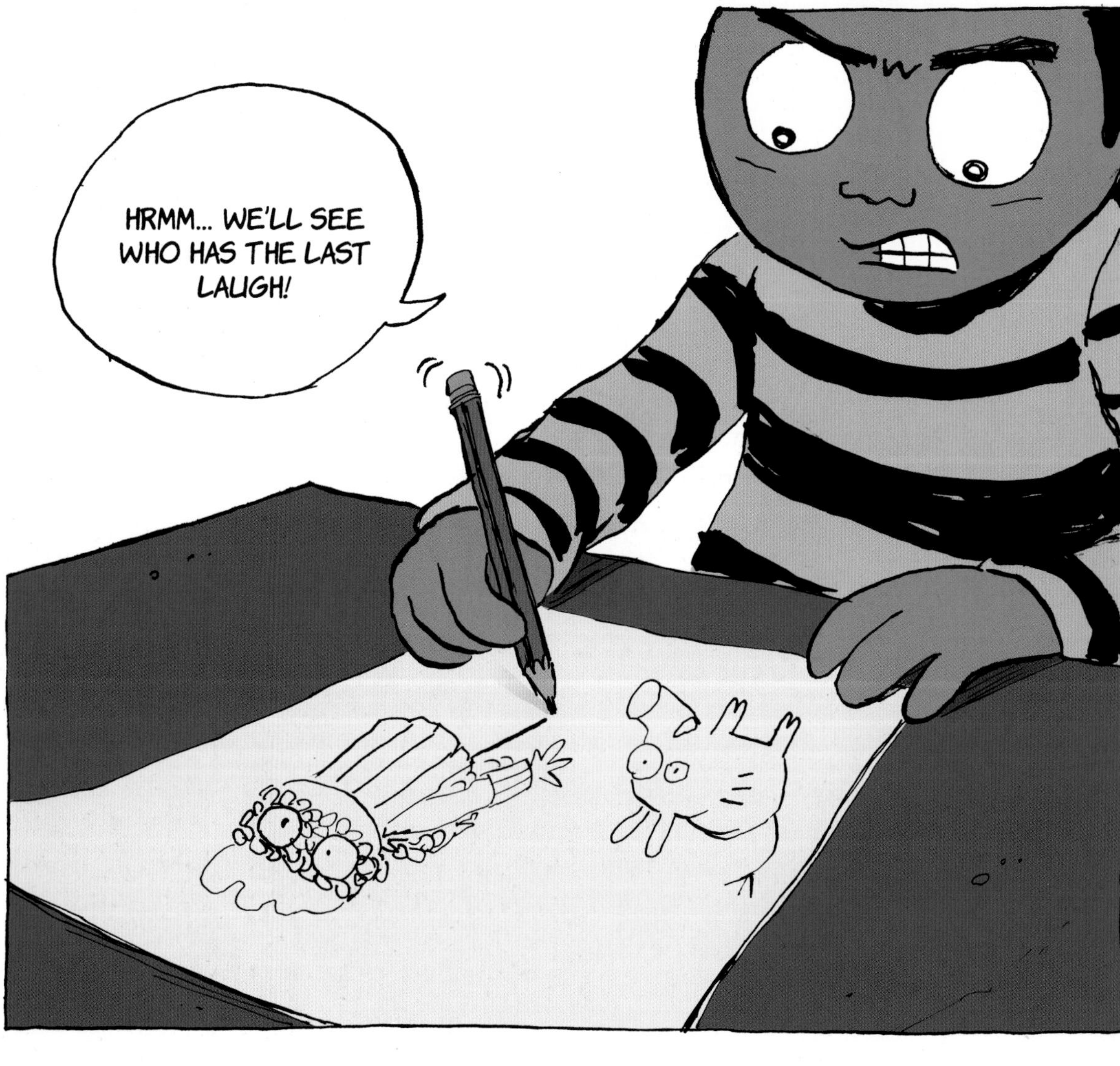
HRMM... WE'LL SEE WHO HAS THE LAST LAUGH!

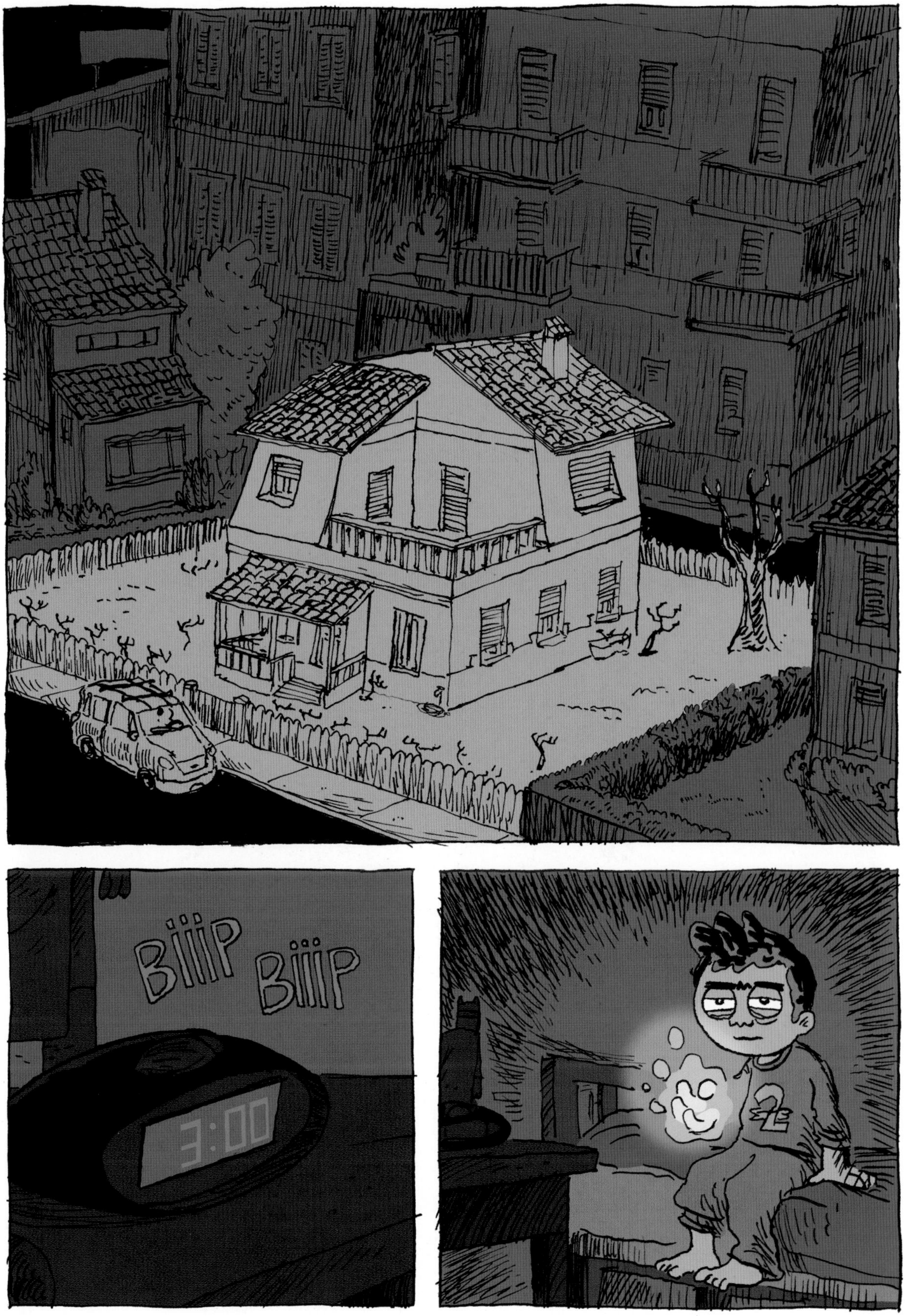
BIIIP BIIIP
3:00

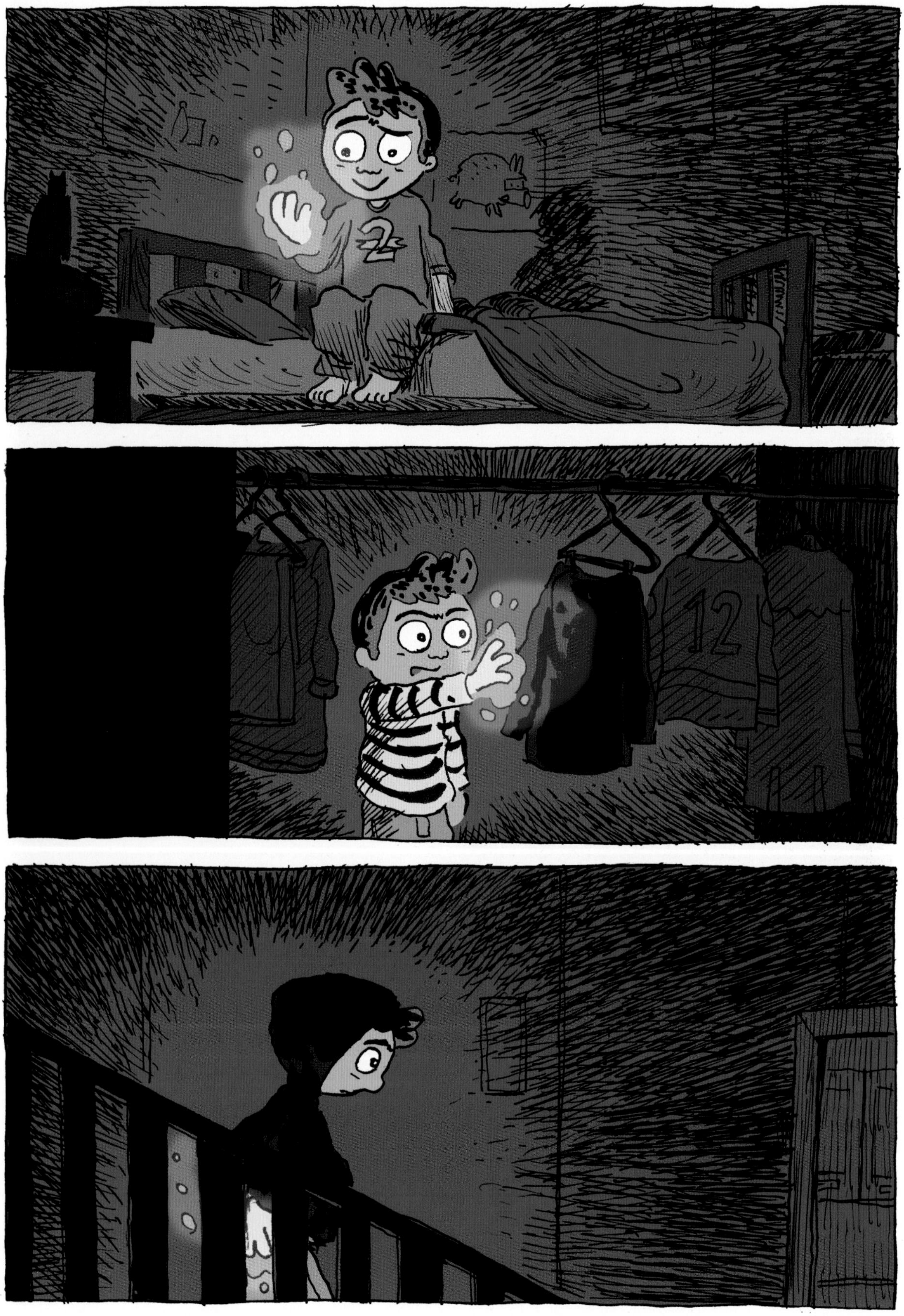

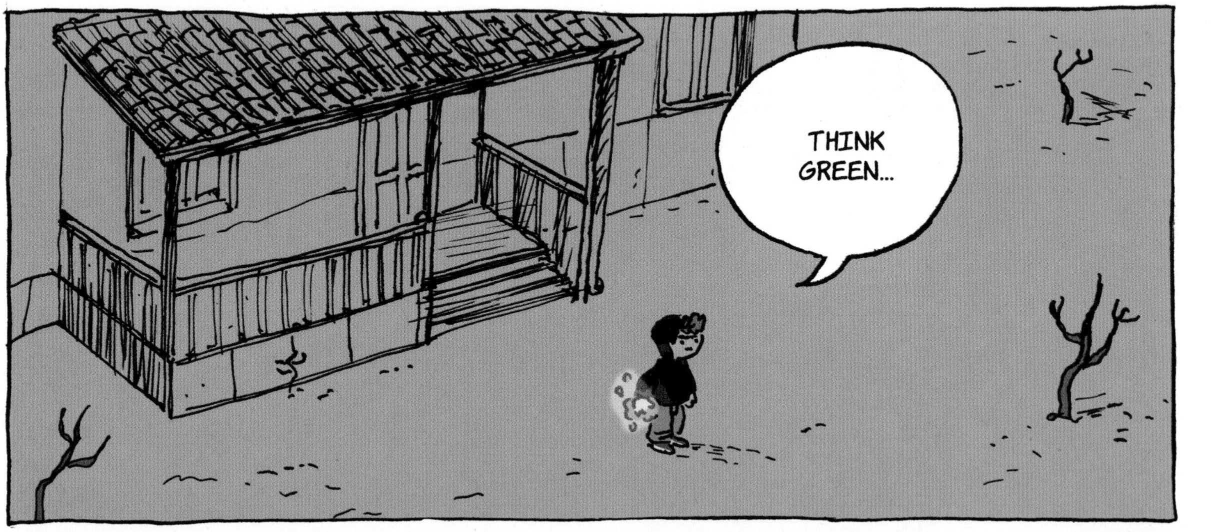
THINK GREEN...

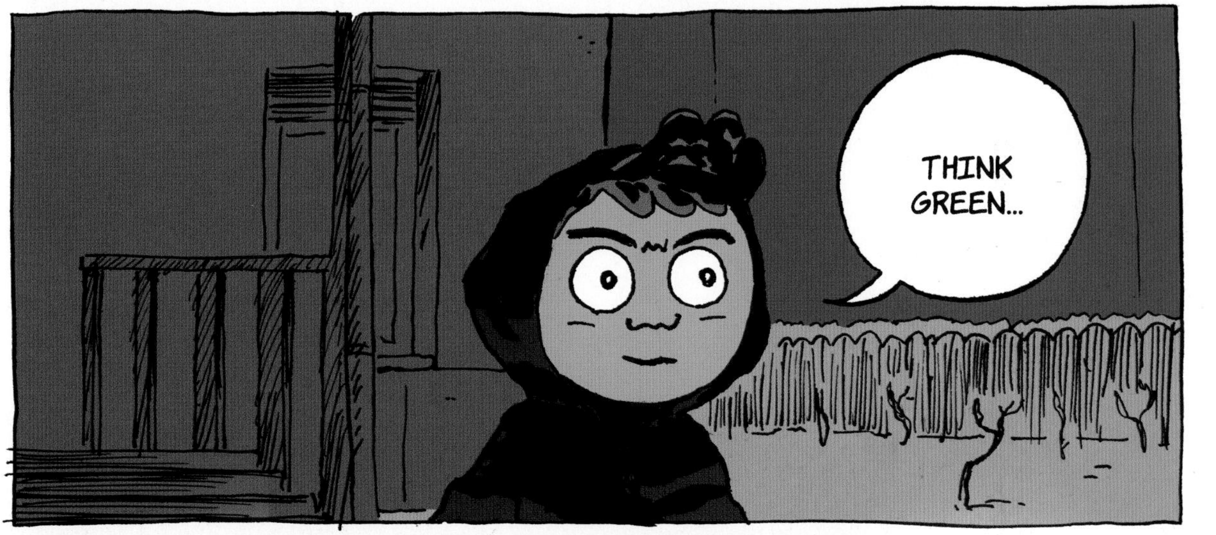
THINK GREEN...

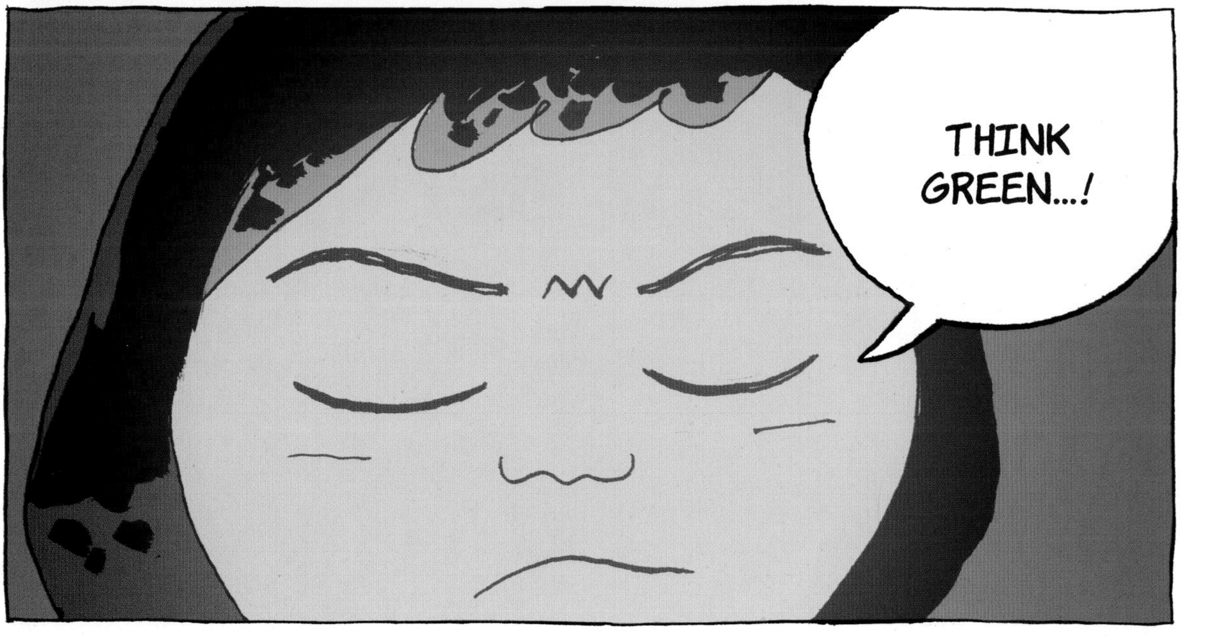
THINK GREEN...!

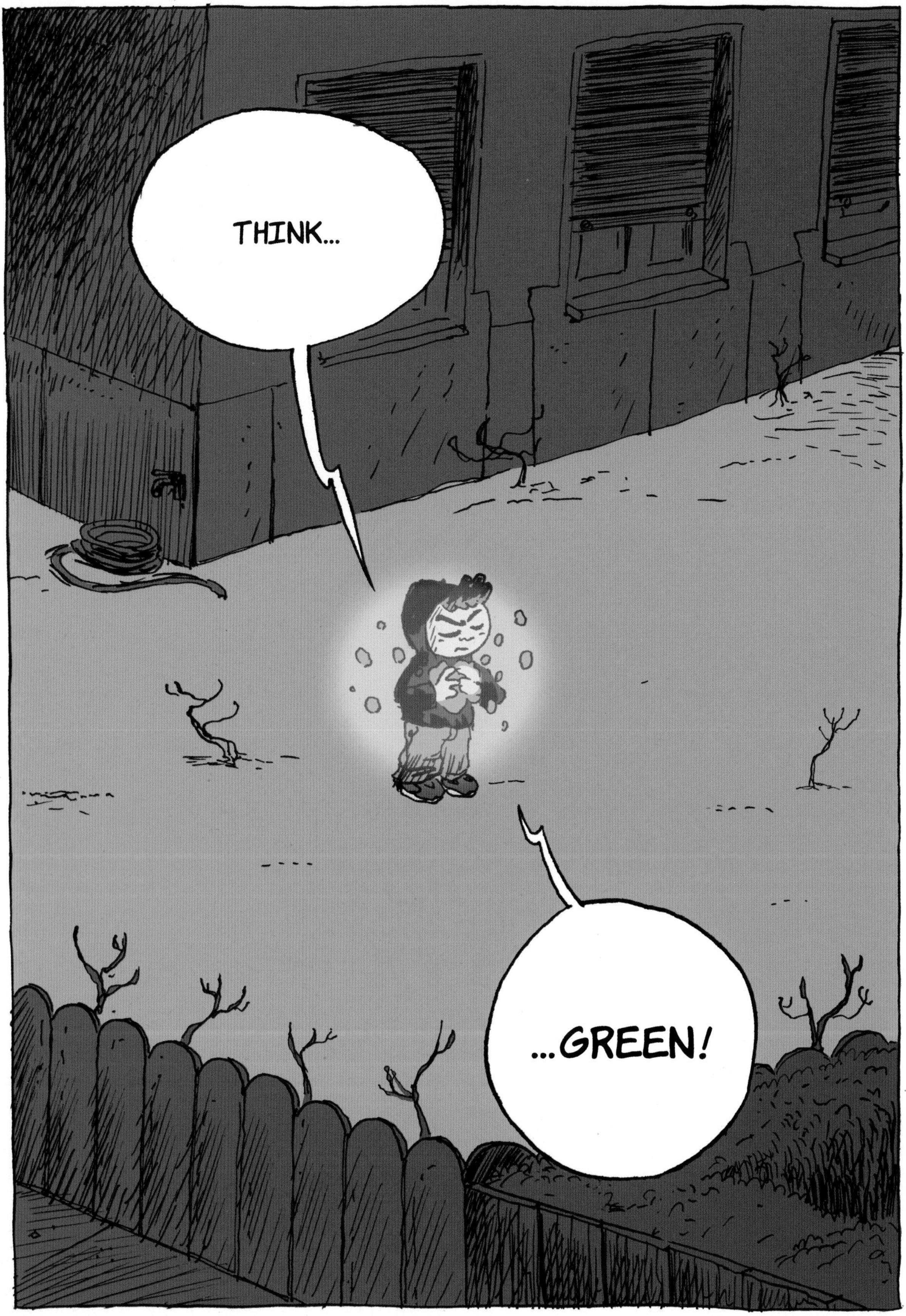
THINK...
...GREEN!

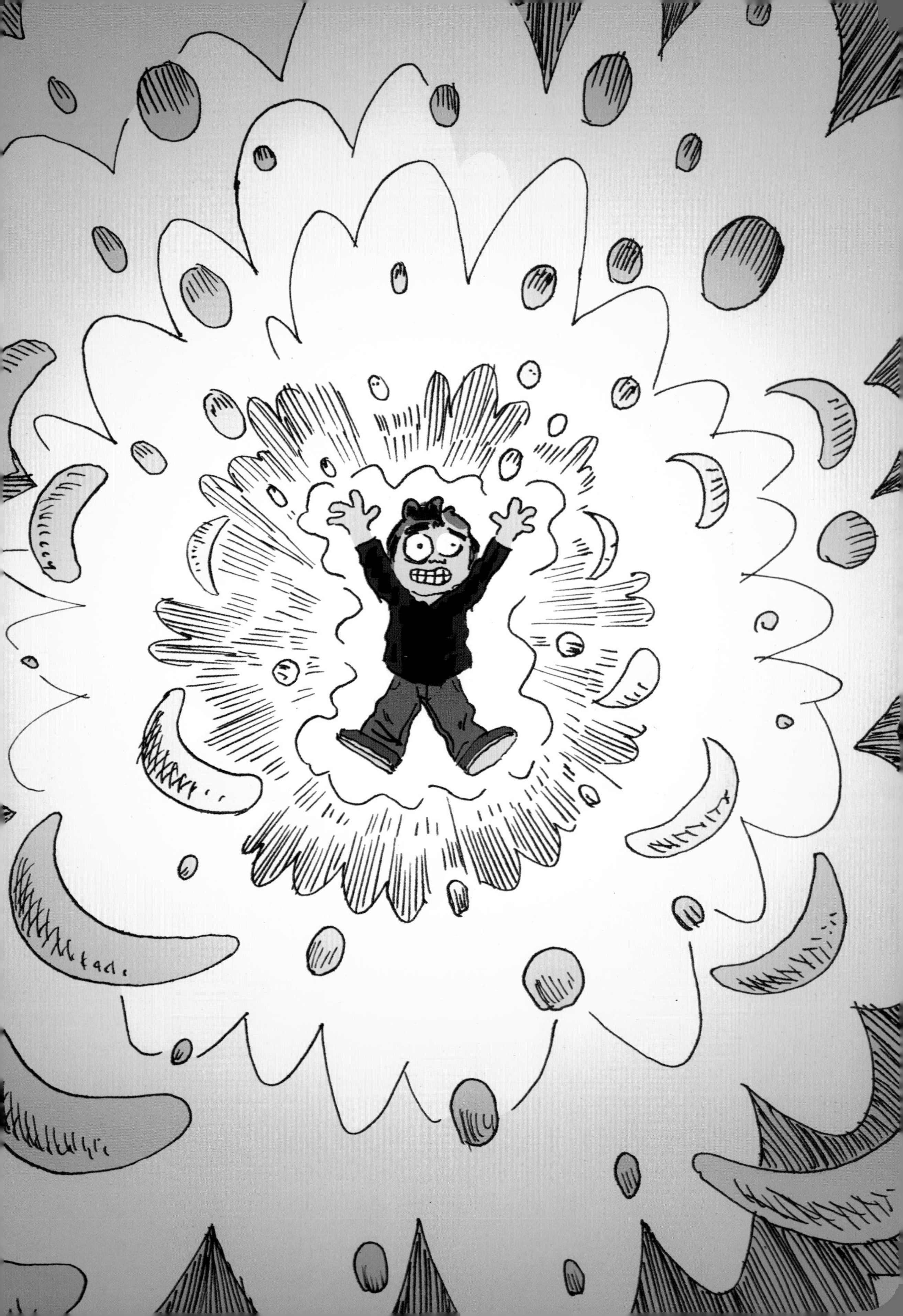

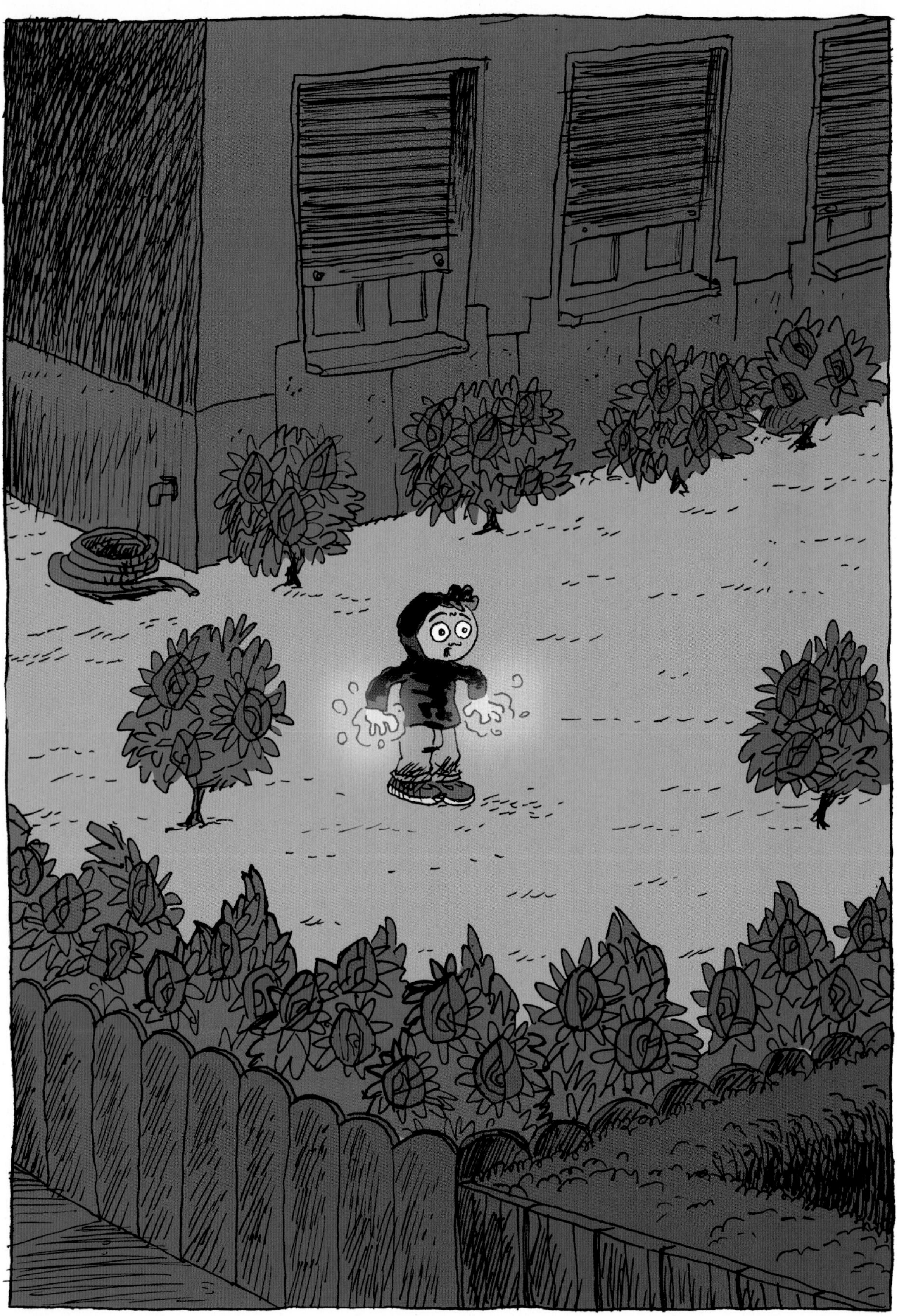

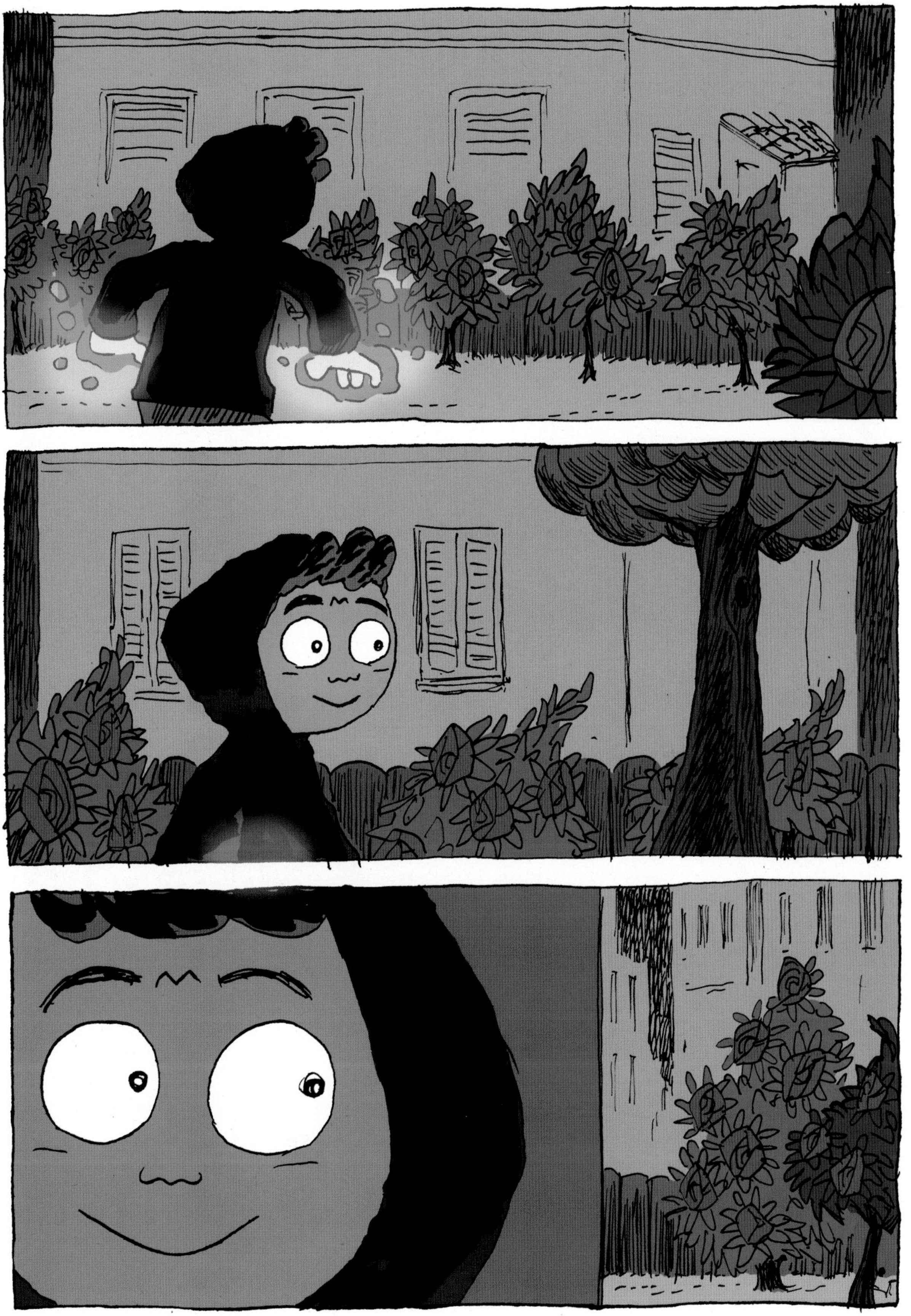

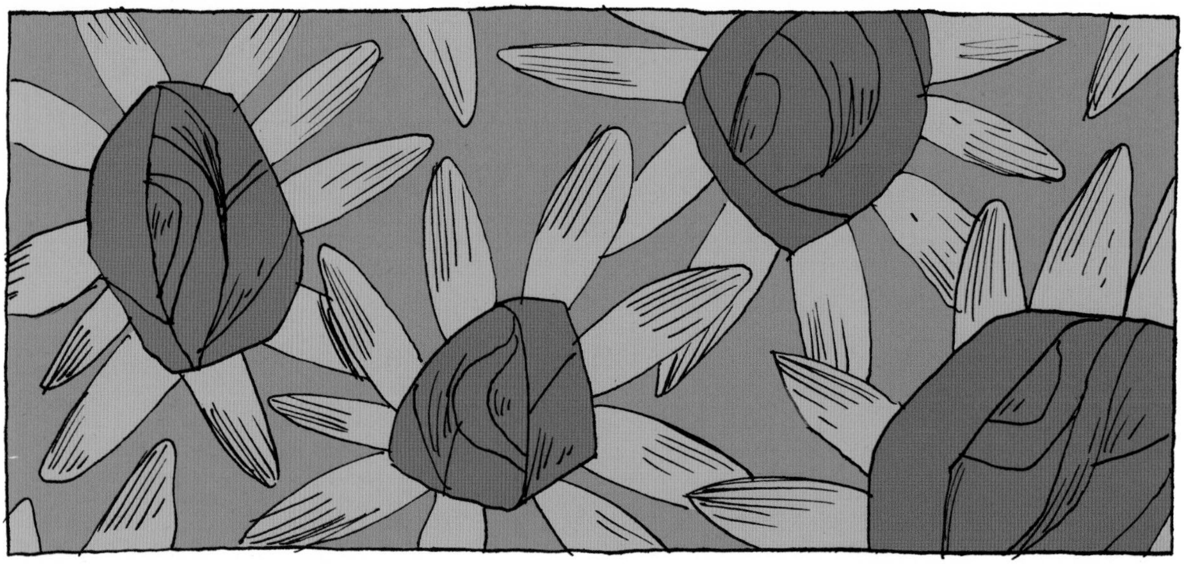

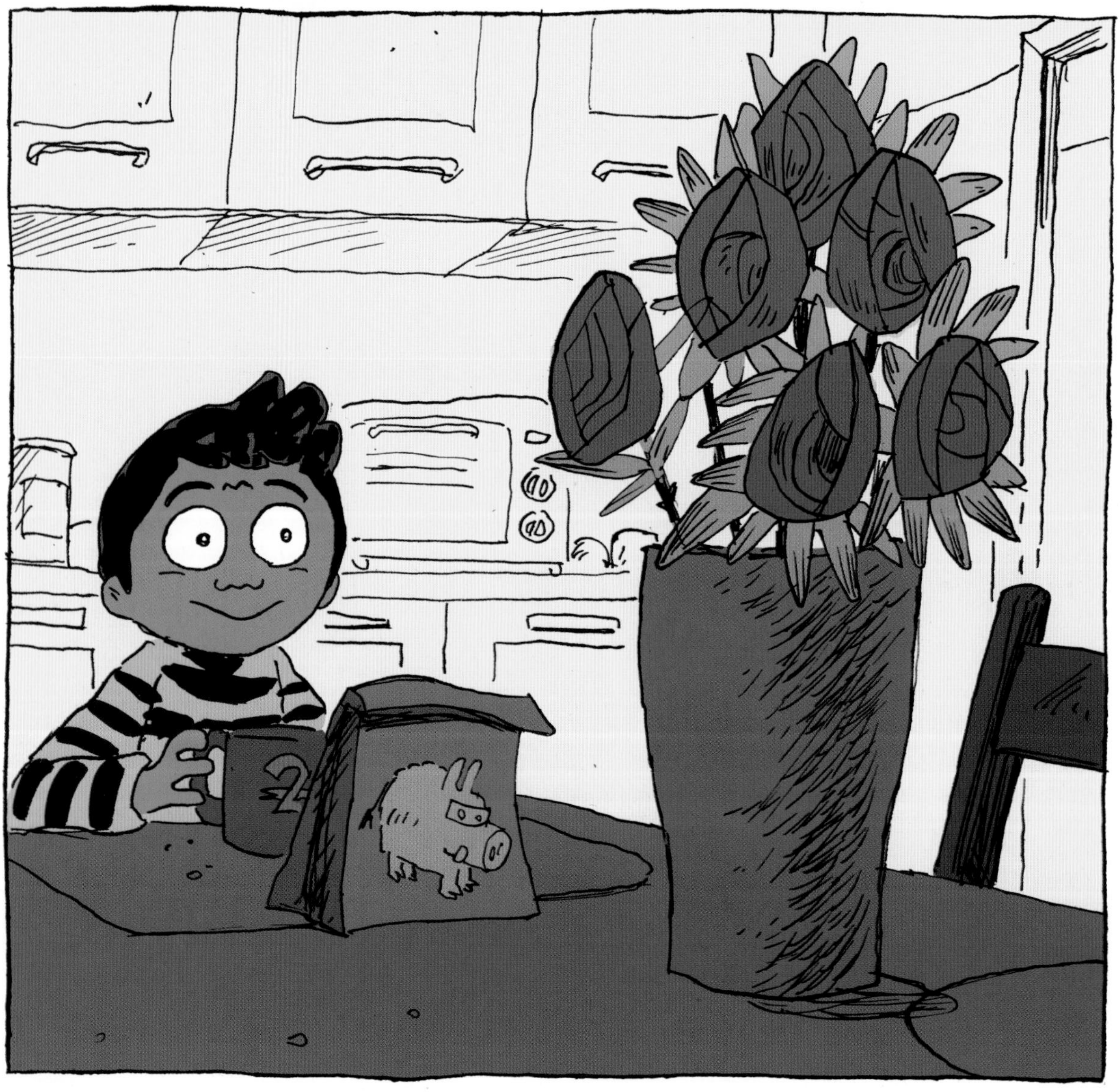

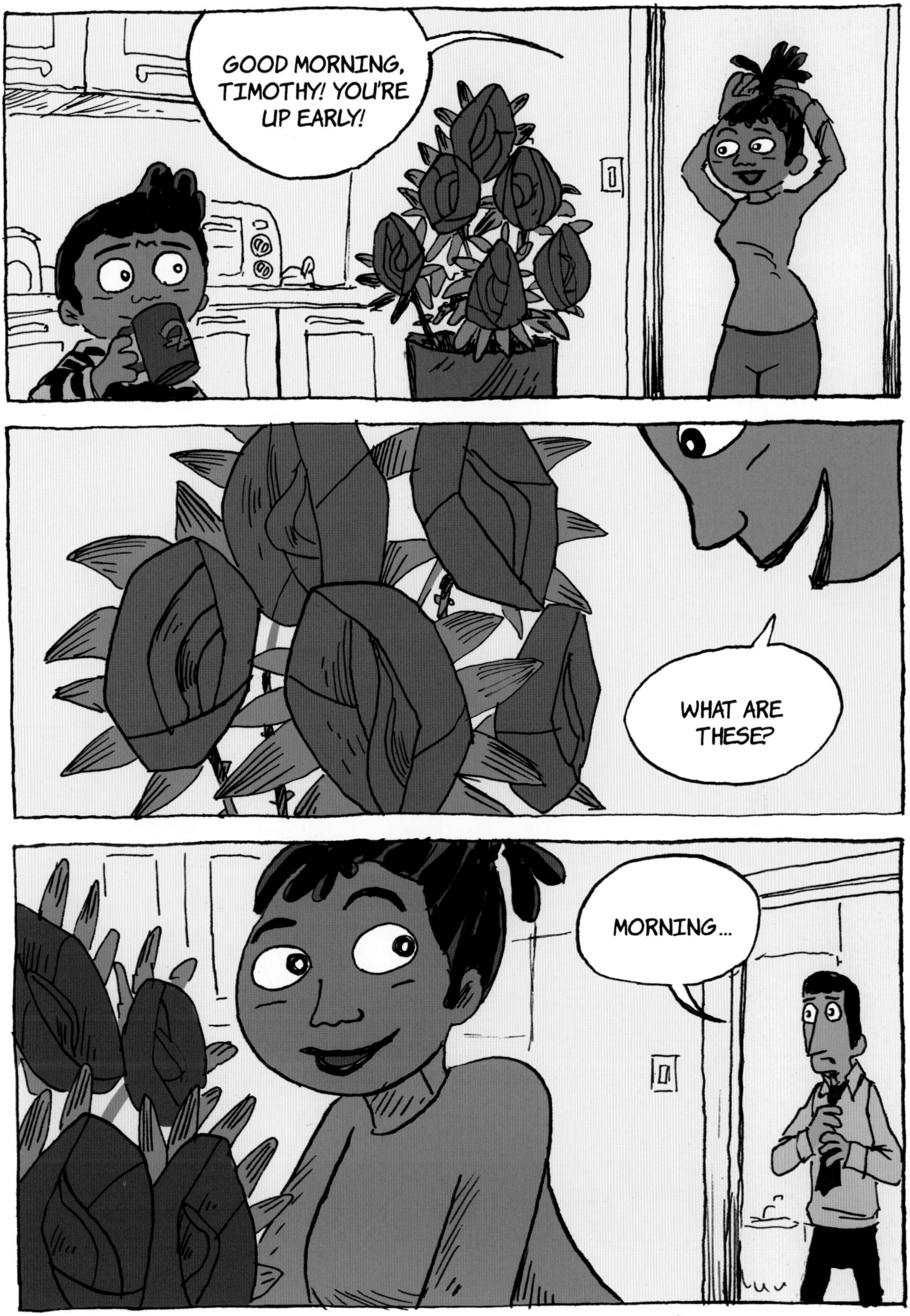
GOOD MORNING, TIMOTHY! YOU'RE UP EARLY!
WHAT ARE THESE?
MORNING...

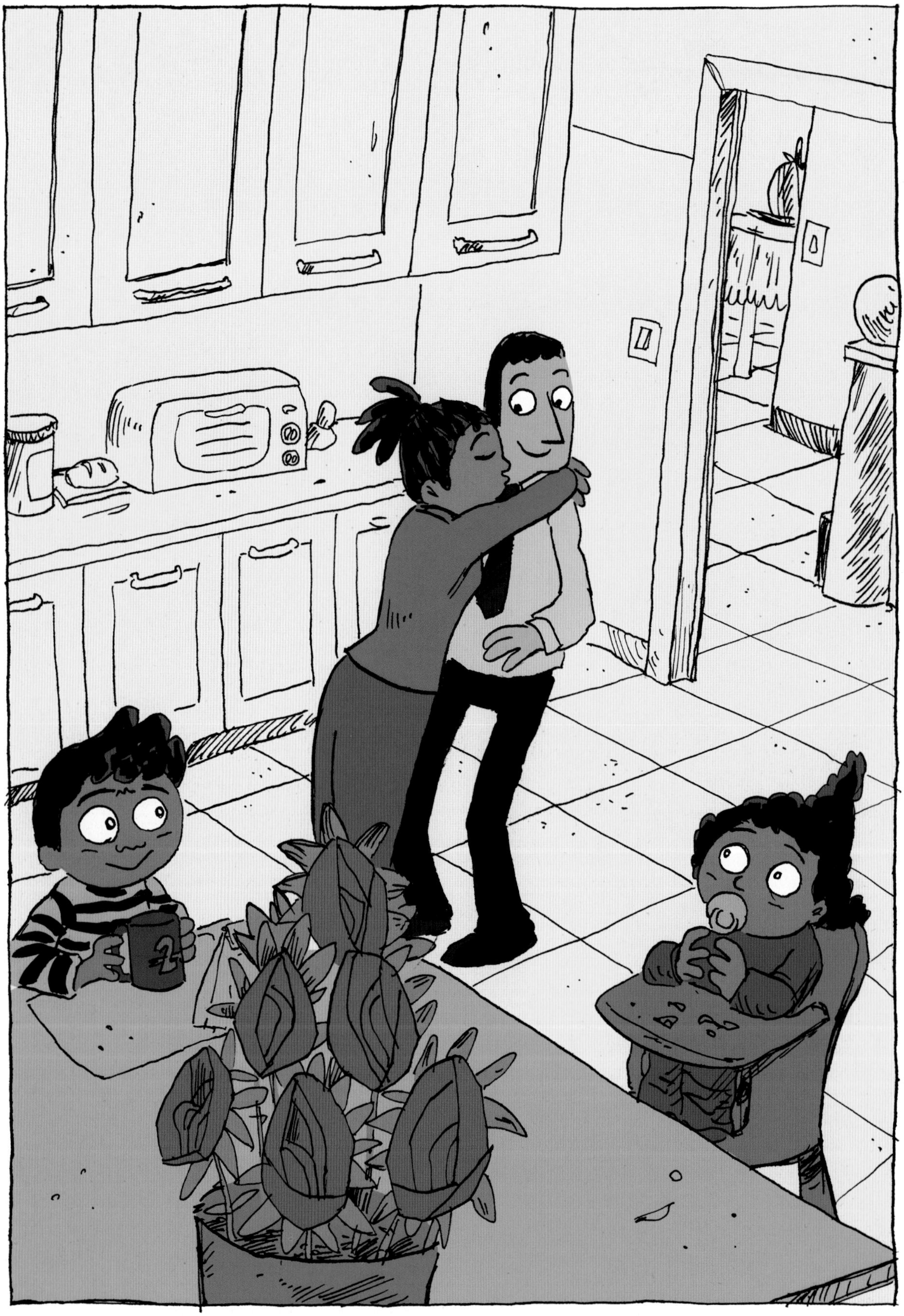

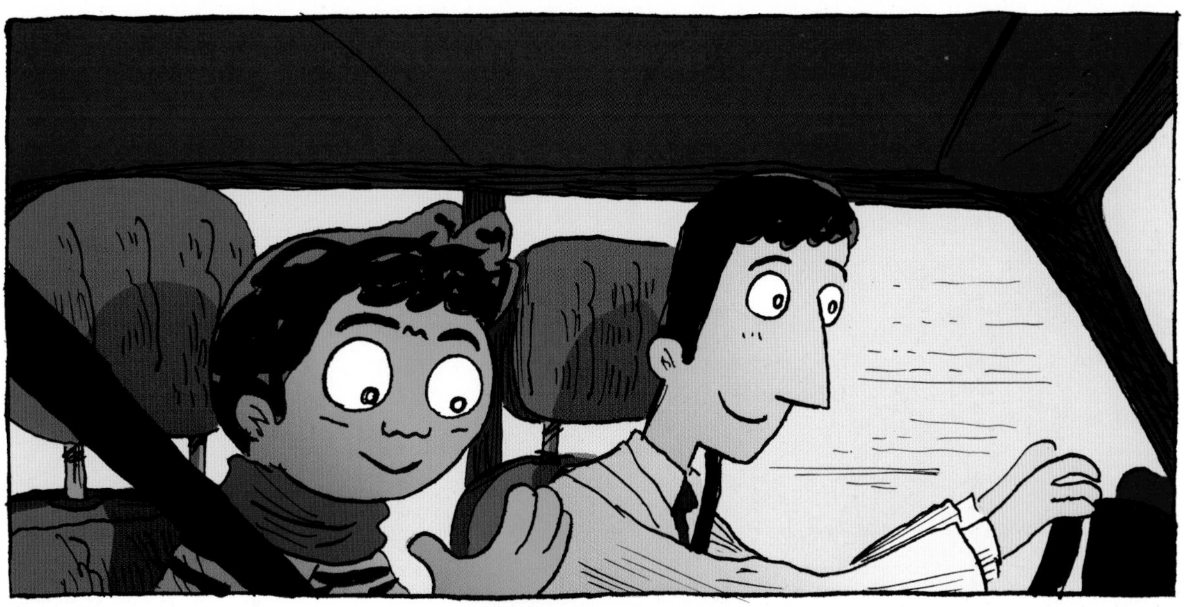

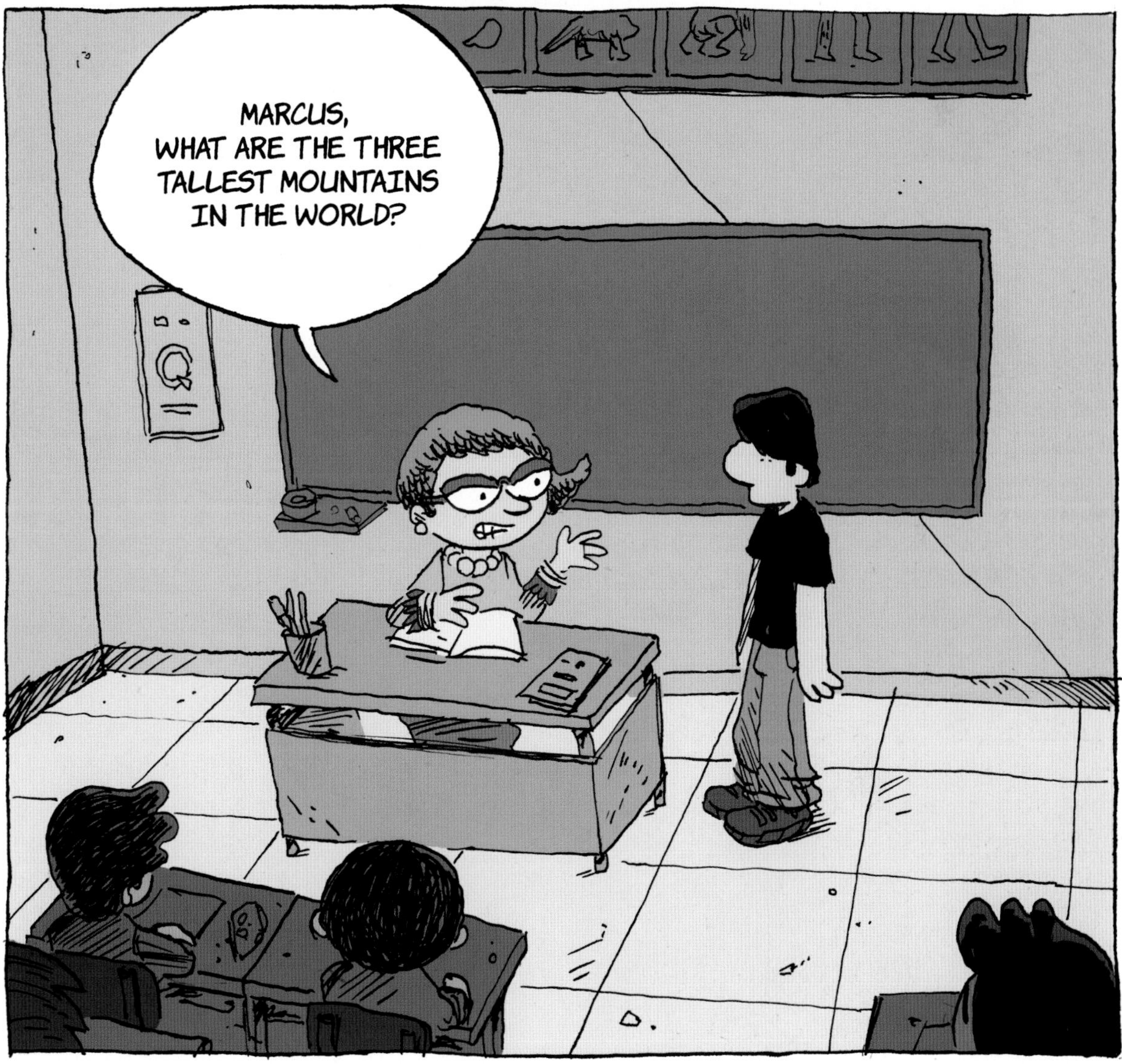
MARCUS, WHAT ARE THE THREE TALLEST MOUNTAINS IN THE WORLD?

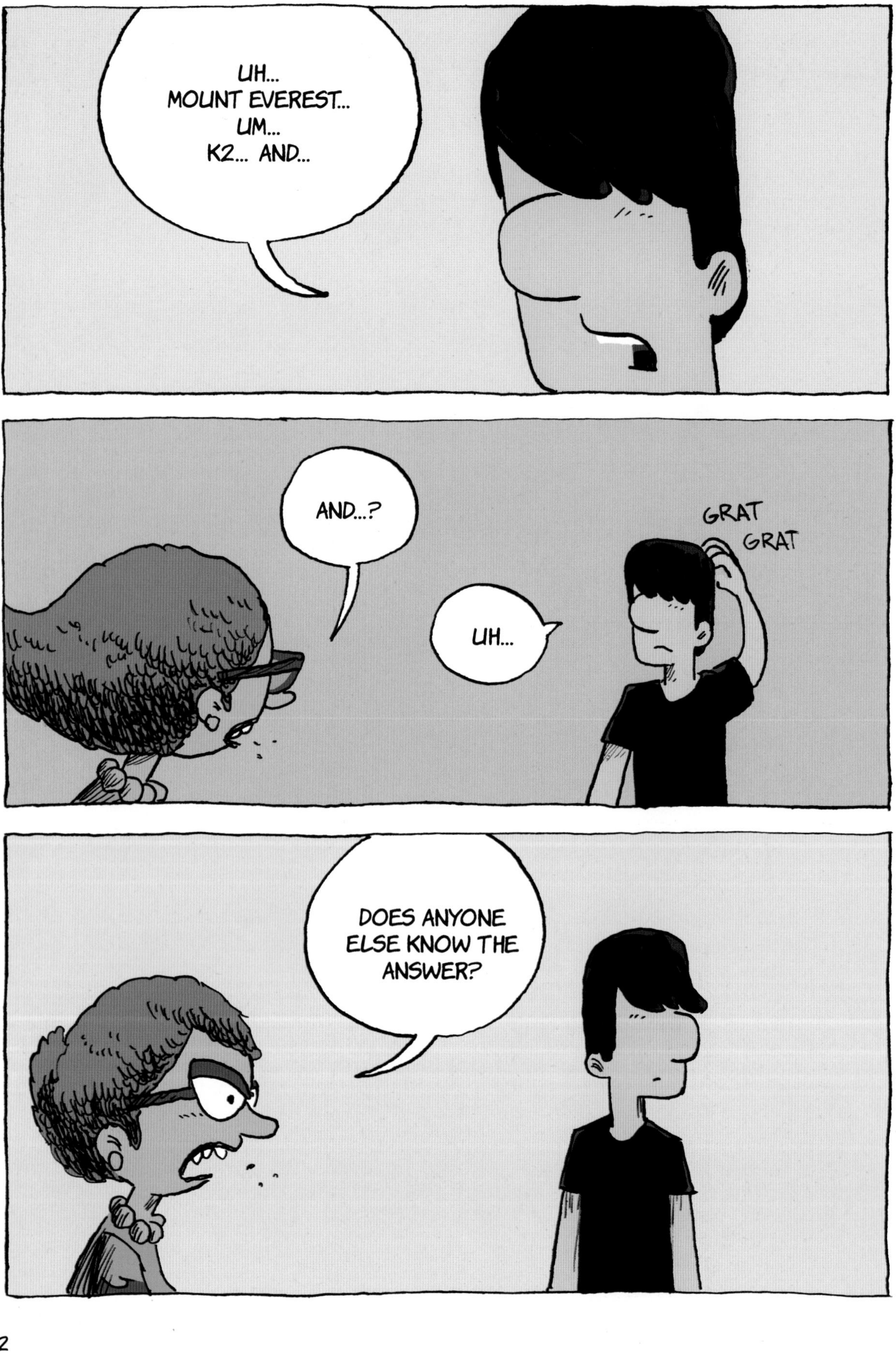
UH...
MOUNT EVEREST...
UM...
K2... AND...
AND...?
GRAT
GRAT
UH...
DOES ANYONE ELSE KNOW THE ANSWER?

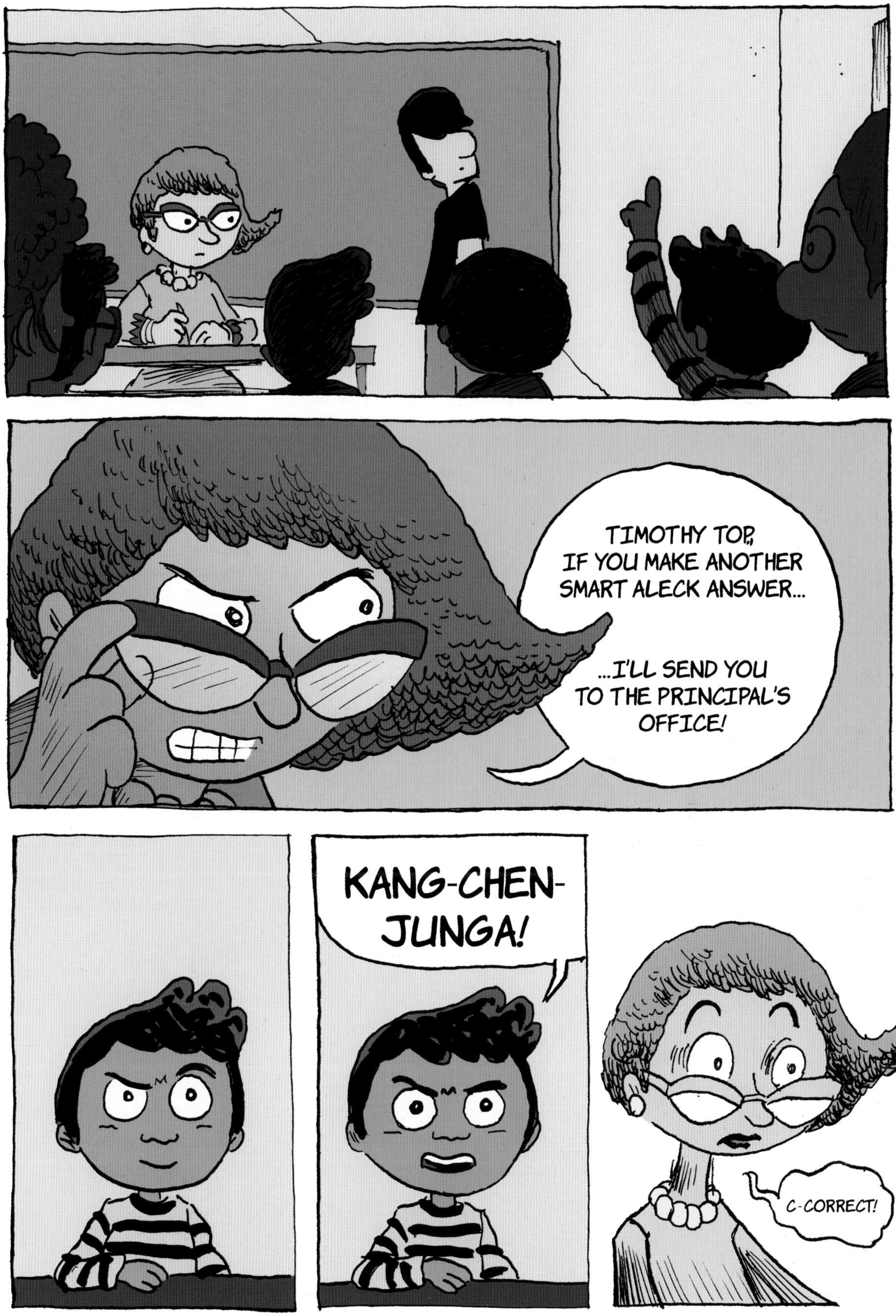
TIMOTHY TOP, IF YOU MAKE ANOTHER SMART ALECK ANSWER...
...I'LL SEND YOU TO THE PRINCIPAL'S OFFICE!
KANG-CHEN-JUNGA!
C-CORRECT!

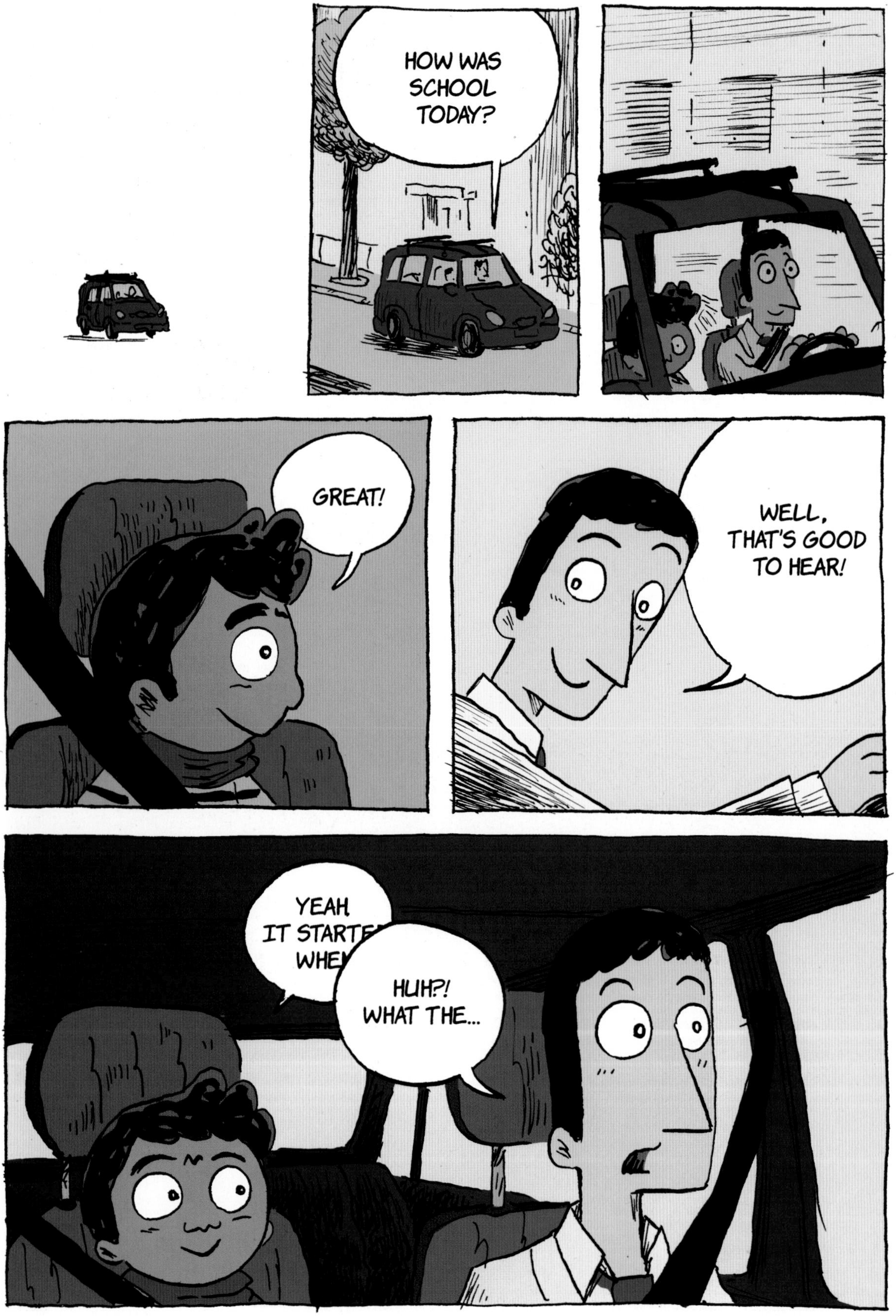

HOW WAS SCHOOL TODAY?
GREAT!
WELL, THAT'S GOOD TO HEAR!
YEAH. IT STARTE WHE
HUH?! WHAT THE...

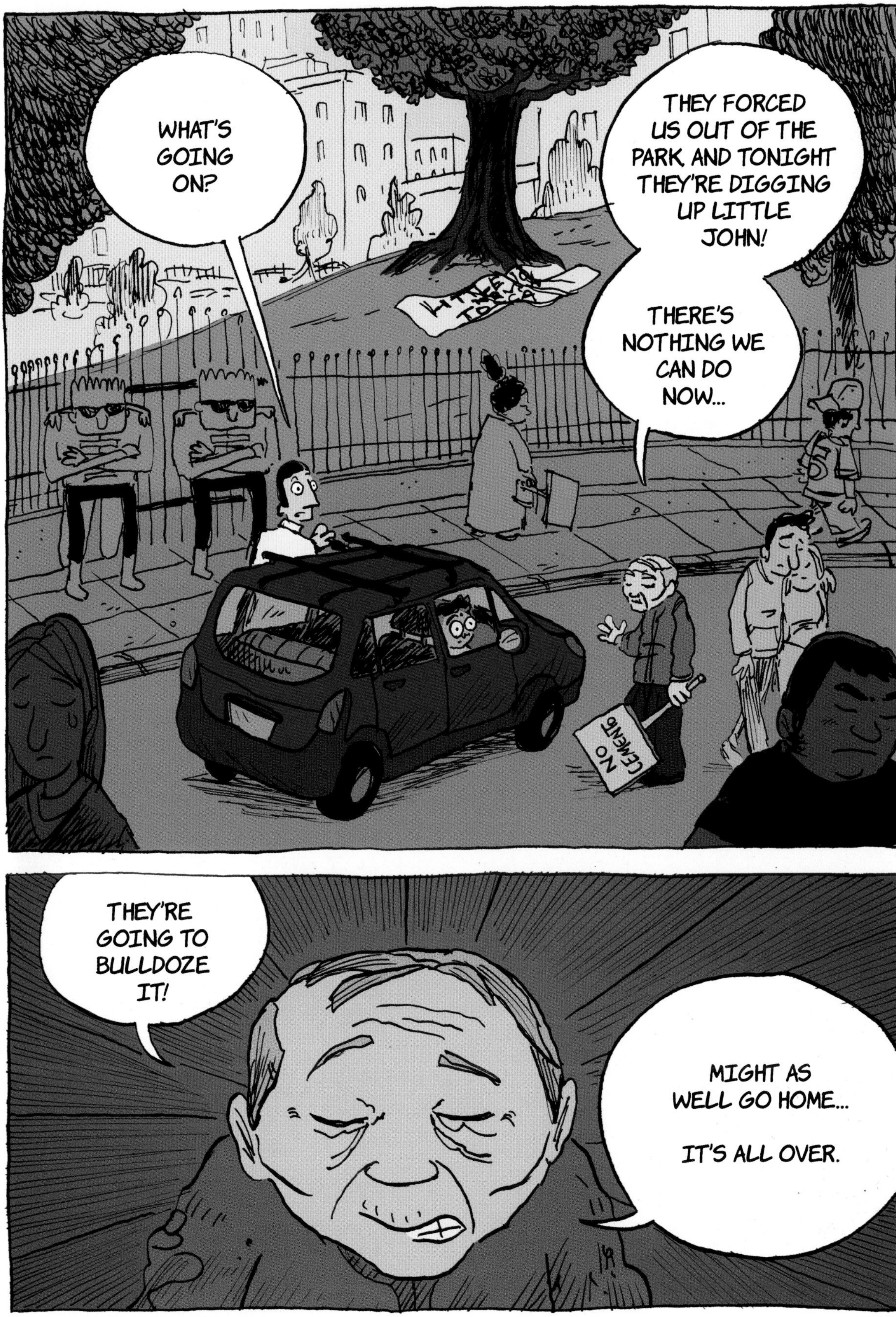
WHAT'S GOING ON?
THEY FORCED US OUT OF THE PARK, AND TONIGHT THEY'RE DIGGING UP LITTLE JOHN!
THERE'S NOTHING WE CAN DO NOW...
THEY'RE GOING TO BULLDOZE IT!
MIGHT AS WELL GO HOME...
IT'S ALL OVER.

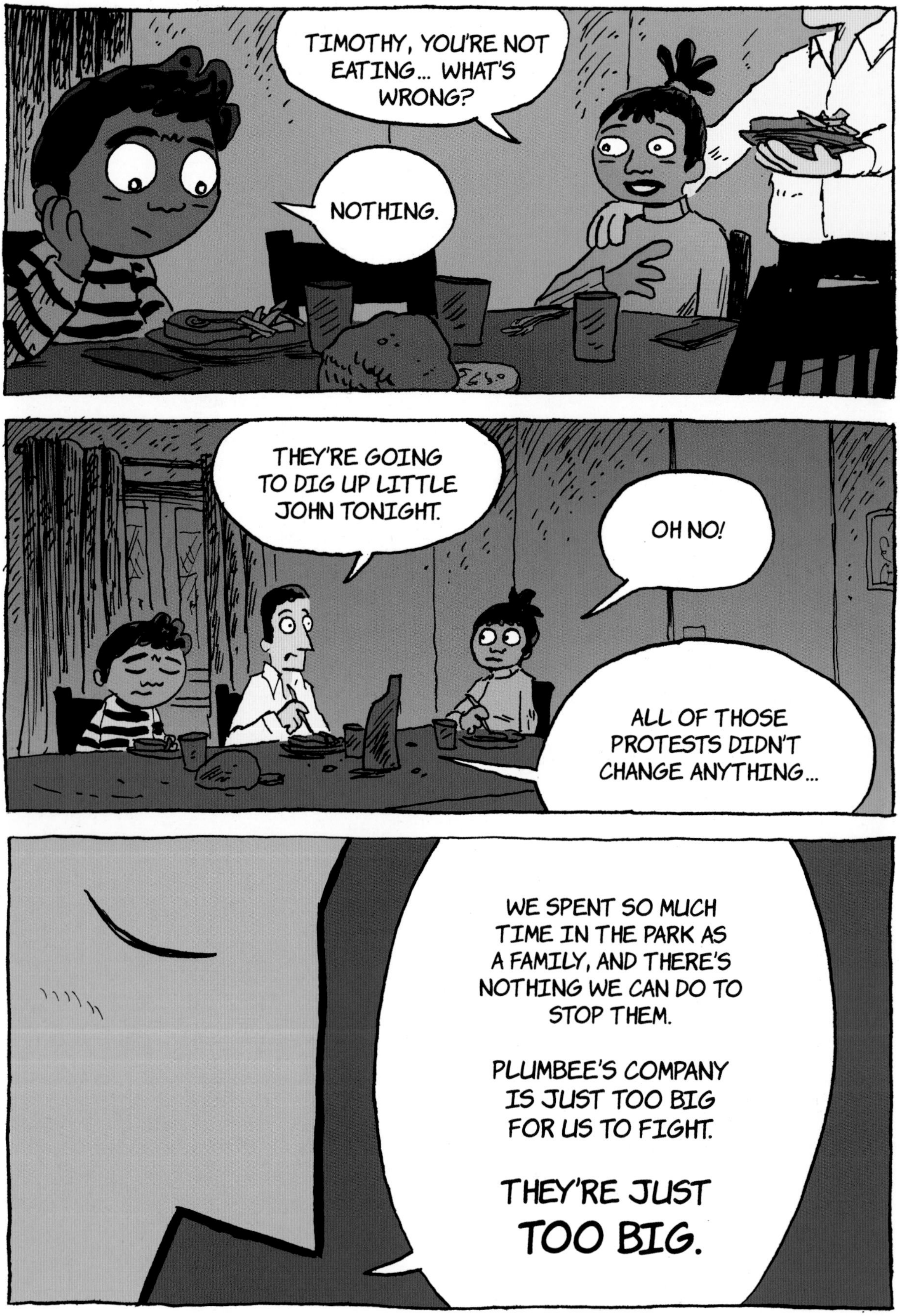
TIMOTHY, YOU'RE NOT EATING... WHAT'S WRONG?
NOTHING.
THEY'RE GOING TO DIG UP LITTLE JOHN TONIGHT.
OH NO!
ALL OF THOSE PROTESTS DIDN'T CHANGE ANYTHING...
WE SPENT SO MUCH TIME IN THE PARK AS A FAMILY, AND THERE'S NOTHING WE CAN DO TO STOP THEM.
PLUMBEE'S COMPANY IS JUST TOO BIG FOR US TO FIGHT.
THEY'RE JUST TOO BIG.

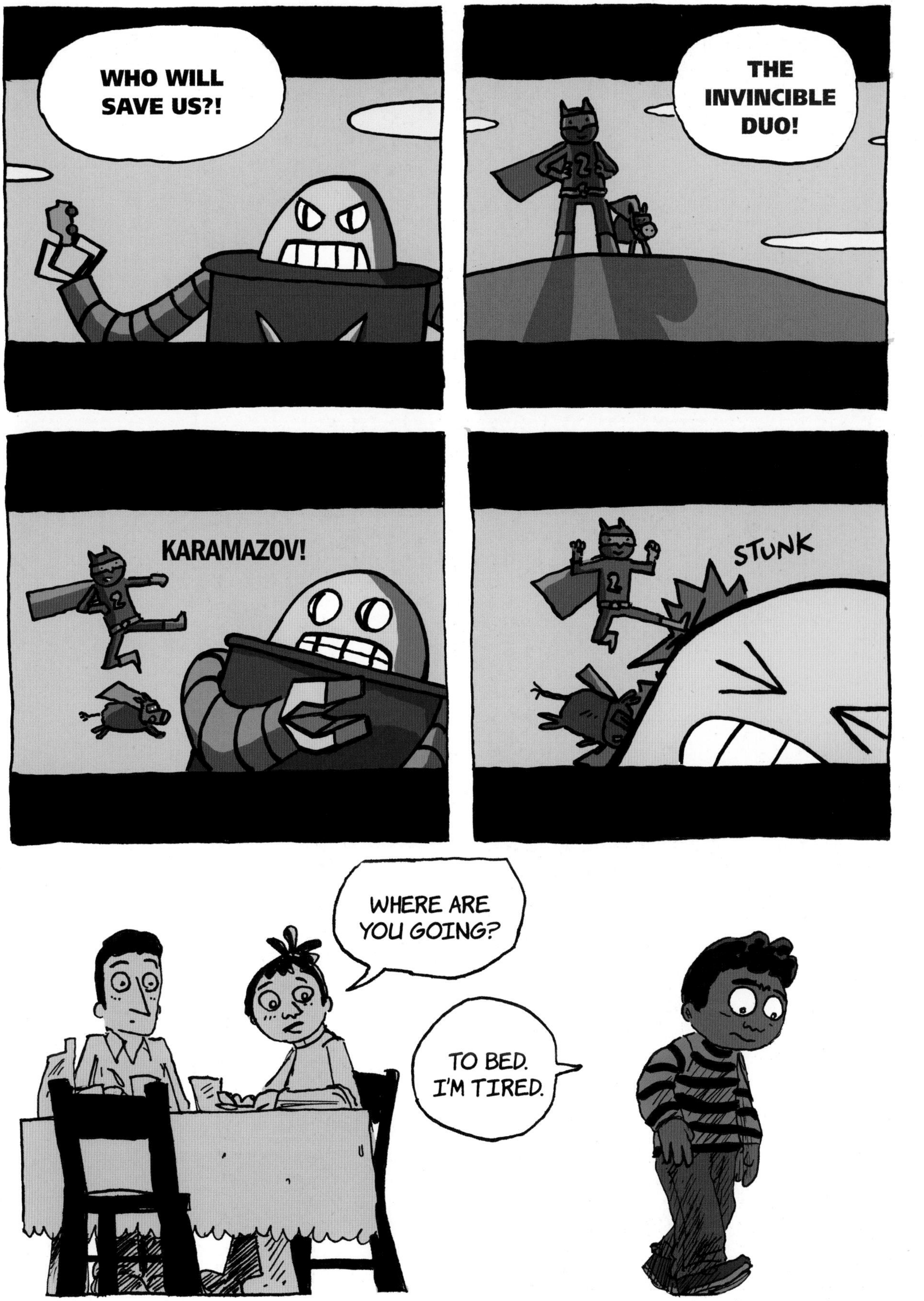

WHO WILL SAVE US?!
THE INVINCIBLE DUO!
KARAMAZOV!
STUNK
WHERE ARE YOU GOING?
TO BED. I'M TIRED.

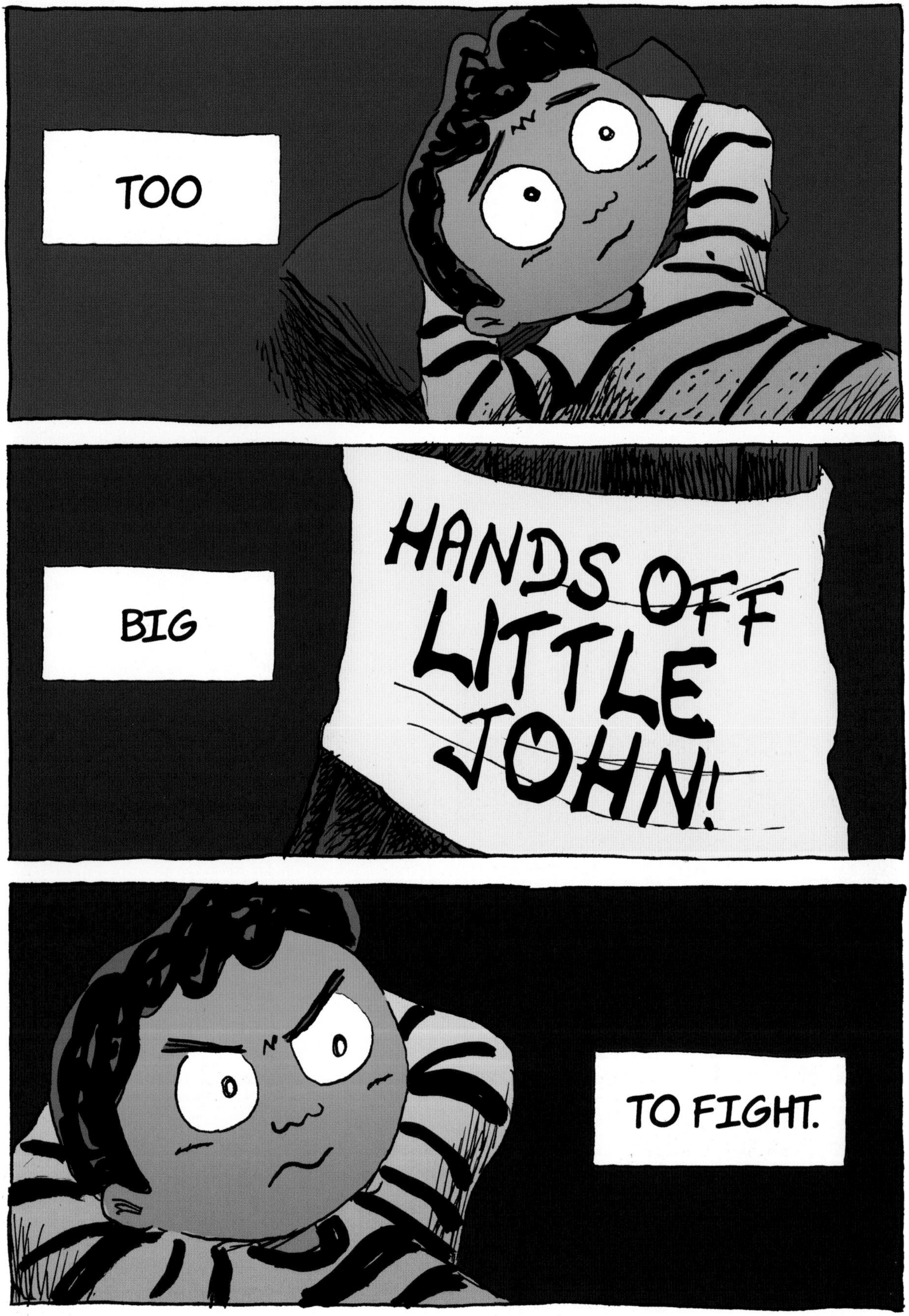
TOO
BIG
HANDS OFF LITTLE JOHN!
TO FIGHT.

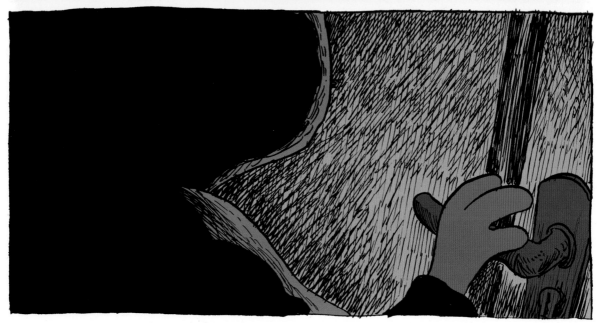

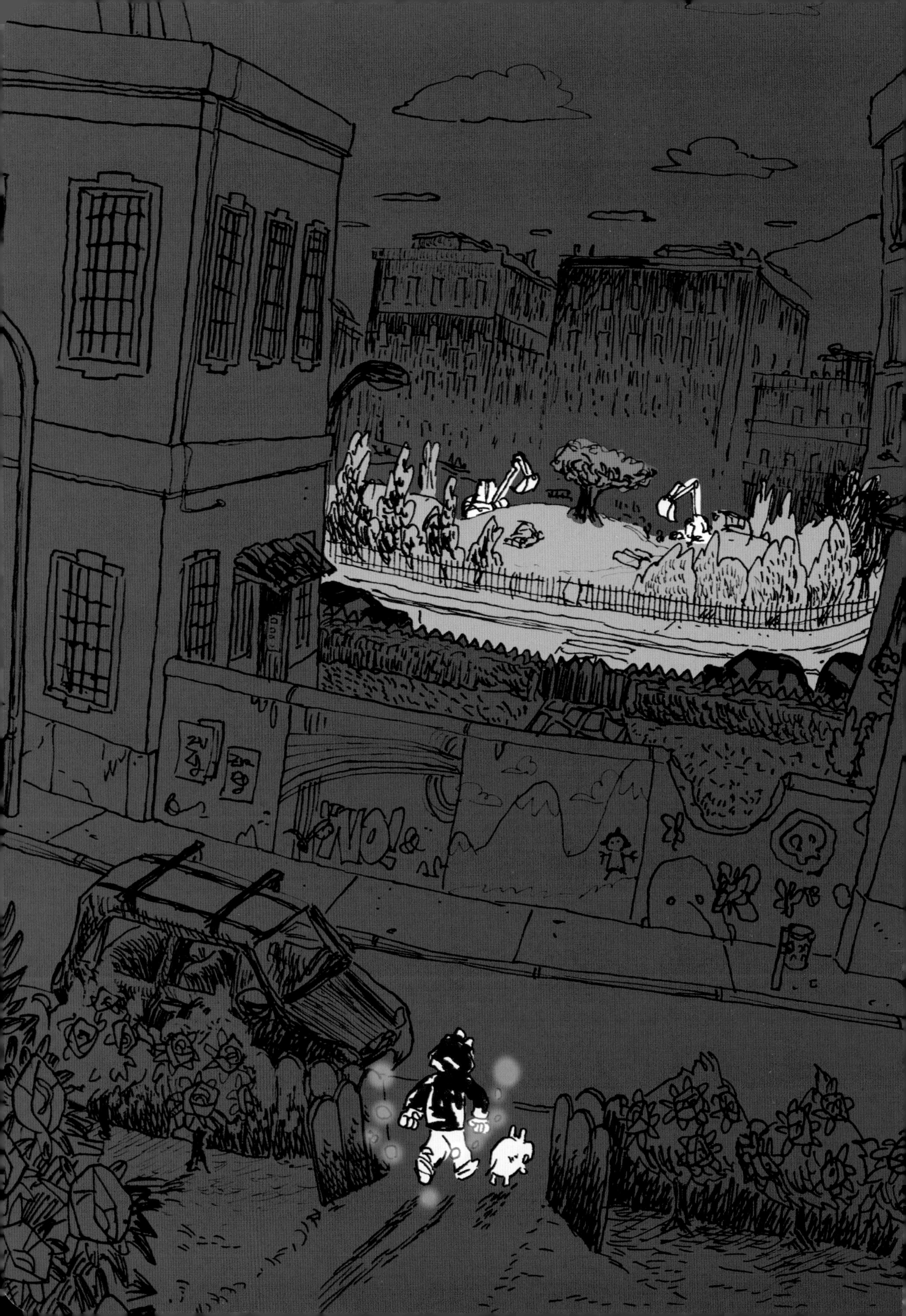
NO!

CHAPTER THREE
MISTER PLUMBEE

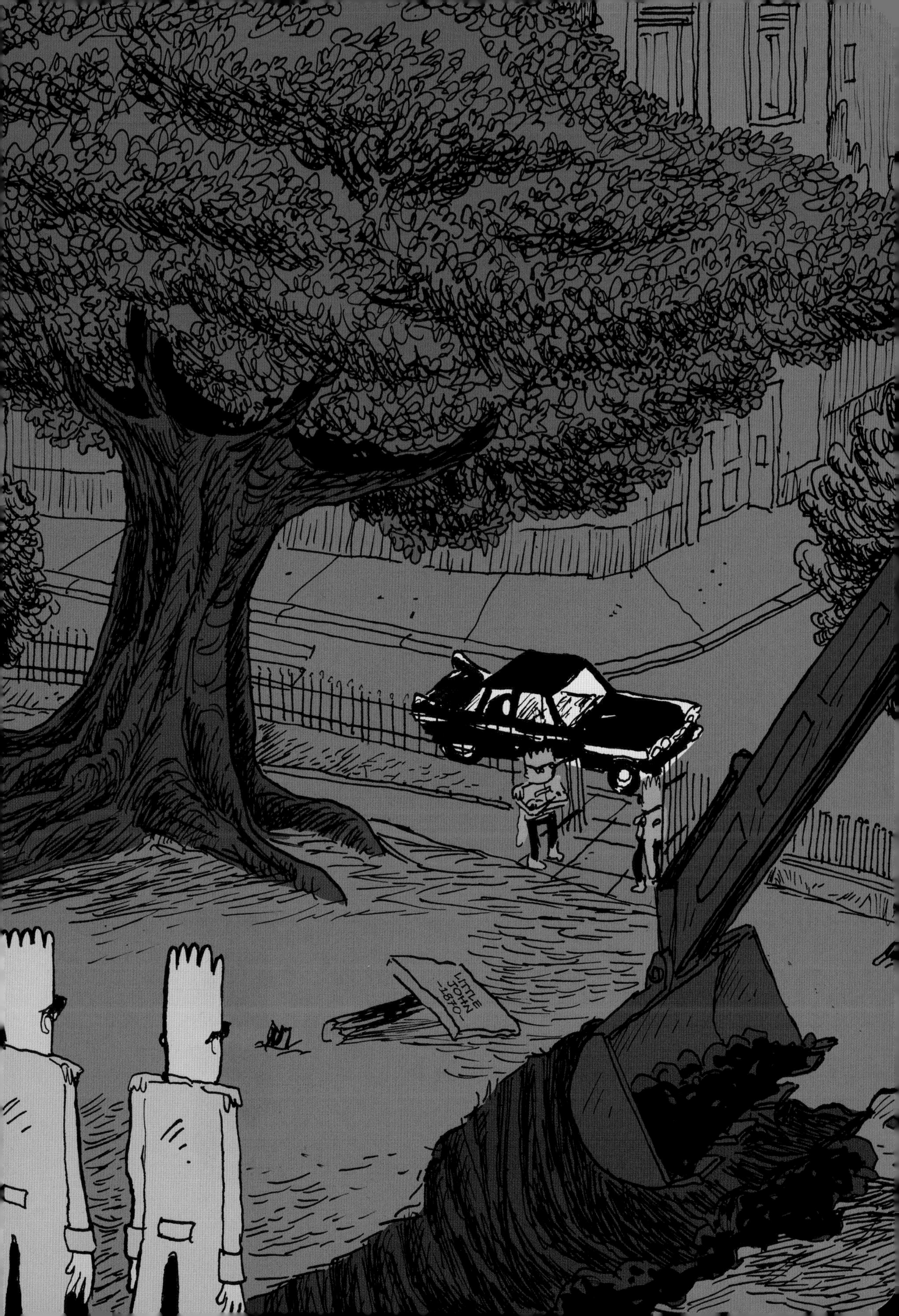
LITTLE JOHN -1870-

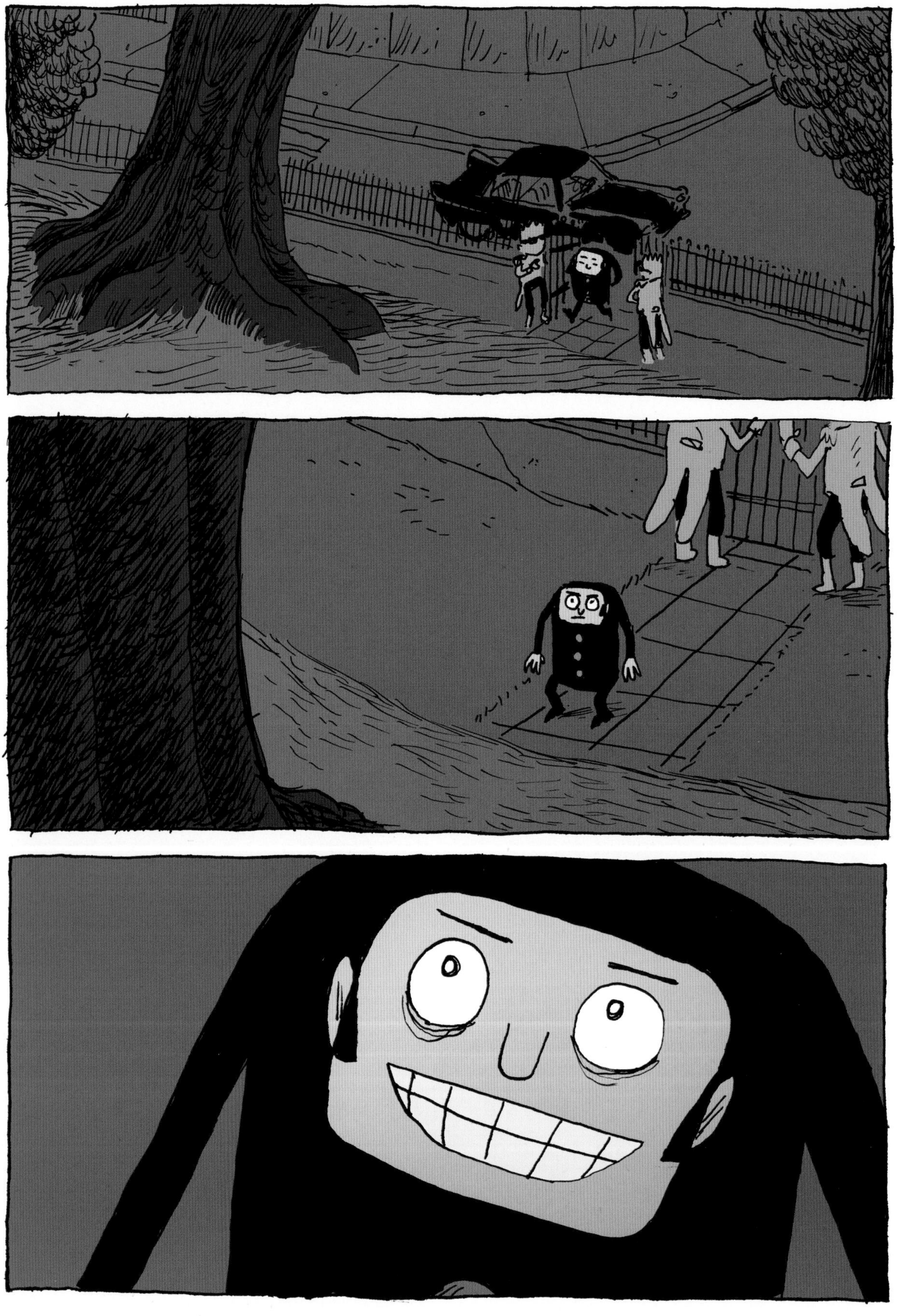

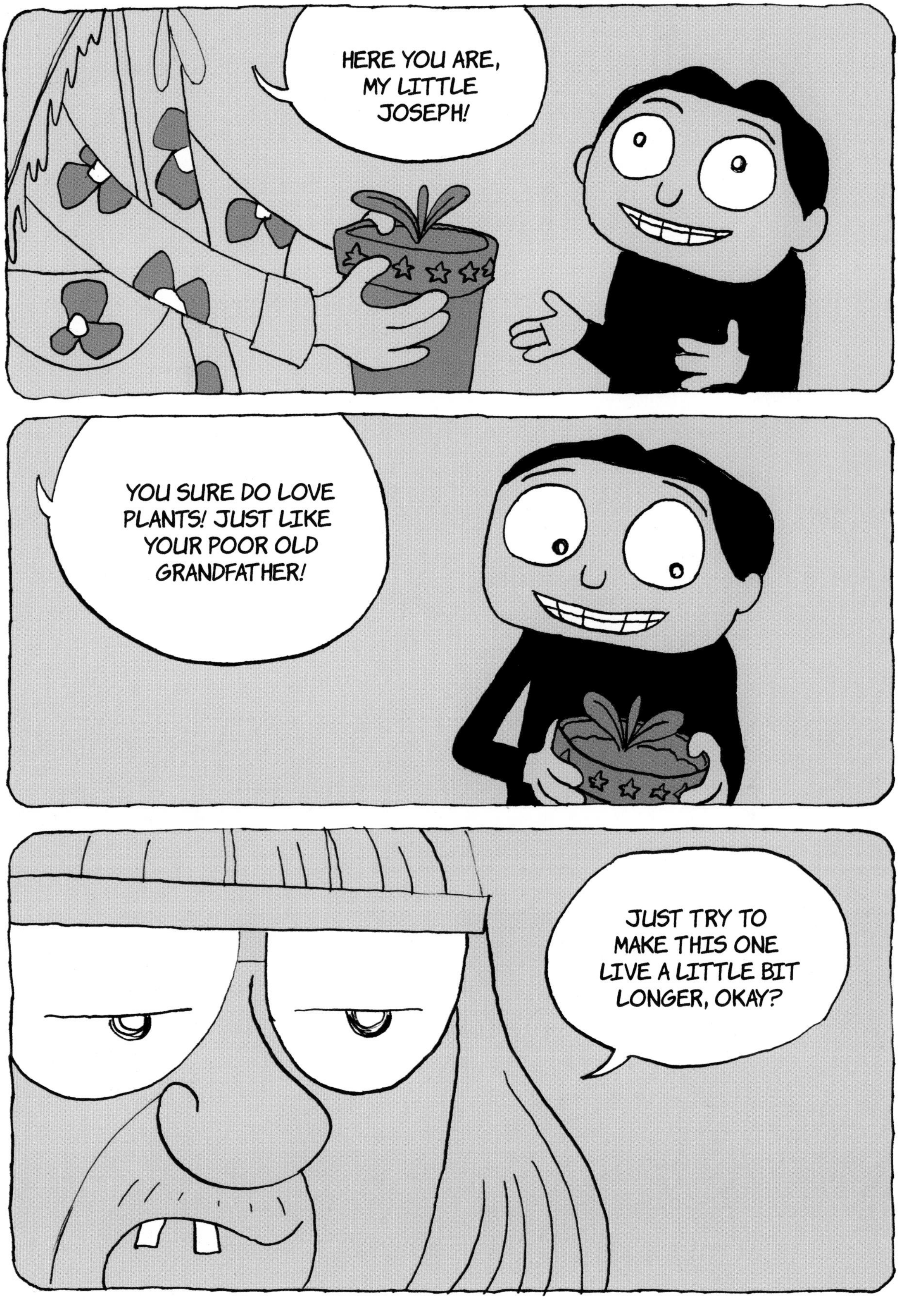
HERE YOU ARE, MY LITTLE JOSEPH!
YOU SURE DO LOVE PLANTS! JUST LIKE YOUR POOR OLD GRANDFATHER!
JUST TRY TO MAKE THIS ONE LIVE A LITTLE BIT LONGER, OKAY?

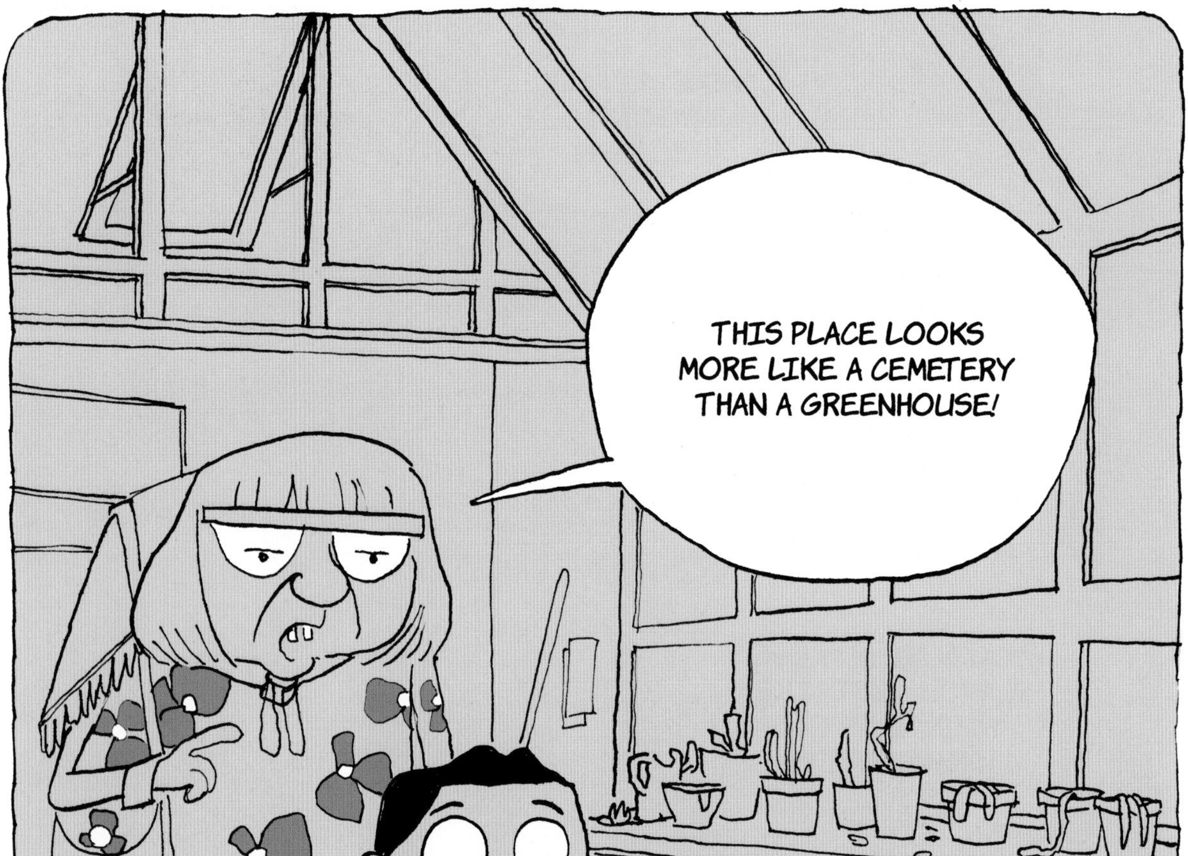
THIS PLACE LOOKS MORE LIKE A CEMETERY THAN A GREENHOUSE!

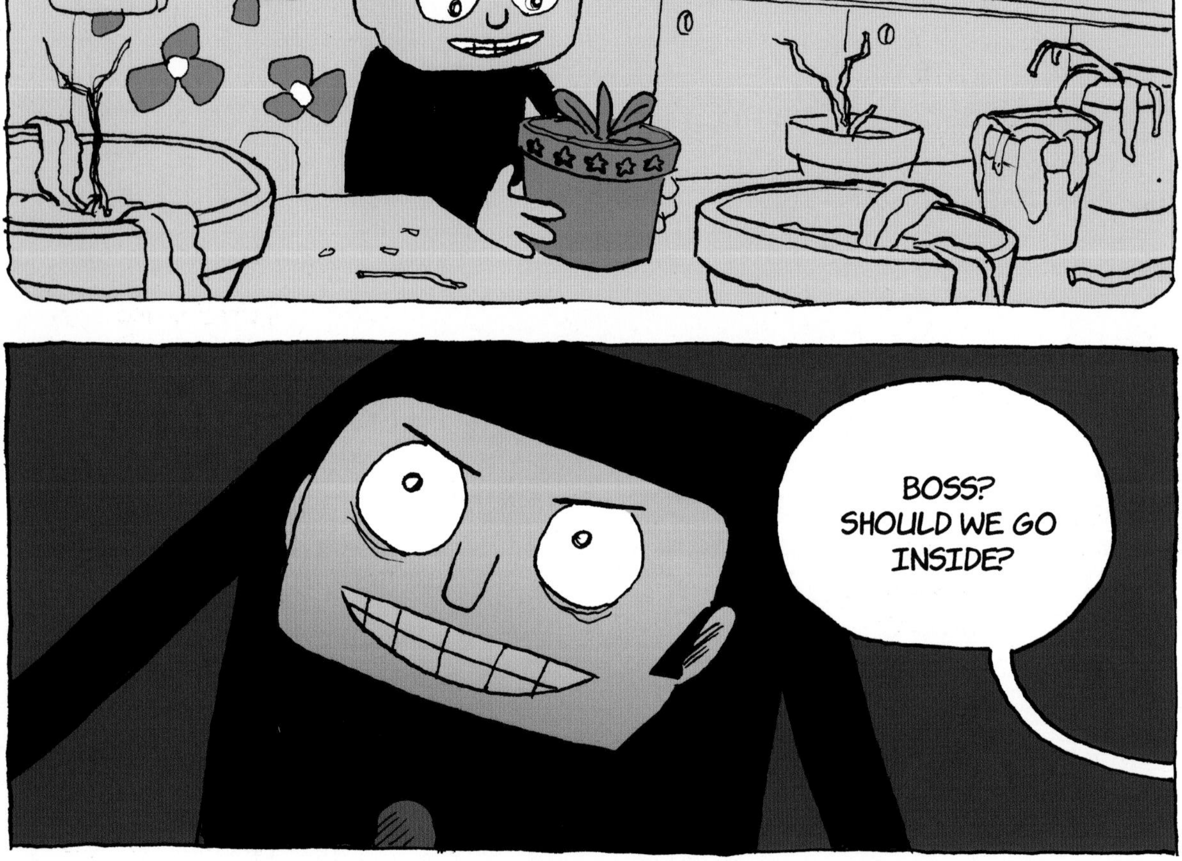
BOSS? SHOULD WE GO INSIDE?

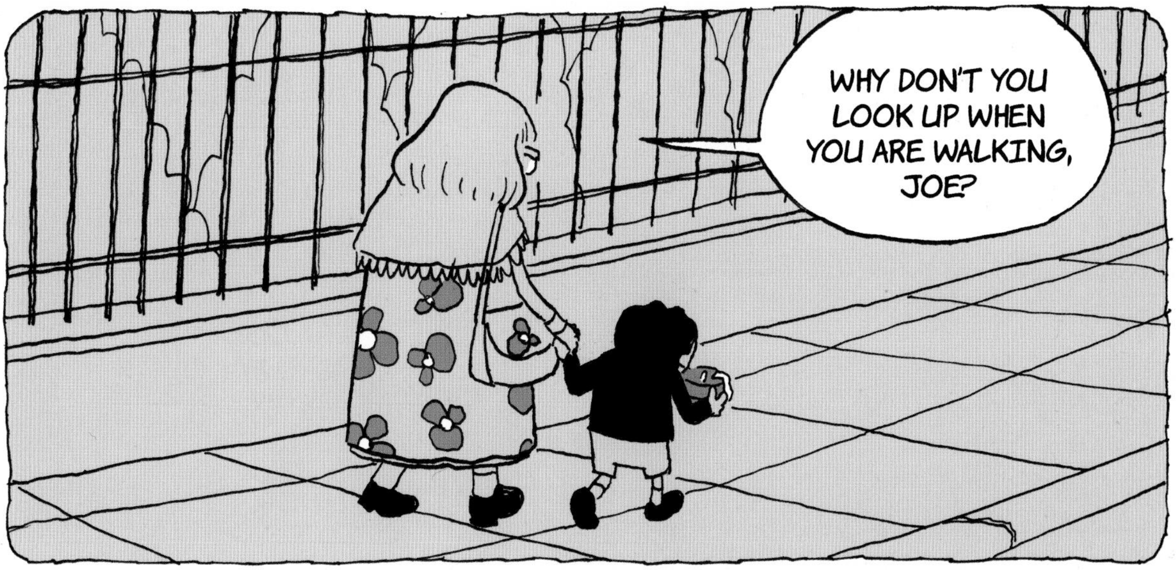
WHY DON'T YOU LOOK UP WHEN YOU ARE WALKING, JOE?

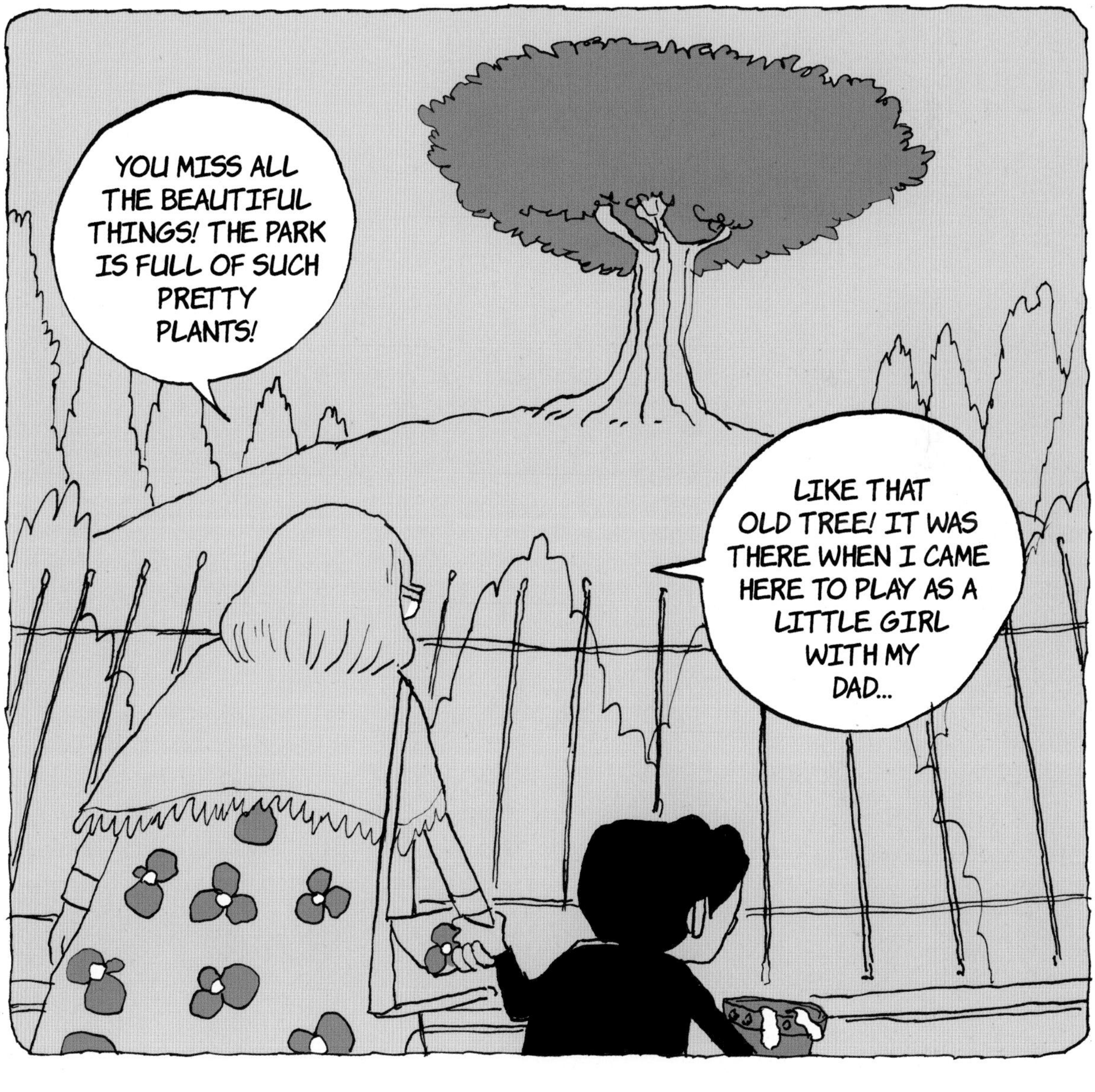
YOU MISS ALL THE BEAUTIFUL THINGS! THE PARK IS FULL OF SUCH PRETTY PLANTS!
LIKE THAT OLD TREE! IT WAS THERE WHEN I CAME HERE TO PLAY AS A LITTLE GIRL WITH MY DAD...

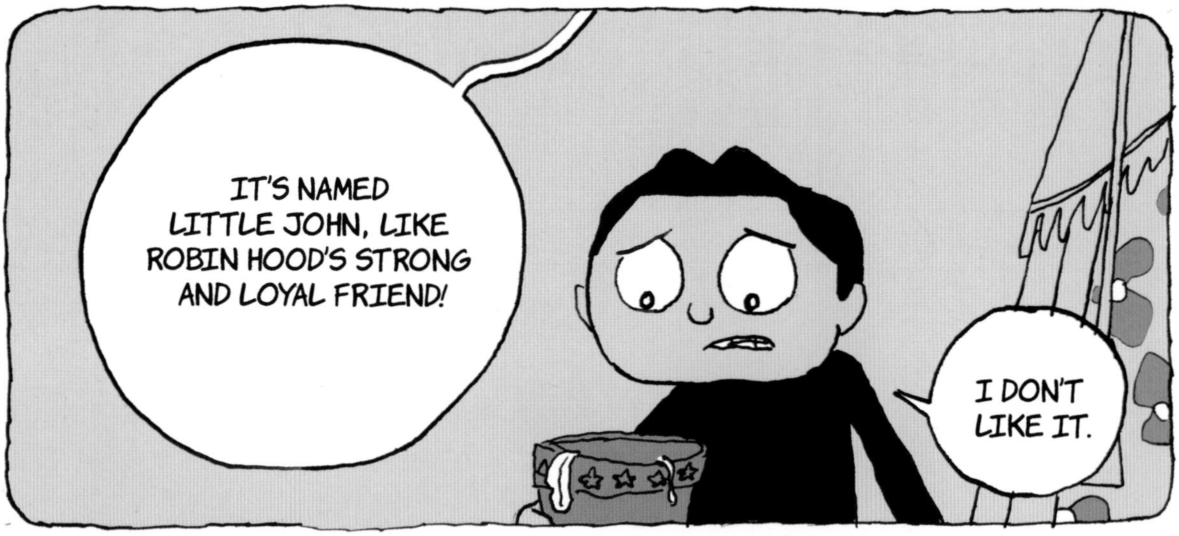
IT'S NAMED LITTLE JOHN, LIKE ROBIN HOOD'S STRONG AND LOYAL FRIEND!
I DON'T LIKE IT.

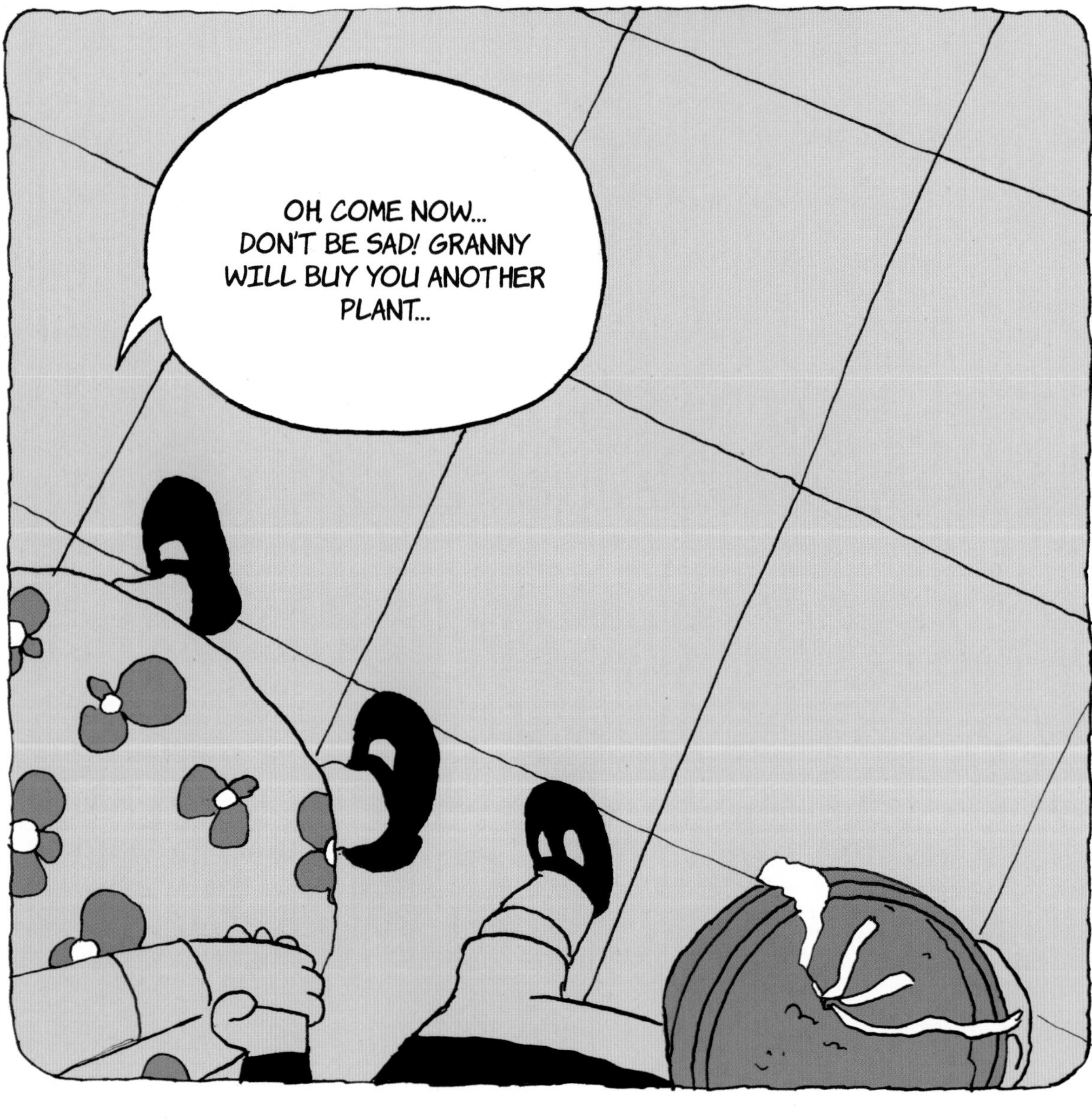
OH, COME NOW... DON'T BE SAD! GRANNY WILL BUY YOU ANOTHER PLANT...

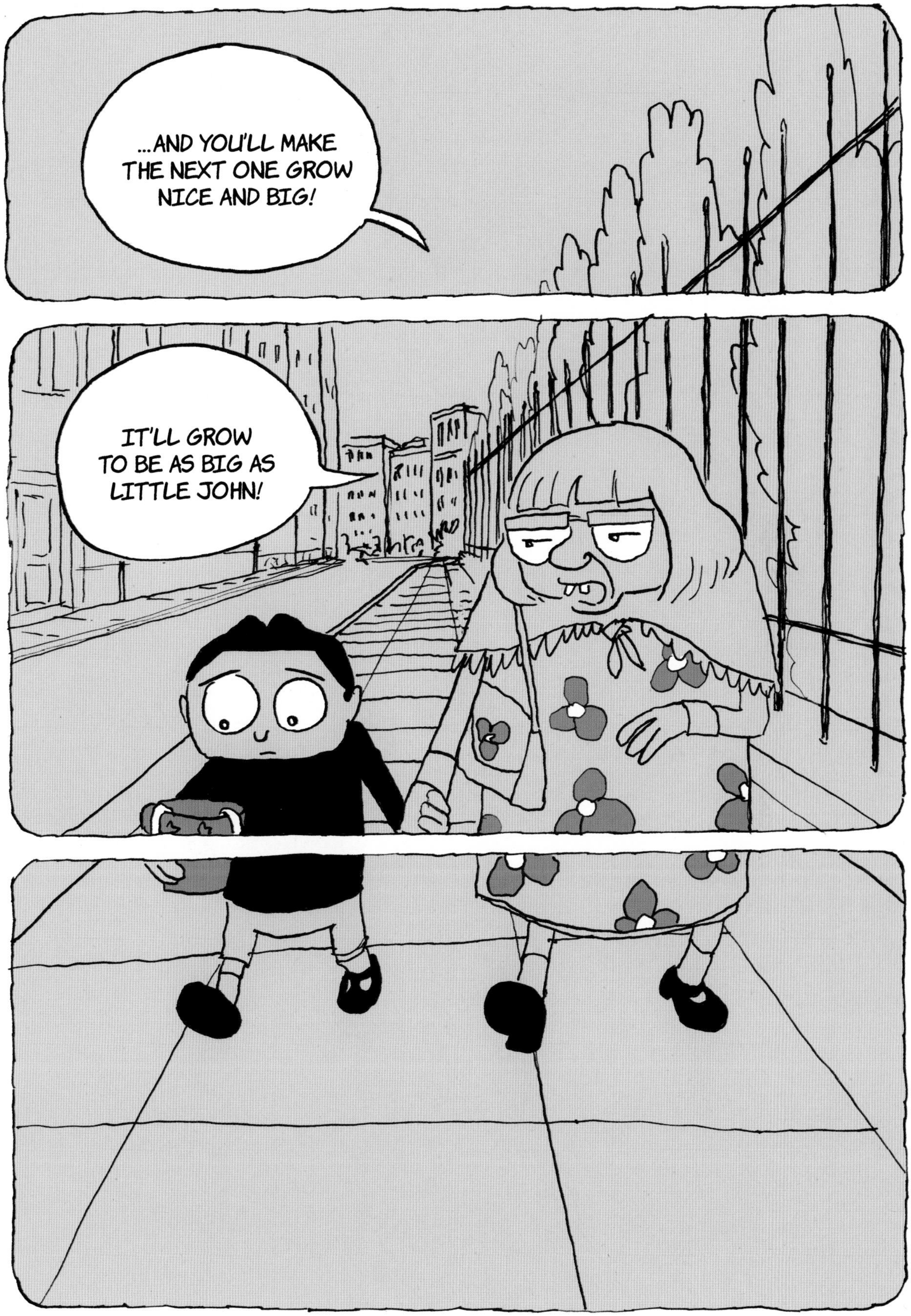
...AND YOU'LL MAKE THE NEXT ONE GROW NICE AND BIG!
IT'LL GROW TO BE AS BIG AS LITTLE JOHN!

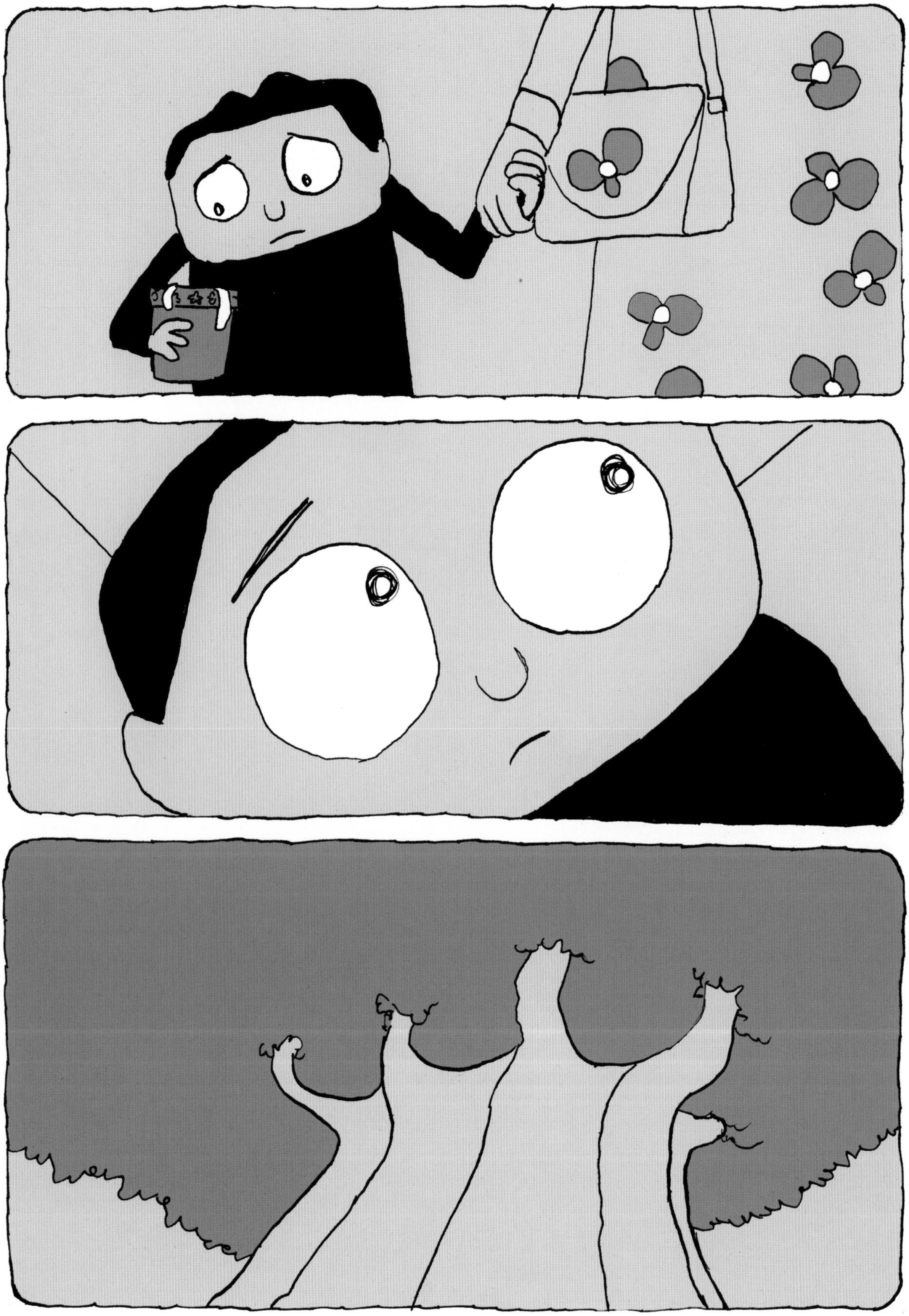

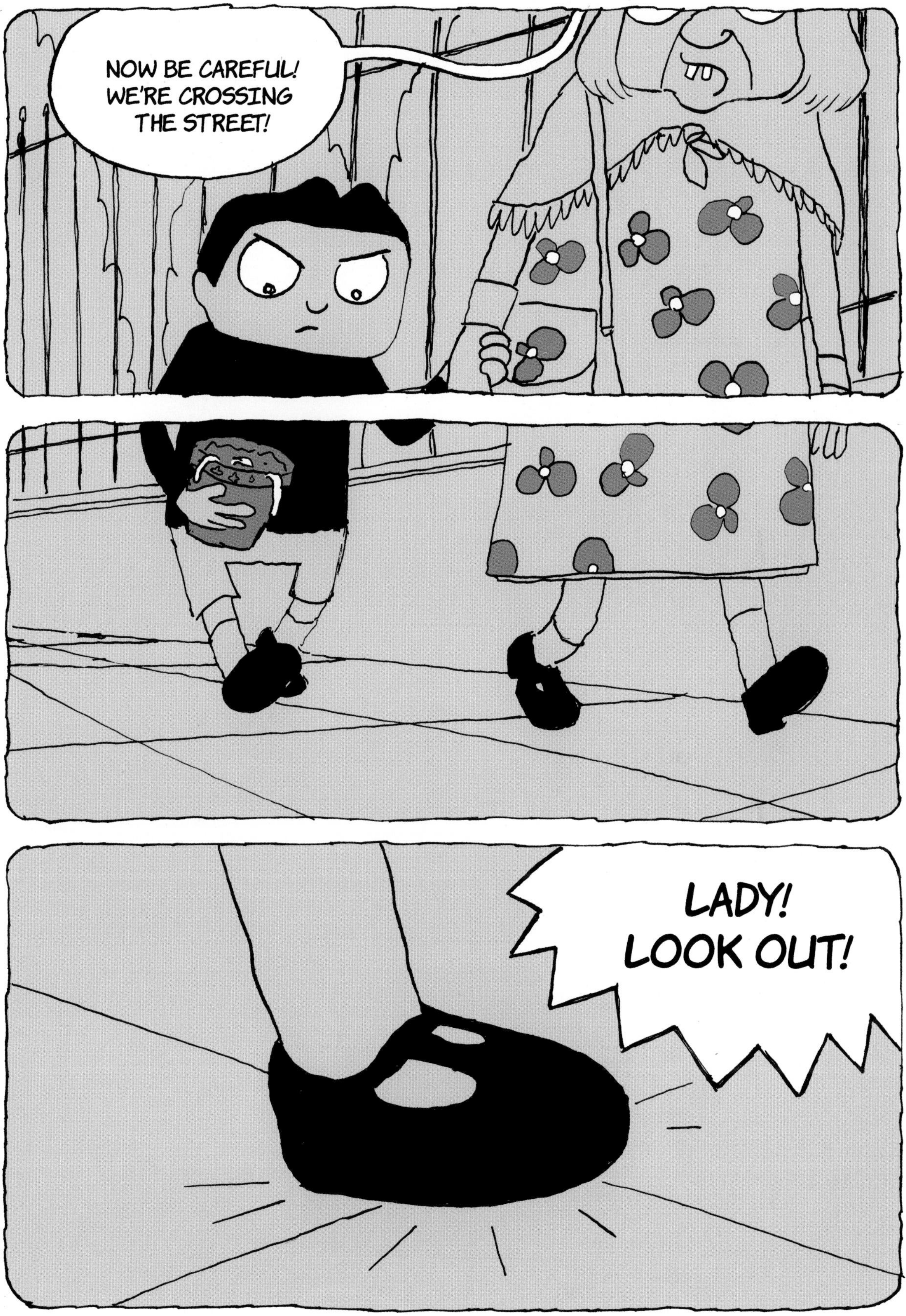
NOW BE CAREFUL! WE'RE CROSSING THE STREET!
LADY! LOOK OUT!

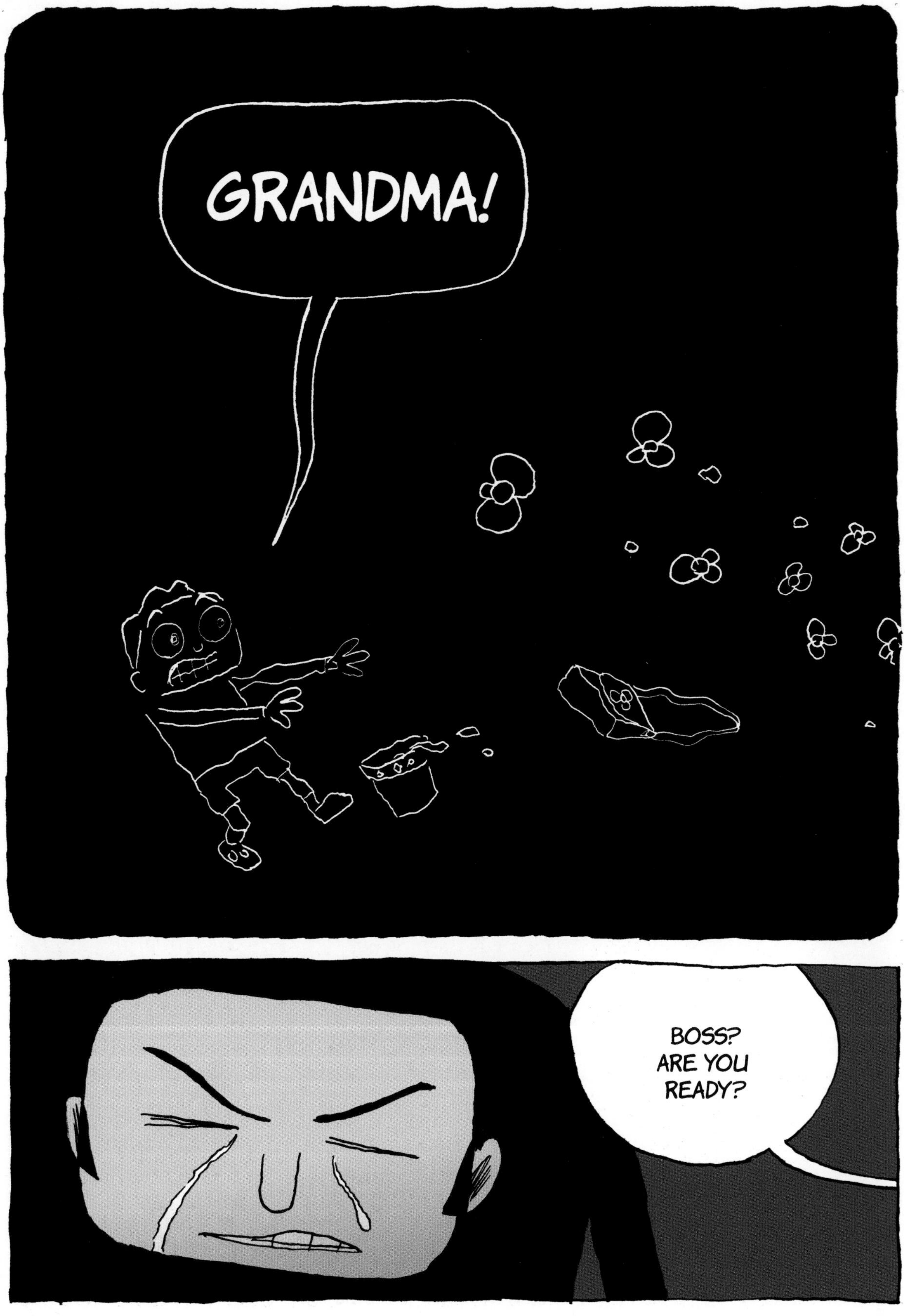
GRANDMA!
BOSS? ARE YOU READY?

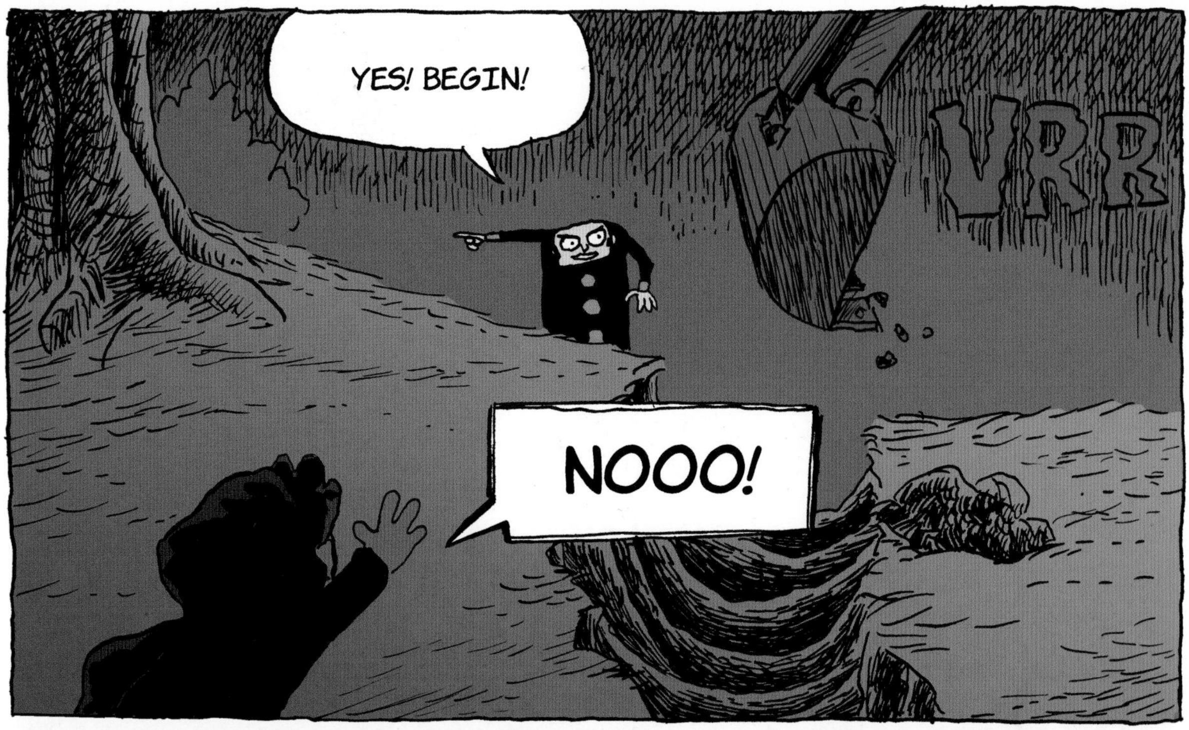
YES! BEGIN!
VRR
NOOO!

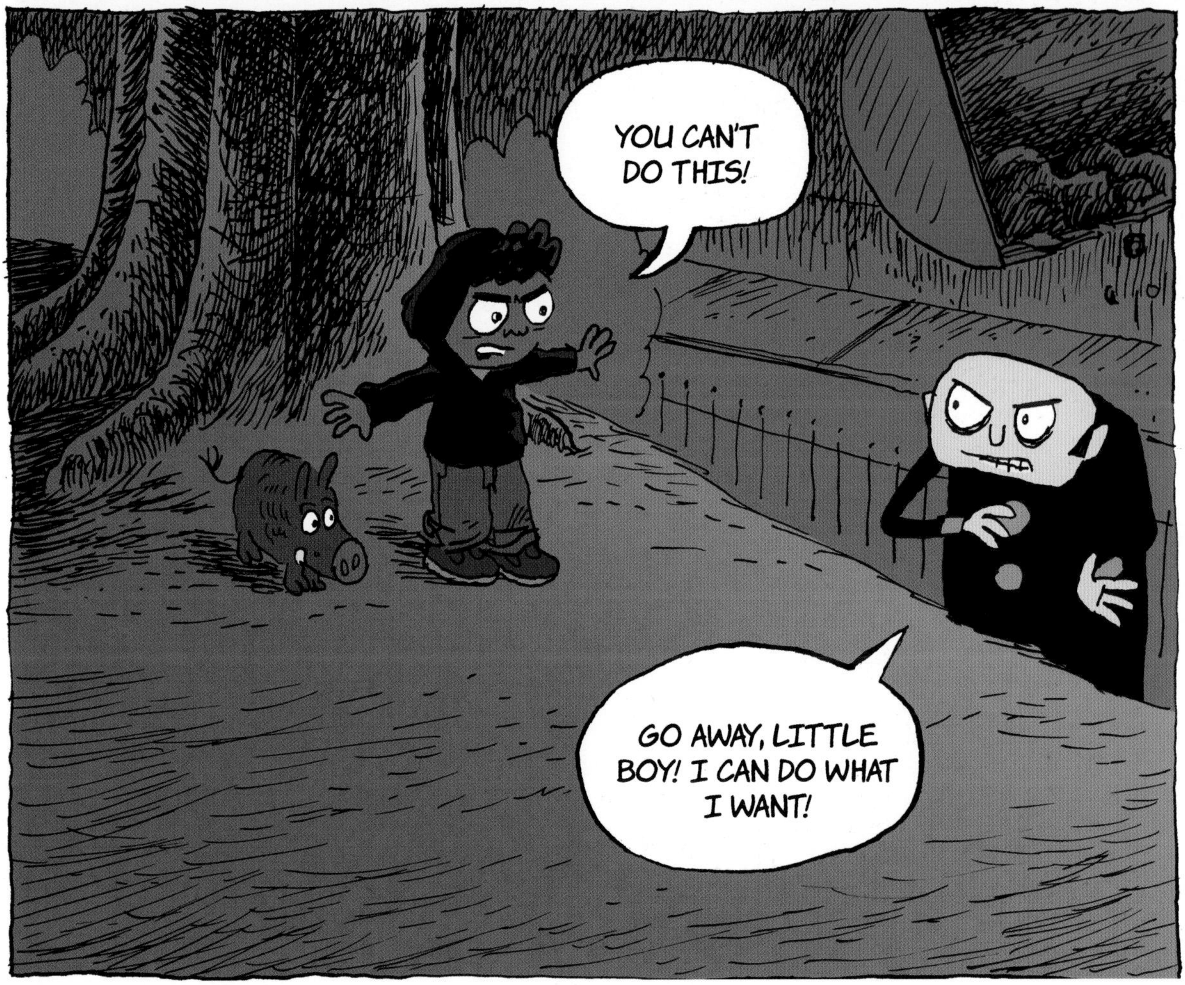
YOU CAN'T DO THIS!
GO AWAY, LITTLE BOY! I CAN DO WHAT I WANT!

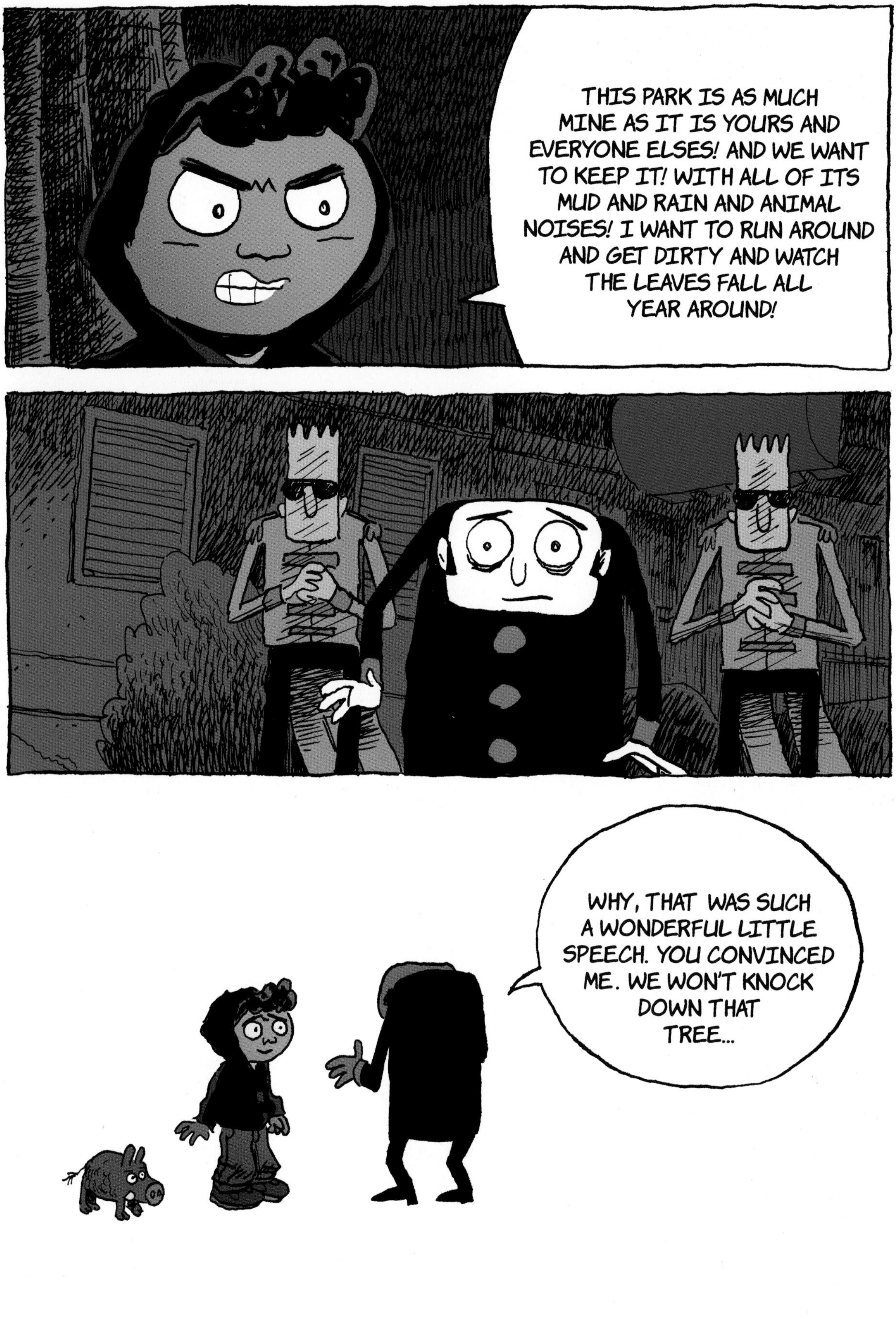
THIS PARK IS AS MUCH MINE AS IT IS YOURS AND EVERYONE ELSES! AND WE WANT TO KEEP IT! WITH ALL OF ITS MUD AND RAIN AND ANIMAL NOISES! I WANT TO RUN AROUND AND GET DIRTY AND WATCH THE LEAVES FALL ALL YEAR AROUND!
WHY, THAT WAS SUCH A WONDERFUL LITTLE SPEECH. YOU CONVINCED ME. WE WON'T KNOCK DOWN THAT TREE...

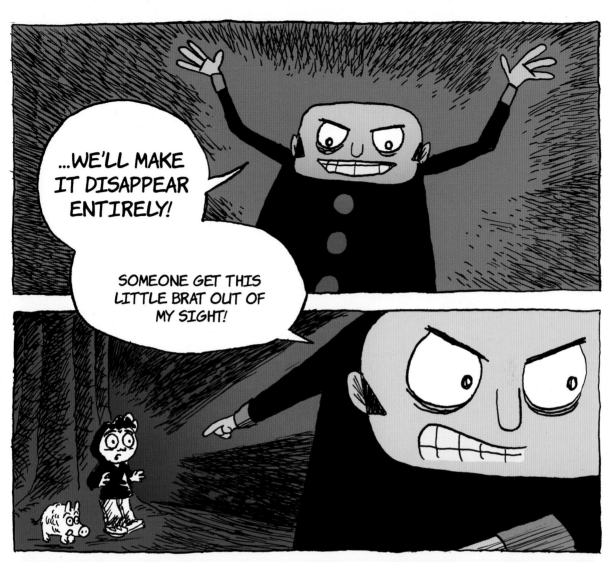

...WE'LL MAKE IT DISAPPEAR ENTIRELY!

SOMEONE GET THIS LITTLE BRAT OUT OF MY SIGHT!

NOOOO

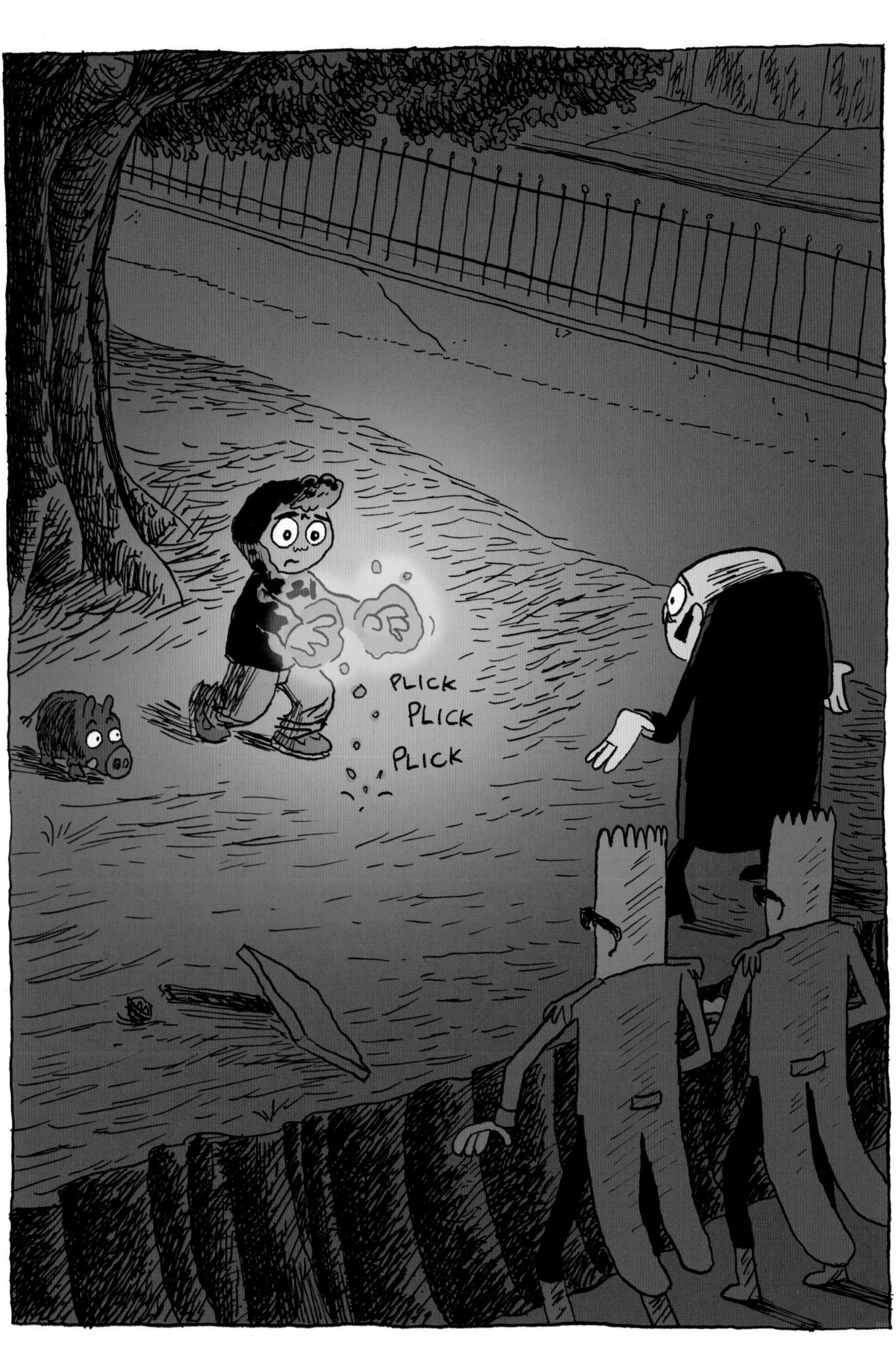
PLICK
PLICK
PLICK

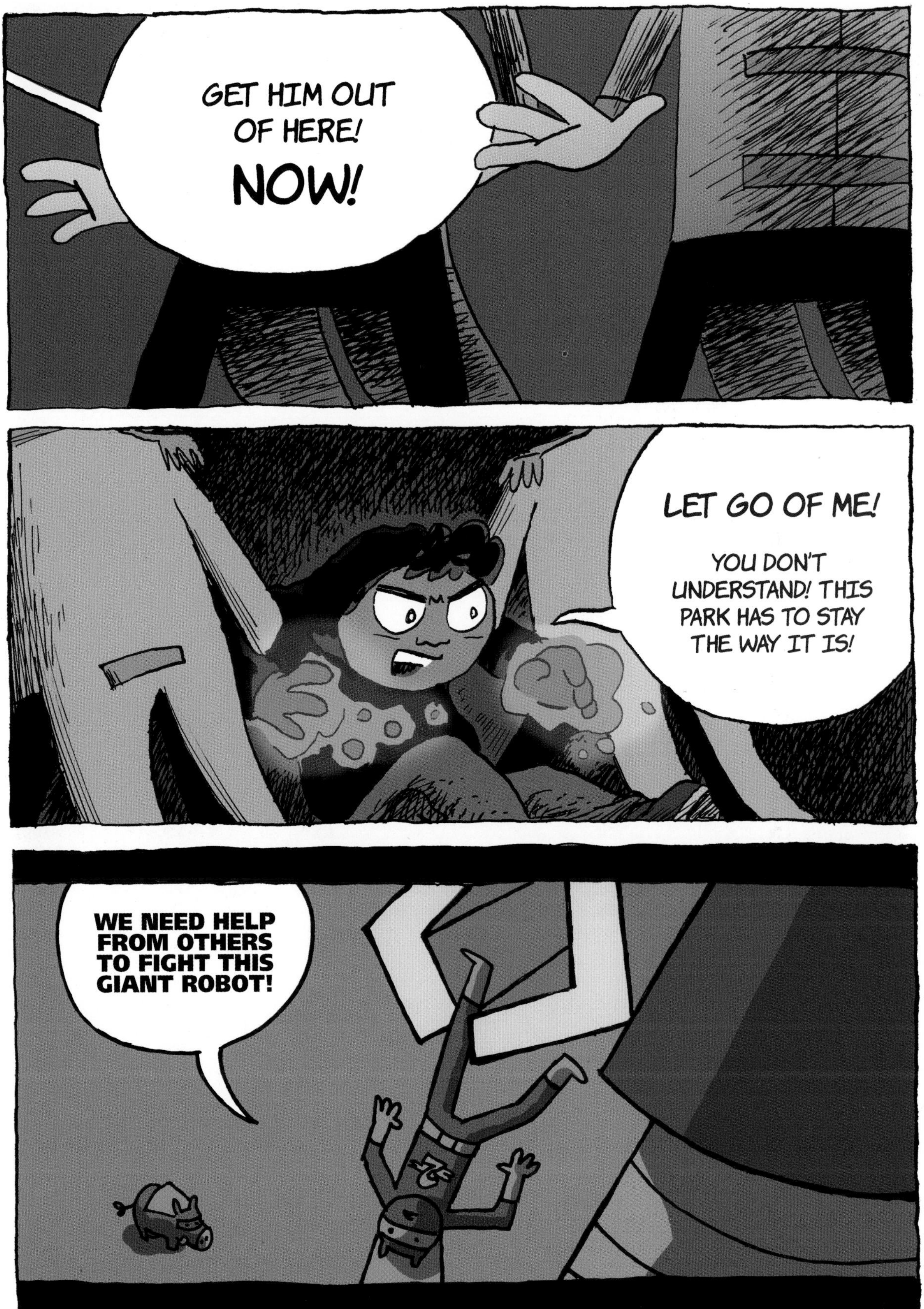
GET HIM OUT OF HERE! NOW!
LET GO OF ME!
YOU DON'T UNDERSTAND! THIS PARK HAS TO STAY THE WAY IT IS!
WE NEED HELP FROM OTHERS TO FIGHT THIS GIANT ROBOT!

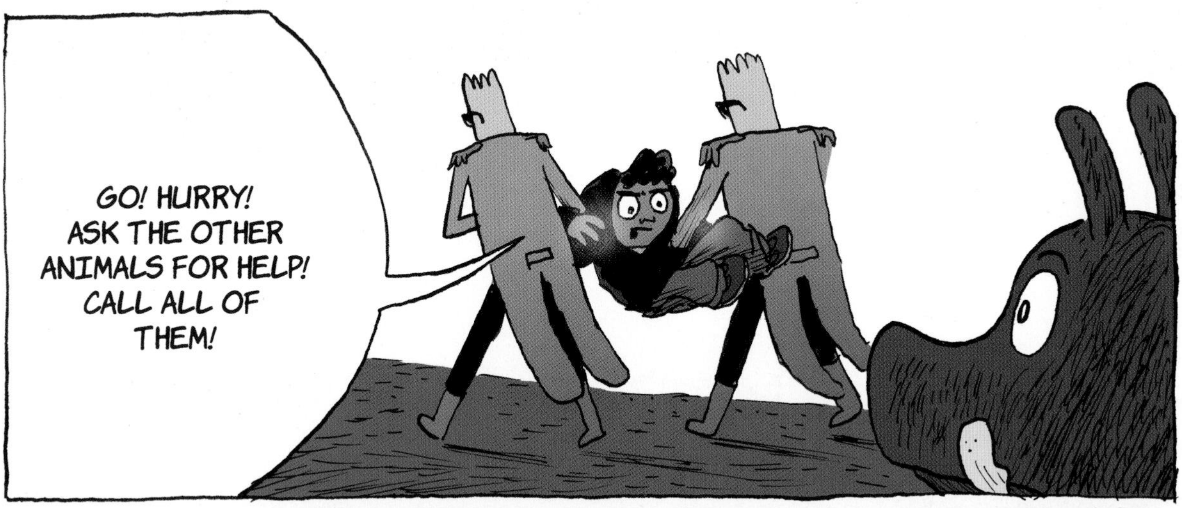
GO! HURRY! ASK THE OTHER ANIMALS FOR HELP! CALL ALL OF THEM!

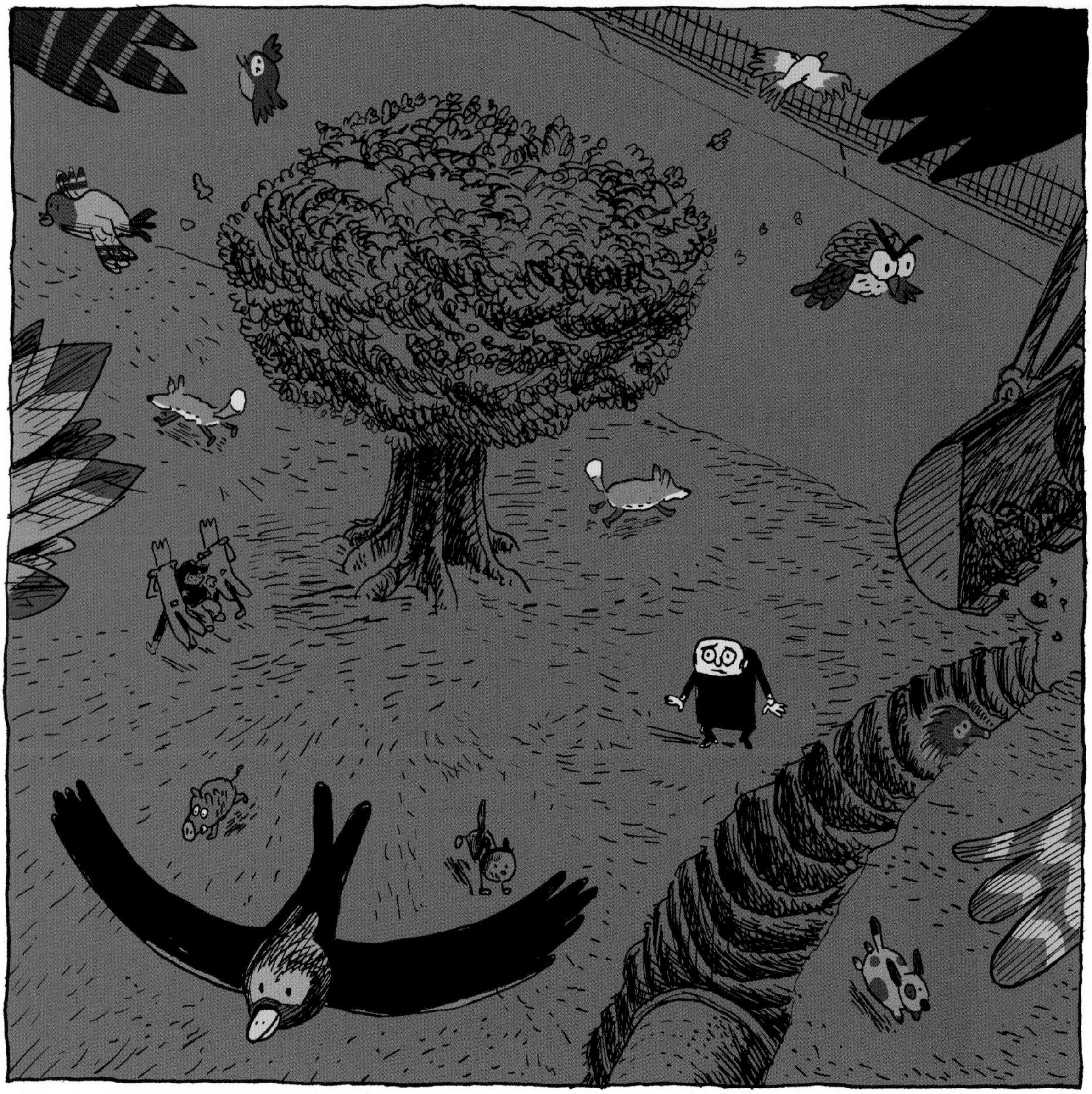

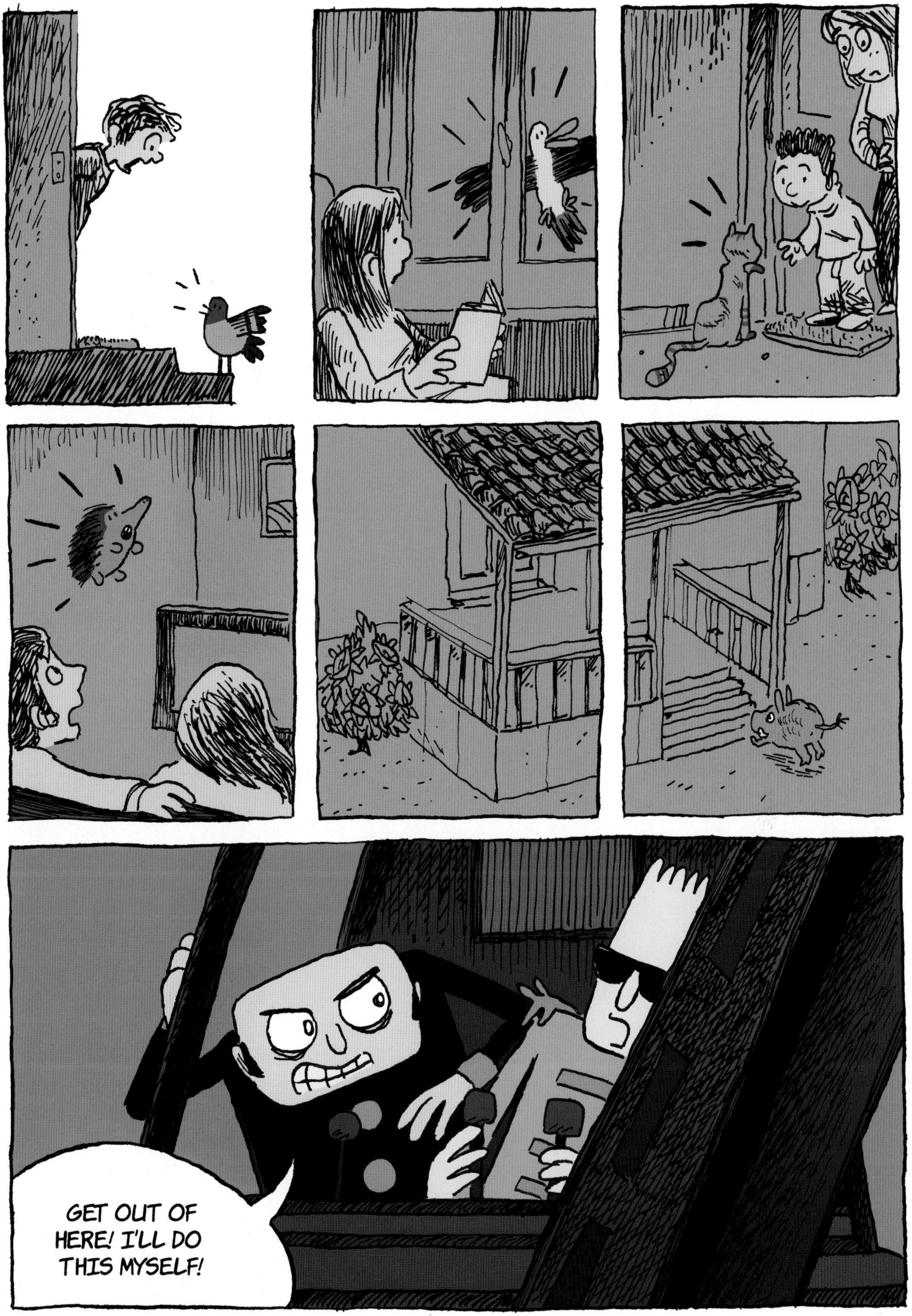
GET OUT OF HERE! I'LL DO THIS MYSELF!

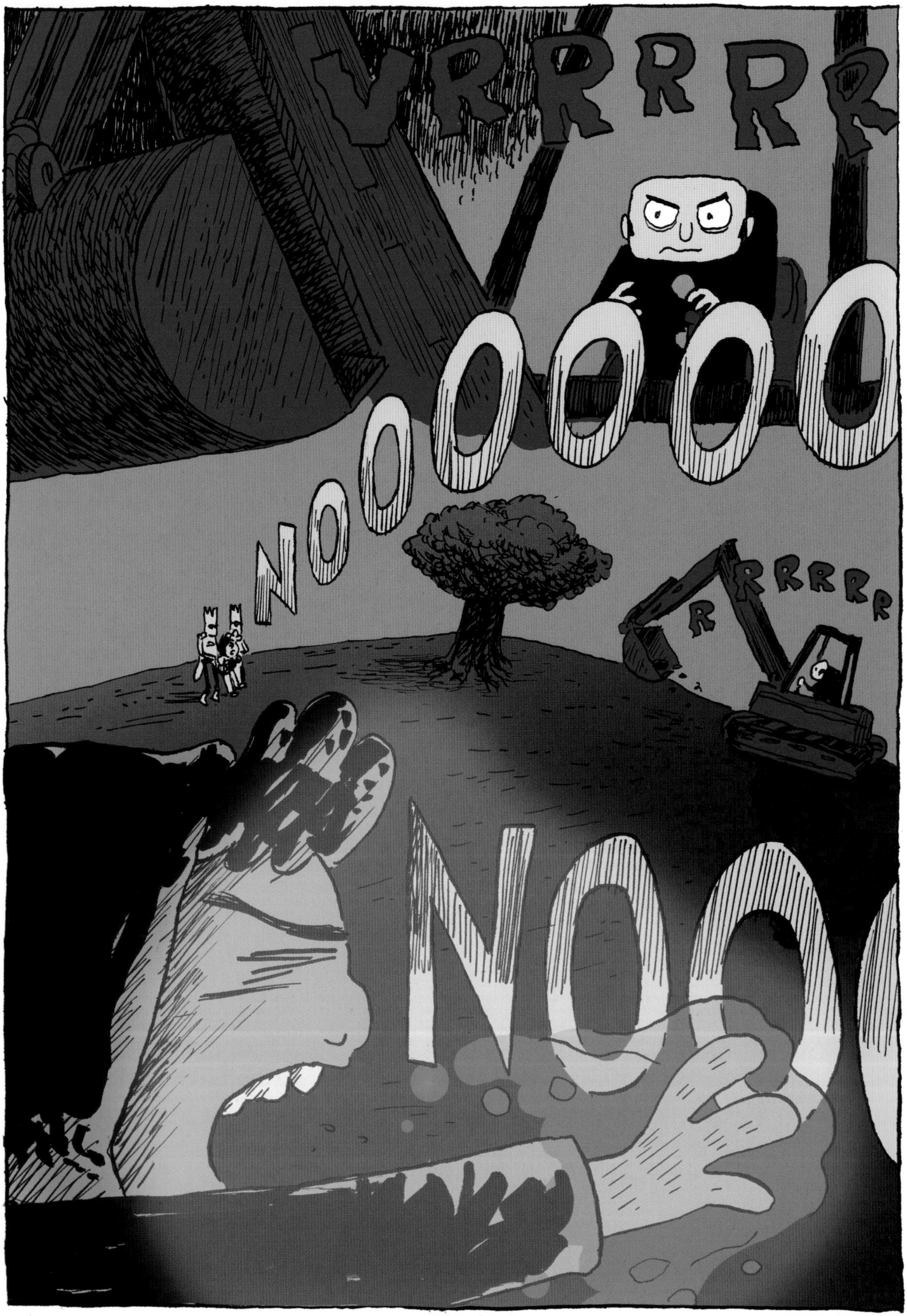
VRRRRR
NOOOOOOOO
RRRRRRR
NOOO

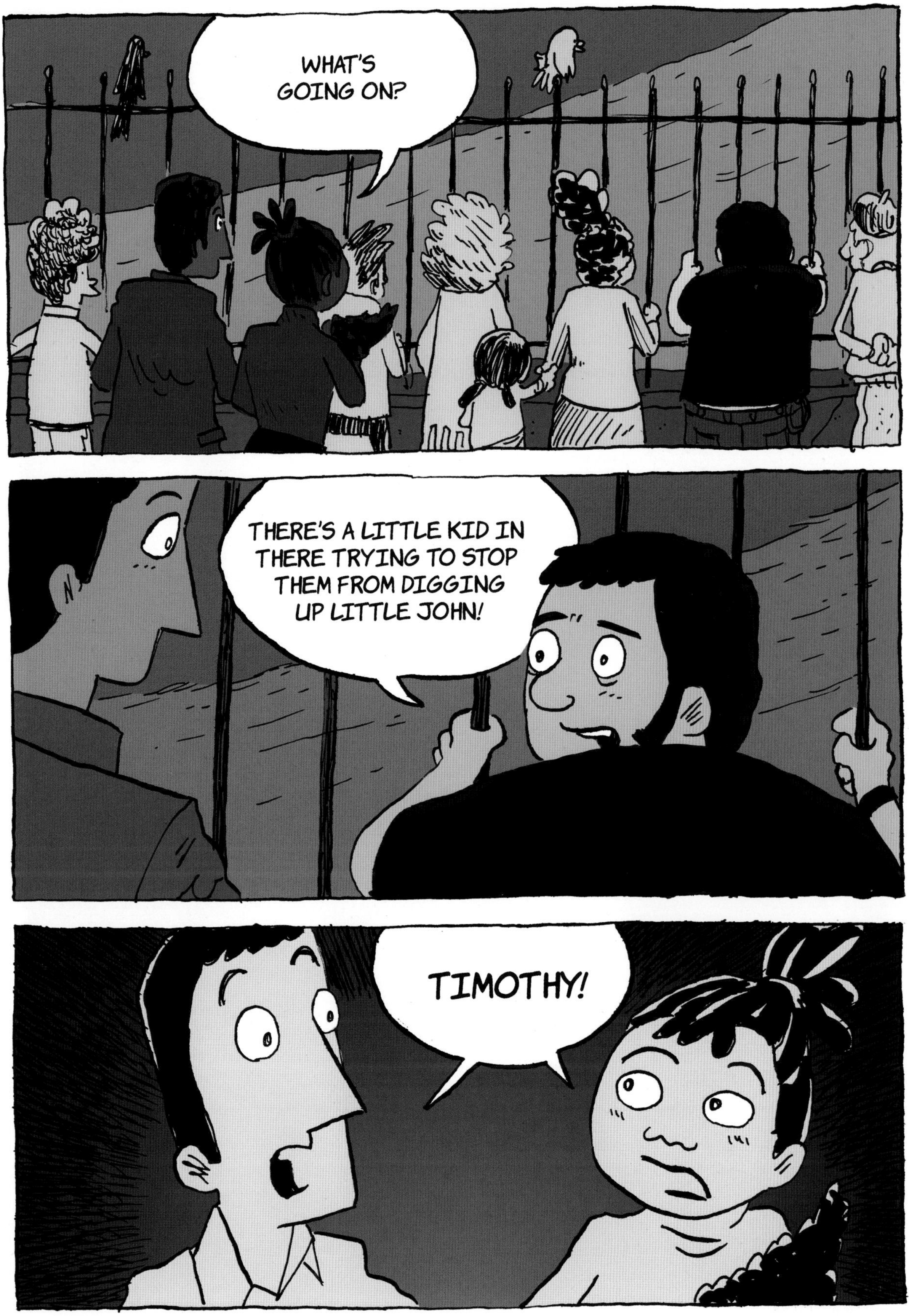
WHAT'S GOING ON?
THERE'S A LITTLE KID IN THERE TRYING TO STOP THEM FROM DIGGING UP LITTLE JOHN!
TIMOTHY!

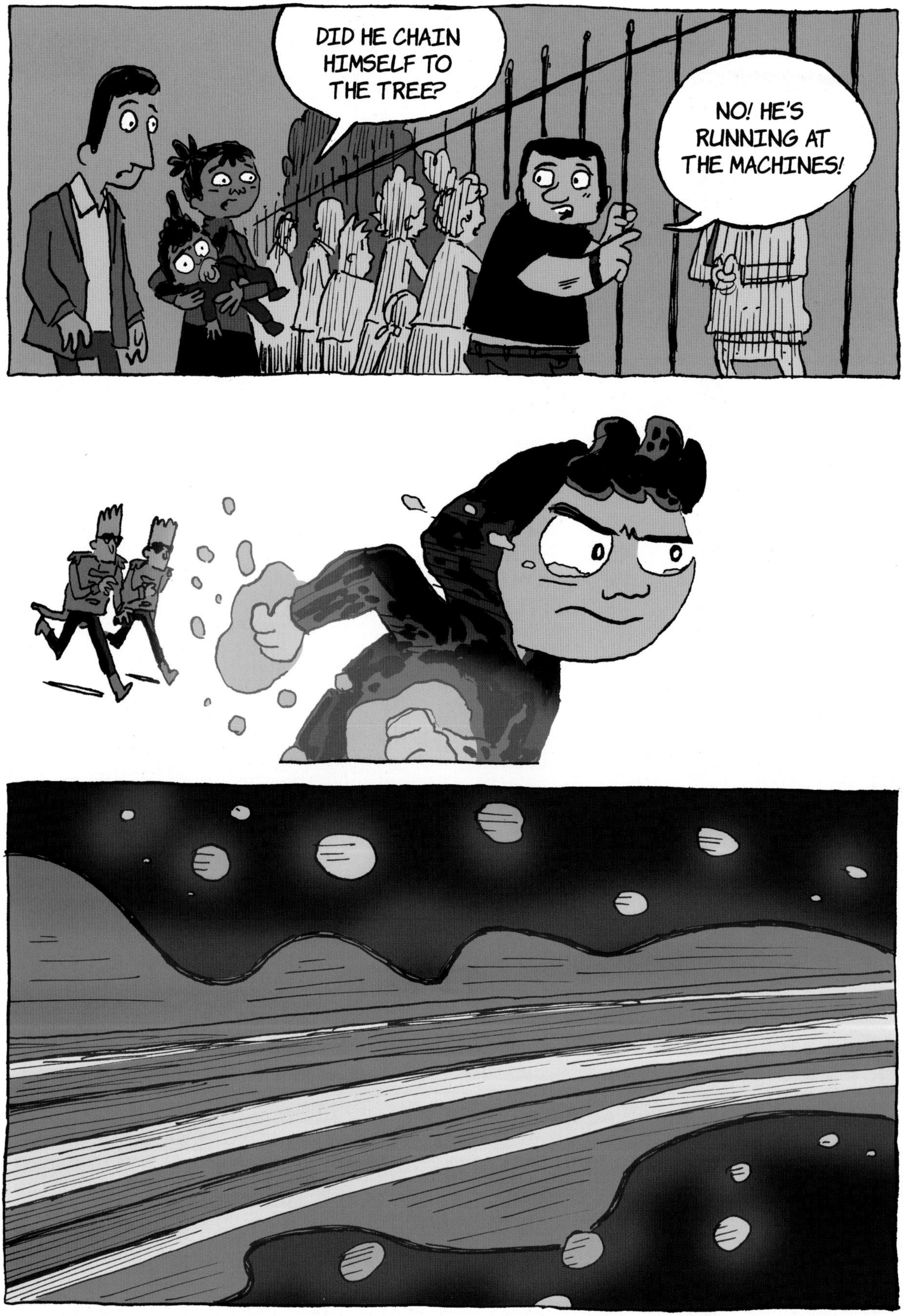
DID HE CHAIN HIMSELF TO THE TREE?
NO! HE'S RUNNING AT THE MACHINES!

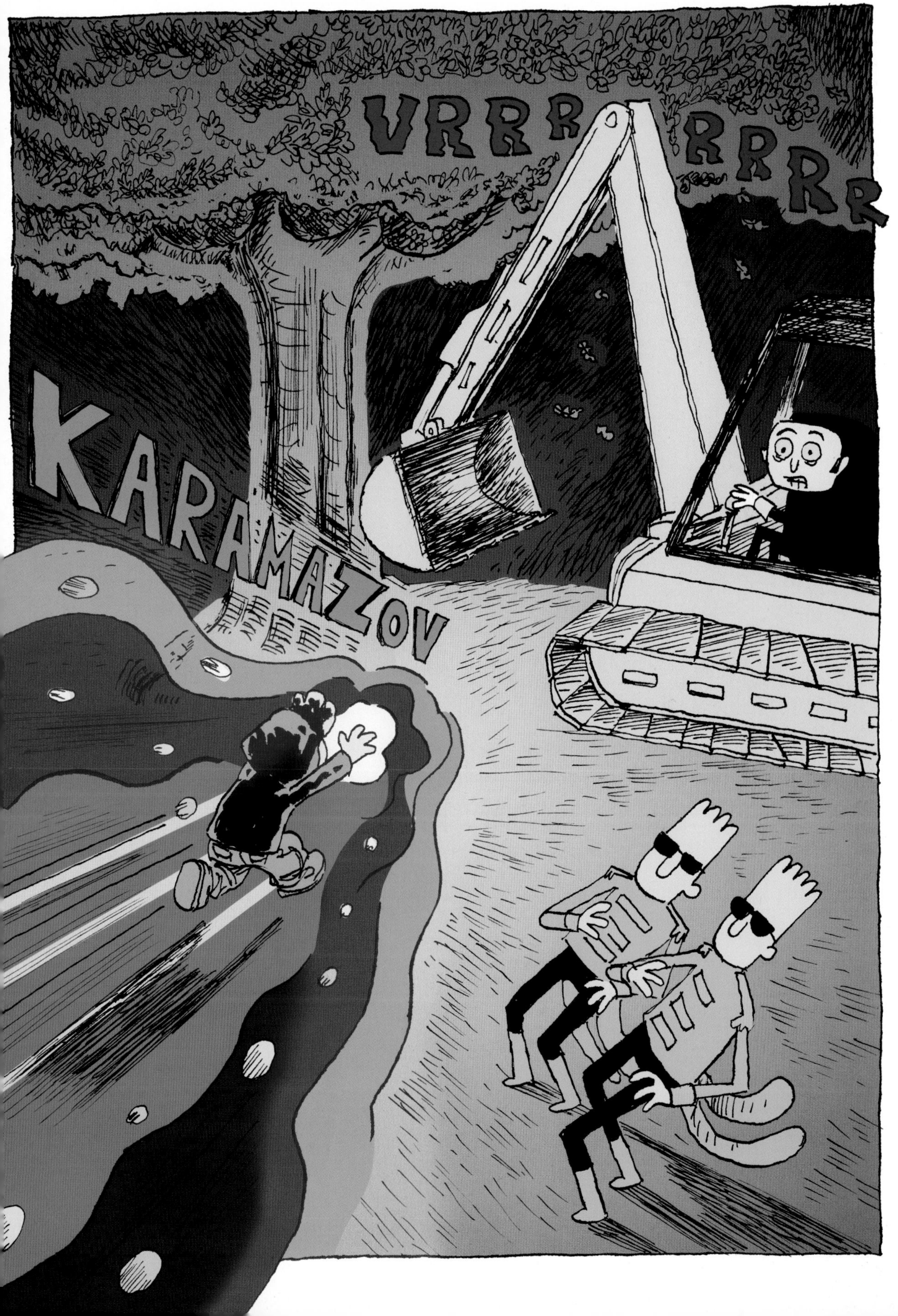

VRRRRRRRRR
KARAMAZOV

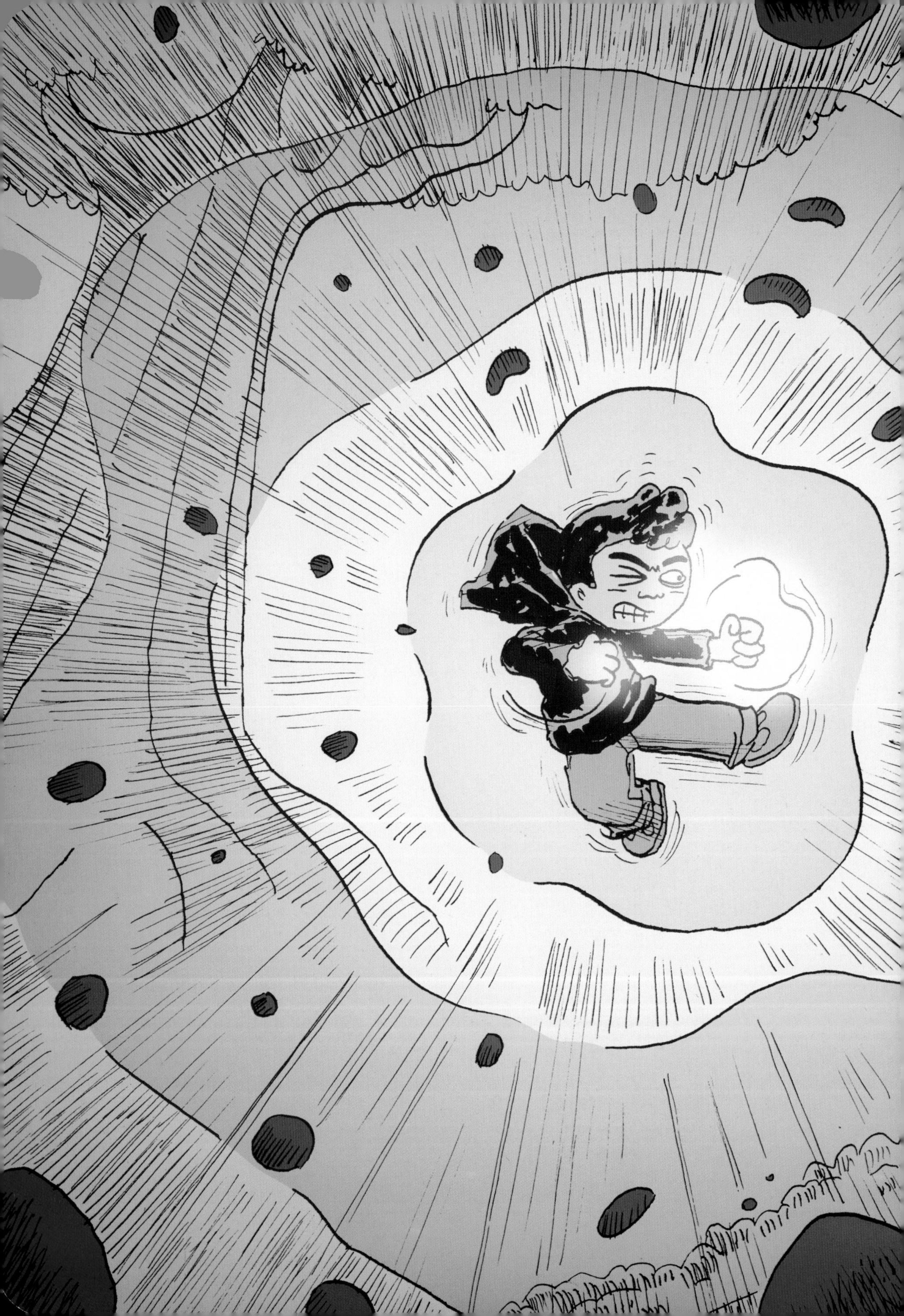

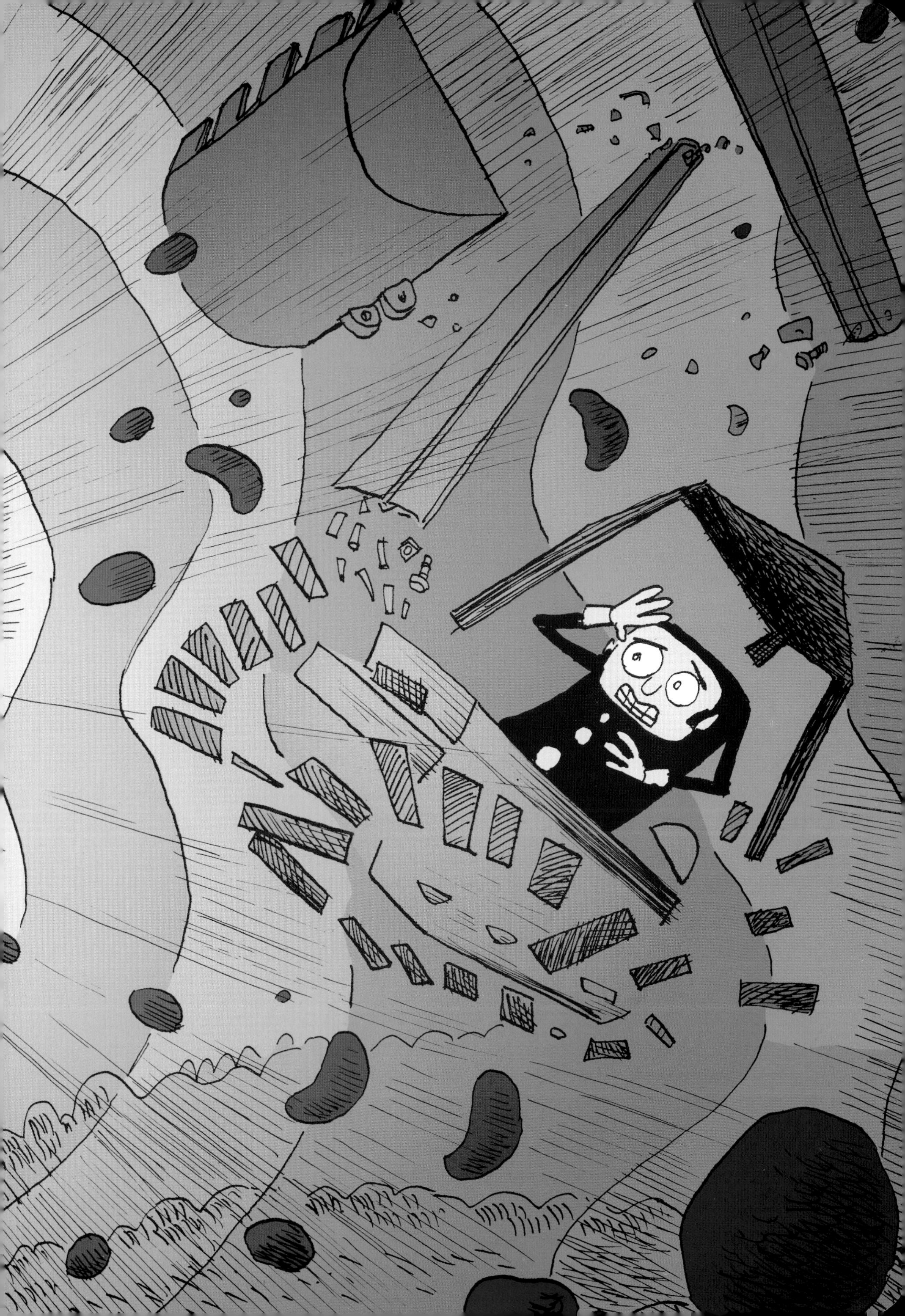

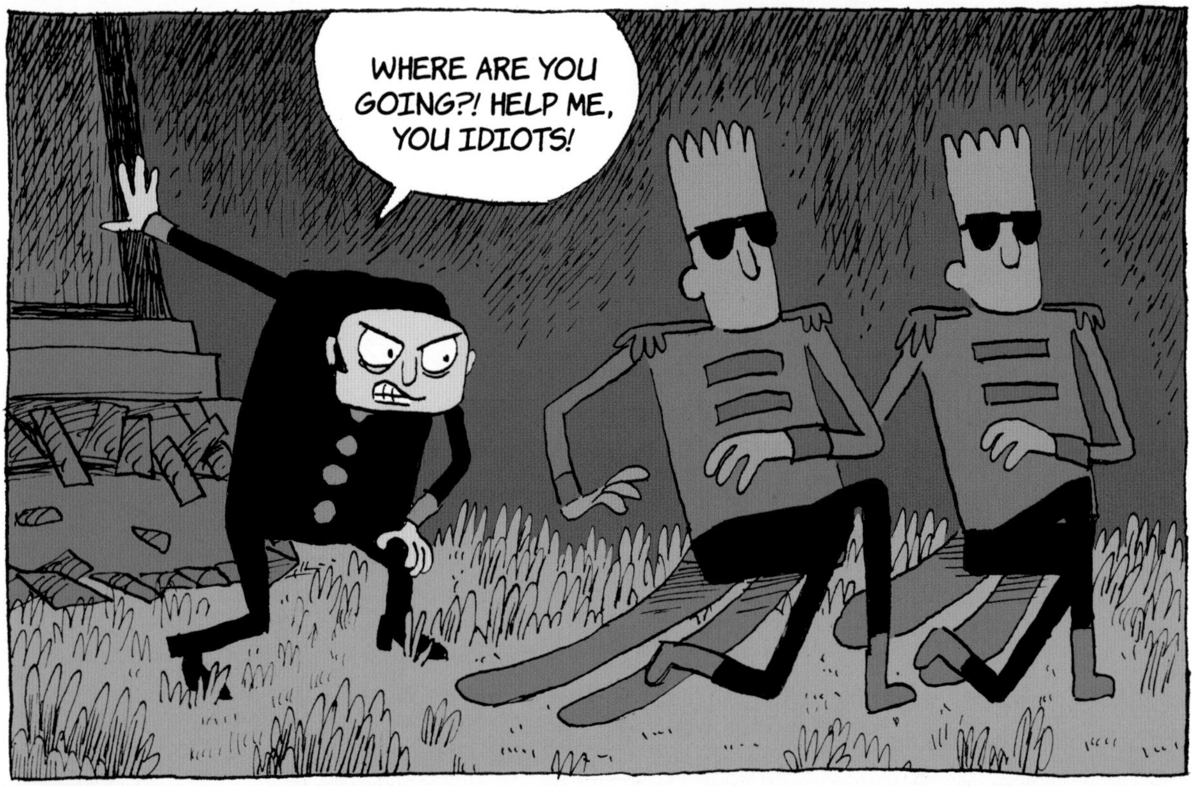
WHERE ARE YOU GOING?! HELP ME, YOU IDIOTS!

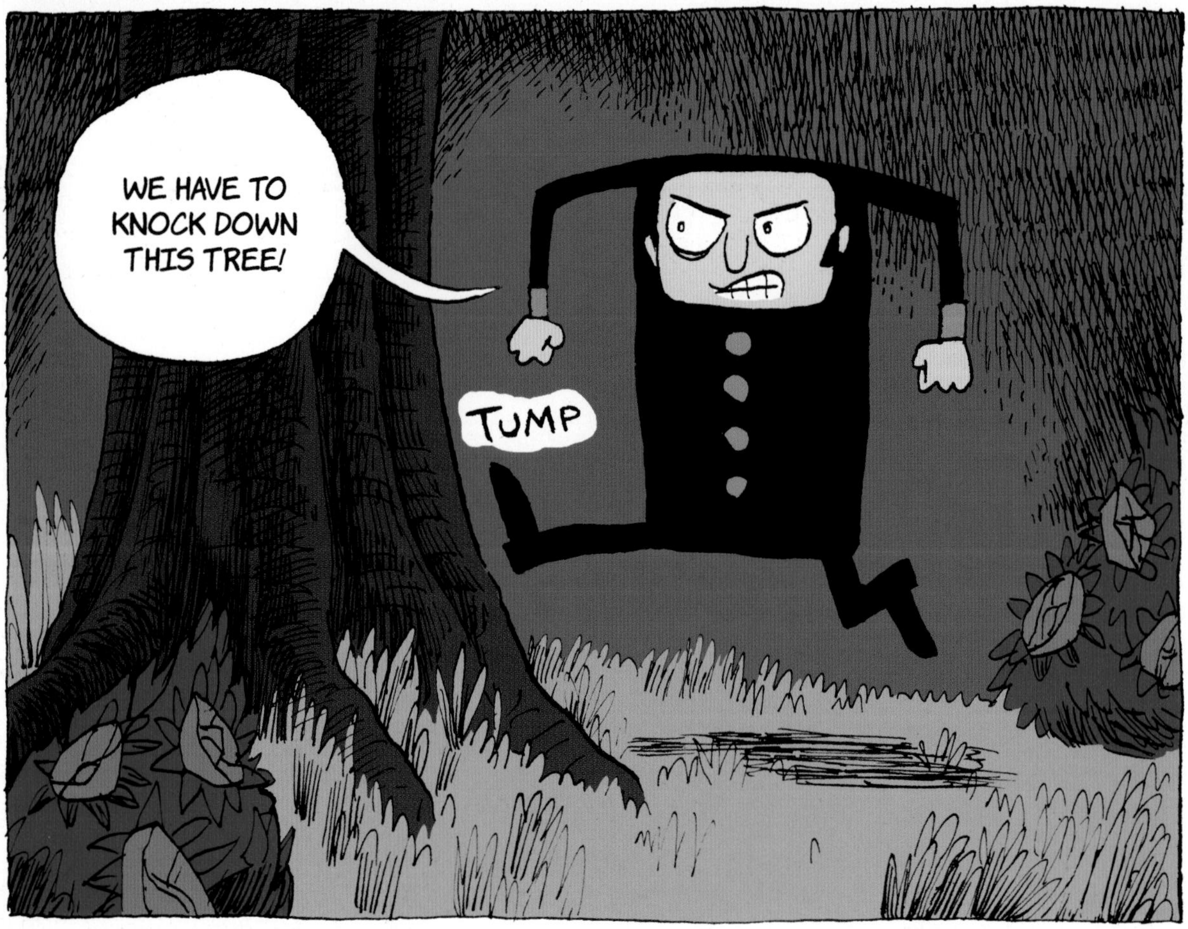
WE HAVE TO KNOCK DOWN THIS TREE!
TUMP

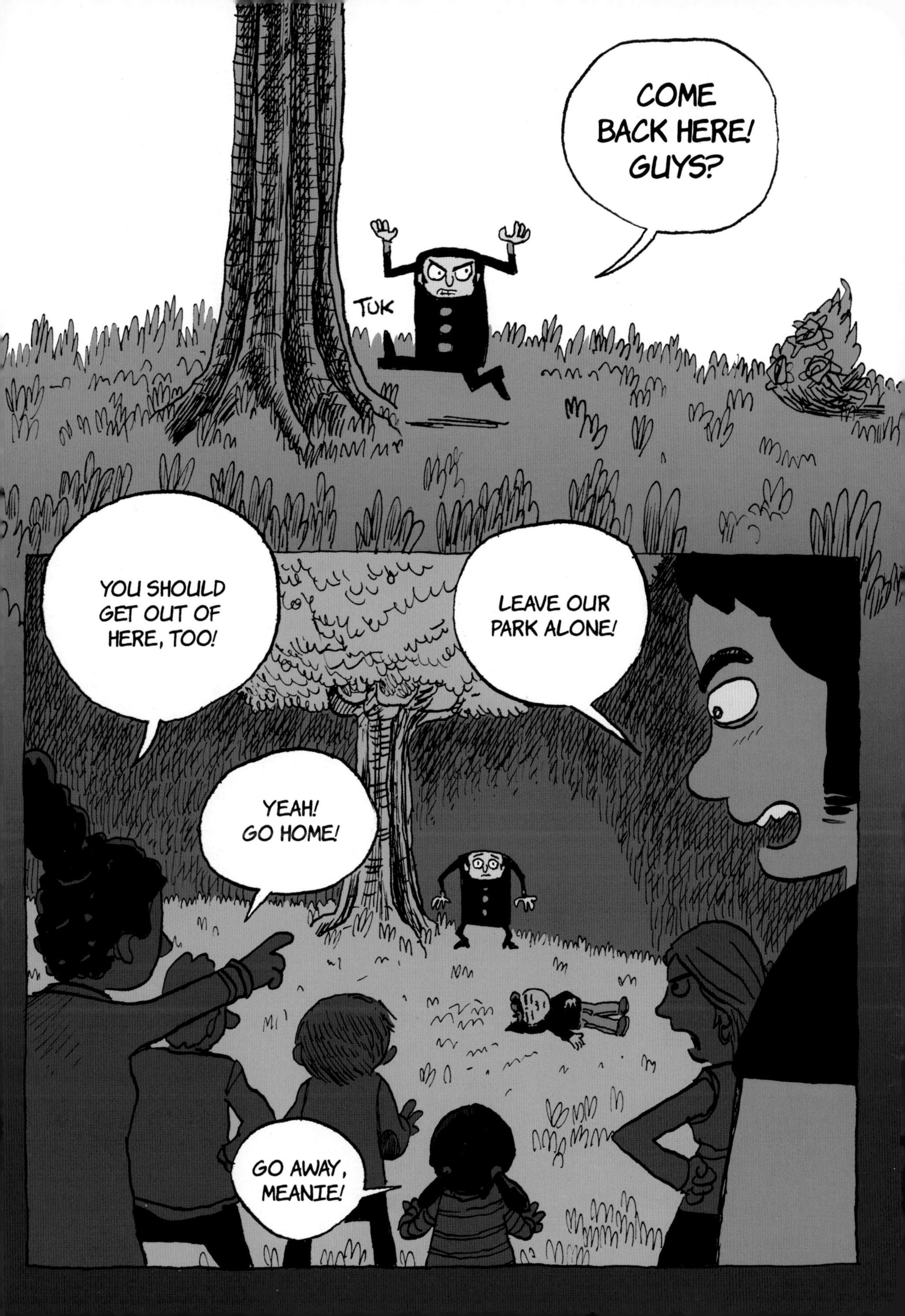
COME BACK HERE! GUYS?
TUK
YOU SHOULD GET OUT OF HERE, TOO!
LEAVE OUR PARK ALONE!
YEAH! GO HOME!
GO AWAY, MEANIE!

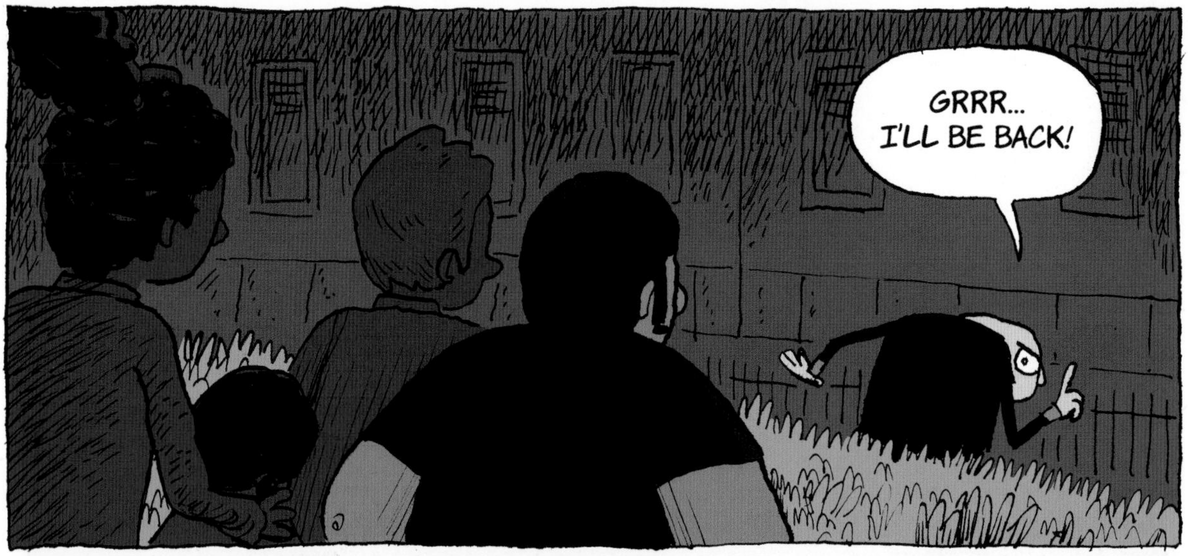
GRRR...
I'LL BE BACK!

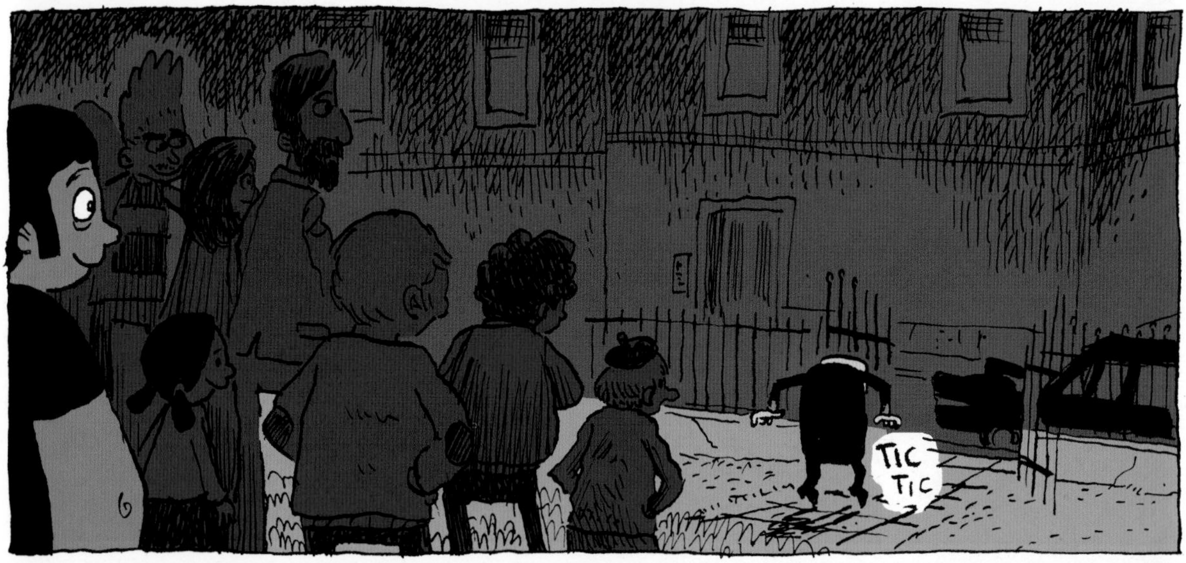
TIC
TIC

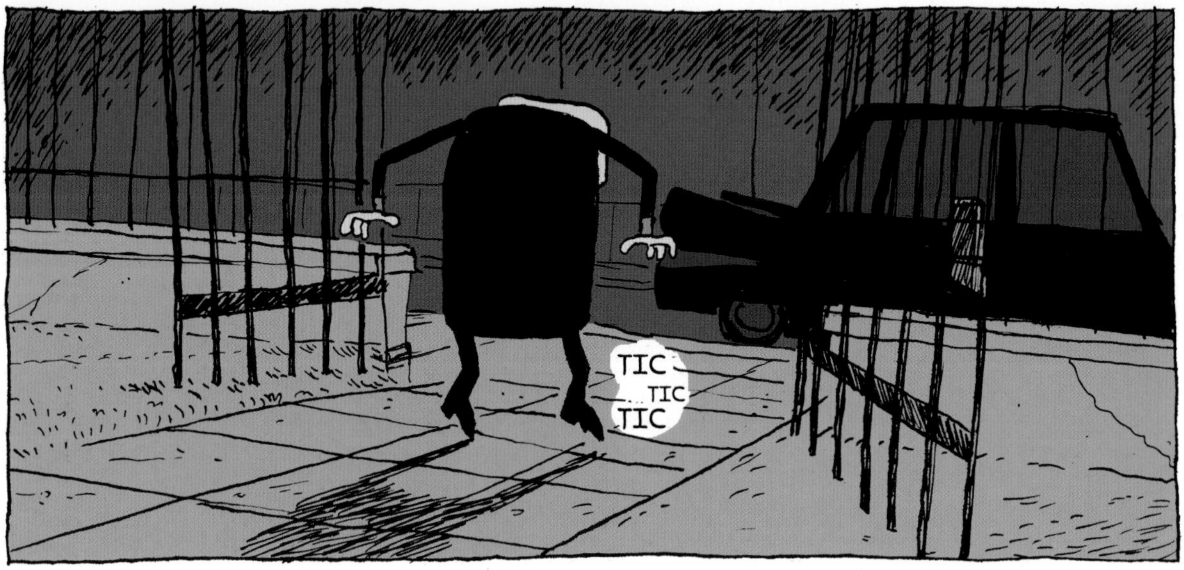
TIC
TIC
TIC

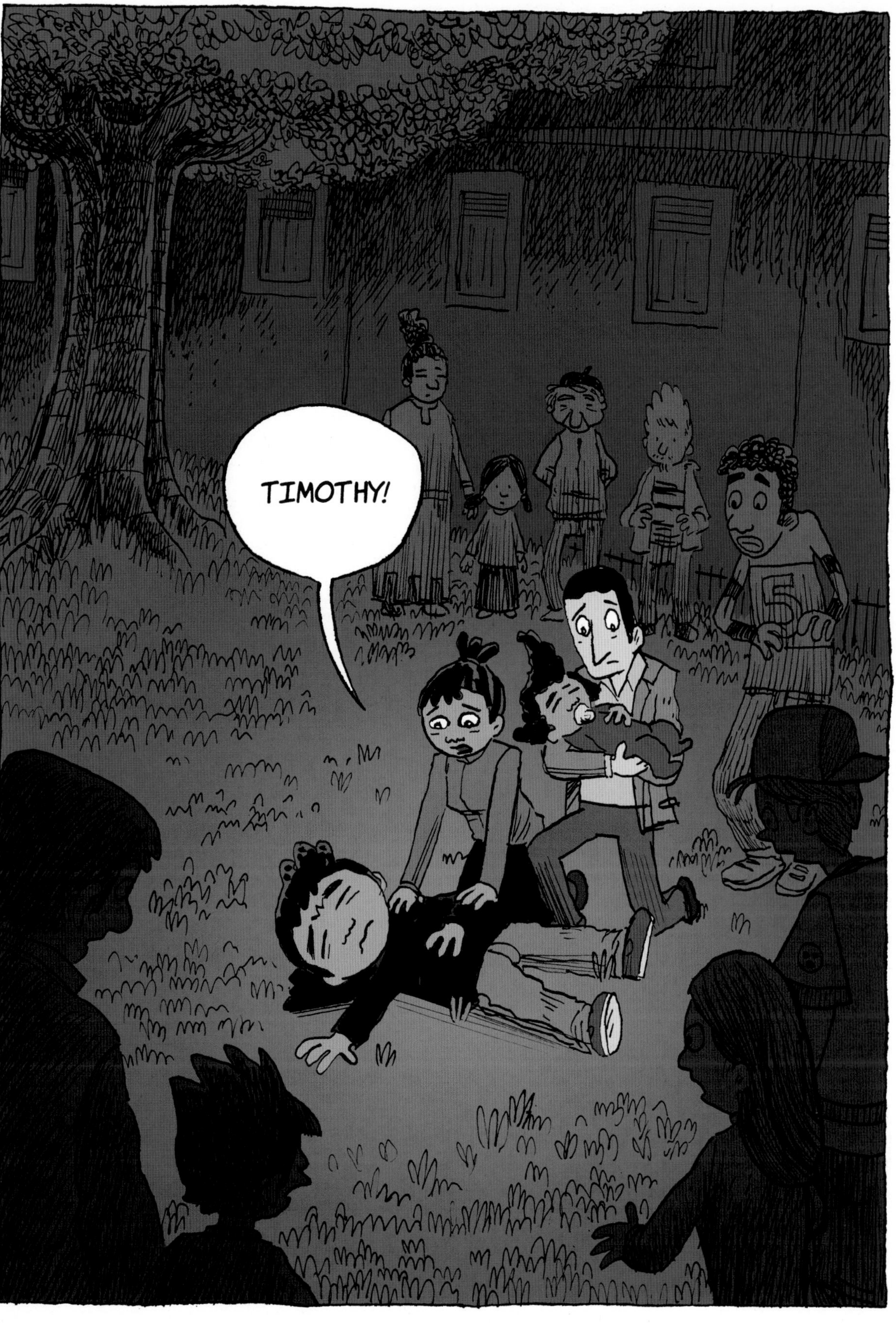
TIMOTHY!

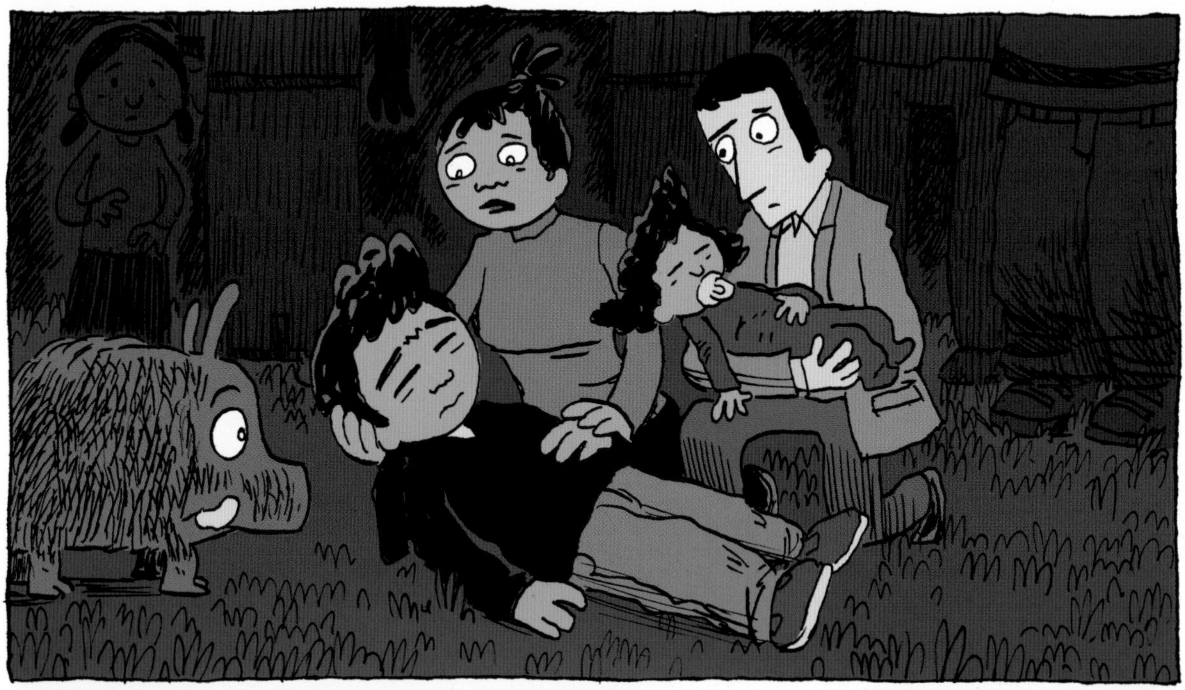

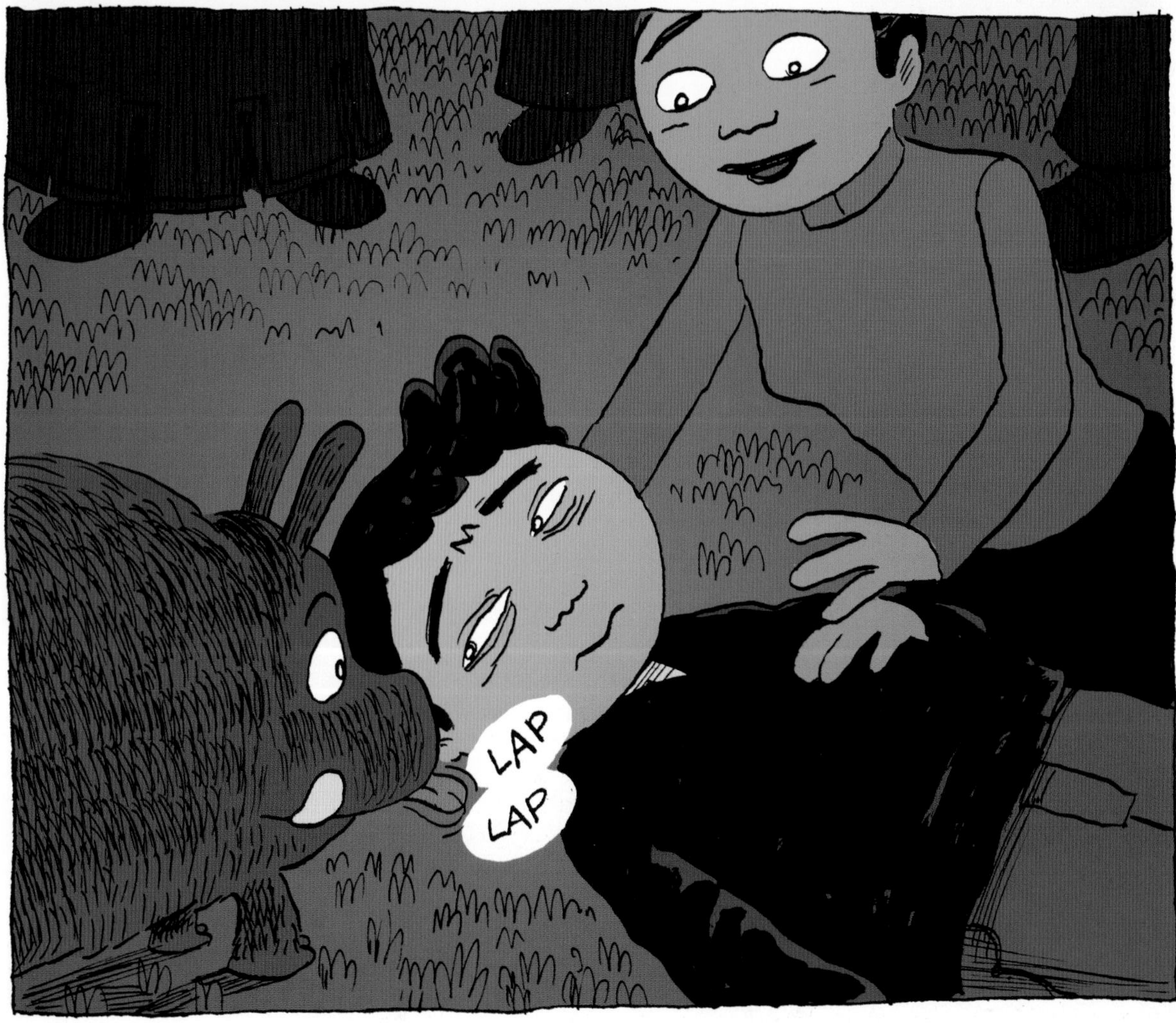
LAP
LAP

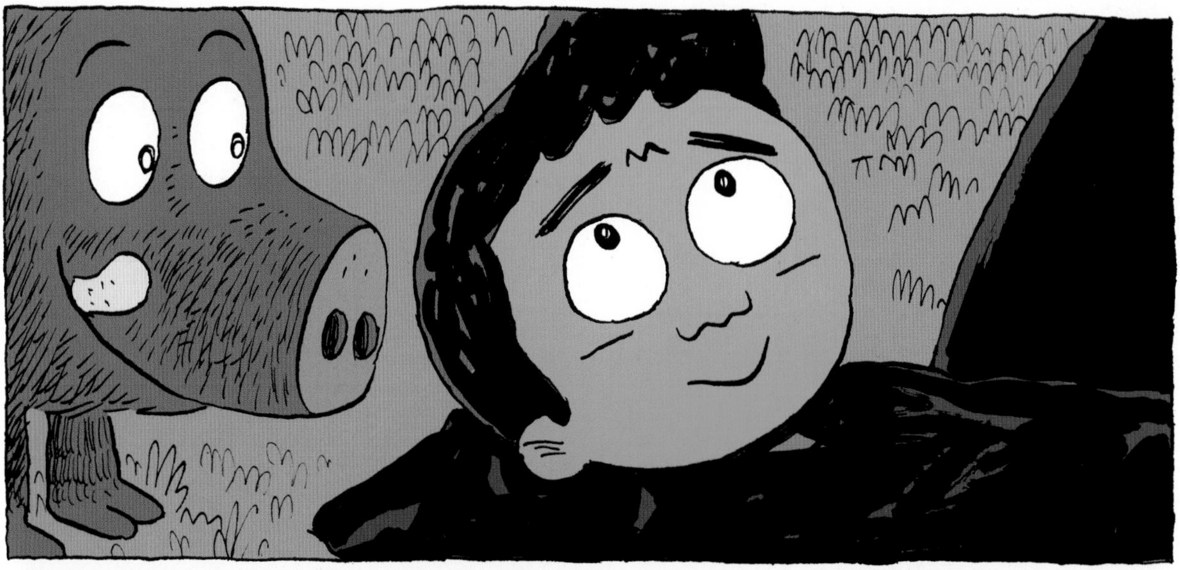

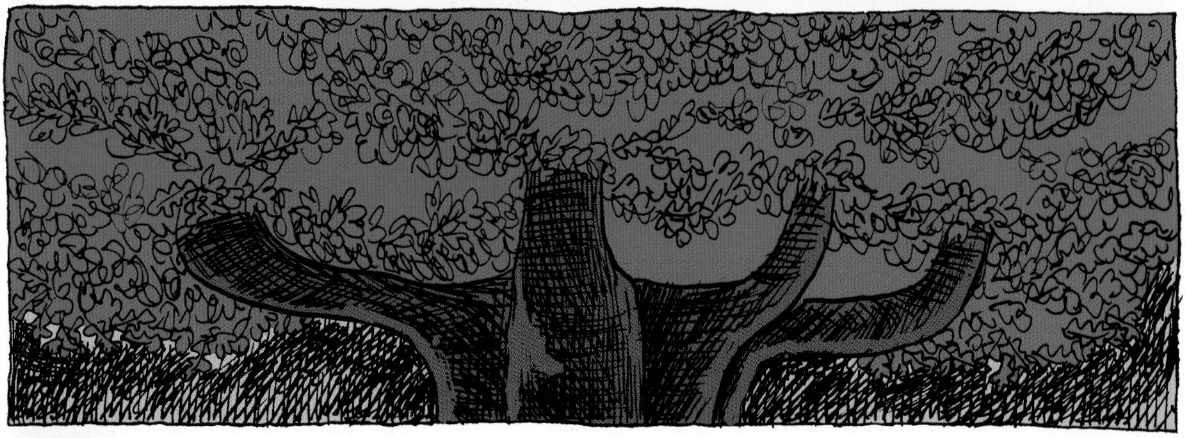

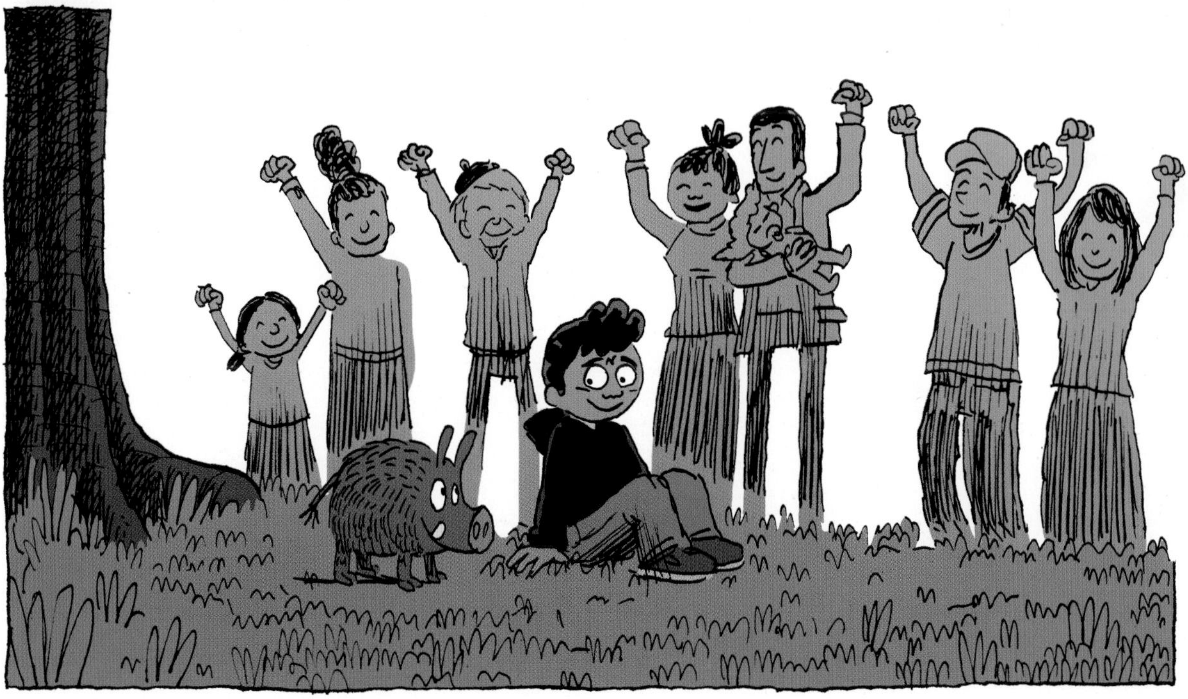

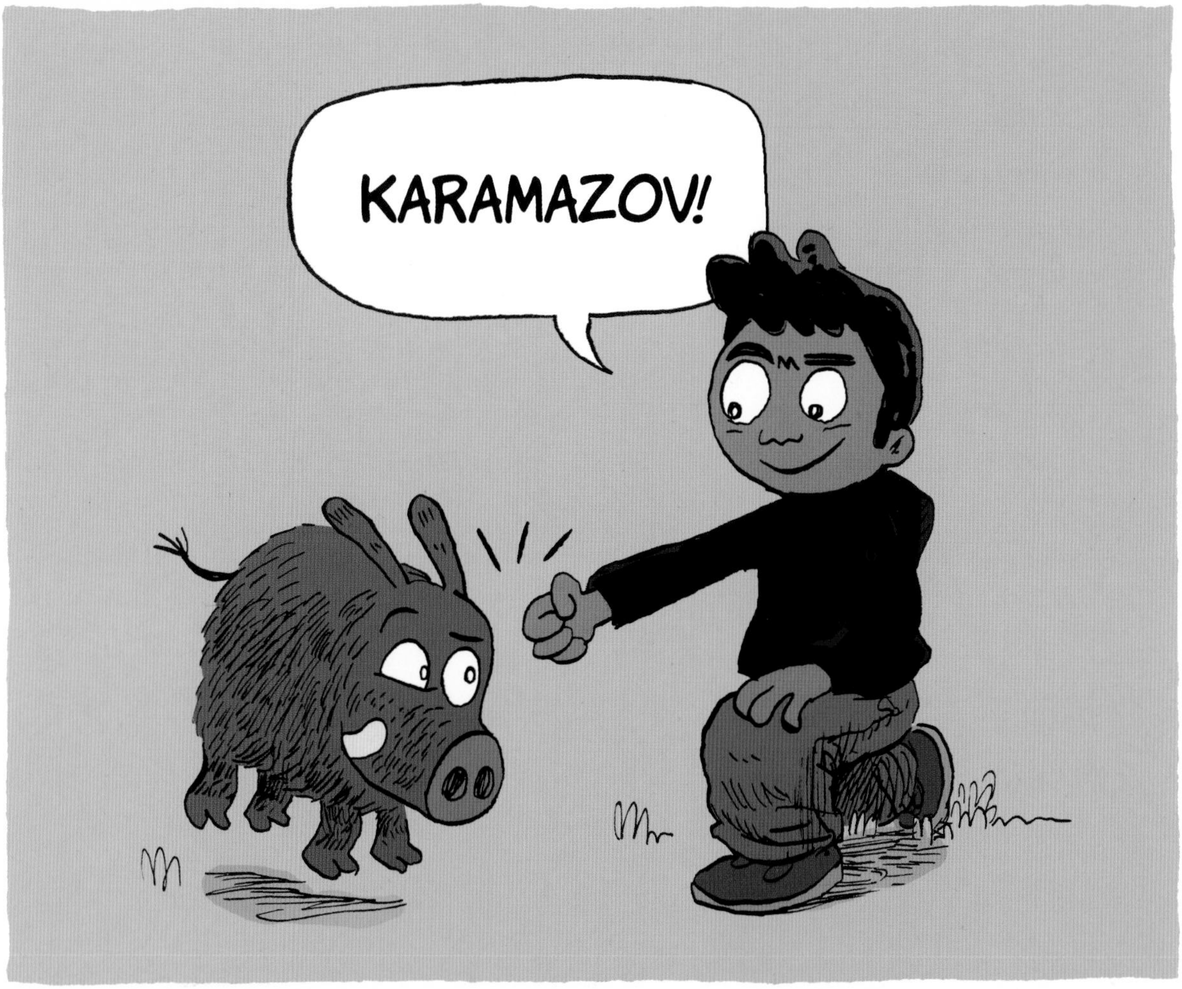
KARAMAZOV!

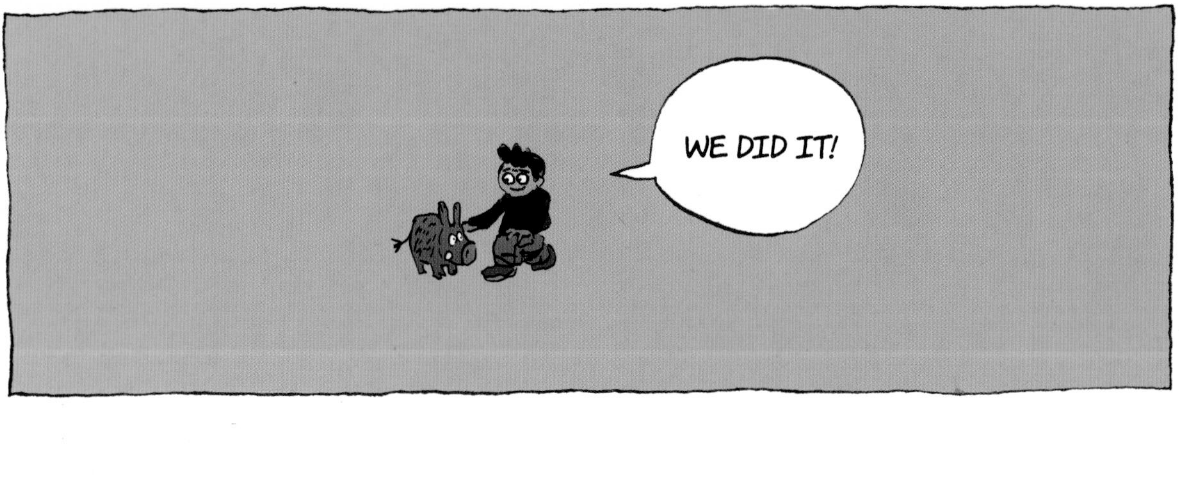
WE DID IT!

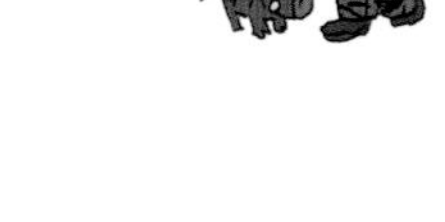
POOT

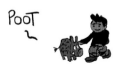

EPILOGUE

NEW LIGHTS

8

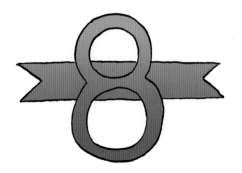

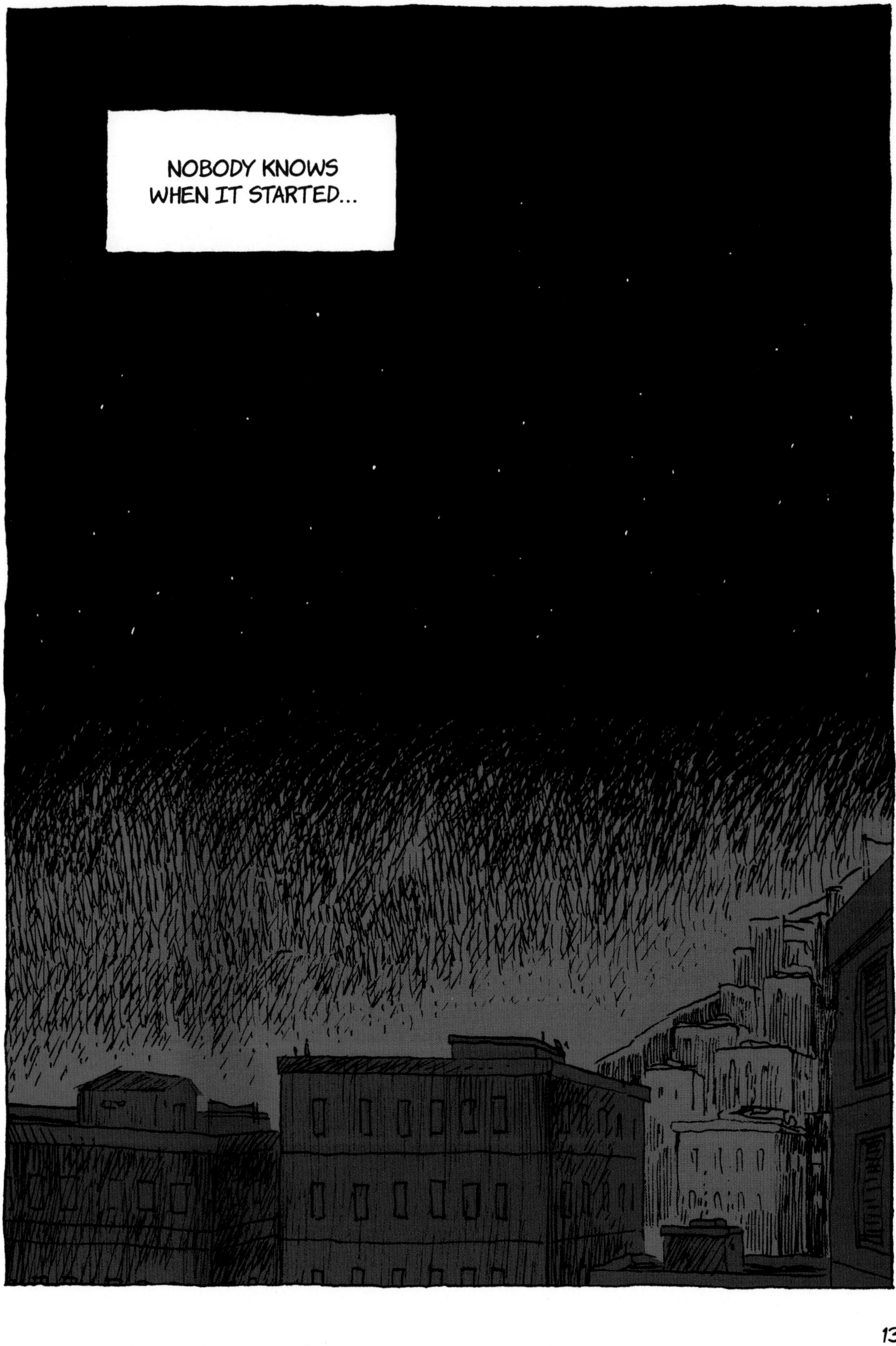
NOBODY KNOWS
WHEN IT STARTED...

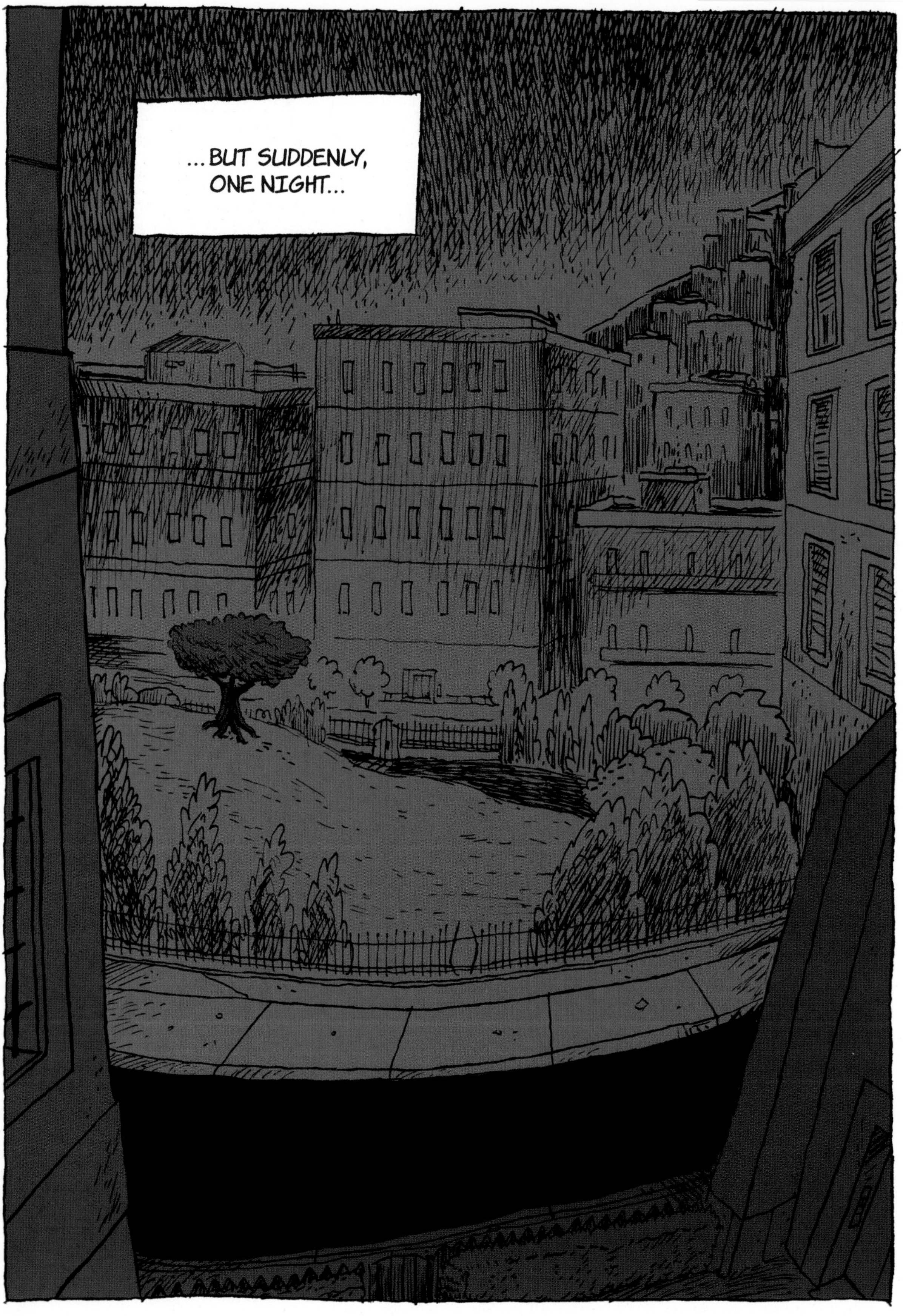
...BUT SUDDENLY,
ONE NIGHT...

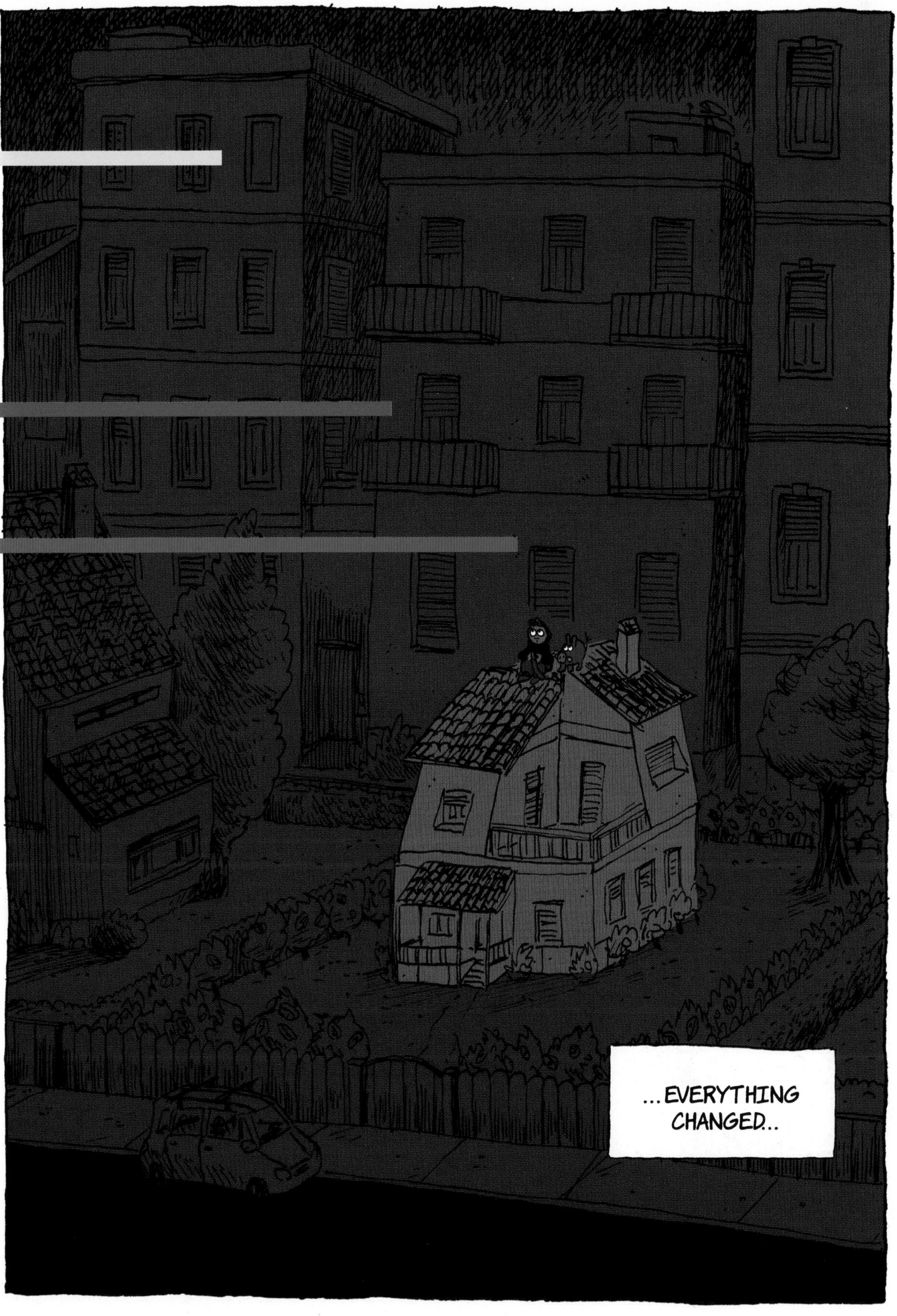
...EVERYTHING CHANGED...

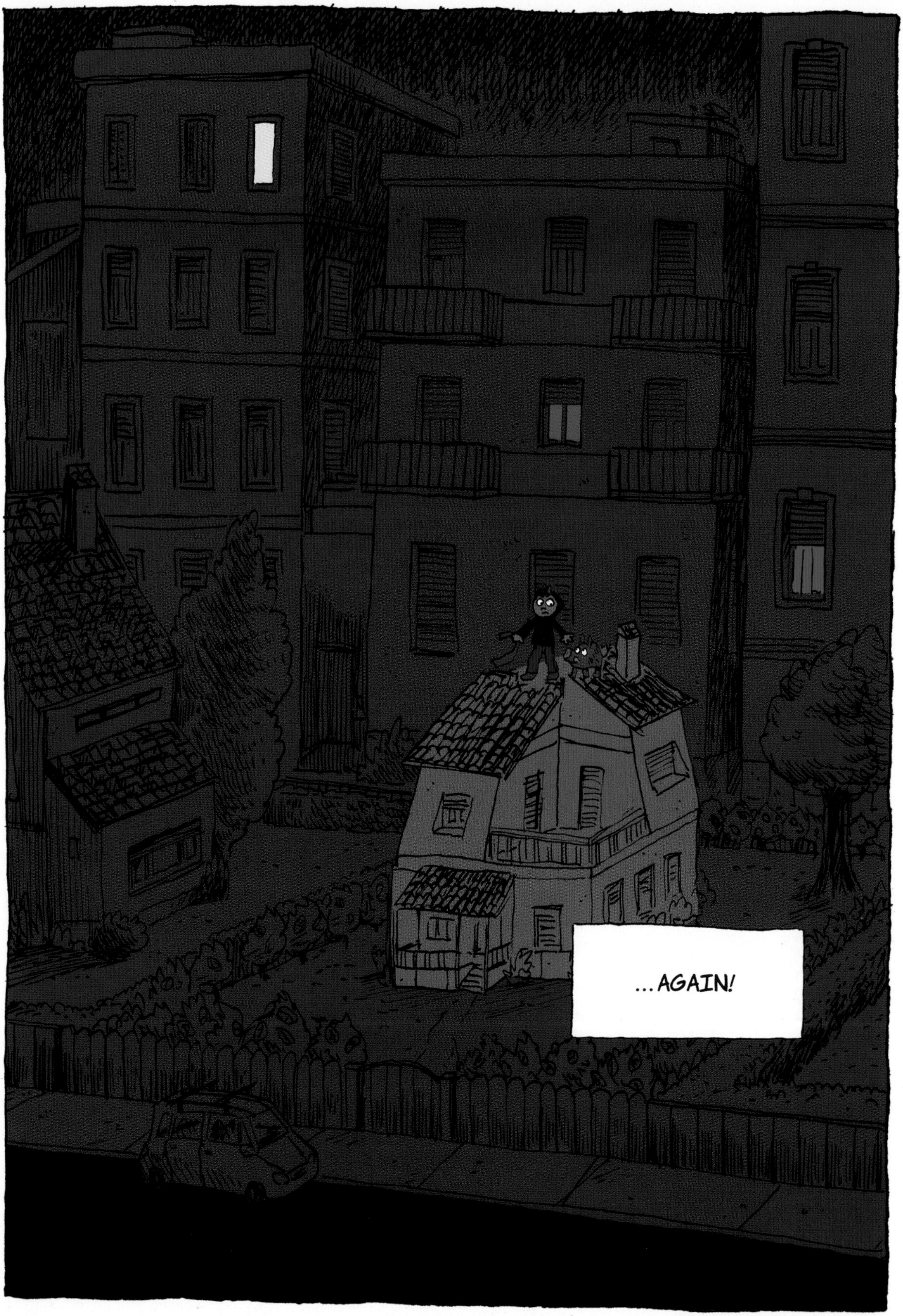
...AGAIN!

TO BE CONTINUED

TIMOTHY'S ADVENTURE CONTINUES IN
BOOK TWO: THE YELLOW WHALE!